12/15
12/31

Kate Griffin was born in the City of London within the sound of Bow bells, making her a true-born cockney.

She studied English Literature at Royal Holloway College, the University of London, and trained to be an English teacher. After leaving teaching she trained to be a journalist and worked in local newspapers for over a decade before moving into PR.

She now works for Britain's most venerable heritage body, The Society for the Protection of Ancient Buildings, situated in Spitalfields, a brisk walk from Wilton's Music Hall.

Kate lives in St Albans with her husband, Stephen.

Kitty Peck and the Music Hall Murders began life as an opening chapter submitted to the *Stylist* Magazine/Faber and Faber crime fiction competition. It beat over 400 entries to the winning spot. A sequel is under way.

Kitty Peck and the Music Hall Murders

KATE GRIFFIN

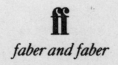

faber and faber

First published in 2013
by Faber and Faber Limited
Bloomsbury House
74–77 Great Russell Street
London WC1B 3DA

Typeset by Faber and Faber Ltd
Printed and bound by CPI Group (UK) Ltd, Croydon CR0 4YY

A CIP record for this book
is available from the British Library

ISBN 978–0–571–30269–7

2 4 6 8 10 9 7 5 3 1

For my husband Stephen, and my mum, Sheila.

Prologue

On the day of my mother's funeral Joey had to break the ice in the basin before I could wash my face. And then he had to comb my hair, button me into my one good dress, tie the laces on my boots and force my rigid fingers into Nanny Peck's old woollen gloves.

My brother had to do a lot for me in them days. I couldn't move, I couldn't talk and I couldn't even think. After the funeral I just sat on my bed for days staring at a patch of mould on the wall. I was twelve years old.

Nanny Peck had gone the summer before and I reckon that's when Ma gave up. She'd never been strong, but after we buried the old girl, Ma became hollow. First the laughter stopped, then the singing, then the stories and then everything. I don't think I heard my mother make a sound in the month before she died.

Eliza Peck was locked up in there somewhere, but we couldn't find her.

I suppose that's why Joey was so worried about me and why he took me with him to The Gaudy. You might think that the halls are the very last place where you'd want your little sister to find work, but he knew I'd be kept busy there.

I thought about that patch of mould on the bedroom wall that first day. It put me in mind of the constellation of little black moles scattered over the eyelid and right cheek of Swami Jonah. The old magician terrified me when we was introduced, though the truth of the matter is that the most exotic thing about Swami Jonah was the broad Liverpool he spoke when he wasn't on stage.

But that's the way of it, you see, nothing in the halls is ever what it seems – you learn that fast enough, or you should do.

I can see quite clearly now that I didn't always pay attention, but I was busy building a new family – of sorts – for myself. I discovered back then that the difference between me and Ma was that I'm very good at closing doors in my head and keeping them locked. I still had Joey and soon there were others too – all of us bobbing around in Paradise on the banks of the Thames.

It must have been a hard thing for a lad like Joey to take the place of mother, father – everyone. My handsome, golden brother gave out that he was cock of the walk, but he was just a boy himself at the time, fifteen, and suddenly responsible for two lives. No wonder it all went so wrong and why it's me, not him, who's sitting here now.

But that's the ending of it, or at least the ending of a part of it. This is the beginning . . .

Chapter One

Lady Ginger's fingers were black. From the flaking tips of her long, curling nails to the crinkled skin just visible beneath the clacking jumble of rings, her hands were stained like a coal boy's.

Not that she'd sully her fingers with anything as menial as a scuttle, you understand. Oh no, Lady Ginger was too grand for that.

She lifted the pipe to her lips again and sucked noisily, all the while watching me with those hooded eyes.

The room was dark and the air smelt like Mrs Conway's special paint box at The Gaudy.

Tell truth, it always makes me feel a bit noxious when I clean up Mrs Conway's dressing table after a show. That 'lucky' cologne she uses honks like a fox in a 'fessional. That's what Lucca says, and he's from Italy where the Romans are, so he ought to know.

Anyhow, I just stood there fiddling with the frayed cuffs of my best frock, waiting for Lady Ginger to say something.

After a moment she inhaled deeply, took the pipe out of her mouth, closed her eyes and leaned back into the pile of embroidered cushions that passed for furniture. The bangles on her skinny yellow arms jingled as she settled into the nest of silk.

I didn't know what to do. I looked over at the man

standing guard in front of the door, but he didn't make a move, just kept staring at the bird cage hanging up by the shuttered window.

I took a couple of steps forward and cleared my throat. If the old woman had fallen asleep, perhaps I could wake her up?

Nothing.

Now I was a bit closer I could see her tarry lips – the fine lines etched around her tiny mouth were black too. It looked like she'd swallowed a spider and it was trying to get out again.

Opium's a horrible thing. Ma always said it was smoke from the Devil's nostrils and that it could coil you tighter than a hangman's noose. Not that Joey had taken any notice of her.

I coughed loudly, but still the old lady didn't budge. I was beginning to think that she might be dead when the parrot went off.

'Pretty girl, pretty girl . . .'

Lady Ginger's eyes snapped open and she grinned up at me – her mouth all wet and dark. No teeth, as far as I could see.

'You are seldom wrong, Jacobin. She's a pretty piece indeed.'

I was amazed.

Lady Ginger's voice was a hundred years younger than the rest of her. All high and fluttery like a girl's. And posh too – very cultured it was. I'd never been near enough to hear her before. Down at the docks when she visits with her lascar boys there's always been too much bumping and shouting to hear what she's saying to them – and, anyway, I've kept a distance since Joey went. When she comes to The Gaudy – not often, mind – she's got her special curtained box near the

4

stage with its own staircase and door to the side alley, so we never see her arrive or leave and we never see who's with her, neither. It's best not to ask too many questions in Paradise.

'So, you are Kitty Peck?'

Lady Ginger shifted on her pile of cushions and pulled herself up into a sitting position. The loose gown she wore swamped her scrawny frame as she adjusted her legs and crossed them. Her feet were bare and now I saw she even had rings on her gnarly toes.

She reached for her long pipe and began to suck again, all the while staring up at me.

Then she spoke in that odd little voice.

'I had dealings with your brother, Joseph, wasn't it? Fair like you, and handsome with it. Now what became of him, I wonder?'

I didn't answer. We both knew what had happened to Joey, even though his body never come ashore.

'Cat got your tongue, Kitty Peck?' Her eyes narrowed and she smiled. Then she reached for an ebony writing box next to the cushion pile, the bangles on her arms clacking and jangling as she hauled it onto her lap. Opening the lid so that I couldn't see inside, she began to rummage.

'Well, I can't say I blame you for not wanting to talk about him. A bad business, that was.'

My belly boiled and I had to fight the urge to say something I'd regret.

'Joey's been . . . gone for two years now, and I miss him every day.'

'Do you now? Miss a murderer? What a loyal little sister you are, Kitty Peck.'

Murderer?

He'd worked for The Lady, right enough – and everyone in Paradise knew what that meant – but Joey wasn't no murderer. He couldn't even put a half-dead bird chewed up by a cat out of its misery. He'd left that sort of thing to me.

I opened my mouth, but nothing came out.

Lady Ginger grinned wider, her eyes glinting in the thin candlelight.

I could see her more clearly now. It was the closest I'd ever been to the woman who put the fear into half of London, and as I stood there I realised with a shock that she was a faker.

All this time I'd thought she was a Chinawoman, but that plait, those fingernails, those clothes, those jewels – they were just a costume. Lady Ginger was as English as I was.

'Still, loyalty is a quality I value,' she continued, producing a green leather case no bigger than a matchbox from the depths of the writing box. She flicked open the shagreen lid with one of her long black fingernails and shook three tiny red dice into the palm of her hand.

'Do you know what these are, Miss Peck?'

I shook my head.

'They are the future.' She raised her open palm so that I could see the dice more clearly. Now I looked, these wasn't like the dice played by men at the back of The Gaudy. Instead of the usual dots, the faces were covered with golden patterns.

Lady Ginger closed her fingers and shook her fist. I could hear the dice clicking against her rings.

Then she spat three times on the wooden floorboards next to her cushions and dropped the dice into the triangle formed by the glistening blobs of black saliva.

She stared down for a moment and then she began to chuckle. 'Come closer, Kitty Peck, and tell me what you see.'

Now, she's not a woman to cross. For all I wanted to back out of that stinking room, skiddle down the winding stairs and get as far away from Lady Ginger's Palace as possible, I didn't want to rile her. So I bent down and looked at the dice – all three showed the same pattern.

I reached forward to take up the nearest one, but – quick as a limelight flare – she lashed out, scratching my wrist with one of them curled nails.

'No one touches the dice but me. However, I will allow you to read them. What do you see?'

I rubbed my wrist and cleared my throat. 'Nothing, Lady. Not numbers leastways.'

I stared hard at the golden swirling shape repeated on the top of the three red cubes and realised that the pattern had a head and what looked like wings.

'It might be a dragon?' I ventured.

Lady Ginger swept up the dice and poured them back into the green case. Then she stared at me.

'You show promise, Miss Peck. Very few people are able to read the I-ching by intuition alone. It seems I have chosen well. And the dice confirmed that – although three dragons warn of an element of *risk*.'

She reached for her pipe and sucked noisily again until the little carved bowl at the end began to glow and a thin trail of sickly sweet smoke coiled up into the air. All the while she looked at me and I was reminded of Mr Fitzpatrick at The Gaudy when he's assessing a new girl for the chorus.

As it turned out, I wasn't far wrong about that.

'How old are you, Kitty Peck?'

'Seventeen, nearly eighteen.'

'And what do I pay you for at The Gaudy, exactly?'

'I work backstage, Lady. I clean up, I help with the costumes and I assist the performers, 'specially Mrs Conway, between her pieces.'

At this Lady Ginger seemed to choke on her pipe, but then I saw she was laughing. 'Old Lally still at it, is she? I must talk to Fitzpatrick about that. It's high time we put her out to grass. I'll not pay for stringy meat and nor will anyone else.'

I shifted uncomfortable like. Everyone knew that Mrs Conway and Fitzpatrick had a special arrangement and I certainly didn't want to be the cause of any trouble on that account.

'Mrs Conway is a very popular turn,' I said. 'There are Johnnies waiting for her outside every evening.'

Lady Ginger smiled, but it wasn't a friendly look. 'As I noted, so very loyal, Miss Peck. Show me your legs.'

Next thing I know, she's reaching across and poking at my skirt with her pipe. I had to hold it up for fear of becoming incendiary. I didn't want to be a second Lucca.

So, there I was standing with my skirts pulled up to my knees and Lady Ginger staring. I felt my cheeks blush as red as the rouge in Mrs Conway's paint box and I looked over at the man by the door. He appeared to have his eyes closed, so at least that was something.

'Very elegant,' Lady Ginger said. 'Can you dance?'

'I'm not sure. I dance for the fun of it, but not like the Gaudy girls, if that's what you mean?'

Lady Ginger nodded. 'Fitzpatrick tells me you have a voice. Drop your skirts now.'

It was true I loved to sing. Whether I was sewing costumes up in the little room at the back of the stage or clearing glasses and unmentionables from the hall and the boxes, I couldn't work in silence. Sometimes Lucca calls me Fannella – which, apparently, means linnet in Italian, though I don't like to be compared to one of those sad little brown birds kept in cages.

'Do you have a head for heights?'

Well, that flummoxed me. I'd never really thought about it, but then I remembered the time me and Peggy Worrow was sent up the rope gantry at The Gaudy to drop paper petals over Mrs Conway as she sang about lilacs and bluebells – all got up like a shepherdess she was. Peggy went whiter than a cod fillet and had to be helped down again by three of the hands, while I'd stayed up there for the view.

So I nodded. 'Yes, Lady – I think I must have.'

'Well, Kitty Peck, I have made my decision.'

Lady Ginger laid down her pipe and reached to the back of her neck for her plait. She pulled the thick grey snake over her right shoulder and began to twist it. For the second time that afternoon I was struck by her peculiar girlishness – not just the voice, but her mannerisms too. They wasn't what you'd expect of an old woman.

'Your brother was a sharp lad. Some might say too sharp for his own good. I wonder if you are as intelligent?'

I knew that wasn't possible. Joey had been the cleverest person I'd ever known. He'd had all his letters before he was six and he taught me to read too. He had Ma's way about him when it came to a story – he'd start to speak and everyone in the room, whether it was a stand-up gin house down by

9

Pennington Street or backstage at The Gaudy after a show, would gather round and listen. I'd watch the looks on their faces, proud to have a brother who could charm words out of the air like Swami Jonah could magic cards from his empty hands.

Joey knew about every country in the world and what's more he could pick up a foreigner's way of talking as fast as most men could pick a brawl. And it wasn't just words neither, he had a head for business. He must have done, because after Ma went he'd made sure we wanted for nothing. He was out working all hours and sometimes he'd bring me back a gift – perhaps a ribbon, some lace – pretty things for a girl to treasure.

Lady Ginger was wrong, my brother had been a wonder. There was no one who could touch him.

I looked down at the floorboards and wrinkled up the material of my skirt in my left hand. I didn't want her to see my eyes.

'Fitzpatrick tells me you are a bright little puss. He tells me you have . . . *potential*.'

She stopped twiddling her plait and reached out to her writing box again. The candlelight in the room caught the moony glow of the mother of pearl pattern on its ebony lid. I still couldn't see what was inside, but I heard her fingernails scrabble and the bangles clatter.

Eventually she took out a small leather pouch and then passed it from hand to hand as if weighing its contents.

'Clary Simmons. Esther Dixon. Sally Ford. Alice Caxton.'

She said the names slowly, clearly and distinctly each time

she weighed the pouch, and I shuddered. Everyone in Paradise knew those girls.

Clary had worked the chorus at The Comet, Esther and Sally were dancers at The Carnival and little Alice had done general duties at The Gaudy. All four of them worked at music halls owned by Lady Ginger and all four had gone missing.

Now, you might think that's not unusual for a theatre girl, and sometimes you'd be right, but not with these. Esther had a baby and Sally looked after her old dad who was crippled after an accident down the docks broke his back. Neither of them would leave Paradise of their own accord.

And then there was Alice. Both her parents had been taken by the diphtheria last winter, leaving her an orphan at twelve like I was when Ma died. But Alice didn't have a brother, just me and Peggy at The Gaudy.

We did our best – I'd got her a room at my lodgings so I could keep an eye on her, and Peggy, who was what you'd call a natural maternal type even though she was just a year older than me, was always finding her warm things from the back of Mrs Conway's closet.

Alice needed us, but we was glad to help. Skinny as a new-born chick she was, with round glass-green eyes and a plait of dull hair wound about on the top of her head so it looked like a mouse sitting up there. She worked hard, but even though she often did the rounds as a tray girl, dodging between tables full of drunken gents at The Gaudy, she wasn't the sort to draw attention, if you get my meaning. Tell truth, I doubt that a man would have looked twice at her bony little body.

She'd gone missing three weeks or so back now and it didn't make sense.

Alice had no one except me and Peggy – and Lucca who took her to his church on Sundays. If she'd gone away somewhere she would have taken her things with her, but her room – two floors down from mine – was exactly as she'd left it that night of her last shift.

It was the smallest room at Mother Maxwell's, more like a cupboard really, but that's all Alice could afford.

Ten of us lived there in all, all of us girls, and all of us clean and decent – Mother Maxwell was most particular about her boarders. That is to say, most particular about boarders who could pay up weekly. When Alice didn't come back the old codwife made me go through her room for pennies, but there was nothing there except a Bible and her clothes. A thick brown skirt Peggy had taken for her was laid out on the bed with half its hem taken up and another yard still to go. The needle and cotton was on the wash stand.

No, we all suspected that something very dark had come across little Alice and across all them girls, but the theatre is a superstitious place at the best of times so no one liked to talk of it. Anyway, Paradise has its own rules and Lady Ginger makes them all.

She watched my face for a moment then continued. 'I don't like it when my property is interfered with, Kitty Peck. You, of all people, must know what happens to those who ... disappoint me. Joseph failed me and that failure cost me dearly. In fact, I rather think your family owes me a considerable debt – and as you are the only one left now, who else to pay it back?'

She grinned widely, showing sticky black gums.

'In recompense you are going to find out what happened to those girls. It's not good for business and it's not good for my reputation when unexpected things happen on my territory.'

Lady Ginger stared up at me, her brilliant black eyes flicking over every part of my face. I could almost feel them move on my skin like a louse. But this time I didn't look away. There was a challenge in her look, something expectant – and part of me flared up.

'Whatever Joey did or didn't do, he paid a heavy price, as you well know. This is none of my business. If you really want to find them girls you need to put the police onto it. Why don't you just . . .'

'Why don't I just *what*, Miss Peck?'

She spat out the words and drummed the pointed fingernails of her right hand so hard on the floorboards that little marks appeared in the wood. I realised then that she was furious. The way she said 'what' would have made a pisspot freeze over in July. She might have been tiny as a bird and old as a 'gyptian mummy, but she was terrifying.

'If you truly imagine that I would allow the police to set foot in Paradise to investigate my affairs, then you have proved yourself to be as foolish as your brother. I am disappointed already.'

She closed her eyes and took a deep shuddering breath. A moment later she continued. 'However, the dice suggest I should test you. You will work directly for me now, just as your pretty brother did before. Here.'

She opened her eyes and tossed the pouch over to me and I caught it involuntarily. It was full of coins.

'You'll need better clothes. That dress is a disgrace.'

I gulped. 'But I wouldn't know what to do, Lady. Please, I couldn't . . .'

'Silence.'

She scrunched herself up into a knot of skin and bone in the midst of the cushions. 'This is not a request, Kitty Peck, it is an order. Like your brother, you are my property and I have made plans for you. Fitzpatrick knows what to do. He will explain everything after this evening's performance. Go.'

The man standing guard at the door stood to one side and shifted the heavy velvet curtain so that I could see the gloomy landing and the top of the staircase.

I stood there for a moment, my heart racing.

Once I get through that door, I thought, I'll start running and I'll run until I'm as far away from Lady Ginger's Palace as it's possible to be, and even then I'll keep going. I'm not going to be a second Joey. I started to back towards the door, gripping the coin pouch in my hand. I even had money to help me escape.

The grey parrot started up again with that 'pretty girl, pretty girl' racket.

Lady Ginger smiled, leaned back into the cushions and picked up her pipe. Just as I reached the door she called out. 'By the way, Miss Peck, I think you should know that if you fail me in this you will never see your brother alive again.'

Chapter Two

Alive.

That word kept clanging in my head like the shift bell at the docks. I hardly took in the gloomy warren of rooms off the landings as I skittered around and around the carved oak staircase down to the musty hallway.

At the bottom of the stairs two Chinamen with identical scars on their faces and plaits down their backs pulled open the double doors without a word. I tumbled down the steps of Lady Ginger's Palace into the frozen alleyway, missed my footing and toppled forward, scraping the palms of my hands on the stones.

My head swam as I pushed myself upright – all this time Joey was alive somewhere and I never knew. What had she done to him?

Joseph failed me and that failure cost me dearly. In fact, I rather think your family owes me a considerable debt – and as you are the only one left now, who else to pay it back?

I stood up, leaned against the blackened brick wall of The Palace and took a deep breath. My heart was beating so hard it felt like a bird trapped under my ribs. After a moment I straightened up and turned to find Lucca staring at me.

'What happened, Kitty? What did The Lady want you for?'

He stepped forward and offered me a paint-spattered rag. 'For your hand – it is bleeding.'

He cocked his head to indicate the graze across my right palm. As he moved, the long black hair that poked out from under his hat to cover the right side of his face parted for a second revealing melted skin that sealed one eye into perpetual dark. I took the rag and dabbed at the torn skin. I can't deny I was relieved to see him, but I was angry too.

'You shouldn't have followed me. Lady Ginger's spies are everywhere, they'll have you marked now . . .'

Lucca shrugged. 'I am a marked man anyway. Come, what did she want? The Lady never asks for anyone by name.'

'Not here – and keep your voice down.'

I frowned and nodded up at the doors. They were closed and the rows of windows were shuttered, but all the same – men said that in this part of Limehouse every cobble was one of Lady Ginger's eyes.

We set off down the alleyway and twisted through the maze of filthy passages. Every so often we stopped and scanned behind in case she'd set a lascar on our tails, but as the streets grew broader and brighter and the crowds grew thicker and louder it was impossible to tell if we were being followed. I didn't even notice the midwinter cold, even though my best dress is made from thin stuff. I suppose fear kept me warm. Eventually we came to the river and I sat down, suddenly exhausted, at the top of a flight of narrow stone steps leading down to the greasy water.

A dead cat, all bloated and muddy, bumped against the foot of the steps as they disappeared into the scum of the Thames.

Fitzpatrick tells me you are a bright little puss. He tells me you have . . . potential.

Lady Ginger's words swam into my head as the cat in the river bobbed past. It was only then that I allowed myself to cry.

Lucca squeezed in beside me on the step and put his arm around my shoulders. I leaned against him and sobbed even harder when he produced another paint-spattered cloth and pressed it into my hands.

'He's alive. Joey's not dead. The Lady says so.' I gulped out the words and twisted the cloth. I felt Lucca's body tense beside me.

'But it's not possible. You would have known – he would have come to you, Fannella.'

His light, accented voice was full of confusion as he continued rapidly. 'They came to the theatre to tell you, remember? I was there when they gave you his Christopher.'

I reached into the neck of my dress and held the little gold medal that was all I had left of my brother.

Two of The Lady's men had come to the theatre that day. I was on stage humming through a mouthful of pins as I adjusted Mrs Conway's Britannia costume and Lucca was painting a circle of wood to look like a shield.

Fitzpatrick came in first and the lascar boys followed.

Now, Fitzpatrick, he looks shifty on the best of days, but that morning he couldn't seem to catch my eye as he mumbled something about terrible news. He stared at Mrs C and she must've known something was up because, quick as you like, she hoiked up her breastplate and rustled off stage left.

I don't remember exactly what Fitzpatrick said next. Something about a fight on the quay, the boat, the water . . . the 'crushed and mangled' body too horrible for a sister to see.

He shuffled away while I just stood there staring at the boards.

It's a peculiar thing, but what I remember most clear about that morning is that as I looked down I caught sight of the fraying straps of Mrs Conway's abandoned Britannia sandals and thought to myself, 'They'll need a stitch before tonight or she'll take a tumble into the pit.'

A moment later, one of the lascars came up. He tossed Joey's Christopher onto the stage and it skittered over the boards until it came to the edge of one of the sandals. I bent to pick it up and when I stood up again he was gone.

I turned the little Christopher in my fingers now and looked out over the water. A fog was coming up.

'The thing is,' I said after a minute, 'I believe her. It's always been wrong this business with Joey. God alone knows what he got himself into when he took Lady Ginger's shillings – he never told me.'

I took a deep breath.

'I know my brother was no angel, Lucca, even though Nanny Peck always said he had the face of a cherub . . .' I smiled and gripped the Christopher tight. 'But Joey wasn't bad. He was just like everyone else round here, and better than most I'd say. There is something, though – that week before he . . . *died* . . . one night I woke up and he was sitting on the floor by the door just watching me in the dark.'

I stopped myself telling Lucca another thing about that night. My brave, handsome brother was weeping like a child.

Lucca was quiet next to me on the river steps, but I could hear all those clever cogs and gears shifting around in his head.

After a moment he sighed and for a second his breath clouded the freezing air. 'So, if you are to see Joey again what must you do in return? What does she want from you, Kitty? No one is summoned to The Palace without bad reason.'

He pulled off the floppy-brimmed hat he wore to cover his scars and began to turn it in his hands. 'I was worried when Fitzpatrick sent you to her this afternoon – that's why I followed, but now . . .'

For the first time that day I found myself laughing. 'And what were you planning to do to save me from Lady's Ginger's boys, Lucca? Drown them in whitewash, perhaps? Duel for my honour with a loaded paint brush?'

I grinned up at him, but his expression stopped me.

'I'm sorry, that was hard. I'm glad you came for me and you're right – she . . . she wants me to work for her. And if she's got Joey, then I haven't got a choice in the matter, have I?'

Lucca fiddled with the hat and pulled at some frayed bits on the edge of the brim.

'But you already work for her at the theatre. I don't understand. What else does she want?'

'She wants me to work direct for her, I think. Like Joey did.'

He turned his hat around again and muttered something in Italian. I stared down at the water where the dead cat was bobbing past again surrounded by a raft of filth trapped by the incoming tide. I knew how it felt.

I watched it twisting round and round, bumping against

the stones, and I never took my eyes off it as I told Lucca everything Lady Ginger said. He nodded when I listed the missing girls.

'We all knew that they hadn't run off. And Alice – she is just a child,' he crossed himself, 'but I'm surprised to hear that The Lady herself wasn't behind it. Who would dare to meddle in Paradise? I don't know if this makes me feel better or worse.'

I snorted. 'And how do you think it makes me feel, seeing as how I'm supposed to find out what happened to them all? Fitzpatrick's in on it too. Apparently, "he will explain everything".' I mimicked Lady Ginger's peculiar fluting voice.

Lucca stared at me with his good brown eye. He probably would have been a handsome lad if it wasn't for the accident – three years ago now – with the limelight flare.

'You say she asked you if you had a head for heights?' he asked.

I nodded. 'And she looked at my legs and asked if I could sing.'

He scratched at some paint caught under his thumbnail and looked out over the river. I couldn't tell what he was thinking. The six o'clock shift bell started clanging down at the docks and a fog horn mourned across the river. Lucca jumped up and jammed the hat back on his head so that it shaded the scar. He held out a hand.

'Come, Fannella, we'll be late. I'm afraid I have a very good idea of what Fitzpatrick's going to do with you.'

Chapter Three

The birdcage was about six foot high and maybe four foot wide. It was made of gold-painted metal and threaded with diamond-studded ribbons that looped between the bars and glittered in the lamplight. I say 'diamond-studded', but actually, the ribbons were decorated with paste glass jewels like the ones I sew onto Mrs Conway's bodices.

'In you get then, girl. Let's try it out for size.'

Fitzy tipped the cage back so that I could crawl inside. It didn't have no door and it didn't have no bottom. What it did have was a swinging perch suspended on chains attached to a hook driven into the canopy at the top.

I just stared.

'Come on, Kitty. I haven't got all night.'

Fitzy was irritated. The show hadn't gone well earlier. There'd been trouble with a group of sailors in the gallery throwing things at the toffs in the boxes. While Mrs C was on stage doing her Nightingale Serenade at the close of the first half, a dozen men were at it like fighting cocks at the back of the hall.

A big French mirror was smashed and one of the gin barrels had been knocked over – leaking a night's takings through the boards down to the cellar below.

Even though we closed up early, setting things to rights had taken a couple of hours. I'd been sent up to the gallery.

Now, people always like to say that sailors hold their liquor well on account of them training their guts at sea, but from my experience – at the end of a mop – there is no job as bad as slopping out the gallery of The Gaudy after we've had a party of shipmates in.

The stink of it!

I was lugging the third bucket of vomit water back down the stairs when Fitzy came to the front of the stage. He shielded his eyes from the flares – we always kept a couple going after an incident so we could see what we were dealing with – and squinted out into the hall.

'Kitty? Is that you with the bucket at the back there? I want a word.'

My stomach clenched tighter than an oyster's shell. Since Lucca and I had got back late to The Gaudy there hadn't been time for anything except pinning and fussing over Mrs C's costumes for the evening. She hadn't been too happy about my absence.

Fitzy's gin-thickened voice rasped out again. 'Come on, girl. Chop chop.'

Fitzpatrick knows what to do. He will explain everything after this evening's performance.

This was it, then. Whatever it was that Lady Ginger and Fitzpatrick had cooked up between them, it looked like I was about to find out. I noted that he'd left it until after I'd done the clearing.

I set down the bucket and propped the mop against a twisted column. When I got to the stage Fitzy had come round the side and was waiting for me at the curtained-off door that led direct from the hall to his offices. It was evident from the dark stains on his striped waistcoat – a garment that strained to contain the consequence of his appetite – that even he had been involved in the aftermath of the evening's trouble.

He was a big man, Fitzy, and generally I did my best to keep out of his way. There was talk that in the old days – after the circus and before he'd got into the halls – he'd been one of the hardest bare knucklers on the streets, but these days it was women he liked to hit. He had a ripe reputation among the Gaudy girls.

'This way.' He pushed the fringed red velvet curtain aside with the end of his cane and opened the door. I'd never been in here before and I was surprised to see it was more like a lady's parlour than an office – all flowers, china, cushions and bits of fancy material hanging over screens. There was even a fat day bed covered with tasselled bolsters stretched out in front of the fire.

'In you go.'

He must have seen my expression, because he started to laugh. 'Nothing like that, my girl. You're not my type – too scrawny.'

He pushed me through the door and walked over to the far wall where a shawl-draped screen all carved like a Chinese dragon stood in front of another door.

'We're going round to the workshop. I need you to . . . *try* something.'

I followed him through a passage that led round to the back of the theatre and then out across the little cobbled yard to the outbuildings where Lucca usually worked on The Gaudy's painted sets and backdrops.

It was late now and the fog that had come off the river earlier had a sharpness to it that promised snow. Fitzpatrick unlocked the wide door and rattled it back letting the familiar smell of paints and turpentine leak out into the night. The workshop was black as a cell at The Fleet, as Nanny Peck liked to say, but Fitzy soon lit a couple of lamps and several candles, and as he did the giant golden birdcage was revealed smack in the centre of the sawdust-strewn floor. He walked over to it and patted it affectionately as you would a favourite dog.

'Marvellous, ain't it? Lovely workmanship. The Lady, she's called in what we might describe as a favour from some friends at The Whitechapel Foundry. It's light as a sparrow, but strong as an anchor.'

He rapped once on the side with his cane and a long, low musical note rang out.

'Lovely tone.'

He paused in admiration as the note died away. 'It arrived on Tuesday on the back of a dray. Took delivery late at night, so I did. Doesn't do to let the competitors see your next attraction.'

He looked over at me and his eyes narrowed.

'Now, as I understand it, Kitty, you and The Lady have had a little tête-a-tête today about some business.'

I swallowed hard and nodded. If anyone was likely to know what had happened to Joey, Fitzy would – after all, he was The Lady's right fist. I felt my heart start thumping under my bodice.

'When I went to The Palace this afternoon, she, that is, The Lady, said my brother was . . .'

'Enough!'

Fitzpatrick's voice was suddenly very sharp. 'I don't want to hear another word about that degenerate.'

'But I have to know. She said he was . . .'

'Dead . . . to the world that young man is. And a good thing too. You, on the other hand, are very much alive and we would like to make use of your . . . *potential* to ensure that all our Gaudy girls and the girls at our sister establishments stay that way too. I know The Lady has already talked to you about this.'

I took a step back. I was angry at what he'd said about Joey, but relieved too. So he was alive then? That was what Fitzy meant, wasn't it? I couldn't stop myself. The old bruiser could be quite handy with his cane when the mood took him, but the words came tumbling out.

'Where is he then? The Lady said I had to help her find them girls if I wanted to see Joey again. I think I've got a right to know what's happened to my brother.'

The workshop went completely silent for a moment. You couldn't hear the creaking of the timbers and you couldn't even hear the rats scratching in the walls, which was unusual because the place was infested with the scabby things.

Fitzpatrick took a step forward and I really thought he was going to land one on me, but instead he just smiled – not in a friendly way.

'Good. I like a bit of spirit and so do the punters. That, Kitty, is just one of the reasons The Lady and I have selected you. But as to talk of rights now, I think you'll find you don't have much say in the matter. Your brother belongs to The

Lady, you belong to The Lady, I belong to The Lady. We all do – that's just the way of it.'

The smell of gin rolled off him and fugged the cold air of the workshop. I noticed his right eyelid twitched as he spoke. We all knew Fitzy liked to end his day with a drop of the hard stuff, but word was out that recently he liked to begin his day that way too.

Paradise was never a rosy Garden of Eden, but in the last few weeks it had become sour as a tanner's pit. As I stared up at him now I realised that it wasn't just the smell of the gin coming off him, there was something else too. Fitzy reeked of fear and that wasn't reassuring.

I stared at the cage. *The Lady and I have selected you.* What for?

I took a deep breath.

'Look, I want to know what's happened to them girls. We all do. Alice Caxton – she's almost like a little sister to me and Peggy. But I don't see what I'm supposed to do. It's a job for the rozzers, not someone like me.'

He started to laugh and I could feel my cheeks going red.

'Come on now, girl, you must know that the very last people Lady Ginger would want to *consult* would be representatives of the law. Paradise has its own rules, so it does. I would have thought your brother would have explained that to you.'

Fitzy came a step closer. 'She always liked a pretty boy, Kitty. I was pretty once, can you believe that?'

He reached forward and caught at a ringlet that had come loose from the knot of hair at the back of my neck. I turned my face away from the stench of his breath. Then I yelped when he pulled hard. 'You look very like him, did you know that, now? But don't flatter yourself. I wouldn't want to touch you, not after . . .'

He broke off and looked over at the cage. 'If you want to see Joseph Peck again you'd better follow the rules.'

I clenched my fists. Keep thinking about Joey, I told myself; he's alive and this is your chance to find him.

I stared up into Fitzy's tiny bloodshot eyes. 'Well, what do you want me to do then? And what, exactly, is that ridiculous thing?'

I braced myself for a slap, but he didn't seem to notice. He rolled the strand of my hair between his finger and thumb for a moment, dropped it, then turned his back on me and walked over to the cage.

I pulled my shawl tighter round my shoulders. It was freezing in the workshop, but that wasn't why I huddled myself up like that. Of a sudden I had a strong premonition about where this was leading.

Fitzpatrick turned back to face me and spread his arms wide with a theatrical flourish. As he did so, one of the shiny buttons that strained across the front of his waistcoat popped off and clinked away into a gloomy corner.

'This, Miss Kitty, is *your* cage and when we have worked with you on your new act for The Gaudy – an act that I confidently predict will be the envy of every hall in London – you will hang seventy foot above the heads of our audience six nights a week and you will twirl and sing for them like a little linnet.'

Do you have a head for heights?

Lady Ginger's peculiar questions suddenly made sense.

'But I'm no turn, Mr Fitzpatrick. I'm just a wardrobe girl. I've never been on stage in my life.'

'I've heard you sing, Kitty Peck – your voice is sweet. Your figure is good – for those what like that sort of thing. I know from the hands that you don't mind the gantry and, of course . . .', his fat lips squirmed into a nasty smile under his faded red bristles, '. . . you have to do this if you want to see your beloved brother again.' He spat out those last words as if they tasted bitter.

'While you're suspended above the theatre singing pretty songs and performing pretty acrobatic tricks you will be our eyes. From your unique vantage point you will keep note of the comings and goings in the hall below – not just The Gaudy, mind, all of them in turn. And if you see anything that might be helpful, you will report back to us.'

He turned back to the cage.

'You'll have to be careful with the paintwork just here on the right, it's still tacky. I've had your boyfriend painting it for the last two days. Nice job he's done too, for an I-tie. In you get then, girl. Let's try it out for size.'

Chapter Four

The feathers on the violent purple tippet that was wrapped tight around Jenny Pierce's throat quivered as she breathed out.

Now, Jenny had a face on her like a flat iron most days of the week, but today the way her heavy jaw was working – all clenched and twitching at the sides – made her look like a boxer in a frock. She was certainly spoiling for a round.

Jenny leaned back against the door, folded her arms and flicked her eyes around the room. She snorted and the cheap feathers under her chin danced about again. 'And you got a fire in here too, Kitty. Aren't we just the lucky little lady.'

Peggy jumped up.

'If you haven't got something pleasant to say to Kitty, I'd bugger off, if I was you.'

She'd been kneeling behind me pulling hard at the ribbons that made the spangled bodice dig so tight into my waist that the first time I'd practised in it I'd fainted. Luckily I'd only been five foot off the ground at the time.

'You know very well why she's got a fire in here, Jenny Pierce. If you was going to dangle over the heads of the punters and do the things she's got to do tonight you'd want a bit of heat in your bones too.' Peggy knelt again and pulled the ribbons tighter. I gasped. 'Sorry, Kitty, but Fitzy was most specific about how he wants you to look tonight – fragile, as if a man could snap you in two with his bare hands, he said.' She shuddered before adding softly, 'The old pervert.'

I took a deep breath, leaned forward and gripped the back of the chair in front of me as Peggy pulled harder.

'It's all right,' I said. 'You can use your foot too if it helps, we wouldn't want to disappoint him, would we?'

I wasn't being sarcastic. I might not have been Fitzpatrick's type, but, unfortunately, Peggy, with her abundant figure and thick dark curls, was. He and Mrs C had a longstanding arrangement, but that didn't stop him walking his dog elsewhere, if you get my meaning – or trying to, leastways. When he was soused, he'd corner Peggy in some dark corner, start pawing at her and then turn rough when nothing happened. A couple of times she'd come to The Gaudy with a black eye or a welt as big as a boot print blooming across her shoulders. We borrowed Mrs C's paint box and tried to disguise the bruises.

Peggy didn't want her Danny to find out. He's a decent lad, but he's got a temper on him too and if he knew what Fitzy had done to his girl he wouldn't think twice about taking him on, and that wouldn't have done anyone any good. Even though Fitzy was twice Dan's age and looked like a badly stuffed couch, he could still throw a punch that would floor a Dutchman. I'd seen him deal with parties of great tall Hollanders, fresh off the barges and ripe on the gin – and if I was to lay a bet on the outcome of one of those encounters I know where I'd put my money.

I suppose it's the way of things that once you've learned to handle yourself on the streets the moves are grained into your head like the choreography of a chorus dance, or like my routine up in the cage. You don't have to think about it, your muscles just know what to do. Of occasion when I watched Fitzy laying one on a soused shipmate I'd get a glimpse of what he must have been. Tell truth, under all that flesh he might even have been Peggy's type – once.

But now she had big Danny Tewson and she was forever telling me that one day soon the pair of them would be packing their things and getting out of Paradise. It was hard to see how that was going to happen. I liked Danny, he was good for Peggy and he was one of the best of the hands in the halls, but Lucca said that if you wrote his gambling debts on separate pages and laid them out in a row you could walk on them from the front steps of The Gaudy down to Kidney Stairs on the river – and then have a good long think about throwing yourself in.

I never mentioned it to Peggy. We was respectful of each other's secrets. It was none of my business what her man got up to, and if she was worried, she never talked about it to me. She was more concerned about keeping Danny in the dark about Fitzy's attentions and I can't say I blamed her.

One time it happened when Peggy was down to do a 'Sylvan Interlude' with two other girls. Not having been further than Lambeth, I can't say as I've seen many woodland nymphs disported with joy, but I'm sure they wear a lot more than the flimsy bits of stuff that passed for a costume. Anyway, she couldn't go on that evening because there was a purple mark the shape of a man's hand – fingers and all – around her throat. I pinned a bit of cloth about her shoulders up to her ears and made her go home. Then I told Dan she'd caught a bad chill and couldn't speak, which was half true.

Don't run away with the wrong idea about Peggy. She

31

wasn't a hard one like Jenny Pierce. Quite the opposite, in fact. Peggy was all warm and comforting, and she fussed over little Alice like a mother. Thinking about it, that's probably what old Fitzy particularly liked about her. My guess is she reminded him of Mrs Conway in her better days – when the two of them was both young and the future was all moonlight and roses. And that made him angry too.

No, Peggy was my friend and the way things had been going in the halls since word had got out about my new act, I was glad of her more than ever. I hadn't told her why Fitzpatrick had selected me to be his cagebird, but Peg was no fool. She knew there was something going on and she was waiting for me to tell her in my own good time.

'Hard as you like. Pull again, I'm ready.' I braced myself against the chair and took another deep breath.

Jenny sniffed. She was still leaning against the door. 'Wants you to look fragile, does he? Like something that might smash itself into little tiny pieces if it plummets to the ground?' Her eyes glinted with malice and a nasty smile twitched the corners of her mouth.

Peggy stood up again; she still had the bodice ribbons tight in her hands and I jerked up and away from the chair as she moved.

'You've always been a piece of work, Jenny, but this beats all. Would you really want to swap places with Kitty tonight? Would you want to hang up there in that bleedin' thing? It might be covered in all them pretty ribbons and twinkling jewels, but I'll tell you what it is, it's a death trap without so much as a net or a rope to save you when . . . if . . .'

Peggy faltered and her grip on the ribbons slackened. 'Sorry, Kitty, I didn't mean . . .'

The room was silent for a moment except for the sound of the little fire crackling away in the grate. It was most important that I was kept warm before a performance – Madame Celeste had said so.

*

For the last week or so, even over Christmas, which didn't mean much to me anyway, I'd spent every waking hour in Madame Celeste's cavernous attic learning how to use the trapeze that had made her a star way back when Fitzy started out as a circus hand in Ireland. The old girl drank like a navvy and to look at her now you wouldn't think that someone of such prodigious corpulence could ever have hauled her body up the steps of a tavern, let alone to the platform of a flying trapeze a hundred foot up in the air. But she didn't half know her stuff.

Fitzy said she'd been the most dazzling aerial artiste Dublin had ever clapped eyes on, and the faded, curling circus bills that decorated the shabby stairwell leading up to her attic showed a lithe and beautiful young woman soaring through the air like a painted angel.

Now she was a mound of flesh, draped in what looked like the shredded remnants of some tasselled parlour curtains. Only her glittering jet eyes and the unlikely confection of thick black hair piled up on top of her head hinted at the likelihood of some long-ago connection to the flying girl on the stairwell.

The first thing to say is that Madame Celeste's attic was vast. It must have run across five houses. When I pushed open the little door at the top of the stairs I wasn't expecting there to be so much space in front of me of a sudden – and above me too. It was like one of them optical illusions of Swami Jonah's. He had a magic box that was bigger on the inside than it had any right to be if you looked at it from the outside. He told me it was done with mirrors. Madame Celeste had a mirror, twelve foot high it was, propped up against the wall on the left. There should have been at least one more floor above us, but that had been removed so that I could see the network of timbers stretching out high overhead beneath the underside of the roof.

It reeked of sweat and cat piss in there. It was hardly surprising – when I stepped into the echoing room, a dozen pairs of yellow eyes turned to stare at me. The old girl swayed to her feet, clapped her hands and started to make shooing sounds. As the cats bolted for the stairs, Madame Celeste nodded to herself and patted the leather flask at her hip absent-mindedly – she didn't seem entirely able to focus her eyes on me.

'You'll be Kitty then? Take off your shoes, now, and on you get.'

She gestured vaguely to the centre of the room. As she waved her hand I got a powerful whiff of armpit that hadn't seen a soap bar since the death of Prince Albert.

I knew where she wanted me to go. The attic was a big bare space. A fire crackled in a corner hearth, a pile of empty gin bottles teetered against the far wall and a heap of dusty cushions littered the floor beneath a long rope swing that dangled from the rafters high above. I say swing, but it didn't have a seat – just a narrow wooden bar that swayed gently about five foot in the air.

We started off low, but I still had to use a stool to climb up. At first Madame Celeste told me, 'Lean back, kick out and go as high as you like, just for the hang of it.'

I won't deny it was a lovely feeling as the ropes creaked and the swing rose higher and higher into the spaces between the beams. The old girl just watched me, occasionally taking a swig from the flask. After a few minutes she called out, 'Enough of that. Bring it to a stand, Kitty.'

When the swing was still again, she told me to stand up on it. I scrambled up on the bar and watched as she hefted off to a corner and started to turn a wheel set into the wall. She breathed hard as she worked it. Instantly the ropes jerked and the swing began to rise, six, eight, twelve, fifteen, twenty foot up into the space between the rafters. I clung tight as I got higher and higher, trying not to think that the only thing between me and the floorboards – which were now perhaps thirty foot below – was a wooden bar no broader than an eel.

'Good, Kitty.' Madame Celeste wheezed from somewhere below and to the right. 'You did well. You didn't scream and you didn't look down – always a fatal error. I think you might indeed have potential, as young Paddy says.'

My guts churned, but it wasn't the height that did it. The image of Lady Ginger with her black-stained fingers and spider-trap mouth reared up into my mind. I had *potential* – that's what Fitzpatrick had told her too. And was that what he'd also said about Joey three years earlier?

The wheezing continued. 'While you're up there, I want

35

you to do one simple thing to test your mettle. Sit down on the swing . . .'

I eased myself down to the bar – simple.

'. . . good, that's right. Now take your hands off the ropes and hold the sides of the seat, tightly. Don't look down – eyes ahead.'

Not so simple. Cautiously I did as I was told. The swing wobbled and I shifted to balance myself – all the while keeping my eyes trained on a stain high on the wall opposite me. I could feel the muscles in my arms twitching. My back was damp with the sweat prickling under my clothes.

Joey. I'm doing this for Joey, I thought, gripping harder and concentrating on the brown stain on the wall, which was beginning to remind me of a skull.

'Back straight, Kitty. Good.' The old girl had caught her breath now. 'Right,' she continued, 'I want you to keep hold until I say otherwise and then I want you to lean back and out from the swing so that only the backs of your knees and your hands are in contact with the wood.'

Joey. I could feel his Christopher around my neck as I did as she instructed, wriggling backwards until my nancy was hanging out in mid-air and every muscle in my body pulled tight as a dockyard hawser. The ropes creaked and the swing began to judder and twist from left to right and back again.

'And let go, now!'

The voice was suddenly sharp and loud. I took a gulp of air and felt my fingers slip from the wood. I arched back and felt the swing move forward. My knees tightened over the bar, my calf muscles clenched and my feet pointed downward so violently that the arches hurt. Instinctively I threw my arms out to the sides for balance. Pins fell from my hair and the tight blonde coil that wound round the back of my head came free, sweeping through the vast empty space below me.

Gradually the swing steadied and I found that I was laughing. I can't say if it was the relief of not having dashed my brains out on the boards so far below or whether I was laughing out loud at the fact that '*young*' Fitzy's name was really Patrick Fitzpatrick.

'Well, well, well.' Madame Celeste was puffing again as she worked at the wheel and the swing began to lower. When my hair brushed the floorboards I pulled myself upright. The old girl was smiling – she seemed to be looking more direct at me now.

'Yes. I think we can make a start with you. Take off your dress now and your shift too. We can't have yards of fabric flapping around your legs and over your head, girl, it impedes the flow, destroys the line and is positively lethal. Try this for size.'

She belched, took a gulp from the leather flask and indicated a pile of dark material on the floor by the swing. It was a pair of breeches made of thin material – like a fine lady's hose, only stronger – and a sort of camisole made of similar stuff. They were covered in cat hair. Once I'd got them on, Madame Celeste shuffled around me and nodded to herself.

'You have my body, Kitty.'

I buttoned it as she continued. 'Like me, you are a natural. As Paddy says, you have enormous potential. It's a mighty challenge, so it is, but I will make you the talk of London.'

*

A lump of coal in the little grate popped and spat a burning marble-sized fragment onto the rag carpet. Peggy kicked it back onto the hearth and glared at Jenny. 'Haven't you got somewhere to go? You're all trussed up like a bangtail at a funeral, after all.'

Jenny narrowed her eyes. 'As a matter of fact I do have an appointment myself this evening with a gentleman so I won't be around to see your performance, Kitty. That's why I particularly wanted to see you to send you on your way, so to speak. In fact, me and a lot of the girls here will be thinking about you tonight and sending our wishes up to you.'

Peggy pulled the ribbons so tight that I gasped. 'Ignore her, she's a jealous cow with an ugly mouth on her. We all want you to succeed.'

'Do *we* now? It's a long time since you've had a proper chat with the girls, isn't it, Peg? But then I suppose you've been too busy sucking on old Fitzy's whore-pipe to pay much attention to us.'

Peggy grabbed a scent bottle from the rickety dressing table by the fire and hurled it at Jenny's head. It missed her by inches and smashed against the far wall, filling the air with cheap violets.

Jenny snorted, tossed her brassy hair, stepped over the shattered glass and turned to the door. As she reached for the handle, the door opened to reveal Lucca standing in the gas-lit hallway. He was carrying a large cloth-bound parcel.

'And here's your ugly boyfriend, right on cue.'

Lucca pushed past her.

'Have you finished them?' Peggy's voice was bright and expectant. Lucca nodded and handed me the parcel. I could feel something hard and angular beneath the wrappings as I looked up at him. 'What's this then – a good-luck charm?'

He grinned and shrugged. 'You'll have to open it to see, Fannella.'

'Well, isn't that just the sweetest thing?' Jenny's voice was like sugared vinegar. 'A first-night gift from your doting beau.'

'I am not her beau.' Lucca practically spat the words into her face. There was an uncomfortable silence and Peggy started to tighten the ribbons again.

'That's what *you* say,' said Jenny. 'But we all know that a half-faced milk-turner like you would give his left eye', she paused unpleasantly, 'for a chance with a girl like Kitty. I'm not going until I see what you've brought her.'

Lucca reddened and turned his back on her. 'There isn't much time. Please open it.'

I stared at Jenny and the urge to slap her big shiny face was hard to resist, but I'd already made too many enemies among the girls at The Gaudy to risk her spreading more lies about the high and mighty ways of Miss Kitty Peck. So I just took a deep breath and turned back to Lucca and the parcel in my hands. I began to unwind the cloth and as I did so a single golden feather fell to the floorboards. A second later and I was holding the most beautiful pair of gold and silver wings. Real feathers were worked with painted plaster and mounted on a network of fine wires to create the delicate arcing shape.

'Oh Lucca,' I breathed. 'They're wonderful. Thank you.' I bobbed up to kiss his cheek, but he quickly turned away, conscious, I thought, of his scars and perhaps of Jenny.

'It's nothing. In Napoli, we make these as gifts at *Natale* –

at Christmas – for the little ones. I thought you would need them tonight to help you believe that you can truly fly.' He paused and an odd expression crossed his face. 'And to remind you of Joey – a cherub, remember what you told me? Tonight I thought you might need . . .'

He shrugged and smiled, but he looked worried.

'A guardian angel! Lucca, you are so feeling, and clever with it. They are beautiful.' Peggy cooed as she took the wings from my hands and started to fiddle with the bodice. 'Look, I've made a place to fix them to Kitty's costume just here. Oh!'

She stopped and started to dab at the sequin-strewn netting at my waist. 'I'm so sorry, I must have pulled too tight.'

I looked down and saw little spots of bright red blood seeping out through the silvery gauze and into the fabric of the bodice just above my waist. Some of the glass crystals sewn into my costume had dug too deep into my flesh when Peggy was tightening the ribbons. For a moment the image of a robin flew into my mind.

'Out, out damned spot.' Jenny stared at the stain and smiled. Peggy gasped, dropped the ribbons and covered my ears. We Gaudy girls might not have had much in the way of book learning, but we knew our Shakespeare when we heard it and most particular we knew that the Scottish play was never to be mentioned or quoted aloud unless you were actually on the stage. And even then only if you was in it.

'Lights in ten.'

Fitzy's great red face loomed round the door. He stepped into the now-crowded room, smiled and rubbed his hands together. 'Lovely job, Peggy. A hand's span waist there – very nice. We'll have to think of some way to reward you.'

I felt Peggy's shudder.

'Off we go then, Kitty, through the back so as no one can see you. This is going to be quite a night for The Gaudy, I can feel it in my water.'

He grabbed hold of my hand and yanked me out through the door and into the hallway.

As I passed Jenny she said, very loudly and very slowly, 'Break a leg, lovey.'

Chapter Five

That was almost the last time I saw Jenny Pierce – in the flesh.

Fitzy dragged me along the hall, down the stairs and into the warren of passages at the back of The Gaudy. We had to pick our way through old bits of scenery and a toot yard of props before we came to the door to the workshop out back. Snow was ankle-deep on the cobbles of the yard. Fitzy stepped out, still gripping my wrist, but I held back.

'I can't walk on that – look at my feet. They'll be ruined. And it's bleedin' cold too. Madame Celeste says I have to be kept warm, remember?'

Fitzy turned back and for a moment I thought he might do me one. Instead he looked down at the silver slippers and the ribbons that criss-crossed my legs up to the knee. Highly indecent it was. If my poor old Nan – God rest her soul – could've seen me she would have had something to say about it.

He swore under his breath and took off his jacket. 'Put this on then.'

The jacket smelt of cigar smoke, gin and dirty old man, but at least it was warm.

'Better, are we? Come on now, girl.' He set out across the yard, but I still didn't follow.

'Like I said, I can't go out there with these on my feet. And, anyway, that's not the way to the stage, is it?'

Fitzy swore again, more audible this time, and crunched back. He gathered me roughly up in his arms and started back across the yard with my feet dangling over the crook of his elbow. I could feel Lucca's lovely little wings crush and mangle up under the jacket. I wriggled and started to squawk.

Now, I wasn't a heavy packet by any means, but the cold and the effort of carrying me took old Fitzy's breath away. It was a couple of seconds before he was able to puff out, 'Just shut your trap, Kitty. Someone wants to have a word with you, so do as you're told.'

We went up by the side of the outbuildings where Lucca and the hands worked, and Fitzy turned into a narrow brick alleyway I'd never noticed before. It ran between the back wall of the workshop and the wall that divided The Gaudy's yard from the streets beyond. At the end of the alley a wooden gate stood open and through it I saw a neat black carriage pulled up on the street. Fitzy shouted something and the carriage jerked. Little steps clattered down into the snow.

A moment later and we were standing in front of the open door. The half-shuttered windows of the carriage were misted over, but I could see the pale glow of lamplight inside.

'Come in, Kitty Peck. We need to have a talk before your performance this evening.'

The peculiar, fluttering voice of Lady Ginger was unmistakable. I kicked and twisted about, but Fitzy gripped tighter and more or less posted me through the small door and into the carriage, which rocked about a bit as I landed ungainly on the seat opposite the old witch. The door slammed and one of the horses gave a low whinny.

Lady Ginger stared at me, her eyes glinting in the yellow

light. The carriage smelt of leather and opium, but beneath that there was something else too – something sweet and sour, something like milk on the turn, I thought.

After a moment she spoke. 'I assume that is not your costume, Miss Peck? Take it off. I want to see what I have bought.'

I bit my lip, shrugged away Fitzy's jacket and sat there with my shoulders hunched up and my hands clasped tight in my lap. The lamplight caught on the sequins and crystals sewn into the net of the bodice and my scrap of a skirt. The scandalised voice of old Nanny Peck piped up in my head – 'As naked as a pig in shit, but not as warm!'

Nanny Peck had come over from Ireland in the Thirties, bringing my mother with her. She had a rich turn of phrase – which, in time, had been elegantly supplemented by the language of Limehouse – and a country girl's natural suspicion of anything that smacked of loose morals. Indecent clothing had always been a subject of particular interest to Nanny Peck, but it was odd that I thought of her again now.

Lady Ginger narrowed her eyes and leaned back. She assessed me in a calculating, professional way, moving from my feet to my knees to my waist (I had my hands held tight just over the blood stain) and up to the top of the bodice where Peggy's ministrations with the ribbons had produced two white mounds that looked likely to escape at any moment. Tell truth, I didn't much like to catch sight of them when I looked down – they got in the way of the floor.

'Very nice. Very nice indeed.'

She nodded and leaned forward to adjust the thin gauze stuff on my shoulders, pulling it down so that even more of

44

me showed. The indignant voice of Nanny Peck went off again.

Lady Ginger was wearing watered black satin crusted with jet beads. Her silver plait was wound up on the top of her head and rubies as big as marbles hung from her ear lobes. Her knees were covered in a thick fur rug, not that she needed it. The carriage was as warm and stifling as her room at The Palace.

'Fitzpatrick tells me you are a natural. He tells me that your performance tonight will be a sensation.'

I picked at a nail and nodded. 'I . . . I've worked hard at it, Lady. The moves came easy and I'm not frightened of the heights.'

'So I understand.' She paused for a moment and when she spoke again her voice was crisp as old leaves. 'I trust you have not forgotten why you are doing this?'

I looked up and stared direct into her face. She had a lot of rouge on her cheeks and today her black lips were painted red like the rubies.

'No, I couldn't do that. Lady Ginger, please, my brother . . . I have to know. Is he . . . that it to say, where is . . .'

'Silence!' She raised a hand and the bangles on her arms clattered down into the lace at her elbow. 'That is precisely why I have come to see you – to remind you.'

Despite the cold, I could feel my naked back prickle with moisture against the leather of the seat as she continued. 'I do not want you to *fly* away with the idea that you are anything more than my employee. Even if your performance this evening makes you the talk of London, that is nothing to you, or to me. Do you understand?'

I was silent as she went on. 'Martha Lidgate is missing from The Comet. She hasn't been seen for nine days now. At this rate every girl I run in Paradise will be a memory within a year. So, do you see, Miss Peck, I don't want your head turned tonight. I want you to sing a pretty song, show that pretty body and titillate the punters with the possibility of your pretty death – but, most of all I want you to keep your wits about you, watch the theatre and tell Fitzpatrick what you see. You will have an unparalleled view of every corner of the hall.'

She broke off to cough, dabbing her mouth with a coloured silk square. She settled back, drew up the fur and licked her lips. Now that the red had rubbed off I could see they were stained black.

'If you survive the week without a safety net we will move you and your cage to The Carnival and then to The Comet.'

'But what about Joey?' I blurted. 'You promised. How do I know you aren't lying to me? If he's really alive, like you say, why can't I see him? At least give me something to show he's alive – a letter, he writes a lovely hand, I'd know that anywhere.'

Lady Ginger laughed and coughed again.

'How touching. When you have completed your service, we will consider his . . . situation. But be assured, Miss Peck, that unless you satisfy me, you will never see him again. Now go. Fitzpatrick tells me that the doors will only be opened tonight once you are in position. Apparently there's quite a crowd gathered in the street already. Fitzpatrick!'

She rapped on the side of the carriage. The door opened to reveal Fitzy shivering in the snow.

'About time, so it is. My trinkets are like ball bearings. Come on then, Kitty, there's a cage waiting for you.'

I made to pull the stinking coat back over my shoulders, but just as I turned to wrap it round me Lady Ginger leaned forward, swift as a greased adder, and plucked Lucca's little broken wings from the bodice.

'Shabby and pointless,' she smiled, crushing up the feathers and plaster in her heavily ringed hands. 'Take her.'

Fitzy bent forward and scooped me off the seat. The carriage rocked again and the horses spooked about, eager to be on the move. As he lifted me out I looked down at the feathers scattered around the bottom of Lady Ginger's fur. It looked like a cat had been there with a pigeon. The angel wings Lucca had made for me and for Joey were damaged beyond repair.

The door slammed like a trap and the lascar on the box above us cracked a whip over the heads of the horses. Lady Ginger's carriage rolled off into the snow and Fitzy swore and grumbled as he trudged back into the alleyway to deliver me to my cage.

Chapter Six

As the cage, with me hanging on inside it, was winched into position out from the stage and up higher and higher until it was swaying from the very centre of The Gaudy's painted ceiling over the empty seats, tables and the four tiers of red and gold booths set around the hall, all I could think about was Joey.

To be fair to the old bitch, that little talk had done the trick. I didn't like to admit it, even to myself, but during all those days in Madame Celeste's attic and more recently when we'd practised at night at The Gaudy after the shows and into the early hours, I'd begun to enjoy it.

I was good – I knew I was. And what's more, the hands who'd been specially selected by Fitzy to work the ropes and wires said so too.

Now, they'd seen it all a hundred times or more, so when you hear them all fizzing and boiling up about a new act, you know there's something tasty on the range. God forgive me, but there were actually nights up there in the cage as I practised my twirls, perfected my balances and tried out my voice, when I completely forgot about Joey and Alice and all them missing girls, and allowed myself to imagine a time when I was as free as the bird I was pretending to be, with all London at my feet, so to speak.

To be straight with you, Jenny Pierce and the other girls

in the halls had every right to be jealous. I was beginning to revel in the attention. I loved the danger and the glory of it. There – that's a shameful admission, isn't it?

Now, as I perched up there on my bar listening to the sounds of The Gaudy filling up below, I wasn't thinking about myself any more: I was thinking about my brother, just as she knew I would.

Be assured, Miss Peck, that unless you satisfy me, you will never see him again.

I could feel my eyes stinging – it was the smoke – but I didn't want to rub them because the exaggerated make-up Peggy had spent so long over would be ruined. So I just sat there in the dark with tears streaming down my face.

*

No one knew I was up there at first. The cage was covered with a hood of thin, dark silk with slits at the seams, which meant that I could look out quite easily, but no one could see in. Even if they had looked up, it's unlikely they would have made much of the great dark shape hanging seventy foot over their heads. Fitzy had ordered that The Gaudy's lights be kept low so the cage was lost in shadow and the smoke that rose up from the punters.

I hadn't thought about the smoke. Below me, scores of glowing red dots showed where someone was puffing on a cigarette or a cigar. It looked like an infernal version of the constellations Lucca sometimes showed me when we sat on the steps out back. My favourite was the Plough because it was easy to find. Lucca said his father had called it the *Sette Principi*, which, apparently, meant the sign of the Seven Princes and sounded very romantic to a girl from Limehouse.

The fumes coiled upwards filling my nose and then my lungs with the treacle fug of tobacco. It got pretty thick in that cage under the hood so I gripped the ropes of the swing and leaned forward, hooking my feet around the bars. The cage began to judder about a bit, but after a while it came steady. I pressed my face against one of the slits in the silk and breathed deep.

Below me to the left, The Gaudy's orchestra was filing into the pit in front of the stage. I say 'orchestra', but actually there were only four of them. 'Professor' Ruben the pianist, Tommy and Isaac the fiddle players, who cordially hated each other, and Old Peter, a gloomy Russian. He claimed his skills as a cornet player depended on the amount of firewater he necked back.

'It helps me forget,' he'd told me mournfully one evening at The Lamb.

The girls loved The Gaudy orchestra. They were all proper gentlemen with the soft-eyed sadness that musicians often seem to carry about them. After a show, they always took themselves and their instruments and their sadness to The Lamb two streets away, and often as not we'd join them. Three years ago Joey would be there too, sometimes alone and sometimes with his fancy friends. Where were those boisterous young men now, I wondered?

The raucous sound of laughter came up. Now I could smell the sweet tang of gin in the smoke. It was going to be a full house – word on the street was that The Gaudy was about to unveil something extraordinary. Well, that was Fitzy's word, anyway.

But it was true that my perspective from up there was remarkable. I could see into nearly every part of the hall. Directly below I watched as a well-dressed woman with bright red hair picked her way between the tables. She brushed against a man, apologised, moved on swiftly up the row and deftly pocketed a glinting gold fob watch into the folds of her skirt before trying the same routine on another Johnny. Interesting.

I looked over to the right and saw that the booths on the second tier were already busy. The Gaudy wasn't really a first-rank hall, but it still had a dozen or so boxes for the use of private parties and what you might call gentlemen patrons. A couple of them already had their curtains drawn.

I caught a flash of something bright in one of the booths – a brassy head bobbing up and down in a punter's lap. I couldn't see all of the man because the curtain was drawn up on his side, but I could see Jenny Pierce's purple bit of fluff quivering away as she went at it.

As a matter of fact I do have an appointment myself this evening with a gentleman . . .

I snorted. She might have had a face like a docker's nancy but at last she'd found a use for that nasty tongue of hers, I thought. And it's not as if the 'gentleman' had to look at her. After all, you don't have to watch a kettle to bring it to the boil.

I'd enjoy telling Lucca all about that later. But then I thought better of it because he didn't always appreciate me talking low. In fact, when I tried my new song on him he'd been furious and we'd had a right set-to. I think the wings were a peace offering.

The orchestra started up and the punters began shouting and laughing even louder.

The first act up was Dismal Jimmy, a droll Scot whose convoluted stories were usually a sure way to settle the hall. Only tonight it didn't work. The air was full of hoots and cat-calls as Jimmy finished up and Mrs Conway came on in her Britannia rig. Fitzy had promised her the slot before mine by way of compensation.

'I'm not here for tough old game. Where's the fresh meat?' called a voice from the dark.

'Fuck off, horseface, and give us all a break,' another added, more loudly. He seemed to be speaking for quite a lot of them. People in the gallery started to stamp and the gaslights shook in their brackets.

Within seconds The Gaudy was in uproar and, from my cage, I could see that Mrs Conway was in tears. Fitzy – all shiny buttons and straining mustard velvet – came bounding on stage right, whispered to her and patted her off. Then he turned to the punters and smiled. His big, red greasy face looked like a harvest moon with the pox, so it did.

He waved his hands in the air and called for a 'bit of quiet in the hall'.

The shouting stopped but the stamping continued. Fitzy nodded, more to himself than to anyone else, then he took a step forward and cleared his throat.

'Ladies and gentlemen, it is my great pleasure to present to you this evening a performance of dazzling aerial artistry, a display of death-defying courage never matched before in this theatre or any other. With the voice of a nightingale, the grace of an angel and the body of Venus herself . . .' He stopped and rubbed his hands suggestively as low, appreciative whistles ripped through the hall. 'May I present to you, The Limehouse Linnet herself, Miss Kitty Peck!'

There was a drum roll and the hood covering my cage was whipped free by hands stationed at the ends of ropes at four quarters of the hall. The limelights came up strong and for a second I was almost blinded. I'd never sat in the cage in the dark that long before starting up.

But there wasn't even time to blink. My music struck up and immediately I began to dip and twirl into the first stages of my routine. I'd done it so many times now I didn't have to think. Not about the grips, not about the balances, not about the swaying and creaking of the glittering cage and not about the empty seventy foot between me and the heads of the punters below.

At first they were quiet – stunned, I think. And then the whistles and the cat-calls started up – very appreciative they was. Not like the ones for Mrs C.

And then I started to sing . . .

> I've got a tidy nest
> But I'm looking for a cock
> Who can help me find the key
> To my tiny little lock?
> I lost it in the park
> When I was tugging on a worm
> Now I'm looking for a gentleman
> Who'll do me a good turn.

Chapter Seven

Pickpocketing was a favourite. That red-haired woman I noticed on the first night was a regular dipster. Watches were her thing, but I saw her lift 'kerchiefs, pocket books and even a jewel dangling from a smart lady's ear. I didn't mean Red any harm – she was a grafter, I'll give her that. At the end of that first week me and my cage were moved to The Carnival – a low sort of hall on the other side of Paradise, up Bethnal Green way – and I saw her up to her usual tricks there too. I felt bad, but I thought I'd better mention it to Fitzy.

After that I didn't see her no more.

Red wasn't the only one. There were a couple of bum-fluff lads who worked as a team, plying their marks with beer and gin until they were able to strip him (or her) of anything of value as they sat there and stewed.

A tall, well-dressed gentleman had a very neat way with the lifting of small items. I watched him on several occasions as he deftly unscrewed the silver top of his cane to deposit the objects he'd stolen into a hollow space inside.

Then there were the bangtails – the sort unregulated by Lady Ginger – who frequented the shabby boxes at The Carnival. I'm no prude, but the tricks I saw them turn! I didn't even know that a couple of them were anatomically possible until I had a very frank chat with Peggy one evening after a show. I was glad she generally came with me wherever

I performed and I was glad she looked after my paint box too. There were stories doing the rounds of theatre girls who ended up a ruin when a jealous rival put ground glass or acid into their face powder. Plenty of the girls in Lady Ginger's halls were as hard towards me as Jenny Pierce . . . and I can't say as I blamed them.

And that brings me to Jenny. No one realised she'd gone missing at first. She'd been so tight wound about what she saw as my promotion that it seemed highly likely she'd flounced off in her feathers and war paint just to prove she still had it in her.

We all expected her to turn up any day, preening in a new bonnet or soaked in some fancy cologne. Even when she missed three shows on the trot, risking Fitzy's anger and, most probably a fine, we still thought she was off somewhere licking her wounds like a vicious old she-cat. No, Jenny Pierce could take care of herself and none of us suspected that her absence was anything more than ill temper and a sore head.

Don't mistake me, we was all frightened by the way the girls from the halls were disappearing, we knew something very wrong was happening, but no one spoke about it for fear of bringing trouble to their doorstep. Like I said, the theatre is a superstitious place at the best of times. We all went about our business as usual, but we'd begun to keep our wits as sharp as the knives a couple of girls hid in their purses.

It was the Wednesday, five days after my first show at The Gaudy, that word came from Jenny's lodgings in Rope-maker's Fields. Her landlady, Mrs Skanks, sent pock-faced Bessie Docket – another of the Gaudy girls who called that flea-infested doss-house down near the river home – along to the theatre with a final demand for Jenny's rent.

Now, Ropemaker's was a filthy place and Jenny was welcome to it. Mother Maxwell's wasn't what you'd call smart, but at least it was clean in every way. Mrs Skanks turned a blind eye to the business some of her girls got up to. Tell truth, she was so far gone on the gin most days she probably wouldn't have noticed if an entire ship's crew had walked through her door. But she come to quick enough when the rent wasn't paid.

Jenny hadn't been seen at Ropemaker's Fields – or anywhere else for that matter – since the Friday previous and her landlady thought it only fair, apparently, that Fitzy should pay up for one of his girls. As Bessie told us, still quaking after her encounter with Fitzy, no one at Mrs Skanks's would dare to skip a rent day – and thinking of that woman's freckled meaty arms and fists the size of ham hocks, I believed her.

I didn't like Jenny, but I didn't wish evil on her. I felt guilty, as if her blood was on my hands. *Out, out damned spot.* That's what she'd said in my dressing room that evening. She should have known better than to tempt fate like that. I thought back to that last time I'd seen her in the box with her gent. I didn't give it much thought then and looking back there hadn't been much to see apart from her big yellow head bobbing up and down.

But what was I supposed to see?

For all that I was up there in the cage night after night, watching all the petty thefts and indecencies that gave the halls such a black name, I wasn't picking up on anything that could point me the way to finding out what had happened to Jenny Pierce or to any of them other missing girls.

When I took my crumbs back to Fitzy I could tell he wasn't happy and it didn't make me feel too easy in myself. Tell truth, I was beginning to feel a right nark telling tales on poor types like me who needed to make a living. The problem was I needed to give him something to feed back to the old bitch to show I was keeping my part of the bargain and I had nothing else to offer.

On the evening of my last show at The Gaudy he caught me and Peggy just as we was leaving. He stood in front of the door leading out to the workshop and barred our way.

'Where do you think you're going?' I felt Peggy stiffen beside me, but he wasn't talking to her. I looked up into his coarse red face. The usual aroma of liquor was rolling off him and the remains of something he'd eaten was caught up in the whiskers around his mouth. I gripped Peggy's hand and squeezed it.

'We're going back to our lodgings – we always walk together part of the way now – all of us do. You know it's not safe for a girl alone.'

'Safe!' Fitzy snorted and leaned forward. The stench of his rotten teeth made me catch my breath. He stared at Peggy and I saw his tongue move over his lower lip, then he looked back at me. 'A bit early for you two to be leaving, isn't it?'

I shook my head. 'It's late and it's cold. I need to rest before we move over to The Carnival. Madame Celeste said I should have at least one free day a week, for the sake of my muscles. She was most particular on that, remember? Come on, Peg.' I stepped forward.

Fitzy didn't move, but his little eyes narrowed. 'Have you been going home straight after the performance every evening, girl?'

I knew what he was driving at. It was common knowledge that a lot of girls in the halls offered late entertainment, if you get me, and Fitzy liked to take a cut of their earnings, but that was never part of this deal. I squared my shoulders and looked at him straight.

'I'm not going to wait around making chit chat with the Johnnies, if that's what you mean. Isn't it enough that I'm hanging up there every night all done up as a tuppenny drab, without me actually putting out as one? I'm doing what you want, aren't I?'

'Are you now? We'll see about that.' He grunted and moved away from the door. As me and Peggy stepped down into the icy yard he called out, 'And it's not me you want to be worrying about, is it, Kitty? Think on that.'

As if I'd forgotten. Every night now when they winched the cage with me inside it up from the stage and out over the hall I'd close my eyes, hold Joey's Christopher tight in my hand and promise him that everything would come right. This time I'd see something.

It never worked.

But I tell you one thing – I *was* a sensation, just like Fitzy told Lady Ginger. My act even made a corner of *The London Pictorial News*:

Miss Kitty Peck, The Limehouse Linnet, nightly defies gravity to delight her growing band of ardent admirers. She is our city's most daring and radiant rising star, but this correspondent declares that it is the purity of her voice and the effulgence of her soul that glow most brightly in the East.

Well, that was all very complimentary, but those fine words were accompanied by a bold sketch that showed even more of my legs (and other parts) than that little spangled costume allowed. It made Lucca remark that my 'purity' and the 'effulgence' were probably not the first things that would arrest the readers' attention when they turned to page seven. Lucca had to explain to me what effulgence meant and I thought it was a lovely thing to say, quite the sort of word that Joey might have used.

At least there was one thing that made Fitzy happy – the takings.

Every evening now, queues formed in the streets outside the halls where I performed. I had thought that the success of that first night was down to Fitzy's theatricals with his whispers on the street, the black cover over the cage and all that malarkey, but I was wrong. No, the punters knew what they were getting all right, and they were wild for it. Fitzy had my cage illuminated by strategically positioned limelight flares, and, as the customers filed in, I fluttered about a bit and I gave out as good as I got when they called up to me.

Most of them were respectful, but just occasionally you'd get a drunken Johnny with a really filthy mouth on him. Although there was no love lost between me and the old bugger, I'll admit I was grateful when I saw Fitzy's barrel of a body bumping a half-cut heckler up the aisle and out through the curtains. It didn't do for a girl in my position to get a reputation. Joey had always been very clear on that.

For some reason, the spot just under my cage was particularly popular. Most nights I'd look down and see all these calf-faced ninnies staring up at me. Generally they just looked, but sometimes I caught sight of the odd dirty bleeder fetching mettle. What they was doing with their hands turned me over. I wondered what would happen if The Limehouse Linnet brought the fatty chops she'd had for her dinner up over their greasy little heads, but I reflected that it probably wouldn't be good for trade. No, when that happened I just concentrated hard on my purity and effulgence. Now I knew what they were.

We soon discovered that there was no point in anyone else going on before me. Mrs Conway was right put out and I don't think Dismal Jimmy was too pleased about it neither. The regulars turned quite mutinous until they saw their pay packets, but what could you do? If a punter came into the hall and saw me hanging up there in my little bits of sparkled stuff, he wasn't going to sit through a dog act, a sentimental serenade, a magician and a puppet routine before getting stuck into the main course.

Fitzy worked out that if I opened the evening and closed it a couple of hours later, then everyone (except Mrs Conway) went home happy – 'specially if the chorus came on in the middle and did a nymph routine.

That gave me a lot of time every night to watch from my cage, not that it did much good.

By the time I was due to start at the third of Lady Ginger's halls, The Comet, exactly two weeks after that first night, it wasn't only Jenny Pierce who'd gone missing. Another girl – just fourteen years old – had disappeared from The Gaudy, right under my very cage.

Chapter Eight

Lucca threw another shovel of coal onto the fire. His room, under the bony eaves of a tall, gloomy house just a street away from the river, was damp and always cold, even at the height of summer. Now it was January and the cobbles outside were crusted with hoar frost thicker than a man's finger. I took his coat off the bed and wrapped it round me.

'I don't know why you don't try to find yourself somewhere better than this,' I complained. 'It's cold enough in here to freeze a duck's arse.'

Lucca wrinkled his nose and threw another, very small, nugget of coal into the grate. After a moment he turned to look at me. I was sitting as near to the hearth as possible with my back against his bed.

'You have become coarse since you have become famous.' He pushed his long dark hair back so that I could see the scarred half of his face in the firelight and he narrowed his gaze. 'You never used to feel the chill in here, Kitty. But that was before you dressed as a . . .'

He stopped and pursed his lips, but he continued to stare at me, the fingers of his right hand rubbing at the ridged and melted skin beneath his blind eye, like he was trying to pull it back to see me more clearly.

'Dressed as a what?' I was indignant. 'She gave me money to buy myself some better clothes, so I did. What of it? And

Fitzy says I should look my best at all times – like a lady. I might be up there half-naked in that cage, but I don't want to give the Johnnies the wrong idea, do I?'

I smoothed the skirt of my new blue satin dress. It was cut to the fashion with a snug bodice and tight sleeves that frothed into a billow of lace at the elbow. I shrugged my shoulders so that the lace that was tucked around the dipping neckline came up a bit higher and I pulled the coat tighter round me. Lucca's words had made me feel self-conscious, but worse, I knew he was right.

'I'll wear what I like,' I snapped. 'And I'll mind my language if you mind your manners. You don't own me, Lucca Fratelli.' I stood up, took off his old coat and threw it on the bed, then I rammed a new feathered bonnet down over my curls and turned to the door.

'I might as well freeze in my own room back at Mother Maxwell's.'

Lucca sprang up and caught my hand. 'I'm sorry, Fannella, truly. Don't go, please. I was thoughtless.' He smiled apologetically and squeezed my hand. 'I'll put some more coal on the fire. It seems so long since we talked properly – like before?'

He kneeled in front of the hearth again, poking at the glowing coals with the shovel. The scarred half of his face was hidden in shadow as he got a lively little fire crackling.

Not for the first time I found myself thinking what a good-looking lad Lucca would have been if it wasn't for the accident. No, more than that – he would have been beautiful. His profile was perfect, like one of them statues he was so fond of showing me in his arty books. Lucca had a veritable library

63

piled under his bed – mostly in Italian, although the pictures were lovely.

As I stood there, I noticed how his eyelashes curled and how his lips seemed very firm and distinct and of a sudden I wondered what it might be like to kiss them. Lucca looked up and I saw the melted half of his face again. Would it matter, I wondered? I felt a flush spread up from my neck and across my cheeks.

'That's better, Kitty, you look warmer now – *accogliente*.' Lucca grinned and patted the threadbare carpet in front of the fire. I rustled down next to him, crossing my legs under the stiff satin skirt that peaked up around me like a small blue tent. I kept my eyes fixed on the fire, not wanting to give him the idea that I'd been thinking about anything other than getting cosy.

It was a funny thing, me and Lucca. Apart from Joey, there was no one I cared more about in the world. When he'd come to work at The Gaudy, just after his accident, none of the other girls would talk to him at first. They were afraid of his face, which looked a lot worse then, I can tell you, what with all the flaking bits of skin and the angry red ridges of scorched flesh that stretched down to his collar.

But one evening I was clearing up in the gallery, singing away as usual, and after I'd finished I heard someone clapping from the stage. It was Lucca, who was working late on a painted bit of scenery. That was the first time he called me Fannella.

I suppose I'd just turned fifteen at the time and Lucca was . . . well, I'm not too sure to be straight with you. I'd lay a bet he's never more than twenty now, so he must have been about seventeen then. And that's another thing, see, Lucca never talks about his past, about his accident or about how he came to be here in Limehouse.

He'll talk about his village back home, and about Naples where he was prenticed, and sometimes he'll talk about his family – brothers, sisters and that. But if I was to ask him about where he was before The Gaudy and what brought him to London in the first place, he'll slam up tighter than a whelk. Now, I know better than most when not to press a point. I had enough of that with Joey, so I bite my lip, but all the same . . .

Working in the halls you get a very clear idea of just how dangerous limelight can be. We're all wary of it. Some of the hands have burns running up past their elbows. It's a vicious light, but we rely on it, every night, to make the magic work. Lucca must have had a bad time of it and I wasn't surprised he didn't want to be reminded – 'specially as it took away half his face just when it mattered. For what it's worth, I reckon he ran away to hide at The Gaudy, and I reckon there was someone he was running away from too – someone who couldn't love a ruin.

Lucca sat back and propped the coal shovel against the side of the grate. For some reason at that moment I became very aware of his wiry body on the rug next to me. I shifted and the satin whispered as it settled into a new shape.

'So, what have you discovered, Fannella? What have you seen from your gilded cage?'

I was grateful for the question.

'Nothing. Well, nothing that can help those poor girls, anyway. Did you hear that Maggie Halpern has gone now?'

Lucca nodded. 'She was so little – just fifteen?'

'Fourteen.' I shuddered. 'She went missing on my fifth night at The Gaudy. I saw her too – she was serving the tables in the hall. I watched her trying to get round with a tray. You know what a scrap of a thing she was. I was worried she might drop it.' Truth is I noticed her particularly because she reminded me of Alice – just for a second I looked down and mistook her.

Lucca bit at a shred of skin around his thumbnail. His fingers were stained with paint as usual. 'It makes no sense. Maggie was so quiet. She was a decent girl. Some of the others were grown women and perhaps they—'

'They what?' I asked sharply. 'You knew them. They were *all* decent types – Clary and Sally could be a bit wild, but they weren't dabbing it up for punters. Jenny, well, I give you she had a sideline going as a penny upright . . .', Lucca winced as I continued, 'but the others – no, I can't see it. And there's Alice.'

I stared into the fire and thought of that half-sewn skirt on her bed and the needle and cotton on the wash stand in her tiny room below mine. What had happened to her?

'She was just a child, Lucca, and a good one. There was never any trouble with Alice. Fact is, I often wished she'd shown a bit more spirit, but she was soft as a lamb, you know she was.'

'What does Peggy say?'

I shook my head. 'She won't talk about Alice and not because she's a superstitious type like the others. Peggy won't talk about her because it hurts. Peggy and me were all she had – and you on Sundays.'

Lucca crossed himself – he was a regular at St Peter's over Hatton Garden way where the services was all in Italian. 'When she came to mass with me, she couldn't understand the Latin, but she said she loved the sound of it.'

'She's the worst, and I feel responsible somehow.'

He was quiet for a moment. 'So what is happening to them? Where are they? If they are dead, where are their bodies? If they are living . . .'

I shivered despite the heat that was coming off the little fire now.

Alice Caxton, Clary Simmons, Esther Dixon, Sally Ford, Jenny Pierce, Martha Lidgate, Maggie Halpern.

Those seven girls had disappeared off the face of the earth just like Joey. I'd been up in that cage for nearly two weeks now and I hadn't seen a thing that could help him or them. Lady Ginger's voice crackled in my head. *Unless you satisfy me, you will never see him again.* How could I 'satisfy' her if I didn't know what I was looking for? I reached into the neck of my dress and rolled Joey's Christopher between my fingers.

After a moment I said, 'All I know for a fact is that if I want to see my brother again, I've got to find out what's happening to Lady Ginger's girls.'

Lucca leaned forward and prodded the coals. His hair flopped forward and I couldn't see his face as he muttered something in Italian. Ah, he's thinking it through, I thought. Lucca was a clever one, like I said.

'There must be something. You must have seen something from the cage? Maggie – tell me again, who did she serve, who did she speak to?'

I looked into the flames and pictured the hall. The Gaudy

was packed that night. My act was attracting punters from all over the city so it wasn't a surprise to see that several tables served by Maggie were occupied by toffs. Usually their sort wouldn't be seen dead at a place like The Gaudy – it was better than The Carnival, mind, which was little more than a gin palace with a hall attached, but it wasn't as smart as The Comet neither. It didn't matter, though, people were so wild to see The Limehouse Linnet – and tell their friends all about it – that they were willing to park their tails in the cheap seats with the lesser sorts.

The air had been thick with smoke and with the smell of ale and gin. I remembered seeing Maggie's scrawny arms as she strained to carry the tray. I'd watched her pick her way between the tables and I'd seen the men who didn't budge or give her a second glance as she tried to get by. Maggie Halpern was a colourless creature, her face, her hair, her clothes – they was all a faded shade of brown. No one noticed her except me – and maybe someone else?

I shook my head. 'There's nothing. It was business as usual. No one spoke to her, no one even knew she was there. You know what she was like.'

Lucca leaned forward, resting his forehead in his hands. It was his thinking position.

'And Jenny? What about her? Tell me again, what you saw.'

I went through it all – Jenny in the box . . . her head going up and down . . . the man behind the curtain – Lucca held up his hand. 'Yes! The man she was with – what do you remember about him?'

'Nothing. I couldn't see him proper, remember? And, anyway, how was I to know that was the last time I'd catch sight of her? After that set-to in the dressing room, I wasn't exactly feeling warm towards the old rantipole.' I grinned. 'Mind you, I was going to tell you all about it – how he didn't even have to look at her mug while she was on the job. And how – all the while – he was beating time to Professor Ruben and the boys. I kept seeing the ring on his little finger on the box rail catching the light – up and down, up and down, like Jenny's yellow head.'

Lucca just stared at me. 'There you are, Fannella, you have your first clue – he wears a signet ring.'

I rolled my eyes.

'And so does half of London. Even Joey wore a ring.'

Chapter Nine

'The Lady is not happy, so she isn't.'

Fitzy smoothed the sheet of paper on the desk in front of him and squinted down at the looping black writing through the pair of wire-framed glasses he normally hid in his top pocket. The writing was old-fashioned, very neat, very elegant like, with flourishes and elaborate curls. Even though it was upside down in front of me I could see it was an educated hand – a lady's hand, I thought.

I watched as he traced down the page with a fat finger until he found the bit he was looking for and began to read aloud:

Remind Miss Peck of her obligations. It is almost two weeks now and she is yet to provide anything of use. Moreover, it seems that the mother of the Lidgate girl has approached the constabulary. I need hardly tell you, Fitzpatrick, the consequences of investigation into my business affairs. Fortunately, I have dealt with this as I have had to deal with much else, but it is a source of disappointment to me that, despite providing our song-bird with unparalleled access to my halls – at no small expense, I must add – she has offered little more than general tittle-tattle of the most tame and uninteresting variety.

I reached across the desk and tried to take Lady Ginger's letter but Fitzy slammed his hand down so hard on top of mine that I yelped. He removed my hand from the paper like it was something dirty and carried on.

I cannot but think that you have failed me in this. Perhaps you have not adequately communicated the severity of the situation to the young lady? Or is it perhaps the case that fame has dulled her sense of familial loyalty? If I do not receive useful information soon, I will send my men to Joseph Peck and the cut will be a choice one. Assure her of this and be assured that you, too, will hear from me. I believe it is time to make the true nature of her task plain. I trust you will do this on my behalf and that the girl will deliver.

Fitzy leaned back, took off his glasses and chewed his lower lip. He thumped the letter again. 'She's blaming me, clear as the nose on your face. This letter is a threat to the *both* of us, Kitty. Unless you give The Lady what she wants, it's not only your precious brother who's going to lose his bollocks.'

He was right, of course. To most people that letter might have looked as dry as the sawdust on the floor of a carpenter's workshop, but to Fitzy and me that workshop was stacked with coffins. You only had to bring to mind the old cow's voice saying those words aloud and you could feel the lights shrivel up in your belly. Still, I have to admit there was a tiny part of me that thought to myself: *I will send my men to Joseph Peck* – he was definitely alive, then, somewhere?

Fitzy clicked his yellow fingers in front of my face – they

came so close I could smell the tang of old cigar on them. 'What have you got to say to that?'

I flinched. What could I say?

'I . . . I'm doing my best. I've been up there for eleven nights now with nothing more than stale smoke and gin-breath between me and the floor. I tell you about everything I see – and I've already saved you and The Lady a pretty packet, I know that. What's more, the halls have never brought in as much trade. Mr Jesmond at The Carnival reckons his takings have increased four times over.'

'But it's not enough, Kitty, is it? We both know that The Lady's reputation is what's at stake here. Someone is pissing on her patch, so they are, and she can't afford to ignore that. Think about it. Her name is what keeps me safe. It's what keeps all of this going.' He gestured around the cluttered office with its dainty day bed, flowered cushions and china plates.

'There's plenty of Barons out there with a keen eye on Paradise. The only thing stopping them from muscling in and making life very . . . uncomfortable for us all is The Lady herself – or the thought of what she might do to them.' He produced a square of chequered silk from his pocket and dabbed at his big pockmarked face. Fitzy's forehead was covered with beads of sweat and his left eye was twitching again. He pulled back a drawer and took out a leather flask. He removed the top and swigged several mouthfuls before screwing the silver cap back on again. As he did so, I noticed that his hands were shaking. He wiped his mouth with the silk and tapped the letter.

'These aren't idle threats. If you want to see your brother

alive again – as much of him as possible, that is – you are going to have to start coming up with the goods, my girl.'

I could feel my heart beating double time under my new bodice. Fitzy was clearly a frightened man – and of a sudden it come home to me, very forcible, that there was a lot more at stake than I realised. If someone like Fitzy was worried, what should the rest of us feel like?

'Well?' He stared at me, expectant. His bloodshot eyes were almost lost beneath the forest of ginger bristles that rambled across the bridge of his thick nose. I don't know why, but as I stood there I brought to mind Ma telling me and Joey some Bible story about the Hanging Gardens of Babylon. Very exotic I thought it sounded at the time, although the memory of it now and the sight of Fitzy's eyebrows made me begin to smile. It's odd, but when things are black I often get the urge to laugh out loud.

The blow – hard, vicious and faster than you'd credit for a man who looked like a walrus – caught me across the left side of my head. I stumbled forward and felt my teeth tear into skin and crunch against the wood as I slammed into the desk.

'It's no laughing matter, girl.' Fitzy's face was purple. His breathing came shallow and he coughed as he leaned over and took hold of my hair, dragging my face up so that I could see the spittle catching in the ends of his moustache as he roared. His breath was thicker than the air in a yard privy.

'You're nothing more than property, Kitty Peck, and don't you forget it. You might be a pretty piece up there, night after night, but this is an ugly business. It's not just your fancy brother whose life is at stake here – it's all of us. All of

Paradise depends on The Lady for protection. She owns you, girl. Give her what she wants.'

I pulled free, leaving a handful of hair in his grasp. I could taste iron in my mouth and when I put my hand to my stinging lip it was wet. I could feel the anger boiling up inside me too and before I thought to stop myself the words came out in a spatter of blood.

'I can't make up what's not there, can I? I don't know what's happening to them girls any more than she does. It's all very well for her, but she's not the one with her breakfast hanging out every night over half of Limehouse, is she? Don't you think I'd tell you if I knew what was going on? I don't even know what I'm supposed to be looking for.'

I stood there opposite him, my hands on my hips. I could feel the blood trickling down my chin now, but I wasn't going to cry. I knew from Peggy how much he liked that.

Fitzy's eyes glimmered and he settled back into his leather chair. I heard it breathe out as his big body squeezed into its padded embrace. Then that nasty grin began to twist across his face again.

'That's just it. You see it's not you, exactly, who we need to be doing the looking.' His stubby finger worked down the curling lines of Lady Ginger's letter again and stopped near the end.

'Here it is. "*I believe it is time to make the true nature of her task plain.*"' He looked up at me from beneath his eyebrows, the muscle still working in the corner of his left eye. 'Now what do you suppose that means?'

I shook my head. My ears were ringing and the room was beginning to spin from the blow.

'Remember that little talk we had about you leaving the hall so early after every performance?'

There seemed to be two of him sitting in front of me now and they were both speaking.

'From now on, Kitty, you will stay on and admit callers to your dressing room. I want you to be a little more *friendly* with your admirers. You start at The Comet on Friday and I want you to entertain the gentlemen. Do you understand?'

His slug-like lips disappeared into the straggling ginger hairs of his moustache as the smile spread even wider. 'The Lady wants results, Kitty. Jesus alone knows why you're so devoted to that brother of yours . . .', he spat to one side of the desk, '. . . but if you want to keep him alive and the rest of us safe it looks like you're going to have to put yourself out, so it does.'

The room swam. The thought of allowing any of the Johnnies near enough to breathe on me, to paw at me, to . . .

Fitzy continued, 'Let them in, let them make free with you – I think you know what I mean – and let one of them give himself away.' He tapped the letter. 'The Lady's just reminded me of a very important fact. You're not just up there to watch, you're our *bait*.'

*

It was only when I reached the workshop that the tears came. Danny took one look at me and called out for Lucca.

'What's happened to you, love?' Danny asked, stuffing a bit of turps rag into my hand. 'Your bottom lip's the size of an egg and split too.'

I could feel the blood crusted on my chin and even on my neck. When I looked down I could see spots of red on the white mounds of flesh crushed upwards by the bodice. I didn't think the Johnnies would make much of me now.

'Lucca!' Danny called again, and after a moment Lucca's head appeared over the rail of the workshop loft. I heard him swear in Italian and a moment later he was down the ladder and pushing the hair back from my face.

'Who did this to you?' His face was tight with fury as he took the rag from my hand, spat on it and started to wipe the blood stains. I winced as he dabbed at my lip and my fat, hot tears fell on the back of his hand.

'F . . . Fitzpatrick,' I gulped. It wasn't so much the pain as the humiliation that got me.

'Bastard!' Danny spat on the floor. 'Hit a woman, would he? Someone needs to teach that bloated bag of horse shit a lesson.' I was glad he didn't know the half of it.

'*Pezzo di merda*,' Lucca muttered as he touched my cheek gently. 'You have a bloom coming here too, Fannella.'

I must have looked blank so he corrected himself. 'A bruise. What else has he done to you? Has he . . .? Are you . . .?' Lucca looked over to Danny who nodded, gathered up some stage bits and headed for the door.

'I'll let Peggy know,' he called back. 'She's going to need a lot of paint tonight to cover that mess. Sorry, Kitty, I didn't mean . . . I meant . . . well, you know.' He shrugged uncomfortably and disappeared into the yard.

Once we were alone I broke into great noisy heaving sobs and Lucca folded his arms round me until, eventually, I

76

stopped. My head was aching now from the crying and from Fitzy's blow.

'What happened?' Lucca looked down at me; his jaw was clenched with anger and the scars across his face appeared stretched and white. We sat down on a pile of sacking and he held my hands in his as I explained about the letter. When I got to the bit about the '*choice cut*' I felt his grip tighten.

'And that's not all. Fitzy wants me to put out for them all now. Entertain them – you know what that means. But I've never . . .' I paused and looked down at my hands in Lucca's. 'He says that's the way to flush out the . . . well, whatever it is that's going on. I'm to be the bait.'

Lucca jumped up. 'This madness has to stop. You cannot continue . . . *che farsa!* I will go to him now.'

'No! Wait . . .'

Last thing I wanted was for Lucca to square up to Fitzy. The old bruiser might have been half-cut and more than twice his age, but he'd make catsmeat of him. Besides, if what Fitzy said about people eyeing up Lady Ginger's patch was true we were all in trouble. There were worlds beyond Paradise where the Barons were every bit as ruthless as The Lady herself. And if they moved in, they'd want to bring their own in with them.

I grabbed his hand again and tried to smile, but stretching my lips broke the skin and I could feel blood starting to flow again.

'Lucca, can I come over and visit you at The Wharf to-morrow? They're taking the cage to The Comet after the performance tonight so I've got one day off while they're fix-ing. That's your regular afternoon off, isn't it – Thursday?'

He nodded as I continued. 'You get some coal in and I'll bring a meat pie and a bottle and we can talk. We'll go through it all again. Like you said, there must be something I'm missing, something I've seen but not seen.'

Lucca pulled at the scar on his face. It was a habit of his when he was thinking. Then he smiled. There was a glint of mischief in his eye as he spoke.

'As a matter of fact, I already have an appointment tomorrow afternoon. But I think you might like to come with me. In fact, I know you will . . .'

Chapter Ten

Them breeches itched something rotten. I don't know how men can walk around all day with their legs and parts all crying out for air. I kept wanting to have a good scratch, but looking around me, it seemed that real men didn't seem to find it too bothersome, so I tried to resist the urge.

I looked at other men a lot. I noted the way they walked, confident like – wider than they really was, if you get my meaning? They kept their chins up and they looked on-comers in the eye, instantly sizing them up as a threat, an equal or someone to despise.

When you're a girl – unless you're a dabber out for trade – you keep your eyes low, your shoulders hunched and you walk small. You don't want to draw unwanted attentions on yourself so you keep to the side of the street, by the wall. The last thing you do is strut down the middle like a bantam cock.

But that's what Lucca made me do.

'Watch them, Fannella, and copy them exactly. You are an actress, *si*? It will be easy.'

*

I wasn't going to go at first. When I got to his room at The Wharf and saw all the gear laid out on his bed for me I was for turning on my heels and going straight home.

'What kind of a rig is that?' I asked, scandalled. Tell truth, we all knew a type hanging out round Limehouse of an evening. These girls catered for a different sort of clientele – and you'd be most surprised if you knew quite how fancy the ladies looking for boys who were really girls actually were.

Anyways, I didn't have anything against the Toms – they were only making a living like the rest of us. But that doesn't mean I wanted to join them.

'Is this some sort of a joke, Lucca?'

My voice came out all tight and high.

He cocked his head to one side. 'You wanted us to talk and I am very happy to listen. But I have a life too, Kitty, and I have already made plans. If you want to come with me today, you have to be a man. No woman will be allowed to go where I am about to take you. And we will talk later.'

He smiled. On the good side of his face a dimple appeared, but the other side drew itself into a knot of bumpy flesh between his nose and lip.

'It's your choice.'

Well, I wasn't going to turn down an offer like that, was I?

No woman will be allowed to go where I am about to take you.

We'll see about that, I thought.

Lucca stepped out of the room while I changed into the clothes on the bed. It was fine stuff – breeches, a shirt, a jacket – all a bit on the large size for me, but neat for a man.

I tucked the shirt tails into the waistband and fastened the buttons on the fly and at the collar. Very odd it was – like being trapped. I read once about the jackets with all the ties and flaps that they use on the poor creatures at Bedlam over in Southwark and I wondered if that's what it felt like.

Lastly, I bound up my hair tight as I could stand it and pinned it to the back of my head. Didn't do much good, though. Anyone would know I was a girl, I thought, as a springy blonde curl wriggled free and dangled over my eyebrows.

I called Lucca back in.

'What do you think then?' I turned and faced him, my hands on my hips.

'*Madonna mia.*' The words came as a whisper. He stopped at the door for a moment and then took a step back.

I'll admit it, I was disappointed. 'It's not going to work, is it? I still look like a girl, don't I?'

Lucca shook his head. 'No, it's not that. It's . . . Kitty, look at yourself.'

I went over to the foot of the bed where Lucca had propped up against the wall a bit of broken mirror he'd taken from The Gaudy. I adjusted the slant so that I could see more of myself and stepped back.

I was quite surprised. If it wasn't for the hair and a certain roundness in a crucial area under the shirt, I could have passed for a lad – quite a pretty one, mind – if you didn't look too hard.

'It's not that bad. If it's the hair I could wear a hat?'

He swore under his breath and came to stand next to me. 'Look again. Who do you see?'

I looked again and when I got what he was driving at I caught my breath. 'Bloody hell! I'm Joey, aren't I?'

It was true. The boy staring back at me from the mirror was a smaller, softer version of my brother.

Lucca dipped to fold back the hem on the breeches. 'It's all too loose on you. We need to pin those cuffs too and we can hide your hair with a hat, as you say.' He was suddenly very busy around me, fiddling with the material of the shirt, adjusting the shoulders and poking escaped ringlets back into place.

'You need to stand tall and remember to keep your shoulders back, like this.' He stood behind me and squared my shoulders, then he carried on fussing. I noticed he didn't look at me in the mirror again, but I did and it was very peculiar seeing Joey staring back.

'Now the last things.' Lucca had a little wooden box in his hands now. He flipped back the lid and I saw it was a paint box. He ducked down in front of me and began to dip his fingers into the tablets of colour. Then he squinted up at me like he was about to produce a masterpiece and started to dab at my chin, at my broken lip and at the skin around my eyes.

'Get off!' I yelled. 'I'm not having you daubing that stuff on my face. I know what's in it, remember? You told me all about it – arsenic and anti-whatsit.'

I pushed him away, but he just grinned.

'You mean antimony, I think? But this is theatrical make-up, like Mrs Conway uses. You need to have the shadow on the chin like a man and your eyes are too, too . . . female. There!'

He stepped back and assessed me. After a moment he nodded. 'Now, try this coat.' He went to the door where a jumble of clothes hung from a hook. He rifled through and selected a dark grey overcoat. 'Maybe a little too long, but I don't think that will matter.'

Lucca held it open and I pushed my arms into the sleeves. The coat was made of expensive stuff and it smelt of good quality cologne.

'Lucca, where did you get this clobber?' The question popped into my mind. I'd been so excited about all the play-acting that I hadn't stopped to think about how odd it was that my friend had a wardrobe fit for a toff stashed away in his gaff. He didn't answer. Instead he pulled a flat trunk out from under his bed and began laying out another good shirt.

'Did you hear me? Where's all this from?'

He carried on flattening the shirt out and brushing bits of lint off it. Then he mumbled something about borrowing it all from an old friend. He didn't look at me.

Well, like I said before, Lucca had his secrets. Didn't we all? So I left it.

I pretended to be very interested in an old newspaper when he started changing into his own gear, but I won't deny I took a quick look in the mirror. He was lovely, apart from his face. His skin was dark and golden, and quite exotic, I thought, compared to all the other men I knew. They mostly looked like something shipped up to Billingsgate.

'Have you found it yet, Kitty?'

He adjusted the collar of the white shirt and came over to sit on the bed next to me.

'Found what?'

'The place I am taking you to this afternoon. Here, let me show you.' He took the newspaper – it was *The London Pictorial News* again – and flattened it out on the floor in front of us. Then he began to flick through the pages until he came to the one he was looking for.

'Here it is, Fannella – read it out, you are better than me.'

Now, I was proud of my reading. Joey taught it me and I picked it up real quick. Just occasionally I stumbled over an unfamiliar word, but I always stashed them ones away in my head for future use.

So I began, following the lines with my finger.

LONDON IN THRALL TO UNKNOWN GENIUS

This newspaper demands to know the identity of the master whose hand has brought *The Cinnabar Girls* so perfectly, so p . . . pulchritudinously and so piteously to life at The Artisans Gallery in Mayfair.

Our critic declares that a painting of such importance has not been displayed in London since Her Most Gracious Majesty permitted the public to view a small selection of her own Renaissance paintings at The National Gallery.

Vast in both scale and ambition, *The Cinnabar Girls* is a triumph of tradition. In a world where taste increasingly worships at the altar of mere impression and sensation, this glorious work reminds the viewer of the Golden Age of art. It is no exaggeration to write that in its strength and vigorous physicality, *The Cinnabar Girls* brings to mind those other masters of the flesh – Raphael, Michelangelo and Titian.

Indeed, the very particular quality of honesty and courageous sincerity displayed in every brushstroke that anoints the canvas has persuaded the trustees of The Artisans Gallery to take a difficult, but one must add, understandable decision with regard to admittance.

Only gentlemen above the age of eighteen will be granted access to a work that is guaranteed to disturb and thrill in equal measure.

The Editor of *The London Pictorial News* profoundly regrets the lack of an image to accompany this item, but as many of our readers are female, we cannot expose their more delicate sensibilities to a scene that only the masculine soul could most fully and rationally comprehend.

'Blimey, Lucca, you're taking me to a flesh show!'

He looked pained and rolled his eye. 'No, I am taking you to see the work of an unknown master. Look, here . . .' He stabbed at the newsprint. 'The writer compares the artist to Titian, to Raphael, to *Michelangelo*!'

I knew how Lucca felt about all them Italian painters, 'specially old Micky, so I bit my tongue.

'Well, why do you need me to go with you then?'

'Because you might learn something, Fannella, and because you need to get away from that theatre, away from that cage and away from yourself, just for a short time. Come on.'

He handed me a tall hat and helped me tuck the last straying ringlets up beneath it. Then he took another coat from the hook on the door and put it on, wound a thick scarf around the lower half of his face and reached for his own hat.

He took my hand and led me over to the cracked mirror at the foot of the bed.

'Well?'

I laughed in amazement. We looked like a couple of young swells out on the flash.

He grinned and dropped my hand.

'Remember, when we are out on the street you must walk like a man. Watch the men around us and copy them – no dainty little steps. It is also a matter of the mind, Fannella.' He tapped his hat. 'When we leave this room you must think like a man.'

Chapter Eleven

Thinking like a man wasn't a problem; walking like one was.

When we got out into the stinking alley outside Lucca's lodgings at The Wharf, he made me strut up and down a bit until I stopped what he called my 'cat's tail promenade'. Truly, I never thought about what I did with my derrière when I was out and about until now, but according to Lucca it seemed to have a life of its own.

'Don't sway. You need to take bigger steps, Kitty. And keep your head up – shoulders back, remember. Now, again.'

After a bit I got the hang of it. The boots helped – shiny black leather they was, flat with laces and straps at the ankle. Being on the small side I was used to a heel and at first it felt like my feet were slapping down on the slimy cobbles like a plaice on a fishmonger's slab. But they stopped me walking dainty.

When Lucca was happy with my gentleman's walk, we went to the end of the alley and turned onto Narrow Street.

'This will be a test,' Lucca hissed as a couple of dockers came tramping towards us. 'Keep to the middle. Meet their eyes once and then look away as if they don't register. Walk straight past and don't, whatever you do, look back.'

I froze for a moment; now I was out on the open street I didn't feel so confident. Lucca knelt down and pretended to tie the laces on his boots. 'You must move,' he whispered. 'A man is not a statue.'

Come on, girl, I thought, you're a performer.

I took a deep breath, squared up and did exactly as Lucca said. When the dockers were just past, I heard one of them say something to his mate, who laughed and said loudly, so as we could hear, 'If they're gentlemen customers for Mrs Dainty's clap house, then they've lost their fucking way.'

There was more laughter and then a small stone knocked the back of my hat so I had to adjust it. But we just carried on walking. After a moment Lucca said quietly, 'Good, Fannella. You fooled them. Now you just have to convince the rest of London that you are a man.'

When we got up to Commercial Road I held back for a moment. The street was crowded with men and women jostling for space and the air was thick with dust thrown up from all the carts and carriages. I sneezed, couldn't help myself, and it must have come out girlish, because a begging woman bundled up against the cold in layers of rags looked at me very strange.

Then she rustled up from her patch and started to follow us, muttering and mumbling and picking at the strings that held her bits of stuff to her filthy body. Lucca quickened his step and I kept up, but the woman was surprisingly fast. I could smell her rankness right behind me and I yelped when I felt her tugging at my coat sleeve.

'Spare a penny, *lady*.' Her voice was low, but it was full of malice and the promise of something more.

Lucca span about and loosed a torrent of violent Italian. It was clear she couldn't understand a word, and neither could

I, but she backed away – little eyes glittering from the grubby depths of the shawl wrapped round her head.

'Foreign bastards,' she said, and spat a gobbet of thick greenish stuff onto the stones and grinned. 'Unnatural with it.' The old bunter's voice was loud now and people were looking at us.

Lucca dug into his pocket and threw down a coin. It landed in the little slick of spittle and the woman scrabbled for it.

'Quickly!' he hissed, dragging me away.

The woman didn't follow, but I heard her call out, 'I know what you are.'

'Here.' Lucca unwound the scarf from his neck and handed it to me. 'Wear this. It will hide more of your face.'

'But what about you?' I asked. 'What about your . . .'

He sighed and pulled his hat lower. 'Don't you think I'm used to people's stares by now?'

We walked on in silence for a bit, pushing through the crowd. No one else seemed to notice anything. When we got to a quiet stretch I pulled Lucca's sleeve.

'It's odd, isn't it – the only one who's found me out so far is a beggar woman?'

He shrugged. 'She has the most to gain. A woman like that lives on what she can find, and she found you.'

I nodded. 'And she was female too. Takes one to know one?'

Lucca laughed. 'You have a point. It's why I know you'll pass at the gallery. The men there will be too interested in themselves to truly see anything else.'

'Except your filthy painting?' I grinned, but Lucca just

looked pained. I was amazed at the next thing he did. He stepped into the gutter and flagged down a hack.

He spoke to the driver and then he opened the door and climbed inside, motioning for me to join him. Normally he would have let me go first – Lucca's a proper gentleman as a rule – but what with me being dressed up I supposed it was the correct way of things.

I'd never been in a cab before. 'Are you made of money?' I whispered as I settled into the leather seat.

Lucca just smiled. 'You, of all people, should know, Kitty, that appearances are everything. If we arrive at the gallery as gentlemen, we will be treated as gentlemen. There's just one thing – let me do all the talking, *capisci*?'

The cab bounced about a bit and then jerked forward. Then the driver's voice came down from the box. 'Half Moon Street is it, sir?'

Lucca didn't answer. He rapped the door sharp just once and we were off.

As I looked out at the street I wondered, for a split second, how he knew to do that.

*

The gallery was crowded. There must have been upward of a hundred men in there – all pressing forward for a good hard stare.

Just as Lucca said, as soon as we rolled up in the carriage we were treated as proper gents. A little bald man with an umbrella came tripping down the steps to open the carriage door and then he sheltered us from the thin snow up to the broad entrance where another man whose coat was covered in big gold buttons greeted us with great servility.

Lucca produced a fancy printed card and we were directed up the wide marble stairs.

'First door on the left at the top, sirs, and on behalf of The Artisans Gallery, may I wish you a most . . . enjoyable viewing.'

The stairs were lined with portraits of men who looked like they were trying to digest something fatty. I nudged Lucca and whispered that a particularly red-faced nob leaning against a column and staring out over a field looked like he was trying to hold onto a fart. He ignored me, but just as we were about to enter the room where *The Cinnabar Girls* was on display he muttered 'No talking, Fannella, remember.'

The gallery was long and narrow. It was tall, though, and rows and rows of gold-framed paintings covered every inch of red-flocked wall space. Some of the pictures were so high up that you couldn't make them out at all. I was about to re-mark to Lucca that if I was an artistic type I wouldn't be too happy if my painting was so far away that no one could see it, but there were too many men pushing and shoving around us and I thought better of it. Best to keep your mouth shut, Kitty. And anyway, there wasn't much talking going on in there. It was gloomy as a funeral and twice as serious. In fact it was all so reverent – and it being little more than an old man's prick starter – that I had to have a very stern chat to myself about laughing out loud.

The room had a very distinctive smell. At first I got the whiff of cigars – expensive ones. Just occasionally at The Comet if a real toff had been in a box for the evening you got the memory of his smokes. Sweeter than the usual ones they were, more healthy like, with a sort of warm, comforting richness you couldn't take against. Then there was the smell of soap and cologne. Over at Limehouse you were lucky to see a tin bath and a bar of Wright's Coal Tar once a month – less in the winter, truth be told – but these gentlemen were all very fragrant.

Money smelt clean, I thought.

And then, under that, there was another smell too. One I recognised from the workshop at the theatre – the sharp smell of fresh paint and something else as well.

You could feel the anticipation in the room; the air around us almost crackled with feverish expectation. Whether or not it was the paint I can't say, but it was heady like Lady Ginger's receiving room in there, only a hundred times more potent.

At The Gaudy a year or so back there was a visiting act, Dr Klaus, an Austrian I think he was. He had this painted box on the stage connected up to a length of rope. He passed the rope out into the hall and invited people to hold onto it, then he went back to that box and wound a handle on the side until it started to fizzle and spark. Next thing, everyone hanging onto the rope was yelling and hopping, but they couldn't let go, see, they just found themselves caught there with their hair crackling and their fingers tingling. And everyone in the hall could feel something coming off them, even if they weren't holding the rope. Dr Klaus called it being brushed by the wings of angels, but I didn't think that would leave a burn.

The atmosphere in the gallery put me in mind of Dr Klaus and his painted box again.

The picture we were all here to see was at the far end of the room. The crowd kept surging forward and Lucca and I were carried with it. I couldn't see much over the hats of the gents ahead, but I could see the top of a heavy gold frame stretching across the whole of the back wall. About fifteen foot up it was, and perhaps twenty foot long.

As we got closer I began to see splashes of colour and I made out shapes through the gaps between the heads – an arm here, a leg there, a pair of naked buttocks – no wonder they didn't want women in here with them. From what I could see, and admittedly that wasn't much so far, *The Cinnabar Girls* was highly incidental.

As we got closer to the painting the crowd was funnelled into a zig-zag pathway marked out with red velvet ropes. Another warder with white gloves and even more gold buttons than the man in the hall downstairs herded us in.

A note attached to the entrance of this final approach informed us that this was to '*enable our patrons to appreciate* The Cinnabar Girls *in the most favourable circumstances and to protect the work itself, the composition of which is so freshly completed that in certain sections the paint is yet to dry*'.

We moved even slower now. It seemed likely that around twenty or so 'patrons' at a time got a front-row view and after a couple of minutes of artistic 'appreciation' they was moved on and out through a door to the left.

After ten more minutes shuffling behind the ropes, it was our turn. Lucca and I filed forward to take up our 'favourable' positions and then I looked up.

*

The word 'evil' is a powerful one, isn't it? It's much stronger than 'wicked', which, to my mind, has a sort of larky charm and might come with a wink and a slap on the wrist. No, 'evil' suggests something dark, something wrong, something rotten, something sinful.

The Cinnabar Girls was evil. No other word would do.

It was the work of a devil, and as I looked at it, the clever insulting comments and laughter I'd been planning to share with Lucca died inside me.

The first thing to say is that the painting was huge. It stretched the whole length of the wall and was held within a thick carved frame. Even the gilded fruits and vines that coiled about the scene seemed to have a horrible, over-ripe liveliness to them.

The carved branches dipped and curled so that occasionally they drooped from the frame into the scene, partially blocking the distant stormy landscape that rolled beyond the arches of the ancient red stone marketplace where the Cinnabar Girls – all six of them – were displayed.

The sky was alive. A shimmering, sickly silver-yellow, it seemed to have deepness to it like a pool of water. You almost felt you could put your hand through it – although you probably wouldn't want to for fear of the lightning about to strike out.

Now, this was the clever thing – if you can use that word about something so twisted – along the front of the picture the artist had painted the backs of what I took to be the market 'buyers' – a row of men all dressed up in Roman gear like the pictures in Lucca's books. They were craning for a better view, the muscles in their backs and necks shown tight and sharp. They were straining to see those girls – and we were too.

I flinched as I looked up at them and I felt a trickle of sweat running down my back. And it wasn't because it was hot in there – that gallery was cold as a nun's tit, as Nanny Peck would have said.

No, it was because every poor half-naked girl was trussed up in some impossible, peculiar position. Limbs were tied back or staked out where they couldn't possibly rest in a natural way.

It was an odd thing, but those contorted bodies were displayed, you might say arranged, to show the maximum amount of flesh and the minimum amount of person. It's difficult to describe exactly what I mean, but those girls were meat – like you might see hanging up at Smithfield of a morning.

It was as if the artist wanted to . . . I don't know if this sounds right, but it was like he wanted to *reduce* them to mounds of flesh, shaped in a way he chose.

The word 'hate' kept repeating over and over in my mind. The man who painted these women hated them.

But I tell you another thing, that painting had a horrible power. You wanted to look away and then you wanted to look back again and every time you did you saw something else that twisted the knife.

Take the girl in the middle. She lay on her side with her head turned away from you and her red hair sweeping the stones. Her legs were lashed up behind her and a wooden stake ran between them up to her hands, which were forced back behind her head and knotted to the top of the wood. She looked like a plucked chicken ready for the pot.

On her arms the artist had delicately painted in the marks of old scars, dried and crusted, where her pale skin had been tied before.

Another girl, upright, was chained to a column. I say 'chained' but she was actually wrapped tight around it, her blue-veined breasts crushed against the stone like she'd been flung at it. Her matted blonde hair hung low from her lolling head. Her eyes, although wide open, were dark blanks and her parted lips were red and wet. There was a fleshy lump slick with crimson blood on the stones by her feet.

At the far end a slender girl swung from an archway. Her bound hands were hooked over a metal spike that pointed out from the middle of the stonework. There were weeping stripes across the pale skin of her back, like she'd been whipped. She was so horribly real you wanted to dab at that torn flesh, clean the wound, take her down and comfort her.

A lump came in my throat and I couldn't tell you if I wanted to cry or if I wanted to spew my guts up, right there on the polished wooden floor. I looked at the gents around me in amazement. Couldn't they see it? These girls weren't desirable, they were dead. The only living thing in that picture was the sky and that was all wrong too.

Just above the hanging girl a cloud seemed to crack in two and a shower of dirty gold fell upon the right side of her body so that she seemed to glow. It made her skin seem diseased rather than beautiful, although you could sense how much the artist liked painting her flesh – every brush stroke revealed the curve of muscle or the imperfect stain of a freckle or a mole. There was even a small painted tattoo on the girl's left ankle, just below a circlet of thorns that bound her feet together. A tattoo just like the one Clary Simmons had.

I looked closer . . .

And then I looked closer at all the Cinnabar Girls, 'specially a small naked creature crouched in the far corner of the painting covering her face in her hands. Her mouse-brown hair was braided into a thin plait that hung over a metal collar at her neck and down across her bony right shoulder to the nipple of her flat right breast.

Oh no, please, no.

I looked at Lucca. He was staring up at the left side of the painting and I couldn't see his face properly.

'Moving on now please, gents. Out to the left there. Next group.'

My hair prickled under the hat and I could feel beads of sweat on my forehead as we filed out of the gallery in silence and found ourselves in an anteroom with plush red velvet chairs arranged around the walls. Several gentlemen in our group sat down to . . . contemplate, I imagined. A couple of them dabbed at their drool-bubbled lips with squares of silk.

I dragged Lucca over to a couple of chairs set against the far wall. His face was a blank.

'Did you see?' I hissed. He nodded as I continued.

'At first I didn't realise, but once I really looked . . .'

He nodded again. 'I never thought anyone would rediscover Sicilian Gold. It has been lost for centuries, but now, here in London. It is, truly . . . amazing.'

I stared at him and my jaw dropped. 'You what?'

'Sicilian Gold – the sky, Fannella. It is a technique that has been lost for centuries.'

'No!' The word rang out in the silence and one of the dribbling old gents looked across at us. I lowered my voice.

'I wasn't looking at the paint, you idiot. I was looking at the girls – *our girls*.' I grabbed his arm tightly. I didn't care what the old gent thought.

'Nearly all the missing girls from Paradise were in that painting. Alice too – didn't you notice her? For Christ's sake, Lucca, what were you seeing in there? You're as bad as the rest of them.'

The blood drained from his face. It was like he'd suddenly woken from a dream. Then he moved his hand to his mouth and his shoulders clenched up tight.

'I'm right, aren't I?' I carried on, dropping my voice to a whisper as someone sat in the seat next to mine.

'And I believe I am right in suspecting you to be a young lady.' The voice was posh and silky with it. I twisted round and found myself staring directly into the eyes of the man next to me. He smiled and extended a gloved hand. 'Miss Kitty Peck, I believe. The Limehouse Linnet, no less. How extraordinary to find you here.'

Chapter Twelve

I scanned the room. No one else had heard him. Beside me, Lucca stood up quickly and tapped my shoulder. I rose too. I could feel my face burn as the man continued softly.

'Please don't disturb yourself, Miss Peck. Your secret is safe – although you must allow me to say how very exciting it is to view two of London's most topical sensations . . . in the *flesh.*' He smiled again, stood up and held his hand forward. I just looked down at it.

'It *is* customary for gentlemen to greet each other in this fashion,' he whispered after a moment, adding, 'If you refuse to take my hand in such a public place it may cause quite a scene.'

I reached out. His grip was tight and he squeezed as he pumped my arm up and down. 'Splendid! How surprising to see you here, *old fellow.*' His voice was louder now. Then he turned to Lucca and briefly shook his hand too, but he didn't look at him. He was staring at me all the while.

The man was young, around the same age, I guessed, as Lucca. He was tall with clear, grey eyes and, from what I could see under his hat, reddish gold hair. He was a proper toff too, his gear was top ticket all right – sleek and plush it was, fitted to his frame like a fine lady's glove. It made our get-up look shabby. Standing next to him, Lucca and I looked exactly what we were – fakers.

Lucca caught my eye and nodded towards the stairs. I took a step back from the young gent, but he laughed and gripped my arm quite hard. 'Before you go, you really must meet my friends. Now, where are they . . .?' He turned to the double doors leading back into the room where the painting was on display. He had the nose of a toff too, I noticed, all long and narrow with a bump at the top that made him look like a hawk.

'Ah, there they are. Edward! John!' He called out and waved his silver-topped cane at two young men just emerging from the gallery. 'Come and meet a most interesting acquaintance of mine.'

Lucca tugged at my sleeve, but the gents were over in a second.

'What an extraordinary work, James. How clever of you to bring us here.' The speaker, a dark-eyed man with a well-groomed set of whiskers clambering all over his face, continued. 'But then, you always seem to know the latest thing.'

'Doesn't he just? And who do we have here then, James?' The other man was stockier, fresh-faced and fair. I saw how he flicked his eyes over Lucca and me and then dismissed us. Instead he looked back at the doors where people were still filing out of the room with the painting.

The first gent grinned at his two friends. 'Allow me to introduce . . .'

'Lucca Fratelli and my . . . my cousin . . . Joseph,' Lucca cut in and spoke up for us both. His voice came quick and his accent was thicker than usual. He nodded at the men and offered his hand. Neither of them took it. I could see them both looking at his scar and I felt for him.

'Ah, but there is a great secret here, isn't there, Mr Fratelli?' James – that was what I took my discoverer to be called from what his friends said – whispered something to fuzz-face, who stared down at me and then snorted. 'Incredible!'

James tapped the fair man's shoulder. 'Edward, stop watching the door for my uncle for a moment and pay attention.' He bent a little to pass on the information. Immediately the stocky man stopped searching the crowd and turned to look at me proper. His eyes were very blue with crinkles at the corners as if he laughed a lot. He stared at Lucca more closely now too.

'So, The Limehouse Linnet is bold as well as brave, I see?' He spoke quietly and held out his white-gloved hand; I took it. 'Enchanted.' His grip was warm and friendly as he continued, 'You really must introduce us all properly, James. It's not every day one gets to view the sensations of the season in such *intimate* circumstances.'

'My thought exactly. But, of course, you are quite right! I am forgetting my manners.' James's grey eyes glinted as he gestured to his friends. 'This is John Woodruff.' Fuzz-face nodded at me. 'And this is Edward Chaston.' The fair man smiled broadly.

James added, 'The former is a lawyer – or would be if he could be bothered to apply himself to his books with the alacrity with which he applies himself to spending his father's allowance – and the latter will, one day, be the greatest physician in London . . . so he tells us.'

The men laughed. Edward Chaston slapped his friend on the back in a good-natured way. 'You flatter me, James. But what should Miss Peck know of you? How would you describe yourself?'

'Ah, there he has me. I am James Verdin, dreamer, writer, aspiring artist and . . .'

'And not much else!' John Woodruff snorted. 'But then, when your uncle owns half of London, you don't really need a profession, do you?'

James Verdin smiled tightly. I could see that Woodruff's words had picked at something there.

I was beginning to feel more comfortable with them all now that it was quite apparent they weren't going to expose me. It was actually interesting being at such close range. I don't know why, but a memory of a day long ago when Ma and Nanny Peck had taken me and Joey to the circus camped out on Hackney Marshes popped into my head. Before we went into the tent we walked about outside and saw the lions and tigers in their painted cages. There was something very thrilling to see them dangerous animals looking back at you from just a few foot away, safe in the knowledge that they wasn't going to chew your head off.

'Perhaps we should ask him. Here he comes.' Edward was looking over to the door leading back to the painting room where a tall, older gent in a long fur coat was deep in conversation with one of the button-fronted warders.

'Sir Richard – we're over here!' Edward raised his right hand as the old gent turned and stared across the room. He looked like a faded version of James, but his eyes were keen and chill as the ice on West India Dock.

'We are leaving now!' Lucca's voice piped up loud and urgent. The other men looked at him oddly. 'We go . . . the game, it is over. *Finito!*' He pulled up his collar and began to walk quickly towards the door to the staircase. 'Come!' he called without even looking back. The word was sharp.

'I . . . I have to go.' I bit my lip. 'Sorry, gents, but . . .' I gestured at the way Lucca had gone.

'It has been brief but delightful, Miss Peck.' James smiled as I backed away. 'Off you go. Your peculiar chaperone seems most anxious to be away. And it wouldn't be seemly for you to remain here, alone with us, would it now? Or would it?' He cocked his head to one side.

Now, I don't like to admit this, but right then I found myself noticing the way James looked at me. Quite warming it was. And that had been an invitation, hadn't it? As I stared up at his sharply handsome face I felt a shameful jolt of excitement run through me.

Of a sudden my neck began to prickle under the stiff collar. I was shocked. How could I be thinking about something like that now?

How?

I saw little Alice as she'd been in the painting, crouching naked in the corner hiding her face in her hands. I rolled my fist into a ball and clenched my fingers so tight they hurt. I deserved to be punished.

Despite myself, my stomach gave a flip as he carried on. 'But as we know exactly where to find you, I've no doubt that we shall be able to continue our conversation in the very near future?' He nodded like a little bow and I felt my face flame up as I turned to follow Lucca.

'You are a remarkable performer, *young sir*.'

I heard them laughing behind me as I scuttled across the

polished wooden floor to the top of the staircase. I looked back just once and I saw that the old man had joined them. Now he was staring at me too.

*

Lucca was waiting at the bottom of the marble stairs. As soon as I joined him he turned his back on me and headed out through the doors, down the steps and into Half Moon Street. It was snowing heavily now and it was almost dark.

I tumbled down after him. 'Wait!' I shouted, but my voice was carried off by the wind and muffled by the snow. Good thing probably, because I'd quite forgotten I was a man. The bald-headed flunky on the door gave us both an old-fashioned look as we pushed past.

Lucca trudged on just ahead of me and didn't once look back. His head was low and he'd pulled his hat right down over his face. I crunched up next to him, panting a bit because he was walking fast. 'Aren't we going to get a cab back then?' I asked hopefully. I think he swore.

We must have carried on like that in silence for a good hour. Lucca moving like the Devil himself was on his tail and me sliding and skidding along just behind him. Every time I tried to talk he ignored me and I gave up trying, but eventually I couldn't go no further.

'Lucca, stop. I'm frozen to the marrow. I can't feel my bleedin' feet. Please!'

He paused and turned round. We were in a narrow, quiet backstreet somewhere near Smithfield. A gas lamp on the corner was fizzing. Beneath Lucca's eye a single tear track snaked through the snowflakes on his cheek; it showed up ghostly in the faint light.

It was like he'd hit me.

What a stupid, selfish little cow I'd been. There was me, lapping up all the attention I was getting from the gents, when Lucca was thinking about all them girls – *our* girls, the girls from The Gaudy, The Carnival and The Comet. The Cinnabar Girls.

It was like when I was up in that cage sometimes, so wrapped up in myself and basking in all my glory that I completely forgot what I was supposed to be doing up there – *really* doing, I mean. And sometimes I completely forgot about Joey too.

He was right to be angry. I pulled my bare right hand out from the deep coat pocket where I'd been trying to keep it warm and reached forward to wipe the trail of ice from his face. He flinched.

'Don't touch me.'

'But Lucca, I—'

'You don't understand, no one . . .' He chewed his lower lip and looked down. I saw he was rubbing his hands over and over. He was much deeper than I was, sensitive with it.

I'd *seen* the truth of that picture, but Lucca, now, it was like he could *feel* it all – every lash, every cut, every chain. I felt tears pricking at the backs of my eyes too. I reached for his hands and took them in mine. 'Look, I . . . I'm sorry. I'm sorry about the men back there. I'm sorry about those girls and I'm sorry about calling you an idiot. You're a much better person than me – you're caring, you're kind and you're good.'

He pulled away, made a noise somewhere between a cough

and a laugh and he leaned forward. His shoulders hunched up and his body was all bent and twitching. At first I thought he was having a fit like a 'leptic, but then I realised he was sobbing. He collapsed into a little pile of heaving material right there on the snow and I crouched down next to him.

I wrapped my arms around his shoulders and rocked him back and fro like Ma used to do with me when I was a child and something bad had hurt me.

After a minute or so he quietened and looked up at me. Curls of hair all frosted with snow were springing out from under my hat now and he reached out gently to push them back. He wiped the tears that were streaming and freezing down my face too.

'If only you knew the truth, Fannella,' he whispered. I just hugged him tighter.

'We're both going to know the truth, Lucca. When I tell Lady Ginger about that painting it's all going to come out and it's going to stop. She's one of the Barons, isn't she? They have people working for them all over the city. The Lady has a network of spies – and worse – in places we can't even dream about. She'll find that artist.' I wish I felt as confident about that as I sounded. Sitting there in the snow with Lucca folded up in my arms I had a very bad feeling indeed, like something vicious and cruel was slipping about in the shadows around us.

I shivered, but it wasn't the cold that got to me – I was so numb now I couldn't feel a thing. No, it was the memory of the girls in the picture.

Esther Dixon staked out on the stones; Sally Ford spread-eagled over a wheel; Martha Lidgate down on all fours, her hands all torn and bloody; skinny tattooed Clary Simmons hanging off that spike; and blank-eyed Jenny Pierce chained to the column, that brassy hair of hers all matted with blood and her tongue ripped from her mouth.

These were girls I knew, girls I worked with. I might not call every one of them a friend, but the thought of what had happened to them sliced like a knife, leaving me raw and open. I pictured Alice curled up in the corner again, that great metal collar digging into her tiny neck, and I knew without a shadow of a doubt that she was dead. They all were.

I pulled Lucca closer. 'Come on. Let's get back to Paradise.'

We shifted ourselves and moved off. Huddled tight, we made our way back to Limehouse. Even if Lucca had any more money on him for a cab it wouldn't have made a bit of difference – the streets were deserted.

As we tramped along in silence I kept thinking about Maggie Halpern. She was the only missing Paradise girl who wasn't in that painting. Was that a good thing or a very bad thing?

Chapter Thirteen

I stayed with Lucca that night after seeing the painting. By the time we got back to The Wharf I was so cold I couldn't even talk and I could hardly drag myself up the five flights of stairs to his attic.

I was numb as a corpse from the ends of my toes to the tip of my nose. All I wanted to do was sleep, but Lucca made me stay awake while he tried to build up the little fire. He also made me change out of those stiff wet clothes and dug out some warmer gear of his own for me. Neither of us bothered too much about modesty as we stripped off.

Then, as we huddled up close in front of the fire, the pain in my bones as the feeling crept back through my body brought tears to my eyes. My back felt like it was broken in two and my fingers stung like they'd been scalded in a pan of water.

At first we were quiet, but then Lucca spoke.

'I'm sorry, Fannella. I shouldn't have left you like that with those men.'

I shifted, embarrassed. 'No, you were right. There I was preening like a ninny. And all the while I should have been thinking about that picture and about our girls.'

Lucca shook his head. 'And I am sorry for that too. All I could see was paint, when I should have been seeing the work of a madman.'

'I meant what I said on the street earlier, Lucca. I need to tell The Lady about that painting – she'll know what to do.'

He laughed bitterly. 'Only a monster can catch a monster, *si*?'

'Something like that.' I stared into the flames and thought about little Alice again and about Maggie.

*

'So, you stayed at The Wharf last night then?' Peggy undid the ribbons down my back and helped me to step out of the flimsy bit of stuff. It was my first night at The Comet, but I hadn't been at my best. Nothing had gone wrong particularly, but I hadn't slept much the night before in Lucca's attic and what with that and the thought of that painting running through my head, I hadn't exactly had my mind on the job.

I would have gone straight to The Palace the moment I woke, but when the cage moved to a new hall there were always rehearsals and checks on the ropes and chains to make sure the balance was right. Danny was in charge of all that.

Peggy bent down to pick up my costume and arranged it on a rail. 'Put your wrap on, you got goosebumps. Did you go back to Mother Maxwell's first thing this morning?'

I didn't say nothing. There was nothing to tell anyway. After we'd got proper warmed up in front of the fire we both climbed into Lucca's narrow bed under piles of coats and blankets and cuddled up close. Lucca soon fell asleep, but I just lay there looking at the snow through the little window under the eaves and thinking.

Peggy brushed down the net of my skirt and a couple of

glass beads fell to the floor. 'He . . . he's a nice lad, Kit. I know he looks . . . well, that's to say it's a shame about his face and all. But none of us girls notice any more. We don't. And if you and he are . . . well, we wouldn't think any the less of you. That's all I wanted to say.' She suddenly became very busy with my silver slippers. 'These are getting a bit worn. We're going to have to replace the ribbons soon and the soles are running through at the toe.'

I watched her, quiet, for a bit and then I said, 'There's nothing going on between us, Peggy. He's a friend – and that's all.'

She shrugged. 'Suit yourself. But some of the hands have been talking. Danny says . . .'

The door swung open.

'Out!'

Fitzy stared hard at Peggy and jerked his head. She dodged past him and pulled a warning face behind his back. He slammed the door with his foot so we were alone in the dressing room.

I didn't expect him to come over to The Comet; it was Mr Leonard's territory and the two of them didn't get on. Mr Leonard was lean as a courser and neat as a draper's drawer. He was the opposite to Fitzpatrick in every way you could imagine, and then probably some more. There was no love lost between them, 'specially seeing as how The Comet was the finest of Lady Ginger's establishments. On a point of technicality, Fitzpatrick was the manager of all three halls, with an office at The Gaudy, but we all knew he'd like to see himself ensconced among the cherubs and the fancy giltwork at The Comet on a more permanent footing.

Fitzy was flushed and his broad nose seemed to have sprouted an angry red lump to one side.

'And what's this I hear about you not being up to receiving callers this evening?' His voice was low, but he was boiling up to a rant and I knew why.

I reached across to the chair at the dressing table and quickly took up the wrap. I turned my back on him as I pushed my arms into the sleeves and pulled it tight round me.

'I'm tired. I can't see anyone tonight. I'll be all right tomorrow.'

'*I'm tired*.' Fitzy's voice came from behind. I was surprised at how well he mimicked me.

'Oh, I bet you're tired all right. From what I hear you've been up half the night giving it away for free to that I-tie bastard. Didn't I make it very clear to you that you were to *entertain* in your dressing room after every performance from now on? Jesus knows you've done nothing else for us so far. And what about your sainted brother, eh? The clock's ticking for him, Kitty, but you've forgotten that. Think you've found a new man to protect you, do you?'

I swung round, eyes blazing as he let those words hang there for a bit. I could hear the breath rattling in his chest. Then he started up again.

'Did you not mark the words in the letter? The Lady made it plain as the nose on your face, so she did, that you are to act as a lure to whoever is responsible for what's going on in Paradise. You are bait, Kitty Peck, and it's time to let them bite.'

I suppose I wasn't really thinking, what with being so

tired, but it was what he said about Joey that did it. The dangerous words just came in a rush.

'Well, it's a good thing she made it clear as the nose on my face then, seeing as how yours looks like a plate of chopped liver.'

Fitzy made a noise like a steam hammer down at Grand Surrey. He lunged forward and I dodged the blow, but I couldn't stop myself.

'And even if I was giving it away, which I'm not, it wouldn't be to the stinking old carcasses rubbing themselves off under my cage every evening, or to them drooling cod-faced Johnnies waiting outside the halls. Or to you, you great lump of pig gristle. Oh yes – I know all about Peggy and what you do to her when the drink's got the better of your senses.'

Fitzy's eyes looked like they was about to squeeze out of his face as he lumbered towards me, knocking over a small table where my half-finished tumbler of gin – a regular little pick-me-up after a night in the cage – sat. The glass smashed on the floor.

He pushed my left shoulder against the wall with one big hand and placed the other around my neck.

'You don't need to give anything away to me. Not when I can just take it.'

He kept his hand around my neck and dropped the other to fumble with the buttons on his breeches. I could smell his sour breath and the meat stench of his great dirty body.

'N . . . no. Stop!' I wanted to gag. 'I . . . I have seen something. I know what's happening to the girls.'

Fitzy stopped grunting and fiddling and took his hand

away. He was breathing fast and shallow, but his little eyes were calculating. 'If this is a trick, my girl, I'll—'

'No trick. I promise. I *have* seen something The Lady needs to know about. I want you to arrange a meeting between us. I can't just go to The Palace and knock on the door, can I?'

I knew he'd believe me. No one ever *asked* to see Lady Ginger, though I only said it to stop him. Fact is I was planning on going straight to The Palace the next morning. He stared down at me, that muscle working double time under his eye again, then he nodded and pulled at his breeches.

'If you're wasting The Lady's time or mine you'll regret it.'

I swallowed the urge to rile him. 'Don't you think I know that better than most? I've got something – something important for her – and only for her.'

Fitzy lowered his head, breathed deep and rolled his shoulders. For a moment he reminded me of one of them old bulls dragged live into Smithfield – Joey always said they could smell the blood. He nodded once and stepped away from me. When he reached the door he turned back, his broad face crumpled up like an unmade bed. He didn't look at me direct.

'Peggy – you won't be mentioning her to Lally, to Mrs Conway now? Only . . .'

I shook my head and pulled up the wrap to cover my neck. Fitzy chewed his lip and reached for the handle. 'Don't flatter yourself, girl, you're not my type.' As he went out into the passage I thought I heard him mutter to himself, 'I wouldn't have been able to go through with it, anyway.'

'Deal with it.'

Lady Ginger flicked a heavily ringed hand at one of her big lascar boys. He nodded once, turned and walked back down the length of the warehouse, disappearing behind a pile of wooden crates. I heard his boots on the creaking boards, then a rumbling, scraping noise as one of the wide flat doors was slid back and slammed up shut again.

It was early morning and I'd been summoned to a ware-house down by West India Dock. The old cow was sitting in front of me on a high-backed chair. I say chair but it looked more like a throne. All dark and carved over it was – the wood around her alive with birds and snakes and dragons. She stared at me and scratched her cheek with one of them long-curled black fingernails.

She shifted to the side and folded one leg underneath her on the seat. I was surprised to see she was wearing breeches like a man. Well, not breeches exactly – these were loose and covered in patterns. Lady Ginger was all got up like one of her Chinamen.

'Fitzpatrick tells me you wish to see me?' That voice again – all sugar and flutter. She half closed her eyes, reached out to the side of her chair and clicked her fingers. Immediately the Chinaman standing guard behind produced a thin black pipe from the folds of his tunic. He struck a Lucifer on the back of the chair, lit the pipe, sucked on it for a second or two until the end sparked up and then he handed it to her. The sickly sweet smoke coiled around her. She just held the pipe between her fingers and stared at me.

'Well, Kitty Peck? I trust you have brought me something of value?'

I swallowed. The smoke was in my nose and in my throat. 'I . . . I think I know what's happening to them girls, Lady.'

Something flickered in her eyes. I can't be sure – mainly because of the smoke – but just for a second I thought I saw something like fear there, or perhaps it was hope? Either way she just kept staring at me and raised the pipe to her mouth. When the end was glowing red again and the smoke was rising around her like steam off a laundry tub she leaned back and closed her eyes.

'Continue.'

I told her all about that painting and about the girls from Paradise. I described it in some detail, right down to Jenny's tongue lying there on the stones next to her foot. All the while The Lady sat there, the smoke curling around us from her pipe. After a while the fumes went to my head. I started finding it hard to make my tongue say what I was thinking.

The warehouse started to look a bit odd too. All colourful it became in there and of a sudden, to my mind, the walls looked like they was made from material billowing in and out like some big animal was prowling around outside breathing on them.

I stopped talking and she didn't move. It was like that first time at The Palace over again, when I thought she was dead. No such bleedin' luck.

Lady Ginger took a deep, shuddering breath, leaned forward in her chair and snapped open her eyes.

'It is not enough.'

'But I thought you could . . . They're our girls, Lady, all of them were there in the picture, except Maggie Halpern and God knows what's happening to her.'

'Precisely. God, if He exists, might well know, but I do not. You have fed me scraps.'

'That picture, Lady – it's what you need. The artist was unknown, I give you, but surely you can—'

'Surely I can what, Miss Peck? Are you telling me what to do?' That voice might have sounded like it came from a little girl sucking on a violet pastille, but something in her tone made the skin on my back prickle and the hairs on my arms stand guard. The words dried in my mouth as I swallowed and looked down at the wooden boards.

'Bring me more and bring it soon or your brother will regret it. I want names and I want detail. Lure them in and then I will deal with it. I believe Fitzpatrick has already told you this.'

'But that's not fair.' I couldn't stop myself, perhaps it was the smoke. 'I'm doing my best. I'm risking life and limb for you in that cage every night – and it's not even as if that's done any good, is it? I mean, I found this out without all that Limehouse Linnet malarkey. And it *is* useful information. You owe me now.'

The warehouse was completely silent. The Chinaman behind Lady Ginger's chair took a step back. I saw he was looking down at his black velvet slippers. Then she began to laugh – a thin wheezy noise that turned into a cough. She leaned forward and spat something black and sticky onto the boards.

'Good, very good indeed. You are so like your brother sometimes. It amuses me.' She settled back into the chair and began to drum the nails of her left hand on the arm. All the time she stared up at me and she didn't blink.

'Very well. In the light of what you have told me today I am prepared to grant you a little more time. Scraps are better than nothing, after all. Now, let us see what the I-ching has to say.' She rested the pipe on the arm of the chair and from her sleeve she produced the small green box. She flicked open the lid and poured the dice into her palm.

Like last time she spat twice more so that three gobbets of black spittle formed a sort of triangle on the boards, then she rattled the dice in her ringed hand and emptied them into the space between the little slicks of saliva.

'Once again, Miss Peck, tell me what you see.'

I knew better than to touch this time. I knelt down and looked. My head felt thick now, like it was wrapped in a muslin shawl. There was a ringing sound in my ears too.

'What do the dice tell you, Kitty Peck? Look and listen.'

I stared, more to keep the old bitch happy than anything else. The dice showed a different pattern to last time – stripes and dots. At first I couldn't make anything out, then I began to see a shape, no . . . a number. I say see, but here's a thing, it was like I could hear it too, although it must have been the shift bell ringing out at the docks.

'Four,' I said. 'It's a four.' The Chinaman behind her chair took another step back.

Lady Ginger nodded. Her face was a sallow blank. 'Four is a powerful number in the Orient, Miss Peck. It is the number of misfortune – the number of death. You may leave now and perhaps you will reflect on the message you have just received. You might, for example, wish to reflect on the death –

or *deaths* – that will surely follow as a consequence if you fail me.'

She raised the pipe to her black lips again and took a deep pull before blowing a single smoke ring into my face. I began to cough.

'You will not speak about the painting. Rumour can be a very a dangerous thing. I would not wish Paradise to be . . . unsettled by tittle-tattle. Do you hear me?' I caught the way her black eyes shifted towards the Chinaman. He bowed his head.

So, that last order hadn't just been for me? I remembered what Fitzy said about the Barons. Lady Ginger's rivals were circling, waiting for her to show a sign of weakness. I nodded and turned in what I thought was the right direction. My head was so full of the opium smoke now that I couldn't even remember the way to the door. Then her voice came again.

'Before you go, I have a gift for you. Call it a lucky charm, if you will. Come here.'

She held out a small ribbon-bound box.

'Open it.' She grinned and I saw a sticky black wetness stretching like a slug trail between her parted lips.

I took the box, freed the ribbon and tipped something bound in cloth into the palm of my hand. As I unfurled Lady Ginger's gift I noticed that the cloth was patterned red.

First I didn't know what I was looking at. Then I screamed.

It was a finger hacked off at the lowest knuckle. The poor bloody thing still had a ring on it. Joey's ring.

Of a sudden the colour drained from everything around me, leaving a fog of grey. It was as if a layer of paint had peeled from the warehouse walls revealing nothingness. I looked down at the finger and it seemed to shrivel and fade in my palm. As I stared, my own hand began to disappear too. I took a step towards The Lady – all I could see was her black mouth, the lips moving and forming words I couldn't catch because my ears were full of clanging like a Sunday morning at St Anne's. Then somewhere beyond the churning inside my head I heard her voice.

'You told me that your brother had a lovely hand, Kitty Peck. You said you would know it anywhere. And so I think we have an understanding – if you fail me in this, you will also fail him. You may go now.'

Chapter Fourteen

I sat on the swing and held Joey's Christopher and his signet ring tight in my hand.. I shuddered when the thoughts came again of what she'd done to him, of what he must have felt when her men came to him with a knife. I pushed the images out of my head, but they were replaced by a sense of hopelessness. I thought I'd brought good information to Lady Ginger, but it wasn't enough. I held the chain forward and looked down at the golden ring. I'd added it to the Christopher to keep him close.

I wondered where he was – somewhere in Paradise, that was my guess. Outside the halls, The Lady's interests stretched across the docks and into the streets beyond like the silky threads of a spider's web. She only had to twitch one of them black-nailed fingers to trap a soul. Joey was caught out there somewhere and he was relying on me to free him.

I closed my eyes and tried to picture him, but instead of his face I kept seeing that ragged stump of a finger. The Lady had cut him, like she said she would, and it was my fault, I hadn't done as she wanted.

But what did she want? I'd told her about the painting and she called it scraps.

Bring me more and bring it soon or your brother will regret it.

When I stumbled out of the warehouse the sharp air

wiped the opium from my head, but nothing became any clearer. My first thought was to throw that bloody little package into the river and I went to Limehouse Pier. But as I stood there looking into the muddied water, turning the box over and over in my hands, I couldn't do it. Instead, I stuffed it into my pocket and took it back to Mother Maxwell's, where I hid it under a floorboard until I could think straight.

What was I supposed to do with his finger? Bury it, burn it or keep it? The first seemed a bit premature, seeing as how the rest of him was clearly alive somewhere. The second seemed to be lacking in proper respect, and the third was plain unnatural. Like one of them relickys Lucca told me about.

By all accounts, there was a church in his village back home where once a year you could kiss the dried-up foot of an old nun. The rest of the time it was kept behind the altar in a golden case with a garter of little pearly flowers around the ankle.

I brought Joey's Christopher up to my lips and kissed it.

'Did you hear me, Kit? We need to have a good look at these chains.' Danny was attaching four metal hooks to loops at the base of the cage and adjusting the big central chain that dragged me out from the stage, up and over the hall every evening. It was ten minutes to doors open and we were running late.

I tucked the Christopher and the ring back into my bodice. 'Why, it's not dangerous, is it?' I pulled at my costume on the right side where bits of glass sewn into the fabric were digging into my armpit. 'It was making a grating noise when I did the song yesterday, but that's to be expected, right?'

Danny scratched his chin and peered at the chain. 'Needs oiling, I think – that's all. But it's best to be careful. We've already replaced the guide ropes twice.'

'I know – and it's thanks to you and all your fussing that I always feel quite safe.' I grinned, and added, 'Safe as any girl dangling seventy foot up without a net to catch her.'

He shook his head. 'You got guts, Kitty. There's not many girls – or hands, for that matter – who'd do what you do up there. Peggy says she can't watch.'

I liked having Danny about. Like Peggy, he followed me and my cage from hall to hall and worked on the fixings and placings for every night. Mind you, I suspected it was Peggy he was really looking out for, not me.

'Kitty, can I ask you something?'

Here it comes, I thought, he's going to ask me about Lucca too. I leaned back on the swing, braced my feet against the boards of the stage and looked at him askance. 'Asking's for free, but that don't mean you'll get an answer, Danny Tewson.'

Tell truth, I was a bit uncomfortable with all the speculation going on about me and Lucca. I shouldn't have stayed at The Wharf that night two days ago, that was clear. But what was worse was that since then I hadn't seen him at all. He'd gone to ground like an injured fox, and for some reason I felt responsible.

Danny bent down and started tying a thick rope to one of the hooks. He didn't look up as he spoke.

'Word is that you've been made to do this, Kit; that Fitzy's got something over you. Peggy says—'

'Peggy says what?' That came out sharper than I intended.

I hadn't breathed a word of what was really going on to anyone except Lucca.

Danny looked up. He must have caught the tone of my voice and regretted mentioning his girl. 'Nothing. She hasn't said anything. It's just she thinks you've been . . . that you . . . you're scared of something. And we know it's not the height or stage fright, so what is it?'

When I didn't answer he carried on. 'And it's not just you. Peggy says Fitzy's terrified – like he's got Ol' Nick himself breathing down his neck. She says he's lashed out at Mrs C – hurt her bad, you know? Makes him feel better to take it out on someone. I caught her yesterday with a pot of Holloway's.'

I didn't think Peggy was actually using it on Mrs Conway.

Danny spat on the boards and muttered something. 'And all them girls going missing too. I'd get her away from this life if I could, but where could we go? We're all trapped in Paradise like them rats in the workshop – ain't we?' He looked direct at me, scanning my face like he was trying to read something there.

I was grateful for the sudden rush of light from the flares along the front of The Comet's curved stage.

'In five now, fast as you like! Shouldn't that cage be up now? Put some back into it, lads. Chop chop!'

Dapper Mr Leonard looked at his golden pocket watch and then squinted at me in the cage. 'Good house waiting outside to see you, Kitty. Put a bit more oomph into it than last night, eh? There's a good girl.'

I gripped the ropes of the swing and hooked my slippered feet around the bars as the cage jerked from the stage and began to swing up and out. As it moved higher the big chain that connected the cage to The Comet's plaster ceiling began to grind and scrape, setting my teeth on edge.

Danny's right, I thought, that does need oiling. Actually, thinking on it, Danny had been right about quite a lot of things. Fitzpatrick was scared and if a man like him was worried, then God alone knew how the rest of us should feel.

The chain overhead grated and creaked as the cage locked into position. It juddered about a bit, but I was used to that by now. The Comet was wider than The Gaudy and The Carnival and I had a very clear view here. I unhooked my feet from the bars, swayed back and settled onto the swing. From the stage Mr Leonard nodded towards the double doors at the back and punters began streaming into the hall. As usual there was quite a crush to get to the seats right under me. I noticed that Leonard had been packing more tables in – the gin girls could hardly get round with their trays. It reminded me of the last time I saw Maggie and I shuddered even though it wasn't cold up there.

And all them girls going missing, too. Danny's words came into my head. Was he here this evening, the man who was doing this?

I watched as one of the side boxes filled up with a party of gents. They're well off their normal beat, I thought, as a tomato thrown up from somewhere in the middle of the hall splattered a sleek fur collar. There was laughter and a huge cheer as a toff poked his head over the rail and got another direct hit. I could see he was about to get right narky, but then he caught sight of me in my cage and his face went all soft and moony.

I was reminded of the men at the exhibition, washed and

starched on the outside, they was, and filthy on the inside. After all, anyone who could enjoy that picture was as bad as the man who painted it – whoever he was.

I badly needed to know the answer to that question.

'*Unknown genius*', that's what *The London Pictorial* had called him. Right there and then I had a sudden thought about that, but at the same moment my music started up.

Off we go, Kitty, I thought, as I hooked my knees over the swing, leaned back, stretched out my arms and began to twirl and sing.

*

'You were good tonight, but now you look done in.'

Peggy peered at my face and offered me a grease pot and a bit of rag. 'I can usually do wonders with a paint box, but there's not much you can do when someone's tired as a dog.'

I shook my head. 'I've got to stay on. Fitzy says I've got to entertain the Johnnies.' I didn't tell her why. Just the thought of it made my mouth go dry.

Peggy made a face. 'You need to rest up, Kitty. I was saying to Danny . . .'

'Yes – just what have you been saying to Danny?' I was sharp. 'From what I hear, you two have been having quite a chat about me when I'm not around. I don't discuss your affairs with anyone so I'd appreciate it if you returned the compliment.'

Peggy pursed her pretty lips. 'I . . . *we're* just worried about you, that's all. It's not normal all this – you up there every night, the moving from hall to hall each week and as for Fitzy, well, he . . .'

She stopped herself and bustled about picking up bits of stuff from the floor.

I was sorry.

'I . . . I heard about that, Peg. It wasn't Mrs Conway, it was you, wasn't it? Is it bad?'

'So, I'm not the only one with a big mouth then, am I?' She undid the buttons on the high collar at her neck and pulled the fabric open. 'Don't say anything to Dan. I can't let him see this.' The bruise that circled her throat and reached even deeper, I supposed, was patched with purple, black and green.

'Looks worse than it is,' she said, buttoning up again.

'Is it?'

Peggy sighed. 'No, actually it hurts like hell. But if I stand up to him he gets angry. It's not as if he can even . . . that's when . . .' She fell silent.

I thought of that time in my dressing room a couple of days ago and reached for her hand. 'I don't know what to say.'

She shrugged her shoulders. 'I'll cope with Fitzy. I have to. Do you want me to wipe that stuff off your face or will you do it?'

'Don't worry. You get off. By the way, your Dan says he's going to oil my chain for me next week.' I arched an eyebrow.

'Does he now? We'll have to have a chat about that an' all.' Peggy grinned and threw the bit of rag at my head. At the same moment the door opened and Mr Leonard appeared.

'Callers for you, Kitty. Make them welcome – Fitzpatrick

is very keen that you should receive. I'll send them along in a minute.'

He scanned my costume with a professional eye.

'You might want to adjust the neck on that – give them a show, there's a good girl. And you, Peggy, she needs a dab of rouge, don't you think? And maybe a touch more lamp black round the eyes? Remember, sit straight, talk nicely and smile. This is business.'

Not the sort of business you mean, I thought, as Peggy fussed over me with the paint box.

'Do you want me to stay with you, Kitty? I don't mind. You've never done this before, have you?'

I looked down as she painted my eyes and I clasped my hands so tightly together that the knuckles showed white through the skin.

Fitzy's words swam in my head. *You are bait, Kitty Peck, and it's time to let them bite.*

The door swung open.

'The Limehouse Linnet in her bower. How charming.'

James Verdin stepped into the dressing room. He had to dip a little to get through the door and then he swept off his hat and bowed. 'Edward, John – our bird is on the nest.'

His two companions from The Artisans Gallery followed him into the room, which, of a sudden, seemed to be extraordinarily warm, and crowded with it.

Edward Chaston immediately removed his hat. 'A delight to meet you once again, Miss Peck.'

John Woodruff just stared at Peggy. He looked like a puppy when a particularly juicy bone is placed just out of reach.

'Manners!' James poked his friend with the silver-topped cane I'd seen before. John dragged his eyes away from Peggy.

'Forgive me, Miss Peck. Delighted to renew our acquaintance, as Edward has already said. And, if I might add, that was a most inspiring performance this evening. My congratulations.'

'Bravo indeed.' James grinned broadly showing even, white teeth. Now he'd removed his hat I could see his lean, angular features very clearly. He looked like a superior type of sighthound and his gaze was fixed on me.

'It was the first time for you, wasn't it, Woody? Edward and I have already seen Mistress Kitty in her cage on at least three previous occasions, haven't we?'

Edward nodded and smiled. Even though the room was dim I thought again how blue his eyes were as he spoke.

'You perform with grace and poise, Miss Peck. James did not have to work very hard to persuade me to accompany him—'

'Although we've never been to this particular venue, what do you say to it, Eddie?' I noticed that as he interrupted his friend, James took in the dressing room and found it severely wanting. I wondered what he'd make of the rooms backstage at the other halls; after all, The Comet was the finest of the three.

'I say that beauty can be found in the most unlikely places.' Edward turned to John Woodruff and said, 'So, what did you think, Woody?'

John Woodruff shrugged and laughed. It was a thin, high sound – more like a schoolboy than a grown man. 'Well, as I have often observed, our friend Verdin has a knack for finding the most extraordinary people and places for us to enjoy. And tonight has been no exception.' His gaze returned to Peggy, whose eyes were almost as large as saucers. 'I trust that you will introduce us to your lovely companion, Miss Peck?'

I could feel my cheeks burn as I stood up, hunching my shoulders forward to try to pull the neck of my costume higher and reduce the amount of my flesh on show. Of a sudden I felt cheap. I would rather have been dressed as a boy again.

'G... good evening, Mr Verdin, gents.' I stumbled over the words. 'This is my friend, Miss Peggy Worrow...'

Now, Peggy and I had seen our share of Johnnies queuing out back after a performance, but none of them had ever been quite as fine and quite as bold as this bunch. The fact they all seemed to know me already wasn't lost on Peggy, who started rolling her eyes the moment John's back was turned. I couldn't blame her, but I didn't want her to know what Lucca and me had been up to neither.

'... who is just *leaving*,' I continued, nodding my head at the door.

Peggy's lips went quite tight and then she piped up, 'But I can happily stay here with you, Kitty, if you feel you need me.' She pulled a face that suggested I would most definitely be feeling that way.

'No, that's not necessary. I know that your Danny will be waiting for you.'

'Only if you're sure, Kitty?' It was an appeal, not a question. I ignored it.

'Perhaps that odd-looking foreign chap will be joining us?' Edward seemed to find his suggestion highly amusing. He grinned at me, his eyes all twinkled up like we was sharing a joke, and then he winked. Peggy's black eyebrows shot up faster than a firecracker.

So much for secrecy.

'P . . . Miss Worrow is leaving us now,' I said, rather firmly, avoiding her eyes. As Peggy left the room – with obvious reluctance – John Woodruff actually patted her nancy. 'Danny, is it? Lucky dog.'

I was glad when she was gone – it would make it easier to cope with her questions later – but now I felt like I was standing there naked in front of them. I pulled the shoulder straps a bit higher. I wasn't usually lost for words, but tonight I was dumb as a haddock.

'Please sit down, Miss Peck, we seem to have disturbed your toilette.' James gestured towards my chair with his cane and I sat down again. 'You must forgive this intrusion, but after meeting you at the gallery under such intriguing circumstances, I confess that I . . . that is to say my friends and I, have talked of little else.' Edward smiled and made a slight bow and John made a snorting noise as James continued. 'And as Woody here had not yet seen you perform – in the traditional sense – we decided to arrange an excursion. So here we are. I am happy to say that your performance tonight was every bit as thrilling as we had led our friend to expect. Bravo once again.'

He began to clap his white-gloved hands together and the other two joined in. I couldn't tell if they was making fun of me or genuinely appreciating. I felt my cheeks burn up under the stage paint.

'Thank you very much,' I said when they'd finished. Then

I thought I should add something more so I went on, 'It's very kind of you to come. I'm esteemed you all enjoyed yourselves.'

John smirked beneath his crawling whiskers and covered his mouth with his hand and Edward looked at the floor.

'Tell me, Miss Peck, or perhaps I might call you Kitty . . .?' James ignored his friends and sat down on the only other chair in the room. He placed his hat on the boards beside him, pulled off his gloves, undid his coat and pushed his thick coppery hair back from his high forehead. He was the only one who made himself at home like that. The other two stayed gloved and buttoned like they were anxious to be on the move.

'. . . we have all been wondering why you went to the gallery last week.'

He paused and stared at me expectant. I wasn't sure how to answer, but as I looked at his face and saw the way his grey eyes caught the light I knew I wanted to say the right thing.

I swallowed. 'I . . . I'm very interested in art.' I concentrated on James. Out of the corner of my eye I saw 'Woody' poke Edward in the ribs. Edward stared at his shoes, but I could see his gloved hands clenched tight together like he was trying to stop himself laughing out loud.

I was furious. They were mocking me. I don't know where it came from but that article about *The Cinnabar Girls* in *The London Pictorial* reared up in my mind, word for word it did. That and some old painter stuff Lucca had gone on about.

'*Michelangelo, Raphael and Titian* – they're my particular interest,' I said, warming up. 'When I read that the painting *reminds the viewer of the Golden Age of art* – that being the Renaissance – *in its strength and vigorous physicality*, I had to see it. And my friend Lucca, Mr Fratelli, well, he's an artist too, sort of, so we went to the gallery together.'

'Well, I never! You are the most extraordinary young woman.' James Verdin sounded amazed. He beamed, but the other two gents carried on their smirking.

The lines around Edward's eyes puckered up as he spoke. 'It seems that Miss Peck is an art-lover, James. How appropriate.'

'Edward flatters me. But it is true that I paint – or try to. Tell me, what did you make of *The Cinnabar Girls*, Kitty?'

I chewed at the inside of my lip. I knew what I made of it all right, but what was the right thing to say? How did that piece in *The London Pictorial* go again?

'I thought it very *ambitious*,' I said after a moment, shooting a glance at each of them in turn to make sure of my answer. James grinned and Edward nodded. He didn't seem to find me so amusing now.

'Ambitious, yes, but successful too, don't you agree?' James was very fired up about it. 'Ambitious suggests that the artist has gone beyond the limits of his talent, but *The Cinnabar Girls* is a masterpiece. It is the work of a genius. What do you say, Edward?'

Edward shrugged. 'I know very little of art, James. I am a mere physician, after all. John is your man – he has a keen appreciation of the female form.'

John seemed to be more interested in the gin bottle on the table.

'You can pour yourself one, if you like,' I said.

He raised the bottle, sniffed at it and began to cough. 'I fear I must decline your generous offer, Miss Peck. In fact I rather think it is time we moved on. It is late, gentlemen, and I have business to attend to.'

James laughed. 'Business, Woody? Would that be a legal matter or something more . . . pressing?'

'Bound to be the latter – I hope she's worth the trouble you'll get from your father.' Edward nudged John's shoulder.

'Oh, she's trouble all right, but the best kind.' John turned up his coat collar and moved towards the door. 'And a thousand times more educational than those gloomy old medical books of yours, Edward.'

He seemed to have entirely forgotten that I was there. 'Come on, James, Eddie. We can take a hackney back into town.'

'You must forgive our friend's impatience. I fear he is not a connoisseur.' Edward cocked his head to one side and grinned. 'Thank you, Miss Peck, for a most interesting evening. I congratulate you on your many talents. You are an ornament to the arts.'

James stood and bowed. He took my hand and kissed it. 'We will not tire you any longer, Kitty. You must be exhausted after your exertions this evening and we have been thoughtless. Perhaps you will allow us to call on you again – we could continue our dialogue on art? It would be a great pleasure.'

As I stared up my breath caught in my throat for a moment. All of an instant I was very certain indeed that continuing anything with James Verdin would be a great pleasure.

Chapter Fifteen

I was in the workshop down The Gaudy looking for Peggy next day when Lucca turned up again.

Now, I thought I should have a little talk with Peggy because it struck me that she might have quite a lot to say about my visitors. And I wanted to be sure that if she did have a lot to say, she said it to me and not to nobody else, apart from Danny. (He'd probably heard it all by now.)

Anyway, Peggy wasn't at her lodgings, so I pushed on to the workshop.

She and Danny sometimes shared a bottle and bite together mid-afternoon of a Sunday and I thought I might find them together. In the halls we didn't much keep to a regular timetable. All the same, even if it was just a bit of boiled bacon and a slice or two of bread, we liked to keep up the appearance that it was a different day to all the others.

But the workshop was quiet – just an old carpenter working on a bit of flat painted up like a garden. Mrs Conway was very keen to do her song about Valentine's Day and turtle doves choosing their mates. By my reckoning it was about thirty years too late for the old bird to be trilling out that one again, but she was a trier – you had to give her that.

I started back across the cobbled yard when I heard a whistle – Lucca.

I turned round and there he was coming in from the back

alleyway – that one Fitzy had carried me down that time I saw Lady Ginger in her carriage. Lucca was bundled up in a heavy coat. It hadn't snowed for a couple of days now, but the ground was all crusted over with yellow ice.

I was pleased to see him, I won't lie. I wanted to tell him about Joey and I wanted to ask him something most particular. Even so, I was annoyed too – what with him going off like that and not telling me.

'And where've you been?' I planted my hands on my hips and gave him the arrow.

He nodded his head at the workshop. 'Not here – inside.'

'Old Bertie's working in there.'

'He is . . . *sordo*, deaf. He won't hear us. Come.'

I followed him through the wide door and slammed it behind us. Lucca began to climb the wooden ladder to the floor above. Bertie looked over and winked at me. Then he made a sucking noise that was supposed, I thought, to sound like a kiss. He gurned and nodded his head at Lucca's legs just disappearing overhead. He only had one tooth left at the front of his mouth.

Jesus! There's another one who thinks we're a pair, I thought, feeling a sudden rush of heat at the memory of James last night. What would it be like to kiss him?

I tried not to think about that as I tucked in my skirt and followed Lucca up the ladder.

When I got to the top I couldn't make out where he'd gone. There were old props, rags and piles of painted stuff all over the place. It reeked of paint and turps up here too, but there was no sign of Lucca. Then I saw a little glow of light from a hatch at the far end of the loft and I went over, bending double to squeeze through into the space beyond. I'd never been in here before or knew it existed.

'Welcome to my studio, Fannella.'

Lucca had lit a small lantern and was attempting to light a candle stub in a saucer on the floor. It kept fluttering about in a draught before dying.

'It is a poor space for an artist, but it is all I have.'

The walls were covered with paintings and drawings – people, animals, trees, houses, all very beautifully done.

'I never knew you had all this up here.' I stepped over to the wall where a sheet of paper was pinned to a beam. 'Who's this then?'

The boy in the drawing had thick curling hair and wide dark eyes – sad they was and deep like they burned out of the paper and into the wood behind. You could swear they'd leave a mark there after you took the paper away.

Lucca looked over and a shadow seemed to pass over his face. It was the flickering of the candle he was still trying to light.

'No one – I copied from a book.'

'He's good. Come to it, they're all very good, Lucca.' I moved along the wall and looked at a drawing of a running horse. Close up it didn't look like much, just scratchy lines. But if you stepped back it all came together as a tangle of wild limbs and mane whirling across the paper.

'Blimey – you really are an artist. You're wasted here.'

Now, we all knew Lucca was good, but apart from the odd sketch of hands or some of the girls and his general paint work for the halls, I'd never seen his proper stuff before, although he talked about it often enough.

Lucca shrugged. 'I thought it was time to show you. After seeing . . .' He stopped for a moment. 'After the gallery and the painting, I thought I should be more honest about myself, my art. That's all, Fannella. I have nothing to be ashamed of.' He sounded almost angry.

Lucca looked around at the pictures pinned on the beams and spread out across the floorboards behind him and, just for a second, again I thought he looked . . . it's difficult to say it exactly, but he looked haunted. Not like he'd seen a ghost, but like a ghost was looking out of him.

He reached into the folds of his coat, brought out a large book and placed it on the boards in front of him.

'We can talk here. Come, see this.'

I shook my head. 'I need to talk to you first. She did it like she said she would – The Lady, she cut off Joey's finger and gave it to me. I went to see her yesterday to tell her about the painting and the girls, but it didn't do no good.'

The tawny skin of Lucca's face paled to sallow ash. 'Surely that's enough? You have given her information, now she can . . .'

'She can *what*?' I mimicked the old cow's voice. 'She said I'd brought her scraps, and that she wanted more. Then she gave me this.' I reached into my bodice and drew out the Christopher and the ring.

'It's Joey's.' I held the ring forward so that the gold sparked in the candlelight. I blinked hard. 'I had to pull it off his . . .'

Lucca swore under his breath and then he stepped forward and hugged me. We stood close like that for a moment and I saw our breath mingle in the cold air.

'So what now, Fannella?'

I looked down at the ring in my hand. 'That's just it. I

don't know what to do next. I had some callers in my room last night after the show ...'

I stopped myself. Of a sudden I didn't want to tell Lucca that James Verdin had come to see me.

'And?' Lucca looked anxious. 'Did any of them try to ...'

I shook my head and didn't catch his eye as I went on. 'They was just ... admirers. I don't see how I'm going to find anything out that way, despite what Fitzy and Lady Ginger might think. She said she was prepared to give me more time, but I don't trust her. She's already hurt him. The only thing we've got is that painting and she didn't want to know.'

'That is why I wanted to show you this.' Lucca knelt down and tapped the book lying on the boards. It was old and the leather cover was decorated with gold fancy work.

'Where did you get this then?' I sat next to him crossing my legs under my skirt.

He didn't answer so I pulled the book over and turned to the first page. A square label was gummed onto the paper: *From the Library of The Fellowship of British Landscape Artists*.

'So you nicked it?' Lucca had told me before how he had a knack of 'borrowing' books. Most of the books under his bed was 'borrowed'. A lad like Lucca couldn't afford fine print.

I tried to smile. 'Well, that's a nice thing for a Sunday, isn't it?'

He shrugged. 'I needed to show you something, Fannella – and anyway no one has looked at this for years. Why shouldn't I have it?' He stroked a long brown finger across the cover and immediately the curling golden patterns in the leather glowed. He loved them old books and he certainly had a knack for getting hold of them. I sometimes wondered what would happen to him if he was caught.

'Come on, show me then.' I rubbed my chapped hands together. 'And after that I've got something I want to ask you.'

He began to turn the pages all reverend like it was a bleedin' Bible. The book was full of pictures just as I expected – all protected under sheets of thin paper that crackled as he smoothed them back.

'Here – look.'

He angled the book and moved the saucer with the candle so that I could see it more easy. 'Do you see?'

I shook my head. 'See what? It's a field, isn't it? And a mountain – and that dollop there could do with a few more clothes.'

Lucca sighed. 'The sky, Fannella – look at the sky and the river – there.'

He traced the line of the water through the picture. Even in the print it seemed to have a particular shine to it. Like the sheen on a toff's coat. I thought about James again, of a moment, but then I got what Lucca was driving at.

'It's the paint! The Sillian Gold you was on about at The Artisans?'

'Sicilian Gold,' he nodded. 'Now read from here. He pointed to the lines under the picture.

I leaned a bit closer. The writing was cramped and the page was stained at the bottom making it difficult to see the words clearly. I followed the lines with my finger – starting off slow.

'"C . . . Corretti's masterpiece, *Pers . . . Persephone in the Fields of Elysium*, painted for The House of Bagnia in

Palermo" – blimey, Lucca, why don't they have normal names like the rest of us? – "was destroyed in the great earthquake of 1693. Acclaimed as the artist's most successful use of Sicilian Gold on the m . . . mon . . . monumental scale, the loss of *Persephone in the Fields of Elysium* is considered one of the greatest tragedies of art. Even in 1693 it was known as the last of the artist's five great commissions to have survived. When Corretti died in 1534, the secret of Sicilian Gold ex . . . expired with him. Although many have tried to recreate this remarkable, some said "magical" pigment, all have failed. The only certainty that remains is that the process was r . . . riven with danger and involved sub . . . substances of the most toxic nature. Corretti himself was just twenty-four at his death. Fellow artist Br . . . Branc . . . Brancazzo wrote that his body had grown old before its time. This fac . . . facsimile was created from contemporary drawings of Corretti's original work now securely lodged in the collection of the Counts of Bagnia."'

I stopped and looked at Lucca. 'It's poison then, this Sicilian Gold. That's what toxic means?'

He nodded. 'Nearly all paints are poison. It gives them depth, sometimes the colour and often it helps them stay to the canvas.'

'Like arsenic?'

Lucca nodded again. 'But Sicilian Gold was different. When I was an apprentice in Napoli it was . . . *leggendario* . . . a legend? They said Corretti had found a way to make the most perfect and beautiful paint. His works were admired and feared because they seemed to be alive . . . *soprannaturale*. But they were also feared because the paint itself was deadly. There are old stories about his works bringing misfortune –

people thought they were unlucky. It's why they were all destroyed. This . . .' he pointed at the picture in the book, '. . . was the last, but then the great earthquake . . .'

'Destroyed that too – so all we have now is this copy and the story about the paint?'

Lucca nodded. 'And after he died no one found the way to make it again.'

He closed the book. 'Until now. I went to see *The Cinnabar Girls* again.'

It was like someone gripped my backbone and gave it a twist. I shuddered as I thought about that picture.

'I don't know how you could go back there. That thing was evil . . .'

'It wasn't easy, Fannella, but I had to see it again to be sure.'

'To be sure they was all in it? I thought that was bleedin' obvious. No, I think all you were interested in was that old yellow paint.' I was furious with him.

'Exactly – I had to see it again to be certain and now I am. The painter *is* using Sicilian Gold. He has found a way to make it again – three hundred and fifty years after the secret was lost. He is not merely a great artist . . .'

I opened my mouth to let something ugly out, but Lucca raised his hand.

'For all that *The Cinnabar Girls* is evil, just as you say, it is the work of a master. The artist is an alchemist as well as a genius.'

'A what?'

'*Alchimista* – in English you say alchemist, like a magician, *si*?'

'No, I don't see. But I tell you one thing, if he is a magician

141

he's bloody good at doing the disappearing act. I've got to find out who he is, Lucca.'

I rubbed my thumb over an old nail poking up through the boards. 'The girls in the picture, do *you* think they're still alive?'

He didn't say anything, so I knew what his answer was.

I pressed the ball of my thumb hard down on the nail so that it hurt. 'This isn't just about Joey any more, is it? I keep dreaming about Alice with that little plait hanging over her shoulder and that collar round her neck. Maggie Halpern – if he's got her as well then what . . .'

'What will he do next?' Lucca paused for a moment. 'I was afraid to tell you this, but there is talk of a new work. The artist is painting again. One of the attendants told me that The Artisans Gallery has negotiated for exclusive rights to show his next work.'

'What else did he say? Did he know anything about him? Who he is? Where he's from? There must be something?'

Lucca shook his head. 'I tried to find out as much as possible, but there is nothing more to tell. He has demanded total secrecy. The attendant told me that *The Cinnabar Girls* was delivered and hung by unknown hands in the middle of the night. No one from the gallery was allowed to be there. The only certainty is that no one knows anything about him.'

I felt a rush of excitement. 'Well, I reckon that's where you might be wrong. That's the other thing I want to talk to you about. Remember that newspaper piece you showed me, the one with all that guff about the *unknown genius*?'

Lucca nodded.

'It went on, didn't it? The first line was "*This newspaper* demands to know the identity of the master whose hand has brought *The Cinnabar Girls so perfectly, so pulchritudinously and so piteously to life at The Artisans Gallery in Mayfair.*"'

'Yes, that's exactly right. You have a remarkable memory, Fannella, but I don't see . . .'

'No, listen again, *"This newspaper demands to know"*. If anyone's in a position to know anything they are. I reckon they're working on it now. Even if they don't have a name I bet you a bottle of Fitzy's best porter they've got something on him.'

Lucca picked some paint from under his thumbnail. After a moment he turned to look at me, watchful. 'You are much more intelligent than your brother, Kitty, you do know that, don't you?'

I was exasperated. 'Don't be ridiculous. Everyone knows Joey had, no . . . *has* a brain like a watchmaker. But what do you think? Will you come to the offices of *The London Pictorial News* with me, please?'

'When?'

'Tomorrow morning, first thing. And I'm not going out dressed as a Tom again, if that's what you're thinking. No, this will be a visit from Miss Kitty Peck, The Limehouse Linnet.'

Lucca grinned. 'Of course I'll come. That's a performance I wouldn't want to miss. But you don't need to buy me porter – I prefer champagne.' He arched his eyebrow.

I snorted. 'Like you've ever had a taste of that, Lucca Fratelli.'

Brushing down my skirt, I stood up. 'Got to be off now. I'm due at The Comet for six tonight. Danny's been fretting over the chains and wants to adjust the balance while I'm sitting in the cage.'

I stepped over to the ladder and was just about to start down again when a thought occurred. 'Lucca, what does *"pulchritudinous"* mean exactly. Is it something dirty?'

He coughed, but I think it was a laugh. 'It means beautiful – like you, Fannella.'

Chapter Sixteen

Sam Collins was skinny as a broom handle. He had to keep flicking his brown hair out of his eyes to see us proper. That could do with a good trim, I thought.

'I can't tell you what a pleasure this is, Miss Peck. As soon as Peters told me you were in the office downstairs I asked him to bring you up to see me immediately. You and Mr . . .?'

'Fratelli. Lucca Fratelli.' Lucca offered his hand and Sam shook it warmly.

'Excellent, excellent. Well, please sit down, both of you.' He gestured at the two chairs in front of his cluttered narrow desk. 'Can I offer you tea? Peters makes a horrible pot, to be frank, but it's warm and brown and with an extra spoon of sugar you don't always notice the under tang.'

He spoke faster than anyone I'd ever met before. The words tumbled out from his mouth like matchboxes coming off the belt at Bryant & May's. He tapped his fingers on the table too – a right bundle of nerves he was – I noticed they were all stained over with ink.

'I must say it's very exciting to meet you, Miss Peck. What a treat on a dull Monday morning. I have to confess that I am something of a follower. I was there at The Gaudy on the very first night, you know. And I've been back several times since. You are extraordinarily brave and very talented. Did I offer you tea?'

'No thanks to the tea.' I smiled. Despite all his twitching and gabble I already liked Sam Collins. There was something very open about him and I noticed that he didn't bat an eye when he looked at Lucca. I thought that was good of him.

When we'd arrived at the offices I wasn't sure what to expect. Certainly I thought they might be grander than the slender four-storey building we found in a side passage off Holborn. I'd dressed up proper for the occasion in my best blue, with all the lace at the neck, and I had a fur borrowed from the wardrobe. But looking at the piles of dusty papers tottering behind the front desk and at the harassed, pinched faces of the grey clerks scurrying around like mice in a church organ, I realised that *The London Pictorial News* wasn't exactly a top-drawer publication.

Peters – that was the man who met us at the front desk, I assumed – asked our business and as soon as Lucca said my name he was off up the stairs like a Sunday afternoon customer at Mrs Dainty's.

A minute later he was back, all smiles. 'Mr Collins would be vewy happy to wecieve you. If you would just come this way, sir, madam.'

I'd never been called madam before. Lucca poked me in the back as we made our way up the dingy stairs. Peters rounded the corner of the staircase above and disappeared. Then his voice came again: 'Office on the wight, if you please.' It was obvious that there wasn't room for all of us on the cramped landing.

I knocked on the door and Sam Collins called out, 'Enter, enter.'

I'd thought at the time that he sounded very young to be

an editor. Now as I sat there in front of him he grinned at me like a schoolboy.

'I fear you have made the right decision about the tea. Now what can I do for you, Miss Peck, Mr Fratelli?' He looked from one of us to the other and beamed.

I cleared my throat and adjusted my bit of fur. 'Are you the editor of *The London Pictorial*, Mr Collins, only you don't seem . . .'

'Ah, there you have me. Smoked already! You would make an excellent journalist, Miss Peck. No, you are quite right. I am not the editor of this esteemed publication. At this very moment he is . . . gathering information at The Lion and Seven Stars, three streets away. I am merely a humble correspondent, but as Peters – and, look here, I may as well admit it – *all* of the boys downstairs know of my deep appreciation of your talents, he knew he could not turn you away without me seeing you. And perhaps you have something for us? A freshly minted song, perhaps? A sensational new act? An exclusive?' His inky fingers drummed away as he stared at me.

'Well, thing is, it's not exactly news we're interested in. Not news for you, anyways.'

Sam looked a bit down, so I carried on quick. 'Although now we've met – and you being so partial – I'll obviously make sure that you get a first crack on anything I might be doing down the halls. That's a deal.'

He brightened up. 'Well, that's very considerate. Thank you, Miss Peck. And what would you require in return exactly?' There you see, Sam Collins might have looked green as a leaf in April and he might have had more tics and twitches than an inmate at Bedlam, but he was a sharp one.

I nodded at Lucca and he took over. 'Would it surprise you to know that we are interested in art, Mr Collins?' Sam raised an eyebrow under that fringe as Lucca went on. 'It should not. Although it is true that we work in what some might regard as the lowliest field of expression, my friend and I have a keen interest in all forms of artistic endeavour.'

I grinned into my fur. Lucca had a lovely way with words sometimes. And with his accent he sounded much more cultural than I ever could. If it wasn't for the scar he could pass anywhere. He carried on, 'We have an appreciation of painting in particular and, if possible, we would very much like to know the identity of—'

'Ha! You and the rest of us.' Sam thumped the desk. 'You want to know who painted *The Cinnabar Girls*, don't you?'

We nodded in unison.

'If I knew, don't you think *The London Pictorial* would have printed the name by now? The story would be an absolute scoop, as I believe my American counterparts might say. No, I'm afraid I have nothing to offer, unfortunately.'

'But you are trying to find out who painted it, aren't you? Your paper *demands* to know his identity. I read it.'

'Did you, Miss Peck? I wrote that.' Sam grinned from ear to ear and for a moment he stopped all that twitching and flicking. 'So I was thinking', I carried on, 'that you must be investigating that painting a bit behind the scenes. You are trying to track him down, *smoke* him, aren't you?'

Sam nodded. 'Without much luck so far I have to admit. But I have some promising leads and hopes of—' He broke off and stared at me through his fringe. 'But why would this be of any interest to *you*?' His eyes narrowed and he looked at Lucca. 'Why?'

Of an instant I had an idea – a good one. 'Listen, Sam, I'll give you a proper "scoop" if you give us the gen when you get it.'

He cocked his head to one side like a spaniel. 'Go on.'

'I'll give you some information about me if you promise to let us know anything you find out about the painting and the artist, *before* your paper prints it.'

Sam blew his cheeks out and drummed away. 'It had better be a bloody good story for a deal like that, if you'll excuse my language, Miss Peck.'

Lucca grinned at me and then nodded across at Sam. 'It is a bloody good story indeed, if it is the one I think.'

*

'What's this filth?' Fitzy waved a crumpled copy of *The London Pictorial* under my nose. We were alone in my dressing room at The Comet. I knew what it was all right. Sam had read it back to me once he'd got it all down.

SONGBIRD SPREADS HER WINGS

Word has come to this publication of the latest daring escapade of Miss Kitty Peck, The Limehouse Linnet. Not content with delighting and alarming her many admirers night after night with her captivating and courageous display, London's favourite aerial artiste has stormed the

149

bastion of masculinity, gaining access to The Artisans Gallery in Mayfair to view *The Cinnabar Girls*.

Readers will recall that this sensational painting – by an as-yet-unknown hand – is widely thought to be so stimulating to the artistic sensibility that gentlemen only are permitted access. Proving that she is as audacious in life as in performance, Miss Peck donned male attire to gain entry to the gallery. Remarkably, despite her considerable feminine charms, our songbird in disguise evaded every point of possible scrutiny and avoided detection.

This newspaper declares that the fortuitous conjunction of the brightest stars of the current artistic firmament must have been a moment of celestial celebration. Speaking exclusively to *The London Pictorial News*, Miss Peck commented that *The Cinnabar Girls* was 'vast in both scale and ambition', precisely echoing the views of this correspondent.

Above the story there was a quarter-page drawing of me all got up as a toff, although if I'd seen a gent with a shape like that I think I might have had a few suspicions about what was going on underneath.

'Unnatural, so it is.' The veins on Fitzy's temples seemed to bulge and the network of spider legs that crawled out over his cheeks pulsed red. 'I should have known better. Your brother is dirt and you're no different.' He crumpled up the paper and threw it to the floor.

'*I need to see The Lady. I know what's happening to the girls.*' Fitzy mimicked my voice again, adding in his own, 'Now I find you've been cavorting around London, pandering to your own perversions when you should have been at work. When The Lady reads this – and she will, mark my words – I wouldn't want to be in your shoes, so I wouldn't. Most particular about morals, she is. You should have asked your brother about that before . . .'

'Before what?' He was breathing like a wounded bear. I could tell he was winding up to lash out at me, but he'd talked about Joey and I couldn't stop myself.

Fitzy paused and seemed to consider. 'Before his *accident*, Kitty.'

I stepped back, but I didn't take my eyes away from his. 'I think I've got a right to hear a bit more about that. You and The Lady seem to know so much about Joey, but all I get is scraps from the pair of you.' I heard myself echo Lady Ginger's words and they tasted bitter. 'What has he done?'

'Never you mind.' Fitzy spat on the floor and muttered something under his breath.

'There you go again. Why do you talk about him like that? He's my brother.'

He snorted. 'I wouldn't want to admit to that, Kitty.'

Now it was my turn to spit – and I caught him straight between the eyes. For a moment he was still, then he lumbered towards me, but I had it all ready. 'Wait!' I grabbed the little chair from the dressing table and held it up in front of me, legs first, to fend him off.

'The Lady knows all about that picture and about me going to see it done up as a Tom. What you need to know is what I told her. Our girls – all our missing girls – was in that painting. All of them – tortured and twisted about like prime cuts of meat at a butcher's shop. The only one that wasn't there was Maggie – Maggie Halpern from The Gaudy. Go see it yourself if you don't believe me. You're a man, aren't you, after all?'

That last line came out a bit more challenging than I intended. I had to duck Fitzy's great paw as it hammered down on the chair instead of my head. He rubbed his hand and stared at me, his watery eyes calculating.

'Lady Ginger was pleased,' I lied, 'but she wants more. She's told me to find out more and that's what I'm trying to do. So you just take your grubby mind and your dirty great fists out of here and let me get on with it. I'll do my job and you do yours.'

I wasn't sure if that was going to lead to another wallop, but it seemed that last bit about The Lady being pleased with me pulled him up. He chewed at the tips of his yellow-stained bristles where they draped over his upper lip.

'And another thing,' I said, 'that write up in *The London Pictorial* won't do trade no harm neither. They'll all be in here tonight now, seeing as how I've titillated half of London.'

After a moment he nodded. He might have been terrified of The Lady like the rest of us, but he wasn't afraid of filling his pockets. He moistened his fat lower lip. 'You're to stay on here for another week. We can take more at The Comet than the other two halls put together. That's something at least.'

'Is that Lady Ginger's idea or yours?'

'I've consulted her.' He stared down at the page of the newspaper, which had crackled open again on the boards showing the drawing of me dressed as a lad. 'You're very like Joseph there, Kitty, did you know that?' The muscle under his eye started to twitch again. 'I'd keep that page if I were you. Unless you do as she wants, there'll come a day when that's the only way you'll be able to picture what your brother looked like.'

I bent down to pick up the paper. He was right. If I tried to call Joey to mind these days the face that I saw was blurred, like he was looking up at me from underwater. Every time I thought of him he became a little less distinct like he was wearing away. And it wasn't just him; when I thought about Alice now, all I could see was the girl in that painting.

It was as if Fitzy read my mind.

'Another one's gone missing this week, so that makes eight.' His words felt like the blow I'd just managed to dodge.

'Who's it now?'

'Polly Durkin – chorus at The Gaudy. Know her?'

Course I did. Before I spent six nights out of seven hanging up in a birdcage, me and Peggy had looked after Polly's boy, Michael, on occasion when she needed to go out of a night. Tell truth, we didn't ask what she did, but we reckoned she was supplementing her earnings the best way she knew, if you get my meaning. It didn't make her a bad person; more a good mother, to my mind.

Fitzy grunted. 'Time's running out, Kitty.' He turned his back on me to open the door, but he couldn't get out into the little passage to the stage because, of a sudden, it seemed that half of Covent Garden was out there trying to get in.

Great pink blooms bobbed about in a forest of green leaves all tied up in a ribbon bow the size of a cartwheel. The flowers moved forward and Fitzy had to stand back as Danny pushed into the room. Some of the petals dropped onto the boards as he shifted through the narrow doorway.

'Bleedin' hell. What's that when it's at home?'

Danny's muffled voice came from somewhere in the middle of the ambling fernery. 'Just come for you they did, Kitty. From an admirer – someone left them at the door.' He propped the flowers up against the wall and the room seemed smaller by half. It smelt like a tart's doss-house too.

'There's this an' all.' Danny reached behind and produced a roll of paper that he'd stuck down the back of his breeches. He handed it over and I picked at the thin black cord that tied it together.

It was a drawing of me. My head and shoulders beautifully done and very much to the life. My hair was all piled up on top and my eyes, fringed with lashes like a boot brush, looked out to the left as if I was thinking about something a lot finer than where tonight's meat pie was coming from. It was a pretty thing – drawn very delicate with fine curling lines and light pen strokes. The smooth skin of my shoulders had a lovely quality. Almost like you could feel something alive and warm there if you touched the paper. I felt a flush creep over my cheeks as I wondered who had sent it. I found my-self thinking – no, *hoping* is more accurate – that it might be from James Verdin.

'I reckon he's caught you to rights there.' Danny looked over my shoulder, and even Fitzy came over for a squint. 'He's got your name wrong, though.' He pointed at a spidery word beneath my shoulder. 'Philomel – who's she then? I'll give you this though, girl. You draw up nice, so you do.'

He snorted. 'After that piece in *The London Pictorial*, you'll have every moon-calf who fancies himself half an artist on your tail, Kitty. But don't go getting any ideas – there's work to do.' I noted he seemed to have got over his objection to my dressing up as a gent and was now very much alive to the financial benefits of my notorious reputation. 'Out the way.' He pushed past Danny and thumped off along the passage.

Danny peered around the tiny room. 'Peggy here tonight, then?'

His question caught me by surprise. I hadn't seen Peggy for a couple of days now and I was expecting Danny to tell me why. Even though I'd missed her on the past couple of evenings when the Johnnies came to my room, I assumed there was a good reason why she hadn't turned up. We didn't live in each other's skirts, after all, and I'd heard that a couple of the girls at her lodgings had the winter fever.

I shook my head. 'Last time I saw her was when she laced me up on Saturday. And then again after the show . . .'

I broke off for a moment when I pictured James, glossy as a new-minted sovereign sitting right there in my dressing room that night, and felt my neck and cheeks flush over. Bloody hell, get a grip on yourself, girl. I busied myself with the pots on the dressing table. 'I thought she was with you, Dan. Everything all right there?'

He shook his head and clenched his fists.

'Saturday was the last time I saw her too.'

Chapter Seventeen

After the show that night I didn't go back to my dressing room. I didn't care what Fitzpatrick and Lady Ginger wanted me to do, I needed time to think.

If what Lucca had said – that the unknown artist was working again – was right, then he'd need a fresh supply of models. I hoped to God I was wrong, but I thought I knew who those models were. I couldn't sit there tonight in my dressing room making small talk with a queue of bare-faced, gin-fuddled Johnnies wondering if Peggy was out there somewhere with a monster. Because that's what the man who painted *The Cinnabar Girls* was, whatever polite society might think. And to my mind, there was nothing polite about what he'd done.

There'd been several evenings now when I'd welcomed gentlemen callers. Some of them wanted to paw at me – and I got very deft at dealing with them – some wanted a cosy chat and some, the younger ones who were still wet behind the ears, just sat there and gawped. They didn't half go a fine shade of puce if I spoke to them direct. But none of them made a move against me.

After I talked to Dan, just before the night's performance, I'd bundled up my street clothes and left them off to the side of The Comet's stage. When they pulled me and my cage down at the end of the evening I waited for a bit of hush and then I slipped behind an old bit of scenery stacked up against the back wall to change. I needed to get out of there sharpish. I kicked the costume – a pile of greyish screwed-up netting – further back behind the scenery. I'll pick that up tomorrow, I thought. It didn't look nothing now – or if it did it brought to mind one of them cases left behind by a big moth. It was something empty, tattered and dead.

Saturday was the last time I saw her too.

I shuddered like someone had pulled the last stitch through my shroud – that was one of Ma's sayings when she had the feeling on her. Mind you, that came so regular we all ignored it. But tonight I had the feeling on me all right.

I heard a couple of the hands shouting out to the orchestra boys. They were off to The Lamb for a long one and you couldn't hold it against them because the next day was a Thursday when the hall was dark. There wouldn't be another show at The Comet now 'til Friday. It's an odd thing, but Paradise kept its own time. Lady Ginger's halls were always closed on Thursdays and as far as any of us knew, no one paid much attention to our blasphemous Sunday openings. Then again, Lucca always said a full purse could buy a lot of things, including a blind eye.

When all the calling and tramping around died off I made my way out through the back to a door that led out to an alley. It was over the other side to the stage door where, sometimes, the punters who couldn't pluck up enough courage – or shillings, more like – to get access to my room hung around like a fart in crinoline. That was another of Nanny Peck's fine old sayings.

I thought of the old girl now as I wrapped her plaid shawl

around my head, tucking stray curls under the folds. (It didn't do to look too attracting on the streets of an evening.) What would she have made of all this? If Nanny Peck had still been here, she'd be the first person I'd turn to for sense, not Ma.

Now that's a funny thing, I reflected, as I pushed the door open a crack and looked out into the alley. Joey and me couldn't have asked for better when it came to loving, but Ma wasn't exactly . . . well, I may as well admit it, she wasn't exactly the strongest of souls. Very fine and very delicate she was and people used to say how the pair of us was the living spit of her. But I tell you one thing, we might have looked like her, but I reckon we took after our Pa – whoever he was – in ways of thinking. Considering the empty shell Ma became after Nanny Peck died, it was no bad thing our minds were strong.

I don't remember Pa, Joey didn't neither. We both knew better than to ask Ma about him because that would lead to a black day. Nanny Peck said we were never to speak of him and so we didn't. Tell truth, it wasn't unusual for a family round the docks to lack a father – plenty of men were taken in accidents involving the river or the loads.

I don't think my father was dead, though. Every second month or so, Nanny Peck would take herself off on her own for an afternoon and when she came back, she always brought a purse full of coins with her. She called it 'family business' but shut up tight as a limpet if we asked where she'd been. I suspected he had a wife and most likely another family – that wasn't unusual neither. I can't say as I worried about the matter a great deal. To my way of thinking you can't fret over something you've never had. We were loved, that's what matters.

The alley was deserted so I pulled the shawl tight and slipped out. It was late now and the night was clear. At the end I could see the moon, not quite full, hanging just between the gap in the buildings at the entrance. If I was a poetical type I might have said it looked like a shiny penny about to be dropped into a slot – even the nibble of shadow at the side made it look like it was being held up there between the fingers of a giant hand.

I stopped for a moment. That's just how I felt. Like I was being held over the edge of something deep and deadly, and any moment now I'd be dropped right in it. I don't mean being up there in the cage without a net to catch me – that was nothing. No, I mean the feeling that I wasn't in control of my life no more. The feeling that something or someone was playing with me . . . playing with us all.

Peggy – that was the worst yet. How many days had she been gone, then?

I counted on the fingers of my right hand with my thumb. Not today, not the day before, not Monday. Like I said to Danny, Saturday was the last time I'd seen her. And by his account it was pretty much the last time he'd seen her too.

But that wasn't long, was it? God knows Peggy had good reason to do a vanishing act – even for a short while. What with Fitzy taking it out on her, who could blame her?

I knew that wasn't right, though – Peggy wasn't the sort to do a runner. I thought about Sunday. The morning after that visit from James, I'd gone over to her lodgings near St Anne's to have a little word, but her landlady, old Ma Stebbings, said she weren't there.

'With the hours you people keep, how am I supposed to keep track? And it being the Lord's day an' all?' She screwed up her mouth and wiped some invisible speck from her white-starched apron. Honest to God, that apron was so stiff with the stuff, Peggy said it could stand up on its own in a corner.

I remember the sour face on the old crow as she stood there on the step. Right Methody she was and not too happy when her girls made friends . . . 'specially male ones. She didn't much approve of us theatricals. But she liked our money all right.

Looking back, I suppose I should have twigged that Ma Stebbings was suggesting that Peggy hadn't come home that night. So, if something had happened to her, it had happened after the show when I'd been sitting there mooning over James Verdin.

I took a deep breath and walked quickly to the end of the alley. It was biting cold, but I didn't mind that. I wanted to think and I needed a clear head and all my wits about me. The chill air helped. Lucca often warned me never to walk the streets alone at night, but he hadn't come over this evening. I think he assumed I'd be going back with Peggy and Danny. It was no matter – I could look after myself. I proved that every night.

The front steps up to the entrance of The Comet were over to my right now. The lamps were out. I turned my back on the hall, kept my head down and made my way up the street in the opposite direction. Within a couple of minutes I was in a shabby quarter. At the sound of my footsteps a ladybird stepped out from a doorway, hopeful, only to melt back into the shadow as soon as she realised her luck was out.

I passed her pitch, not looking at her full on.

'Trade's as dead as a corpse's prick tonight, love, so if you're thinking of working this patch you'd best move on.' I heard her gin-tight hiss behind me and I quickened my step.

At the far end of the street there was a ragged black mound in the gutter. It was a man so far gone that he'd disgraced himself where he lay. Steam came off the little pool forming around him and the sharp tang of alcohol and piss filled my nose as I stepped over him. He didn't even know I was there.

This was Lady Ginger's Paradise.

I snorted and the air in front of me fugged up with my breath like I was a dragon in one of Nanny Peck's old stories. That's what I'd seen that first time I looked at The Lady's dice – three dragons. What had she said? *An element of risk.* She wasn't wrong about that. And then last time when I'd seen the number four, *the number of death.*

I wasn't superstitious, not like Ma and Nanny Peck least-ways, but I didn't rule anything out neither. Jenny, Clary, Esther, Sally, Martha and Alice – they were the Cinnabar Girls and they couldn't be alive if that painting was a record of what had happened to them. But did the dice mean the future or the past? Alice, Polly and now Peggy – perhaps it wasn't too late for them?

I had to know more about that painting. It was all I had to go on. Sam had promised that as soon as he had anything he'd let me know. But how long was that going to take?

I'd reached a crossroads now and a hack clattered past, spattering my skirt with dirty slush. It was the only sign of life. Apart from the occasional lamp glowing dully behind shutters or window blinds, the streets were dark, and silent too.

Think, Kitty, I told myself, think. What would Joey do?

I found I couldn't answer that question. Tell truth, since the beginning of this business I'd begun to see that there were a lot of things about Joey that I didn't know. There – it was the first time I'd said that, put it into proper words.

When I thought he'd died, I'd missed him so bad that at first the grief of it felt like a real pain, as if there was something ripping me apart deep inside. But when Ma went, Joey had forced me to live and that was a lesson well learned.

I made myself go out to the halls every day, I made myself talk to the girls, I made myself sing as I sewed costumes for Mrs C and cleared vomit from the floors, and although it didn't make the pain of losing him go away, it made it different. That vicious tearing became a dull ache and you can live with that, it becomes a part of you.

See, if you think about an ache you feed it and it hurts you the more, but if you don't dwell on it, most of the time, it sleeps. I'd let Joey sleep, but now he was awake again inside me. Only this wasn't the brother I thought I'd lost. It was someone else, someone Lady Ginger and Fitzpatrick knew – a shadow in the mist.

I didn't know what Joey would do because I didn't really know him any more.

I felt hot tears streaming down my face and I had to keep rubbing at my eyes with the backs of my hands as I trudged along. The tears kept coming and soon I was aware of a noise, a high-pitched wail that kept stuttering and faltering before building up again. That was me too. I was going off like a flood warning down the docks, but I couldn't stop. I could hardly see and I could hardly breathe.

'Kitty?'

The hand on my shoulder froze me in my tracks. A great spurt of something like anger ripped through me and the next sob died in my throat as I shrugged myself free and span around, eyes blazing and every muscle strung up for a fight.

It was James.

Even though he was dressed in a long, dark coat with the fur collar pulled up over his chin, I could still tell it was him all right. His grey eyes glinted in the darkness and I could see his copper hair where it poked out from under his hat at the sides. He frowned, two parallel lines forming between his straight eyebrows.

'Good God, what the devil is wrong?'

I tried to answer, but my mouth just opened and closed. I felt the tears beginning to prickle at my eyes again as I stared up at him.

'My dear girl!' He held his arms out to me and I took a step forward. I couldn't help it – at that moment the thought of being all folded up with Mr James Verdin was the most comforting thing in the world. But then I recollected where I was and got a hold of myself. I pulled away sharp, wiping my nose with the back of my hand.

'Here, please take this.' He offered me a silk 'kerchief that smelt of leather and lavender. As I dabbed at my face I'm shamed to say that the very first thing that came into my head was the fact that I probably looked like a herring girl standing there in Nanny Peck's old plaid shawl with my eyes all red and watered up. Last thing I wanted was for James to see me like that. I wasn't the darling of the halls now – there was no theatrical magic to blind a gent to reality out here. No, I was just an ordinary working girl going home down an ordinary working street and he had no right to be here with me. I could feel my cheeks burn as I sniffed and took another step back.

'What are you doing here?' I was quite surprised at the tone of my question, but if James noticed I was being less than friendly, he didn't show it.

'It's quite simple, Kitty, I followed you.'

'You what?'

'I followed you. After the performance tonight – and may I say that you were as . . . enchanting as ever – I tried to see you in your room again, but a boy said you'd already gone. I was bitterly disappointed; I'll happily admit it to you. I waited outside for a few minutes in the hope that the boy was wrong or lying, but when they extinguished the lamps and I heard them barring the doors, I knew it was fruitless.

'I was about to light a cigar and flag down a hackney when I saw you emerge from the passage on the far side of the hall.'

'How did you know that was me?' I was feeling a bit more with it now. I planted my hands on my hips and stared up at him. He really did have fine eyes.

'You have a most unmistakable . . .' He broke off, smiled and cocked his head to one side. 'You are unique, Kitty. I would know you anywhere.'

Now, I won't lie, that hit the spot. And something in the way he was looking down at me made me feel very snug, but I wasn't going to let on.

'Never mind anywhere. Why are you sniffing around here? It's well off your normal beat, I reckon. We're not in Mayfair now, Mr Verdin.'

'James, please. As I tried to explain, so clumsily, I wanted to see you again. Did you like my gift?'

I felt my belly flip and a stab of excitement sparked deep inside. I'd been right then.

'So it was you. I wondered.'

He actually looked embarrassed. 'What did you think? It's not much, but I wanted to show . . .'

I smiled at him now. 'It was a lovely thing to do. Thank you . . . James.' I liked saying his name aloud. I offered him the 'kerchief back, but he shook his head. 'No, please keep that too.' He frowned as he looked down at the patterned silk square. 'When I followed you I must admit I wasn't sure what to do, but then when I heard you crying . . . Kitty, what's wrong? You sounded so, so . . . desolate.'

I stared up at him confused as to what to say.

'Desolate, it means sad, so very sad,' he explained. 'Are you in pain, in some sort of trouble?'

Well, that was one way of putting it. I chewed my lip and looked down. What would James make of this business with Lady Ginger's girls and that painting? *The Cinnabar Girls is a masterpiece. It is the work of a genius* – that's what he'd said in my dressing room, wasn't it? I wondered what he'd say if he really knew.

And as I stood there thinking about that painting, it came to me of a sudden that I was out on the road in the middle of the night talking to a man I barely knew. What if James Verdin really *did* know something about that picture?

I took another step back and looked around. The street was deserted apart from an old tom cat slinking around in the shadows.

'I've got to go,' I said, all the while thinking that if he tried anything on with me I'd scream loud enough to stir a cemetery. I looked at him narrow, assessing like, but he was just standing there, his eyes all wide and clear. That little furrow had come back between his brows too, as if he was really concerning himself about me. He removed the glove from his right hand, reached forward and gently brushed a tear from my cheek. I felt my skin tingle as he touched me with long tapering fingers that smelt of good cologne.

'If there is anything wrong, perhaps I can be of assistance?' He held his head to one side and smiled.

I had the strong feeling in me then that James was as sweet on me as I was on him.

'Kitty?'

I shuffled my feet and lowered my eyes to the cobbles. 'It's nothing. I've just had a bit of bad news, that's all . . . family business. I was walking home because I needed to think about it, work some things out.'

'Family!' He almost spat the word and I looked up surprised as he continued. 'Then you have my sympathy. Always the cause of the greatest suffering, I find. At the moment I am tortured by both my father and my uncle.'

'Him at the gallery, is that who you mean? Tall gent . . . you take after him in looks?'

'And nothing more, thank God.' James breathed deep and stared across the street like he could almost conjure him up. For a moment I think he forgot I was there, but then he carried on, 'My uncle, the great Sir Richard Verdin, has no children of his own. My parents intend that I should inherit his business. I am the second son, so their hope is that I will make my own way –', he paused and snorted, ' – on the back of Uncle Richard's fortune. My father has cut off my allowance to make this plain to me. But I am an artist. How can I be expected to bury myself alive in meetings, ledgers and figures when there is so much more to see, to feel, to touch, to taste . . .?'

I must have looked blank because he pulled himself up. 'I'm sorry, I didn't mean to burden you with my own troubles. But it seems we might have something in common, yes?' He smiled and his grey eyes caught the light again. I noticed there was something hard to them behind the brightness.

Now, it was clear as the boil on Fitzy's nose that James Verdin and me had about as much in common as Mrs Conway and Queen Victoria, so I wasn't sure what to say next, but he was.

'Look, I must be frank. Since that time at the gallery I have thought of little else but you. I've watched you perform so many times now that Edward and John have made me a laughing stock. They have even wagered . . .' He stopped, smiled and brushed a snowflake from my shawl. It had just started to fall again.

'I cannot help myself. It's why I came to see you again this evening, why I sent you those inadequate expressions of my affection.' He shrugged, and gestured with his hands. 'Will you take pity on a poor soul?'

I laughed at that – the thought of James Verdin as a poor soul, when he was standing there in a coat that probably cost as much as I earned in two years. I looked up at him and grinned. My tongue did the thinking for me – quicker than my mind it went sometimes. 'Well, you can walk me home, if that's what you mean. It's bleedin' cold standing here. I'm over at Penny Fields near West India Dock.' I was amazed to hear the bold way it came out.

He smiled and bowed. 'Thank you. It will be my pleasure. Here . . .' He unfurled a woollen scarf tucked beneath the fur collar of his coat. 'As you say, it is "bleedin'" cold indeed. I think you might need this.'

I was grateful for the scarf and I wrapped it round my neck over the shawl as we started off.

'Can I offer you this as well – against the chill?' James reached into a pocket of his coat and produced a leather flask with a silver top. It minded me of Fitzy's.

I took a deep swig. It warmed me up all right. I could feel it slipping down my throat and into my belly where it seemed to glow inside me like a fire in a grate. I don't know what it was – not gin, that's for sure; it was too fine for that. It had a sort of flowery sugared flavour to it.

'Is it to your taste, Kitty?'

I nodded. 'It's good – a lot better than the muck they serve in the halls. What's in it?'

James laughed. 'I'm not entirely sure myself. It's the special mixture of a friend, he calls it an elixir. The recipe is a closely guarded secret. I understand it can be quite addictive.'

'I can believe that.' I took another mouthful and rolled the sweetness round my mouth. When I allowed myself to swallow, I enjoyed the sensation of heat and comfort that seemed to spread to every part of my body, even to the smallest toes inside my boots.

'As we walk, you must tell me about yourself. I want to know everything. Your friend with the scar . . . Mr Fratini . . . was it? And what about the lovely Peggy? Woody was very taken with her, you know. I want to know all about you, Kitty, and all about your life. The life of an artist.'

I felt a little jolt of excitement as he put his arm around my shoulders. For the warmth and the boldness it gave off, I took another nip of the lixir. I could feel my heart fluttering like a little bird under my ribs now. James drew me closer and I didn't pull away as he bent down to kiss me – the first time.

I won't lie, I'd been thinking about that kiss for days. And it didn't disappoint neither.

Chapter Eighteen

I'd made a very bad mistake. That much was clear when I woke up.

My head felt like there'd been a dog fight going on inside it. My tongue was as dry and stiff as one of Ma Stebbings's aprons and when I shifted the room seemed to sway like I was bobbing about on a river barge.

Now, tell truth – I'd been something this way before. There was a night at The Lamb a year or so back when Old Peter laid a bet that I couldn't match him drink for drink on the Russian stuff. As it turned out, I could, and everyone was most impressed. Only I didn't feel too clever the next day.

Lucca had come over and stayed with me while I got it out of my system. And when it was clear that I wasn't going to die he'd made it very clear that he didn't approve. 'It's not becoming to a lady,' he'd said, holding my hair back while I leaned over the bowl. 'You can be surprisingly stupid some-times, Fannella.'

I'd been stupid this time all right. There was a long lump in the bed next to me. The only part of James Verdin visible among the rumpled sheets and blankets was the top of his head, coppery hair fanned out on the pillow.

He had his back to me. That was something. I lay there for a moment staring up at a knot in a beam overhead. For some reason my eyes kept slipping away so I had to make myself focus. That made my head hurt even more.

What had happened last night? I remembered changing behind the scenery, going out into the alleyway, the old bangtail warning me off and then . . . then it all became thick as fog. On the little chair by the door I could see James's clothes neatly piled and folded. His coat with the fur collar was hung up on a wall hook.

I sat up and my head felt like it might explode. My clothes were everywhere – strewn about the room like I'd done the bleedin' Seven Veils for him. Perhaps I had? I couldn't remember a thing.

Trade's as dead as a corpse's prick tonight, love, so if you're thinking of working this patch you'd best move on.

I'd moved on all right. I remembered feeling sorry for the old girl in the doorway and now it seemed I was no better. I rubbed my forehead. My hands were cold and it helped a bit, but every time I moved my body ached. On the floor next to the pile of blue stuff that was my dress I saw a leather flask. The stopper lay nearby and a little pool of liquid had dripped from the silver-rimmed neck staining the boards.

Something flickered in my mind – a word, 'lixir', was it?

James stirred in the bed. I pulled the sheets tight up to my neck as he turned over and opened his eyes.

'Kitty.'

He didn't smile at me, just stared. I must have looked a wreck.

'Charming.' Something in his tone gave off the strong impression he didn't mean that. He reached to the side of the bed where there was a little stand. I saw that he'd made a tidy arrangement of his things the night before. There was a fob watch and chain, a ring, a stick pin and his cufflinks – all laid out in a row. He took up the fob watch and flicked it open.

'So late already? I must be on my way.'

James sat up straight, pushed back the covers and swung his legs over the side of the bed so that he was sitting with his back to me. I gripped the sheets and pulled them even more tightly. He was completely naked; the clear-marked muscles in his back curved outward like he had the wings of an angel hidden under his smooth, even skin.

I tried to say something, but nothing came. What *did* you say at a time like this?

He stood up and went over to the chair. Even though I felt like hell, I caught my breath. He was as beautiful as one of the boys in one of Lucca's pictures. I wanted him to stay with me, to talk to me.

'Thank you for w . . . walking me home last night.' The words came out cracked and thin. It felt like someone had been rubbing around inside my mouth with a bit of sandpaper.

I felt cheap as the whore in the doorway when he laughed. 'It was nothing. My pleasure entirely. Now I'm afraid I really must be on my way.'

'Y . . . you aren't going to stay on f . . . for a bit then?' I hated myself for asking.

James bent to sort through his folded clothes. 'Sadly, I cannot, Miss Peck. I have an early engagement with Woody and Edward.'

I noticed I wasn't Kitty any more.

He pulled his shirt over his head and walked back to the bed to take up the cufflinks, the stick pin and the signet ring.

I watched as he pushed the gold band over the little finger of his left hand.

'Where are you meeting them?'

It was all that came to my mind. It was clear he wanted to be out of my dingy room quicker than a fox over a yard wall, but I wanted to make it seem – I don't know – clean somehow. Like nothing untoward had gone on and we was just having a polite little conversation.

'The club. As usual.' He smiled at me then, but there wasn't much warmth in it. 'We dine together twice a week. We like to keep . . . abreast of each other's activities.'

So, I was an 'activity' now, was I? It came to me very clear just then that James Verdin had got what he wanted. In fact, he couldn't wait to get away from me now. A snatch of conversation from last night came back – *I've watched you perform so many times now that Edward and John have made me a laughing stock. They have even wagered . . .*

There! I was the subject of a bet and the bleeder had won it. What a stupid little fool I was to think that someone like him might be interested in me. I tightened my fists under the sheets. I wasn't going to make it easy. He was going to talk to me as if I was a proper lady.

'They seem very . . . interesting, your friends. How do you know them?' I winced at the coarse sound of my own voice. I'd never heard it like that before, but James was making me feel dirty and low.

He stood in front of the rickety dressing table, one of its legs propped up on a pile of old books, and looked at himself in the crackled mirror. He licked his fingers and pushed his hair back from his forehead, then he frowned and leaned closer to examine the gingery stubble on his chin. If James Verdin found this situation uncomfortable he certainly didn't show it. On the contrary, he seemed quite happy to have a chat – as long as it was about him.

'I've known them for years. I was at school and, briefly, at college with Woody. The two of us toured Europe together for a year after we were sent down. There was a small misunderstanding with some local girls.' He grinned at himself as he fastened his cuffs. 'He can be wild-hearted, but he's a splendid chap – his wife is a cousin of my mother's.'

Good luck to her I thought, remembering the way he looked at Peggy.

James started to work on his tie as he continued. 'And Edward is . . . I suppose you could describe him as a member of the family, almost. His own parents died when he was very young so my uncle, who was in business with Edward's father, took him in, became his guardian and agreed to pay for the rest of his education, including his medical studies.'

'That was good of him,' I said.

James nodded. 'He still lives with my uncle when he is not at the hospital. Sometimes I think Edward is the only one of us Uncle Richard actually approves of – with all his books and his high ideals. Still, in his favour, at least Edward is good company – when my uncle isn't around.'

I thought of the little lines around Edward's blue eyes – he was certainly someone who found life amusing. He'd laugh at James's story today, that's for sure. They would all find me highly comical. Something itched on my cheek. I reached up and was surprised to find a tear there. I rubbed furiously, but

James had seen me in the mirror. He stopped fiddling with his collar and came over to sit on the edge of the bed.

He was quiet for a moment and then he spoke. 'I was the first, wasn't I?'

I looked down, but he took my hand. 'I am sorry, sincerely. I mistook you for . . . well, girls from the halls have a certain reputation. You must know that?'

I couldn't look at him. 'But I'm not like some of the other girls – and what about my reputation? If Mother Maxwell knew you were here then . . .'

'She keeps this house?'

I nodded. 'And it's a clean establishment. If she finds out you've been here, she'll show me the door.'

'Then I will endeavour to be careful when I leave. I wouldn't want to be the cause of any difficulty for you, Miss Peck.'

I could feel my eyes glassing up again. 'I was Kitty to you last night. I thought you liked me, I thought . . .' Tell truth, I'm not sure what I thought.

James sighed. 'Look, Miss Peck, Kitty – last night was . . . delightful, but you must see that you and I could never . . . That is to say . . .' He paused and looked at me and those distinct furrows appeared between his eyes again. 'This is not what I intended. I have made a mistake and I am sorry. You are a lovely creature, but I have disappointed my family enough without . . .'

He stared around the room taking in the peeling walls, the patch of damp under the window and, most shamefully, my clothes spread out over the boards – one boot was hanging by its laces from a bedknob. He released my hand, stood up and walked over to take his coat from the wall hook. He was twitching to be away.

'Goodbye, Kitty. And . . . thank you for a most entertaining evening. You tell a chap the most extraordinary things when you are . . . well, no matter. Good morning to you.' He smiled, made a shallow bow, plonked his toff hat back on his head and reached for the door handle.

'Wait!' It came out shrill.

He turned. 'What about your flask, there on the floor?' I pointed at the stained boards where the flask and stopper lay. As I moved I accidentally lost hold of the sheet so that more of me was on show than I intended.

James smiled. 'You may keep the flask, Miss Peck. I understand that the silver is of a high grade. It is hallmarked. You may be able to sell it.'

When he'd gone out of the room, I leaned forward, grabbed the boot from the end of the bed and hurled it at the door. Then I was violently sick.

*

I don't know what was in that stuff James gave me to drink, but I was ill for the rest of that day and into the night. It wasn't like that time with Old Peter's firewater, it was ten times worse. Just when I thought there was nothing more inside to bring up, I'd start retching and heaving again. Every muscle in my body felt like it had been pulled out tight like you see the butcher boys doing with the tendons in a calf's leg down Smithfield. My head rang, my neck ached and my eyes burned. But the most uncomfortable thing of all was when the flashes started up of exactly what James and me had been up to.

By the evening my memory had come back all right, but I almost wished it hadn't. I was furious with James Verdin, but even more angry with myself. How could I have been so stupid?

I didn't have Lucca to look after me this time neither. It being a Thursday, it was the quiet day in Lady Ginger's halls and I supposed he'd taken himself off to one of them galleries or exhibitions he was so fond of.

So I wallowed there in my room, feeling used, sullied and sorry for myself. When I finally got out of bed I stood on the stopper by mistake. I was about to kick the thing away when I thought better of it. If James Verdin mistook me for a whore, I might as well get paid for it. Ezra Spiegelhalter over on Stainsby Road would give me a fair price.

I bent down to pick up the flask and got a whiff of the stuff spilled out on the boards. It made me feel noxious again, but I still didn't recognise what it was – not gin that's for sure and not firewater neither. It was almost like a cologne, but under that first flowery sweetness there was a tang of something else, something metallic or bitter.

I thought back to when I met James last night. He'd been very keen to get me to drink up, hadn't he? The lixir had certainly warmed me – in every sense. I pushed the tangle of curls away from my face as another flash started up; the pictures that gallivanted through my head made me close up my fist so tight that the nails drew blood in my palm. That girl hadn't been me, had she? The more I thought on it the more I knew she wasn't.

I understand it can be quite addictive. That's what he'd said wasn't it? Now, that was interesting. From my reckoning James hadn't taken a sip of the stuff. Was that because he knew what was in it? Or because he knew what it did? Or both?

I forced the stopper back into the flask and folded it up in my shawl.

Then I pulled an old blanket off the bed, wrapped it around me and went over to the window to let some clean air into the room. It was dark. I leaned out over the narrow street below and gulped down the freshness like it was a glass of water.

That cut through. So that was romance, I thought to myself?

I watched a couple of women swaying about on the cobbles below. They were half-cut already and the very thought made my stomach churn over again. I most definitely wouldn't be taking in anything stronger than cocoa for the foreseeable.

One of the women rolled over to a man standing in the shadows just beyond the pool of dirty yellow light cast by the lamp on the corner. She pawed at his arm and I heard her cough and slur something out, although I couldn't hear exactly what she said.

The man shrugged her off, stepped back and raised his arm as if he was going to belt her one, but her mate pulled her back just in time. 'Leave him be, he's not worth it. Come on, we'll find some likely ones up on the Commercial.' Her voice was over-loud and ragged with liquor. The women staggered on together a little way until one of them stopped and bent double. Clutching her sides she began hacking away like she'd rack up half her lights right there in the gutter. Her friend waited until the spasm finished. All the while she just stood by, rubbing her hands over and over against the cold, her eyes darting about for trade.

'You done?'

The coughing woman wiped her mouth, straightened up and nodded. They linked arms and lurched into the dark.

I watched them go. Was that going to be my future, I wondered? Joey had always protected me from that world, but I reckon he knew all about it. In fact, considering he worked direct for the old bitch he was probably up to his wide green eyes in all the greasy filth that floated around her like scum on the river. When I thought about Joey now my head fogged up so that nothing was clear any more – and it wasn't the lixir.

Why hadn't he told me what he was mixed up in? Together we could have sorted something out, couldn't we?

Thing with Joey, though, was there was no 'we'. I was his little sister and he was the man. Now I was hanging up there in that cage for him and getting my boots into God knows what and all because he . . .

The fug in my head swirled thicker. What *had* Joey done? Why was Lady Ginger keeping him from me? I couldn't shake the thought that there were so many secrets winding, slipping and sliding around me that I'd become like one of them bound-up girls in the painting.

I took another deep breath and looked up. There were stars winking there now in the gaps between the clouds. They were cold and sharp like The Lady's eyes when she said Joey's name and I realised right then that what I felt was anger too.

I was furious with my bold, beautiful brother for getting me into this business. I loved him, of course, but I hated him for leaving me alone and for making me responsible.

If I failed it wasn't just him who'd suffer, was it? Fitzy was right. Lady Ginger was a name among the Barons, but if she showed weakness any one of them would be waiting to move into Paradise. And when they moved they'd bring their own with them. Where that would leave the rest of us was anyone's guess, but a good guess was that girls like me and Peggy would end up working the streets faster than Old Peter could empty a tankard.

That's if Peggy was alive. I bit my lip; it was bruised where James had kissed it. If I thought hard I could still taste the way he . . .

I froze. Of a moment, I felt as if I was being looked at hard. It was as if something cold touched my face, like brushing through a cobweb in the dark. I rubbed at my cheeks to wipe the feeling away and scanned the street. The gent standing near the lamp had moved. He was closer to my lodgings now over on the other side of the road. The thin light from the lamp didn't touch him there, so all I could make out was the black shape of him. But I knew he was staring up at me.

I shivered, pulled the blanket tight and closed the window.

Chapter Nineteen

By the Friday morning I was feeling a lot better. A bit sore, to be honest, but nothing I couldn't deal with.

I splashed my face with icy water from the basin and looked at myself in the crackled mirror. Did I look different now?

Behind me in the glass I saw the three new dresses I'd bought with Lady Ginger's shillings. They were hanging off a string running across the damp back wall of my room – a row of crumpled headless bodies in fairground colours. What had James made of that?

I'd thought I looked so fine got up as a lady, but tell truth, looking at them empty frocks now with their low cut and their fancy bits at the sleeve ends, I realised I must have looked as cheap as a tuppenny bobtail. Lucca had been right – as usual.

As I buttoned up my old brown frock and searched the room for the other boot, I wondered how much I should tell Lucca about James. That didn't make me feel too good neither.

I went to the workshop at The Gaudy first. Lucca wasn't there but Danny was. He had his back to me and was sawing through a plank across the work bench. I called his name, but he kept on working, so I stepped through the door, walked across the room and tapped him on the shoulder.

'Any news?'

He shook his head and even though it was cold in there, little beads of sweat fell from his forehead to the wood. Then he slammed his fist down so hard on the plank that it jerked up and clattered to the floor, splitting in two.

'She's gone, just like the others.' He turned to look at me and I could see dark circles round his eyes and stubble on his chin. Dan was usually very particular about his looks. It was one of the things Peggy loved about him.

I didn't know what to say. I reached for his arm and squeezed it.

'Kitty, if you hear anything – anything at all, if she gets in touch, you'll let me know, won't you? Even if she's run off, I just want to know she's safe.'

I swallowed. 'That's what we all want to know. And you'd be the first one to hear, Danny, not me. You know that, don't you?'

He rubbed his big calloused hands together and nodded miserably. 'You looking for Lucca, only he's over at The Comet. You need to get over there too, Kit, we all do. There's a gathering.'

'What, for everyone?'

Danny nodded again. 'We need to do a run-through with the cage this afternoon. I've worked on the chain and re-placed a couple of the guide ropes, but you need to get the feel of the balance in case it's different.'

'There wouldn't be a gathering for that. What else is going on?'

He shook his head. 'Some business or other. You better go. I need to finish up here, but I won't be far behind.'

Like I said, The Comet was always thought to be the best of Lady Ginger's halls. It was far grander than The Gaudy, with plaster angels and golden flowers crawling all over its ceiling. Looking up from my cage one evening at all the little winged babies and the curling leaves and petals going on over my head, I wondered if that was why Lady Ginger's patch was called Paradise.

Anyway, it might have been the grandest hall, but it wasn't the most friendly. The Comet girls hadn't taken to me and my cage, and I hadn't taken to them. Now I was going to be hanging up there for a second week on the trot and I wasn't looking forward to it. The thought that Peggy wouldn't be there with me made it even worse.

The thought of Peggy made everything worse.

Dan had said there was going to be a run-through, and frankly, I was glad to have the chance to get up there away from the world. I needed to clear my mind. Being on the swing, twirling to the music without having to give a thought to what I was doing, was actually quite restful to the brain. Tell truth, I actually looked forward to those moments in the evening when the orchestra struck up with my song, because for the next ten minutes it was like I wasn't there no more. I just went off into a sort of trance and did what I trained to do. Madame Celeste had called it '*the state of perfection*' and I'd perfected it all right.

When I got to The Comet I went round the back, but instead of finding the hands working in the yard – as a rule they'd be painting up bits of scenery and building bits of stuff for the novelty acts – everything was quiet.

I went up the steps to the back door, pushed it open and called out, 'Anyone home?'

'Kitty!' Mr Leonard came pattering down the corridor. He didn't look his usual immaculate self. He hadn't managed to do up the buttons on his waistcoat proper and one side of his waxed moustache had the droop, giving him a most comical expression.

'There was an . . . incident last night. My office was ransacked. The Lady is furious and Fitzpatrick is due at any moment. Everyone is waiting in the hall, come along quickly.'

So that was the reason for the gathering.

It must have hurt Mr Leonard to have Fitzpatrick coming over. The Comet might have been the grandest of The Lady's halls, but old Fitzy was the top dog when it came to management. He'd have a lot to say about it, I was sure. It didn't surprise me that Mr Leonard didn't mention the rozzers. In Paradise we liked to deal with things in private. I say 'we', but what I really mean is that Lady Ginger didn't want anyone with a legal cast of mind sniffing around her business affairs.

Mr Leonard trotted up the corridor and disappeared behind a green velvet curtain hung over with a garland of gold tassels, but I still could hear his tinny little voice going on up ahead. 'I suppose I must take comfort from the fact that the assault on my property took place after I'd secured last week's takings. You more than tripled our best and outstripped The Gaudy and The Carnival together – it's why you're here again this week. The Lady was pleased with me. Keep up, Kitty.'

I followed him through the curtain, reflecting that I was a

valuable commodity these days to a lot of people, including James Verdin. I wondered how much he'd '*wagered*' on me? When I thought of his fine grey eyes and his copper hair now, I didn't see stars twinkling and hear birds singing like one of them love-struck maidens in Mrs Conway's songs, that's for sure.

It seemed as if everyone in Paradise was gathered in the hall waiting for Fitzy. The curtain was down and some of the flares were lit. I looked around – the Comet girls were lolling around on little gold chairs at the front, Professor Ruben and the boys were playing cards at a table, Mr Jesmond from The Carnival was talking to Mrs C and some of the hands were smoking or ogling the girls. Swami Jonah was sitting at one of the tables. He didn't have his turban on today and his freckled bald head gleamed. He nodded at me as I came through the curtain. The tease line about his act on all the playbills went through my mind: '*Swami Jonah – he knows you from cradle to grave*.'

Lucca was over on the far side leaning against a pillar.

When he saw me come in behind Mr Leonard he waved. I pretended I hadn't seen him. For some reason I didn't want him to look at me. Would he be able to tell what I'd been up to with James? Was that possible?

I went to the back of the hall and leaned against the rail of one of the booths. Lucca came over, of course. I could feel my cheeks flushing red. He took off his hat and leaned back against the rail next to me.

'There will be no time for a run-through this afternoon, Kitty. By the time Fitzpatrick has finished with us, it will be late.'

I nodded. Thievery in the halls was nothing new. Over at The Carnival the cellar man had been running a very lucral gin racket for a year and a half before Fitzy got wind of it. Every so often we was gathered together for a little talk about loyalty and the consequences of not being loyal. The cellar man at The Carnival, what was left of him, had been fished out of Deptford Creek on the other side of the river. He'd been bound up and wrapped tight in an old oil sheet. Someone had spotted him bobbing against the wall of the Phoenix Gas Works like a big old turd.

I could hear some banging about behind the curtain on the stage. 'Lucca, after the show tonight can I come back to yours – you've heard about Peggy?'

He shook his head and spat into the sawdust. 'Danny told me yesterday. Do you think she has run away or do you think she is . . .'

'I don't know. I want to think she's done a runner, but it doesn't ring true. She and Danny were good and I don't think she'd go off without telling me. She wouldn't.'

Lucca fiddled with the rim of his hat and nodded. 'You are right. Peggy was . . .' He stopped himself. 'Peggy *is* a good woman. She would never hurt Danny . . . or you, Fannella.'

It struck me then that proper friends tell each other things. I looked at Lucca's face, into his bright brown eye, and realised that he was pretty much all I had left in the world. I was going to have to tell him about James – maybe not all of it – but as much as he needed to know. Like I said, to my mind there were too many secrets knotting around us and I didn't want to add to them.

'After the show tonight then, yes?'

Before he answered, the red stage curtains swept back. The sudden silence in the hall was so thick you could cut it with a barber's razor.

Lady Ginger was sitting in that old carved chair right in the middle of the stage. Two of her lascars stood either side and Fitzy was up there too, over to the right. He looked pale as milk and he was rubbing one of his ugly great paws over and over the top of his cane so I imagine that he and The Lady had already been having a little chat.

Mr Leonard gasped and tried to scramble up the side steps to join them, but The Lady raised a hand and one of the lascars went to block his way. She was wearing a black lace dress with a high collar right up to her chin. Around her shoulders was a red China shawl all broidered over, and jewels glinted at her ears and on her fingers. Her face was painted white, but her lips were red as the shawl.

Even though she was tiny as a wren, Lady Ginger seemed to fill that stage. You could feel something coming off her like heat from a fire – although this was the kind of heat that burned and tore at your skin when you touched an icy wall with bare fingers. Her glittering black eyes caught the lime-light as she scanned the room and I swear that every one of us there would say that she stared straight at us.

After a moment she clicked her fingers and one of the lascars lit a pipe for her, like that time at the warehouse. She inhaled deeply and blew a smoke ring that floated up and hovered above her head for a moment, looking for all the world like a grubby halo.

Then that fluttery little voice started up. And don't, for a moment, think it sounded sweet or comical, because standing there listening to her, it was like someone had scratched down the line of your backbone with a jagged cube of ice.

'It has come to my attention that there has been an . . . incursion into my property. I understand from Fitzpatrick here that last night someone entered this theatre and stole several items from the office. This is not pleasing to me.'

She coughed and took another deep pull on her pipe. The bowl glowed up.

'I further understand that some of you have been talking about my business affairs. This, also, is not pleasing to me. Indeed it is something I will not tolerate.' She stared hard at the Comet girls and I noticed that a couple of them looked at their pretty boots. I knew there'd been a lot of speculation about Martha Lidgate. In fact, I'd heard that a couple of the Comet girls had been round to see Martha's ma. I remembered that letter The Lady sent to Fitzy – *Moreover, it seems that the mother of the Lidgate girl has approached the constabulary. I need hardly tell you, Fitzpatrick, the consequences of investigation . . .*

The Lady continued.

'You must understand that I see myself as a mother to you all.' The way she said *mother* brought to mind an old story Joey had read to me once. Something about some old Greek witch – Medea, was it? I think that was her name – anyway, she wasn't much of a mother.

'You are my family and I will care for you, but only if you have the courtesy to abide by my rules.' She clicked her fingers again and the double doors at the back next to where Lucca and I were standing swung open. Six of the Lady's Chinamen came in – all dressed in long dark gowns with plaits hanging down their backs. They walked in two lines to the foot of the stage where they bowed their heads to The Lady.

'Frances Taylor and Sukie Warren, you will stand.'

There was a murmur among the Comet girls up front as two of them rose to their feet.

'Now you will kneel.'

The hall was that silent you could have heard a bluebottle fart. Frances and Sukie sank to their knees, their eyes huge with fear.

Sukie started up. 'Please, Lady, please. We didn't . . .', but Lady Ginger raised her hand. 'Silence.'

Then she turned to look at the hall. 'I want you all to remember that what you see today is the act of a loving mother. Frances and Sukie have . . . disappointed me. And now, in front of their family, they must be punished.'

The Lady sucked on the pipe again and the trail of smoke coiled up around her on that chair.

She nodded at the Chinamen.

'Deal with it.'

They moved swiftly and neatly. Two of them took hold of the girls' arms from behind, while two more leaned across their shoulders and forced their heads to the floor. When the girls were unable to wriggle free the last two Chinamen produced curved blades from their sleeves.

I gasped as the flash of silver caught the lights. I stepped forward, but Lucca caught hold of my arm and hissed, 'No, you cannot.'

The men with the blades bent down to the two girls who started to scream. Through the tables, chairs and people all

I could see was the glint of silver as they slashed and hacked. I could hear the girls sobbing and calling out too, but after a while they fell silent. Everyone else in the room stood absolutely still. A couple of the Comet girls hid their faces in their hands.

'Enough.' The Lady's voice was high and clear. 'You will stand now.'

The Chinamen moved back and Frances and Sukie rose unsteadily to their feet. They were both completely bald – their scalps raw and bleeding where the blades had bitten too deep and too vicious. One of the Chinamen held up a great hank of dark hair – Sukie's – then he dropped it into a lime-light cup on the front of the stage where it sputtered and smouldered.

The sour-sweet smell of burning human hair filled the hall as the girls wept.

'I trust I have made my point.' The Lady was ram-rod straight in her chair, her face a mask. 'When any of you question me, when any one of you displeases me, you strike at the heart of your family. Do you understand?'

The hall was silent.

'Do you understand?' the Lady asked again and received mutterings and nods in reply as she carried on. 'A family is a precious thing, but it is also a fragile thing. There are many who cast envious eyes over my children – many who wish them harm. But I will continue to protect you all, as long as you show me the respect I demand. "Honour thy father and thy mother." That is what the Bible tells us, is it not? If any of you bring dishonour on this family, make no mistake, I will deal with it.'

Lady Ginger leaned back in her chair and closed her eyes, and she didn't open them when she spoke again. 'Now, Mr Leonard, I wish to talk to you in private. Come.'

From the look on Mr Leonard's face I could tell he'd rather be shorn in public like Frances and Sukie than face The Lady alone. The lascar at the top of the steps by the stage moved aside and Mr Leonard climbed up them like they was a scaffold. When he reached the middle of the stage just a few steps from The Lady, the curtains came down.

Chapter Twenty

Just as Lucca said, there was no time for a run-through that afternoon. Tell truth, none of us was much in the mood for it after that little performance. And we weren't exactly in the frame of mind for the evening neither. Mr Leonard didn't re-appear so Fitzy stepped in for the night, ordering the hands around and eyeing up the chorus.

The Comet girls were in a right state. I kept finding fussy little knots of them crying in corners, but when I tried to talk to them they clammed up tight and gave me daggers like I was somehow responsible for what had happened to Frances and Sukie.

When one of them actually spoke to me at all it confirmed everything I suspected. 'We was all right here, Kitty Peck, un-til you moved in with your cage and your high ways.'

Louisa Tyke was stringy as an old alley cat and sharp-clawed with it. 'You've brought bad luck to The Comet – you and your one-eyed, foreign boyfriend.' She spat on the boards near my foot and flounced off.

It didn't help that Fitzy called me into Mr Leonard's office for a little private conversation about an hour before curtain up. There was a pile of jumbled papers on the desk in front of him and the drawers were hanging open – a couple were up-turned on the floor.

'Is this how the jemmy boys left it?' I asked, looking round the room. Behind Fitzy's chair – as formerly occupied by Mr Leonard – there was a big coffin of a cupboard with a lock on it the size of a mastiff's head. Like the drawers it was gaping wide open and inside I could see stacks of paper all done about with strings and ribbons piled up on the shelves.

Fitzy grunted and started to sort through the papers on the desk. He licked his thumb as he turned through the pages. When he'd got to the end of his counting he grunted again, puffed out his cheeks and pulled at the end of his greasy whiskers. Finally he looked up at me and his moist little eyes were redder than ever.

'This room is exactly how Solly found it this morning.' Solly was Mr Leonard's Christian name – in a manner of speaking. Fitzy narrowed his eyes. 'Now here's a thing. Nothing is missing. Me and The Lady have been through this most particular, and now she's got me checking it again, but if anything's been lifted then I'm one of her Chinamen.'

I didn't understand. 'If nothing's gone, why did The Lady come over here today for a gathering?' I looked at the papers and the drawers. 'Looks to me like someone was searching for something.'

Fitzy drummed the leather desk top with his fat, stained fingers. 'Or trying to make it look that way? I never thought I'd see this day, but The Lady is rattled, so she is. Right now she's *talking* to Solly and I wouldn't want to be in that man's shoes tonight if it meant I could swap places with Finn McCool himself. The point is that someone is sticking two fingers up at her and that's never happened before. First the missing girls and now this – someone is putting their mark on Paradise.'

So, that explained all the theatricals with Frances and Sukie. The Lady was stamping her territory in the most notable way, but if nothing had gone missing I didn't see the point of anyone breaking in and I said as much.

Fitzy's face flushed up scarlet. 'It's a direct challenge and a threat. These things are happening right under her nose and they have to stop.' He thumped the desk and knocked the papers to the floor with a swipe of his paw. He stood up and leaned towards me. I could smell the rot on his breath as he held his face close to mine.

'You heard from Peggy?'

I shrank back and shook my head. He didn't say anything for a moment, but that muscle started working under his eye. It struck me then that he might actually feel something for her, after all.

He looked down at the desk top and delicately shifted a glass paperweight to one side. 'At least there's one thing, girl. The cage has worked. You've lured them in, like we wanted. The Lady wants you to pay particular attention to the audience tonight. She thinks they'll be here this evening – in the house. And if not this evening, then sometime soon.'

He paused and stared at me. His eyes darted across my face like he was looking for something. 'She's also under the impression you might recognise them.'

'How did she make that out then?' I gestured at the desk and the cupboard. 'It looks like just another crowbar job to me. Everyone knows The Comet is a good house, so why wouldn't any bob-tag jemmy crew have a go? What makes Lady Ginger think this has anything to do with me and the cage?'

'Take a look at this.' He opened his jacket and reached to the top inside pocket. As he did so, the smell of sweat and stale tobacco rolled most powerful across the desk. He'd never been much of a one for the personal dainties, but recently he'd got worse.

'Nothing was taken last night, but this was *left* here, pinned to the inside of Solly's door, so it was.'

He handed me a plain envelope. 'Open it.'

For some reason my hand trembled. I didn't want Fitzy to see I was afraid, so I tried to mask it, but when I pulled out the sheet of paper inside and unfolded it I covered my mouth with my hand. I couldn't help myself.

The girl in the drawing was me. There was no question of that.

In the picture I was half-naked and huddled up in the cage with a chain around my neck. My shoulders were a knot of bones and shadow, my feet were bare and my toes wrapped around the bar like claws. The artist – if you could call him that – clearly intended the viewer to think of me as a fancy bird kept in someone's drawing room. Only this bird was sickening for something. A pair of mangy wings drooped at my back and a couple of stray feathers etched into the space beneath my perch suggested the drop below. In the drawing, my eyes were huge and beseeching. The artist had worked them over and over in heavy black ink so that they were almost scratched through the page.

I'd been with Joey once when we'd run into a backstreet dog fight. I say run into it, but actually Joey was running an errand – and now I knew who for. We'd got there just at the end when the punters were closing in round the exhausted dogs – the men were baying for blood twice as loud as the animals. Joey had tried to pull me away, but I wouldn't budge. I was horrified and transfixed at the same time. He tried to cover my eyes, but I just shook him off. The point is that one of the dogs – the loser – made a lunge for it and broke through the edge of the ring. Before the men kicked him back I saw his eyes and I knew then that he was dead, even though he was still panting and bleeding and whining.

That's what I looked like in the drawing. The paper shook in my hands.

'What do you think of that then?'

I gripped the paper and said nothing. 'Fold it down again.' Fitzy's voice was brash, almost like he was enjoying this.

I shook the sheet and the last fold flapped down to reveal some writing. The words were scrawled beneath the drawing in large, jagged letters that tore through the paper in places.

At night your cagebird sings an ugly song. The black 's' in the word 'song' had ripped the paper.

And beneath that there was another line etched fainter in a more composed hand like it had been added later as an afterthought.

Fitzy licked his lips. 'Someone of an artistic bent took the trouble last night to break into The Comet and leave that here – nothing else. They're interested in you, girl, just as we wanted. The Lady is particularly taken with that line there – the one about her cagebird. I very much doubt it means her damned parrot.'

I stared at the black writing confused. I'd been performing the song nearly every night for three weeks now, so if someone had taken offence, they'd been a long time working out what I was really singing about.

At night your cagebird sings an ugly song.

I traced my finger over the scrawl and felt how deep the pen had cut into the paper. The first stroke of the letter 'n' in 'night' slashed through the page too.

At night?

A cold thought wormed itself into my head, but it wasn't one I wanted to share with Fitzy. Of a sudden I knew I was going to have to tell Lucca a lot more about James Verdin than I'd intended. I stared at the other neater words, but I couldn't make sense of them. They weren't London English that's for sure.

'Anything to say for yourself?'

I shook my head.

The cane whipped through the air just past my ear and smacked into the desk so hard that it made a dent in the wood. 'Well, I've got something to say to you, Kitty Peck, and it comes straight from The Lady herself. Seven days – that's all you have left, or to be more accurate, that's all your brother has left.'

*

By the time the punters started queuing outside that evening we were running late. I sat down on the swing seat in the cage and braced my feet against the bars.

'You can take me up, lads. I'm ready.'

Four of the hands started pulling on the guide ropes and the big chain connected to the centre of The Comet's plaster ceiling started to grate. I wasn't surprised Danny hadn't remembered to oil it, what with Peggy and everything.

I swung out from the stage over the centre of the hall. I was about forty foot up and the cage was juddering and swaying about as usual. Fitzy must have given the order to open the doors because punters had started to take up their places – a couple of them were already standing just below me and calling up, but I wasn't in the mood for banter.

The limelight flares were firing up along the front of the stage and Professor Ruben and the boys had started up with some jaunty song. If only they knew, I thought. My temples throbbed when I thought of Lady Ginger. Seven days. It was hopeless. I'd failed everyone – all the girls and even my own flesh and blood. Joey was a dead man.

The hall smelt of smoke and gin and bodies. It was almost good to be up here, away from everything that could touch me. I spread out the net of my skirt and breathed deep. It was a rotten world where a girl felt safer hanging seventy foot up without a safety net to catch her than she did going about her normal business.

At night your cagebird sings an ugly song.

When I'd touched that line under the drawing something James Verdin had said repeated in my head – *Thank you for a most entertaining evening. You tell a chap the most extraordinary things when you are . . .* When I was *drunk*, that was what he meant.

What *had* I told him when I was under the influence of that lixir? The more I thought about it, the more it seemed possible to me that it wasn't what I'd done with James a couple of nights ago that I should be worrying about. No, it was what I'd *said* to him. If I'd babbled about missing girls and paintings and he'd recognised what I was saying, then no wonder he was on to me. He could draw too – he'd sent me that picture of my head and shoulders. And now the vicious sketch of me in the cage.

If I was right, then James Verdin was likely a mad man and a murderer.

The cage jerked and I clung tight to the ropes of the swing. The air was thick with smoke, but that was nothing to what was coiling about inside my head.

That couldn't be right, could it? If James really was the *unknown hand* behind *The Cinnabar Girls*, why hadn't he taken me like the others when he'd had the chance? After all, I'd offered myself to him on a platter. Perhaps that was too easy? Was it like a game he was playing – like a cat with a mouse, or a *songbird*?

The thoughts were going round and round my head as the cage swung upwards. There were just a few more feet to go now until it reached the centre of the ceiling. In the four corners of the hall below me, the hands were pulling the guide ropes tight and beginning to lash them to big metal hooks set into the walls. The ropes kept the cage steady, the chain kept it up.

That chain was scraping away so loudly tonight I couldn't hear the orchestra boys below. I hoped it would quieten down a bit once I was locked into place. Not far now.

I looked up; one of the plaster cherubs was right over my head, strumming away on a harp or something. I felt that if I reached out I could touch his little bum – Nanny Peck had a pottery shepherd boy in her room and she patted his shiny round rump for 'the luck of it' every time she went out.

The luck of it! Now, that was something I needed. I pulled myself up and reached out from the swing, but just as I was about to push my hand through the bars, the harp in the boy's hands seemed to quiver. A crack appeared across the strings, snaking out across the instrument and up his arm. I could feel powder on my hand now and a second later a load of the stuff came down from the ceiling, covering my head and shoulders.

I began to cough, rubbing my eyes with one hand and hanging on with the other.

Next thing I know that harp and the cherub's arm were slowly peeling off the ceiling, the harp bouncing on the outside of my cage as it crashed to the floor – the arm just hanging out, the fingers pointing down. Then my cage began to judder and sway – a lot more freely than I was comfortable with – the chain was making a right racket now as it grated around the big hook overhead. The groaning noise sounded like the wooden hull of one of the tall ships down the docks when it's trapped in the ice.

'Kitty! Watch out!'

One of the hands called up as a guide rope broke free from the wall below and snapped up into the air just beneath my feet. The chain linking me to the ceiling above squealed and the cage dropped about five feet, lurching violently to the left.

I lost my balance, slid to the edge of the swing and tipped off the seat. Madame Celeste's voice rang out in my head. *Never let go.* As I toppled forward I thrust out my arms and caught at the golden bars. The cage was hanging at an angle now, with two more of the guide ropes on the right side flailing free below. My breathing came fast and shallow and I tried not to think about the space gaping beneath me. My left knee stung where it had scraped against the inside of the cage when I fell.

I pulled myself further in and managed to wedge my feet between the lower bars. Then I bent low and clung tight. Behind me there was a ripping sound as the last of the guide ropes broke free. Now the cage jerked, tilted even more and began to spin – all the while the chain grating and yowling overhead. I could hear voices – shouts and screams. People were calling my name.

The hall began to smear around me – a dizzying blur of smoke, lights, colours and distorted faces in the boxes.

I could feel my hands beginning to slip as sweat covered my palms. I pushed my slippered feet further into the gaps between the bars and tried to find what Madame Celeste would have called my 'point of balance'. I'd just managed to hook my knees over the bottom bar as a great smiling plaster head cracked off the ceiling above and smashed into a thousand pieces over the table and floor seventy foot below.

Chapter Twenty-one

'Fannella, open your eyes!' Lucca's voice came from somewhere below and over to my right.

I didn't want to look anywhere – it made me dizzy and confused. Madame Celeste had been very clear about what to do in case of an incident. Once she'd even loosened a rope without warning when I was forty foot up to test me. As the little trapeze in her tall, beam-latticed attic had suddenly dipped and swayed, I'd closed my eyes, wrapped my legs around the one taut rope and latched on tight until all the movement stopped. Then I'd slipped down like a rigging boy on a clipper ship.

She was pleased. 'Good, Kitty. You have the nerve. Remember the three cardinal rules: never look down; never let go; and never give up hope. And that last is the most important rule of all, girl. If you ever allow yourself to think you might fall, you will. It's as simple as that.'

Only it wasn't so simple now. I'd been frozen into a crouching position on the inside of the cage for what seemed like hours, only it can't really have been more than a minute. It had stopped spinning, but every time I moved the metal quivered and hummed around me like a cracked bell. The cage jerked and groaned again as something came loose and there was a dry, rustling, pattering sound as more plaster from the ceiling crumbled over my head and bare arms.

'You must look, now!' I opened one dust-crusted eyelid and squinted down in the direction of Lucca's sharp command. He was in a second tier box, perhaps fifteen, maybe twenty foot below. He had a coil of thick rope in his hands. He held it up. 'Look – we can use this.'

I opened my other eye and accidentally, because of the angle of the cage, I looked straight down. That was a mistake – just as Madame Celeste had warned. Instantly the jumble of gawping people, plaster-dusted chairs, tables, broken glass and floorboards below seemed to whirl and fall away. I was about sixty foot up, but when I looked down I felt there was such a space gaping open between me and the hall that I might as well have been about to knock on the gates of heaven itself. I closed my eyes tight and gripped the bars. Pull yourself together, I told myself, if you don't sharpen yourself up the pearly gates likely will be the next thing you see.

I took a deep breath. *I will not fall.*

Lucca's voice came again. 'I need you to catch the end of this rope, but to do that you need to look at me, Fannella.'

I opened my eyes and locked them on Lucca. He smiled and nodded, but his face was paler than the plaster dust over my shoulders. 'Good. Now I am going to throw the rope and you need to catch the end and tie it to the cage. *Capisci?*'

I nodded as Lucca continued. 'But you cannot do that unless you let go of the bars and hang down – like on the swing, Fannella. You must let go gently and lean back. Keep looking at me.'

I took another breath and tried to let go, but I didn't seem able to move.

I gripped even tighter. I could feel panic rising from

203

somewhere deep inside. Under the flimsy costume my back prickled with sweat and my fingers were slippery as eels.

'Please try.' Lucca's voice was tight.

'I can't move.' My words came out as the faintest whisper. There was dust in my mouth and dust in my eyes. The thought came to me that I was being buried alive in the air.

But then something wonderful happened. Even now I can't explain, but it was like someone or something took over for me. As I clung there, not able to move a muscle – not even my lips – Professor Ruben began to play my music softly on the piano. It was just him at first, but gradually the orchestra boys joined in and as the notes danced up into the air around me mingling with all the dust, of a sudden I found I didn't have to think any more, just be.

I let go, leaned back and stretched out my arms, and even though the cage juddered about a bit and more plaster fell from the ceiling it didn't matter. I was perfection. Ringlets swung loose below me and pins dropped to the floor. It was just like that first time again in Madame Celeste's attic. I was flying and nothing could hurt me.

'Catch!'

I caught the end of the rope the first time Lucca threw it across.

'Now tie it to the side of the cage nearest me – just to your right.'

I hooked my feet around the bars to keep me secure and doubled up until I was able to sit once more. The cage juddered and would have begun to spin again if it hadn't been for the rope snaking back down to Lucca in the box. More plaster dust rained from above as I passed it over the thick metal band around the foot of the cage, wound it tight and knotted it several times.

'Yes – that's good, Fannella.'

Lucca pulled the rope taut. He wound the other end around a pillar on the edge of the box and tied it securely while the cage groaned and the chain above me rasped. When he was satisfied it would hold he looked up and grinned warily.

'The next bit is easy. You just have to climb down the rope and join me here in this box.'

I nodded. 'Like you say – easy!'

I reached for the rope with my right foot and wound it deftly around my ankle and lower leg. Then I inched forward and slowly freed every part of myself from contact with the bars until I was clinging to the underside of the rope like one of the acrobatic monkey boys in the seasonal tumbling act over at The Gaudy. Without my weight to steady it, the cage began to sway from side to side, the rope with it. I kept my eyes locked on Lucca.

The hall was completely silent now. If another one of my hair pins dropped, I swear I'd be able to hear it bouncing off the boards below.

'Now come.' Lucca's voice was level and warm.

I went slowly feet first, pushing myself down hand over hand, with my ankles crossed over the rope. All the while the cage kept up its clanking and growling behind me and once I heard a gasp from the crowd as something big fell off the ceiling – perhaps a whole plaster baby this time? Whatever it was it crashed and shattered on the boards below. I didn't look down.

When I was about three foot from the box, Lucca leaned out and caught my legs roughly, dragging me in so that I fell on top of him and the pair of us disappeared behind the painted front.

As I lay there panting with tears of relief streaking down my plaster-dusted cheeks I heard a rippling noise. Quiet at first but then it grew and grew until I could hear clapping, stamping, cat-calls and whistling. It was even louder than that first time I'd performed my act at The Gaudy.

Lying on the floor of the box next to me, Lucca let out a huge shuddering sigh like he'd been bottling air up in his lungs ever since the moment I slipped off the swing. He sat up and pushed his hair back from his face. There were raw bloody stripes across his palms where he'd been holding tight to the rope. He turned to look down at me.

'What's this, eh? There's no need.' He brushed the tears and the dust from my cheeks, pushed a stray ringlet from off my face and kissed my forehead. 'You are safe now. And listen to them . . .'

People in the hall were chanting my name now, over and over. Lucca grinned. 'You must take a bow. They want to see you.'

He stood and offered me a hand. I sat up, and for a moment the little box swam around like I was up there in the cage again. I took a deep breath and clenched my fists. 'The show must go on, eh?'

He nodded. 'Of course, always.'

I wiped my face with the backs of my hands, dusted off my shoulders and my frock and let him help me to my feet. As I appeared over the edge of the box the crowd went wild. I waved and twirled and blew kisses and then I tried to make Lucca take a bow too, but he wouldn't come into the light, no matter what I said. He just stood in the shadows behind me, watching.

*

After my 'performance' at The Comet – the last in that theatre as it happens on account of there not being much in the way of a ceiling to hang from – Fitzy was clear that I'd be moving back to The Gaudy.

'Did you hear them, now?' He rubbed his palms over and over as he stood next to my chair. The room was crowded and stuffy. There were at least twenty men crushed in there with us and more out in the hallway trying to get a view of me. Fitzy had shifted my dressing table back against the wall to let more of them in.

After taking my bows, me and Lucca had made our way through the curtained passages to the dressing room. When we got to the narrow winding stairs at the back of the stage my legs gave way and I'd crumpled up on the lowest step. Lucca had to carry me the last bit of the way, but now he was gone. There were too many people pushing and shoving around and he wasn't one for a social.

I felt Fitzy's rough hand on my shoulder as he stooped to whisper in my ear. 'I've got the hands looking over the cage now, so I have. If it's not damaged – and there's no reason it should be, the boys at the foundry did a lovely job there – we'll have you up at The Gaudy by Monday. Don't want to miss out on all this, do we?'

He straightened up and his piggy eyes glinted in the gas-light as he took in the scene. I felt a stab of anger in the pit of my belly. For all that he was Lady Ginger's creature as much as I was, Fitzy was a scurfy coker out for himself too. Even now, just a couple of hours after telling me I had a week before Lady Ginger '*dealt with*' my brother, he was assessing how much he could sell me for.

I felt like the Queen of Sheba sitting there with a score of Johnnies gazing down at me with puppy eyes. They were yapping so much that I couldn't hear myself think let alone answer their idiot questions.

'What was it like up there, Miss Peck?' One of them caught my hand between his and knelt at my feet. 'Tell us, what was going through your mind as you whirled so perilously above? Did you think you might die?' His fingers were clammy.

I pulled free and wiped my hand on my skirt. 'What do you imagine I was thinking about – buttering up a toasted muffin, or perhaps a nice little stroll in the park with a penny lick?' The young man's cheeks burned as everyone in the room laughed. I felt bad for him, but really, ask a stupid question . . .

'I think we should allow Miss Peck to rest now, gents. Out!' Fitzy thumped on the door behind him to draw attention. He opened it wide and began to usher the Johnnies out into the passage. They grumbled, but I reckon Fitzy knew his songbird was about to turn into a right old crow and that wasn't good for business.

'Remember, The Limehouse Linnet will be back in her cage seventy feet up at The Gaudy on Monday, so tell all your friends about what you've seen tonight and make sure you bring them with you when you come to see her again – as I know you will.'

When the last of them had gone he closed the door, leaned back on it and folded his arms. 'Very nice, very nice indeed. You're a lucky little bitch, so you are. But I won't deny it, you're good for the trade, Kitty. Lady Ginger always had an eye.' He looked at me speculatively, sucked in his cheeks and seemed to chew on his tongue before continuing. 'I tell you what, girl, if you give her what she wants before the week is out – and maybe even if you don't – me and you might have a little talk about carrying on this act of yours. I reckon we could make quite a packet together in Paris – maybe even New York. What do you say to that?'

I was still for a moment, then I answered very slow and deliberate. 'I should say that Lady Ginger would be very interested to hear about that, Mr Fitzpatrick sir. It sounds to me like her old yard dog needs a stronger leash.'

He clenched his fist and scraped a flat yellow thumbnail over the side of his index finger. I could hear the scratching on his dry skin.

His hand jerked out and I flinched, but instead of belting me he reached for the door handle. 'Be at The Gaudy tomorrow by noon. We'll need to do a proper run-through with all the checks before Monday night – we don't want a re-run of today, do we?'

In the dim passage he looked back and narrowed his eyes. 'Seven days, Kitty.'

I ran my hand over the torn skin on my knee where I'd scraped against the inside of the cage. I was beginning to feel the ache of it. Fitzy started off, but I called out, 'I don't see the point in going up again, not back at The Gaudy, not anywhere. How am I supposed to find what she wants in a week when I'm hanging up there every night?'

Fitzy's bulky figure flickered in the doorway; the gaslights were low now.

'There are three reasons why you'll be at The Gaudy on Monday. Firstly, The Lady says so – if nothing else, after this business tonight you're a powerful sign to the Barons that everything is in order in Paradise. If you don't do as she says your brother will be kissing the hull of a packet steamer quicker than that.' He clicked his fingers.

'Second, I say so. I'll not lose out on the takings. You'll be the talk of London now, so you will. If you don't turn up The Lady will hear of it. Is that clear?'

I nodded sullenly and Fitzy turned into the passage. I called after him, 'You said three reasons. What's the other one, then?'

He paused, but he didn't look back. 'I think you already know the answer to that, girl. I've worked the halls long enough to recognise the signs. Take a good hard look at yourself, Kitty Peck.'

The door slammed and I was alone. I looked at myself in the mirror on the dressing table. My stage make-up had smudged into blue-grey crescents beneath my eyes, my face was white with plaster dust and my lips were still smeared with the red paint that showed up my pretty mouth when I sang that '*ugly*' song. I looked like a badly drawn ghost of myself.

'What's happened to you?' I asked the girl in the mirror.

She didn't answer. Diamond tears welled up in her big dark eyes. 'Who do you think you are?' I asked and the tears began to snake down her face leaving glittering trails of lamp-black mascara.

Because the truth is that the girl in the mirror was my guilty shadow. She'd loved being the centre of attention up in that box. When the crowd went mad for her and stamped and called her name she had lapped it up like a kitten with its paws dipped into a saucer of cream. And while she was taking her fill, the thought of her brother and Peggy and Alice had gone clean out of her head.

'Seven days – and don't you ever forget that again,' I whispered to the girl in front of me.

Chapter Twenty-two

You are safe now.

That's what Lucca had said when he'd got me into the box. But he was wrong.

Danny held the rope out. 'See the end there – half of it's frayed and torn, but if you feel here . . .', he ran his fingers over the ragged cords, 'you can tell where it's been cut through smooth with a knife – not all the way, mind, but enough to make it break when your cage began to pull into place. Someone cut into all the guide ropes like this – I've checked them.'

The three of us were alone in the workshop behind The Gaudy. Lucca examined the rope in silence as Danny continued. 'At first I blamed myself, I didn't check over the chain and the hooks like I promised, but what with . . .'

I reached for his hand. 'It's all right, Danny, I know, with Peggy being . . . away and everything?'

He nodded. 'And that's not all, Kit. I went up to the crawl space above the hall between the plaster ceiling and the roof. I wanted to take a look – the way that plaster came down wasn't right. It's only been up six years and it was a craftsman job. The Lady brought in people from France special.'

'What did you find?' Lucca's voice was sharp.

'It's usually dark up there so I took a candle, but I needn't have bothered. It was like the sky at night in the crawl space, what with all the little lights twinkling up through the boards.'

'What do you mean lights?' I didn't catch him at first.

'There were holes, Kitty, bored down through the struts – right down into the plaster – dozens of them, all in a ring round that central hook where the chain connects up.'

I felt the hairs on the back of my neck rise. 'So the plaster work and the boards over my head were deliberately weakened too, like the guide ropes?'

Danny nodded. 'The only thing that kept you up last night was the fact the hook goes right through an oak beam at least a foot thick running across the centre of the hall. Like iron it is. When you aren't up there in the cage there's usually a big old chandelier hanging off it so it has to be strong. That's why we knew The Comet was always going to be the safest place for . . .'

He stopped again and I had a sudden revelation of just how dangerous my act really was at the best of times. I wasn't scared of heights, but I was scared of a murderer.

I looked at the boys; Danny was rolling the fraying rope end between his big hands and Lucca was gnawing the skin at the side of his thumb. They weren't going to say it, so I did.

'That break-in yesterday – Fitzy told me that nothing was taken – did you two hear that?'

Lucca nodded. 'The Lady believes it was a challenge, *si*? The reason nothing was taken was because nothing *needed* to be taken. It was a show. The Barons want to try her. She is old, Kitty – surely her time . . .?' He shrugged and raised his hands.

I pictured Lady Ginger on the stage while Frances and

Sukie had knelt before her. Silent and still she'd been, the only movement the glittering of her jewels and the flint-strike of her dark eyes. She was a coil of vengeful fury and no one in that hall could match her. Lucca was wrong – The Lady wasn't old, she was ageless.

I shook my head. 'That wasn't a challenge to The Lady's power. Someone broke into The Comet yesterday, but the only reason they did was to kill me. They did their best to make bleedin' sure my cage went crashing to the ground with me inside it – and if it wasn't for you I wouldn't be here now talking about it. Don't you see, this isn't about The Lady. It's about me and it's about *The Cinnabar Girls*.'

Lucca frowned and shot an anxious look at Danny whose face was a blank. I caught his meaning immediately. Poor Dan hadn't got a clue about that painting and with Peggy gone missing I didn't want to start explaining anything to him.

'Look, Dan,' I thought fast. 'Could you do something? I won't feel safe until I know that someone I trust has looked over that cage again and checked all the ropes and the links in the chain. I know you're right about what happened at The Comet and, I'll be frank with you, I'm frightened. You remember the other day when you said how I'd got guts? Well, this has shaken me up bad. I'm scared and I need friends like you and Lucca here to look out for me. You'll go and check it all, now, won't you? Please?'

I caught sight of Lucca's expression as I finished up and I hated myself for being such a competent liar. I knew Danny Tewson's weak spot and it was kindness. He wasn't what you'd call the academic type, but he was a natural gentleman.

Even if he had any suspicions about what I'd said to Lucca about *The Cinnabar Girls*, he didn't show it now.

'Of course. I'll get straight to it.' He jumped up and reached for his coat. It was a bright day, but cold with it. 'They're getting ready for your run-through inside. We've had new ropes delivered this morning so I'll go over every inch of them before you're needed.'

When he'd gone Lucca didn't look at me. 'You've become quite a performer, haven't you?' he said quietly after a moment. I felt a guilty flush creep up my neck and spread across my face as he continued. 'Tell me then, how is what happened at The Comet last night connected to *The Cinnabar Girls*?'

So I went through everything and as I spoke I realised that most of it – no, all of it – was about James Verdin.

I told Lucca about James and his mates from The Artisans Gallery coming to my dressing room, about that picture and the flowers he'd sent me, about meeting him again on my way back from The Comet the night Peggy went missing, about getting drunk on that stuff he'd given me and about taking him back to my lodgings.

Lucca sat in silence while I talked. He leaned forward and rested his head on his hands so I couldn't see what he was thinking. When I got to the bit about my lodgings, he stood up and walked over to the far end of the workshop. Then he stepped back and kicked at the wood suddenly and viciously. He spat on the floor twice and I heard him mutter 'Verdin' followed by something in Italian.

The workshop was completely silent.

'The worst thing is that when I was with him and ... under the influence, I think I told him about the painting and the missing girls. Next morning, before he went off to his club, he told me I said "extraordinary things" when I was . . .' I paused and looked at Lucca's back. 'I . . . I've been stupid, haven't I?'

There was no answer. I felt into the deep pocket in the folds of my skirt. I'd taken the drawing of me in the cage from The Comet and I'd brought it with me today, along with the sketch of my head and shoulders James had sent to the theatre.

I'd pinned them to the wall of my room at Mother Maxwell's last night and I'd sat cross-legged on the boards staring at them for a long time. Now I spread them out in the sawdust on the workshop floor, tracing the lines of writing with my finger. In the clear winter sunlight, I was sure. The drawings were by the same hand, and there was something else about them too.

'Lucca, come and have a look at these.'

He didn't move, just stood there with his back to me. I felt even shabbier now than I did when James had left me in my room. 'It wasn't my fault. You must believe me. It wasn't . . .'

'It wasn't what?'

He span round. The mottled, scarred skin of his face pulsed red and white and his eye blazed. 'From the moment you first saw him at the gallery you've been panting after him like a bitch on heat. No – don't deny it. I know you. When you saw him your eyes – they shone like stars. I have seen it before – I know the signs. What did you expect? Did you think he would take you away from all this? Dress you in fine clothes, tempt you with rich food, offer you champagne? Or did you think he would marry you and make you a lady?

Look at yourself. Look at your cheap clothes and your thread-bare life. Look at our world.'

He laughed harshly and gestured round the workshop. 'Those people, they are all the same. You are a bigger fool than . . .' He stopped short.

'*Puttana!*' He spat out that last insult – I knew what it meant – and a little slick of spittle came to rest on the boards near the drawing of my head. I'd never heard Lucca so bitter and so passionate before. The words tumbled over his lips and his accent almost disappeared. He was shaking with anger.

I stood and took a step towards him.

'A bigger fool than who, Lucca? What you've just said, that wasn't about me, was it?'

Something flickered across the handsome side of his face and he dropped his head so that his dark curls fell forward. 'You aren't angry with *me*, Lucca, are you? All that stuff about fine clothes, fancy food . . . and champagne?'

I remembered that time when Lucca told me he liked the taste of the stuff and I'd wondered how a lad like him came to know about it. I thought of that now as I watched him. His head hung low and he'd hunched his shoulders up and forward like he was trying to fold himself away.

He didn't reply so I took a step closer. 'For your information, James Verdin got me drunk with something . . . something that made Kitty go away and replaced her with someone else. I didn't know what I was doing that night, so I certainly wasn't thinking about any of those things you said. I won't deny it, there *was* something about him that took me right from that first time. I thought of him a lot as it happens. And then when he came to see me with his mates he was very charming with it, kinder than them and cultural. He told me he was interested in me as an artist – he lapped up everything I said about that picture and I was flattered. Before he drugged me and made me a whore I . . .'

Lucca looked up. The fire had gone out of him now. He was about to say something, but I reached out and put my fingers to his lips. 'Oh yes, that's what he made me that night and don't think I'm proud of it. Before he made me a whore I'd thought about the smell of him, how smooth his skin was, how his lips might feel on mine, how his hands . . . Well – there you are. Perhaps he was right about me after all. But *you* are wrong, Lucca Fratelli, so wrong. I'm no liar and I don't have any secrets. But maybe you do?'

The sliding door rattled open. 'Kitty, they're ready.' Danny stood in the sunlit yard, his shirt covered with greasy black marks. 'I've been over every inch of ropes and oiled the chain too. It won't make a squeak now. You're in safe hands.' He held up his stained palms and added softly, 'Let's hope Peggy is too, eh? Wherever she is.'

That cut home. Lucca and I were spitting like a couple of yard cats fighting over a sparrow, when there was so much else at stake. I pulled my hair back and began to wind it into a tight knot. I was hard on myself as I forced it into a ball and stabbed it with a pin.

'I'll be with you in a minute. Me and Lucca are just finishing up here.'

'Fitzy wants you now. His mood's fouler than a tanner's pit so I wouldn't keep him if I were you.' Danny frowned. 'You two all right?' We must have looked odd standing close there, rigid as a couple of hop poles.

I tried to smile. 'I'm fine as any girl who's come within a feather's breadth of dashing her brains out, Dan. Tell him I'm coming.'

Through the open door, we watched his shadow disappear across the yard. His feet crunched on the ice-crusted cobbles and then we heard the back door to the theatre swing shut behind him.

'Forgive me.'

Lucca's voice was thick and muffled. He slid down the wall and wrapped his arms round his legs.

'What's there to forgive then?' That came out tighter than I intended.

He began to laugh, but it wasn't a happy sound. I sat down next to him, the swishing of my skirts stirring motes of saw-dust into the golden air. They danced around us as we sat there in silence. He didn't look at me, but he took my hand and squeezed it.

'Lucca, I've got to go. You heard Danny? Fitzy's got the bear's head on him. And I need to change into my practice gear.'

He nodded, dropped my hand and pulled his arms tighter round his knees like he was trying to make himself as small as possible. 'I am not a liar, but there are things ...' He broke off, leaned his head back against the slats and sighed.

'After the run-through, eh? I'll come to your studio up there.' I nodded at the wooden ladder leading up to the space above the workshop where he sketched and painted.

I stood up. 'There's another thing. Joey – the Lady's given me seven days more before she ... well, I don't know what she's going to do to him, but the end will be the same. Someone will find him in the river.'

Lucca stared up at me. 'Seven days?'

'Less now. I can't see my way through this. I don't want to fall out over nothing, Lucca, I need you. You're all I've got left.'

Of a sudden I felt raw and I didn't want him to see my face. I brushed down my skirt. The drawings were on the floor where I'd left them. I walked over, picked them up and took them back to him.

'While I'm gone, have a look at these.' Now it was my turn to laugh bitterly. 'James sent them. He's done a lovely flattering job on my head here, but that was before he had me.'

I handed the first drawing to Lucca. Then I smoothed out the picture of me in the cage and looked at it again. It was a wretched thing, twisted with spite and hate. The lines carved through the paper like a knife through flesh. The person who'd drawn this was furious. Just touching it made me feel sick, but not as sick as the thought that I'd had him in my bed.

'Whoever broke into The Comet last night knows that I know about *The Cinnabar Girls*. Look at this.' I held the drawing out to Lucca.

'See that line there – *At night your cagebird sings an ugly song*. That doesn't mean my act; I think it means what I said to James about the painting and the missing girls. And there's something else. I reckon the person who drew this and the sketch in your hand is the person who painted *The Cinnabar Girls*. Look at the way he's drawn my face in the first one. It's beautifully done – and he makes the flesh of my shoulders seem real, warm, almost like you could feel it. Even this one . . .', Lucca took the drawing of me in the cage from my hand, '. . . has a horrible sort of . . . power. I'm right, aren't I?'

He looked from one drawing to the other and nodded slowly. 'Philomel. Do you know who she is?'

I shook my head.

'It is an old myth. Philomel was a beautiful princess turned into a nightingale by the gods. Some say she became a swallow – but the end is the same. The swallow and the female nightingale they are mute. They have no song.'

'What does that mean then?'

Lucca shrugged, then he looked closely at the foreign words under the picture of me in the cage and frowned. 'When did you get this?'

'Fitzy gave it to me just before I went up last night. It was left in Mr Leonard's room by whoever it was that broke in.'

'So it came after Verdin drugged you and took advantage of you?'

I nodded. I was glad to hear the way Lucca put that.

'Do you know what this means?' He pointed at the neatly written words and read them aloud. '*Magna cadunt, inflata crepant, tumefacta premuntur.*'

I shook my head again. 'So it's Italian, is it? I thought as much. Something insulting – you know, dirty language?'

Lucca looked up. 'No, Fannella, it is Latin from the Bible. In English you would say something like, *pride goes before a fall.*'

Chapter Twenty-three

The run-through was easy enough. Danny had fixed the chain so it didn't make that horrible grating sound no more and, even though Peggy wasn't there, it was almost good to be back at The Gaudy, which always felt more hospitable than Lady Ginger's other halls.

When they let me down I was surprised to find Mrs Conway waiting. We Gaudy girls all knew that Mrs C wasn't to be disturbed of an afternoon on account of it being the time for her 'medicinal'. Peggy used to go round with her prescriptive sometimes, that being half a pint of neat gin straight from the cellar under the bar.

Mrs C wasn't a bad woman, but she liked being a star, even if it was only somewhere quite low in the sky. Since my act had started I'd been a very painful reminder that it was taking longer and longer to burnish herself up of an evening.

After the rehearsal I was itching to go straight back to Lucca. If we could talk everything through, without a row this time, then perhaps we'd see something.

The cage had bumped onto the stage and a couple of the hands had just lifted the side to let me crawl out when Mrs C tapped me on the shoulder.

'I'm so pleased to see you back here, Kitty my love. You must have had a terrible fright.'

I noticed that the dry red paint on her lips was creeping up into all the little lines around her mouth. She was wearing a lot of violet over her eyes, her arched brows were inked in the most unlikely places and the black wig on her head looked like it might jump off if a mouse ran past.

She took in my gear and sniffed. I must have looked like a boy in the same thin breeches and camisole I'd worn during all those rehearsals in Madame Celeste's attic.

'You're thin as a whip. The Johnnies don't like that, remember? Give them a bit of meat, that's what I always say.' She patted my arm, maternal like.

'Tell me, how did you feel up there just now? Did it all come flooding back?'

It hadn't, to be honest. All the time I was up there my mind was turning over what Lucca said.

Magna cadunt, inflata crepant, tumefacta premuntur – Pride goes before a fall.

It was a threat, wasn't it, or a prediction? And it pointed direct to that business with the ropes and the ceiling at The Comet. Kitty Peck – the fallen woman.

But why would James Verdin, brazen as a barrow boy, break into the theatre, meddle with the cage and then leave that picture in Mr Leonard's office when he knew someone, Lucca most likely, would know what those words meant?

He'd already asked if I liked his first picture so why would he send me another one, with a threat scrawled across it? It was almost like an announcement. He might just as well have taken out a page in *The London Pictorial*.

The more I thought about it, the more I began to think that James wasn't the one I was looking for.

Or was he?

He could draw, he'd been hanging around the halls – he admitted that himself – and he'd used that stuff to drug me. Is that how he'd caught the others?

Danny's voice had come up from below. 'Can you go into the dips now? And then we'll try the bit where you twirl upside down. We need to check the weight on that. You ready, lads?'

There was quite a crowd watching. Several of the chorus girls were sitting cross-legged on the stage, the hands who weren't hanging off the end of a rope were leaning against the side wall smoking, and even a couple of the orchestra boys were tuning up in the pit. It was an unusually early start for them, I thought.

They all wanted to see if I still had the mettle for it – and I didn't like to disappoint.

I hooked my knees over the bar, leaned back, stretched out my arms and swung free. I heard the ropes creak as they pulled tight, but the cage stayed locked into place, which is more than I can say for the thoughts in my head.

If James wanted me out of the way, why hadn't he done something about it a couple of nights back? Why would he break into The Comet and set me up for an accident when he could have smothered me in my bed and tipped me into the river?

Think, girl, think, I told myself as I began to spin. All the while I kept my eyes on a single point in the hall just as Madame Celeste had taught me.

Every time that gilded vine on the front of Lady Ginger's box snapped into view I counted.

One: *Philomel*

Two: *At night your cagebird sings an ugly song*

Three: *Pride goes before a fall*

One, two, three: I went through them again seeing the black lines on the paper as I twirled and arched my back. There was something there on the pages, something important.

A smooth transition, Madame Celeste had been most keen on that. When I went from one set of movements to the next she explained that it must always look effortless, like I was a wisp of silk slipping around the bar.

'All the time you're up there you must make them believe you can fly. You must soar, Kitty – graceful, beautiful, seamless. No jerking about and no hard angles – they'll give you away, expose you for what you really are.'

Danny's voice came up from the hall. 'That's enough, Kitty. We don't need the song. We'll bring you down now.'

I pulled myself onto the bar and sat there, my mind ticking like a clock shop, as the cage was winched carefully back down to the stage. Madame Celeste was right about the hard angles. I had to show Lucca.

'You're the darling of *The London Pictorial* again.' Mrs C pushed the newspaper into my hand. 'Page three – a very lurid account of the incident. Most particular that I should give it to you, the boy was. There's another picture as well, although I must say it doesn't look much like you.'

She held it under my nose, but I didn't look at the drawing. There was a line of writing across the top of the page.

My heart started to beat very fast.

'As I said, you really must eat more, Kitty. Now, what with Peggy being away and you being back here at The Gaudy this week I was wondering if you'd help with my wardrobe and hair, like before?'

She patted the mass of black hair on her head. It lurched to the side and stayed there. 'I don't know if you've heard, but I'm revisiting some of my most popular numbers and I'd be most obliged if you—'

I cut her off. 'Sorry, Mrs Conway, but I have to go. I'm late already.' Her crimson mouth crumpled up like a dry old rose as I darted past her into the slips and went to find my street clothes.

I took *The London Pictorial* with me.

*

Once I was dressed I went straight back to the workshop. I slid open the door and called Lucca's name. Old Bertie was shuffling about near the work bench at the back, but there was no one else around.

I stepped inside and pointed upwards to the studio when Bertie caught sight of me. He shook his head and nodded at the door. I wasn't entirely convinced he'd have heard Lucca coming back in again – if he had – so I climbed up the ladder and poked my head over the edge.

'Lucca, you there?'

The little hatch that led through to his private space in the attic was open so I hitched up my skirt, clambered onto the boards and went across. I bent my head and called again.

'Lucca – I need you to come out with me.'

Lucca's studio was deserted. A small cobwebbed window high in the eaves allowed a shaft of direct sunlight to slant across the room and I could make out the papers pinned to the walls. There was no doubt about it, Lucca was good. His drawings were full of movement and character. I recognised faces I knew from the halls, sketched lightly and quickly. It was like he'd caught them unawares in a flash of a moment when they was laughing or talking or thinking. There was a large black book bound up with ribbon propped against the wall partly covering a drawing of Peggy.

She was smiling. Her wide eyes sparkled and her pretty lips were parted like she was about to remark on something. It was so true to the life that I could almost hear her voice followed by her throaty laugh. I missed Peggy something bad, and if that's how I felt, what must Danny be like with her gone? I screwed the newspaper up in my hand.

Something hard balled in my throat.

I tried to swallow and stiffened my shoulders. If I allowed myself to start crying now I knew I'd never stop, not just for her, but for Joey, for the other girls, for me – for all of us. I drew a breath and made a promise to the girl in the drawing.

'I will find you, Peggy, and I'll make this stop. On my life I will.'

I'm not one for hocus pocus – like I said, that was Ma's territory and old Nanny Peck's too – but something made me feel I had to look direct at Peggy's face to make that vow work – to give it a meaning. I tried to move the book to one side to get a better a view of her, but it fell open, sheets of drawings falling to the boards.

I knelt to gather them up, pushing them back between the stiff covers as neat as possible. They were mostly drawings of the boy I'd seen in the sketch pinned to the wall last time.

Thick curls, fine eyes, strong nose – the sort of classical face Lucca liked to show me in his books – the sort of face that Michelangelo might have drawn. I smiled at that. I'd surprised myself. Lucca was a good teacher as well as a good artist.

I wondered again who that boy was as I reached out for the last two sheets. I turned the first over. It was me, asleep. Lucca had sketched me in his bed that night after we'd seen the painting that first time. I knew it was me, even though my face was mostly hidden in a scribble of curls. There were freckles across my nose and my pointed chin rested on a hand just visible on the pillow.

Lucca was a deep one. I turned the last page over.

My brother was standing there naked as the day he was born – only this was clearly several years later. He looked up at me from the paper, his eyes bright and his lips curved into a wide smile. It was the expression on his face that haunted me afterwards. Was it a challenge, or maybe an invitation?

I dropped the sheet like it was something scalding, then I picked it up again. I looked more closely, all the time feeling odd, like I was earwigging on a private conversation. It was a fine drawing – one of Lucca's best, no doubt about that. The soft lines that came together to make the outline of Joey's body feathered across the paper and the smudge of shadows suggesting muscle and flesh made you want to reach down and touch him.

Carefully I followed the line of his arm and neck with my forefinger. Something ached in my chest and my throat felt blocked and tight again. My handsome brother – what was he doing here in this file? My hand went to the neck of my dress and I drew out his Christopher and his ring. I could see the Christopher in the sketch and now I rubbed the real thing between my thumb and forefinger as I stared at the fine young man on the paper.

'What's all this about, Joey? What have you got me into?' I whispered to the drawing and tried to find the answers in his dancing eyes. My bold brother just smiled back at me.

I am not a liar, but there are things . . .

When had Lucca drawn this? It was from life, I could swear. A hundred questions rattled in my head, but the more I thought, the more confused I became – and angry too.

A bell started tolling outside. It was two o'clock. I didn't have time to sit here stewing and waiting.

I pushed my brother back into the black book, tied the string and fled. Tell truth, I was glad to get away.

*

I opened *The London Pictorial* and spread the rumpled paper across my knees. Mrs C was right, that didn't look like me at all. The girl in the picture, clinging on by her fingertips to the bottom edge of the cage, was more generously endowed in crucial areas than I was, although she had managed to cram herself into a costume even smaller than mine. I read the untidy looping scrawl across the top of the picture. '*I have information. Come and see me when you are able. SC.*'

I looked down at the street. It was the first bright day in a long time and people were bustling about their business in the sunshine. If any of them had seen that story no one would recognise me as the plump, doe-eyed doll on page three – not like I'd recognised the Cinnabar Girls.

I wondered what Sam Collins had turned up. I hoped to God it was something useful.

The omnibus juddered as it came to a halt at Colet Place. Over to the left I saw the pale sun caught between the ugly grey towers of Christ Church on Watney Street. I wondered what time it was now. The horses swung their heads and waited as three more passengers climbed up the curved stairs at the back and joined me up top on the garden seats.

It was cold up here, but cheap too. I pulled my shawl tight and blew on my fingers.

FLYING IN THE FACE OF DEATH

Our readers will be delighted and relieved in equal measure to learn of the latest triumphant performance by Miss Kitty Peck, The Limehouse Linnet. Amidst scenes of the greatest damage and destruction at The Comet Theatre, London's most valiant songbird plucked victory from the jaws of death.

While the heavily ornamented plaster ceiling – the work of Frenchmen, we are given to understand – failed above her, crumbling one hundred feet to the floor below, Miss Peck soared to safety at the very moment her gilded cage hurtled to the earth . . .

Not only was the picture all wrong, but Sam hadn't even got the facts right neither.

'A miraculous survival. It is a thrilling, story, Miss Peck. Kitty?'

I sat completely still as James Verdin's voice came from somewhere behind. 'May I join you?'

I didn't answer. A moment later he slid onto the wooden seat next to me. I felt my body go rigid as he nudged up. He smelt of brandy, good cigars and leather and he was wearing the coat with the wide fur collar. I could see it from the corner of my eye although I wouldn't look direct at him.

I offered a silent prayer of thanks that there were at least five others up there with us. James leaned close and began to speak into my right ear. I could feel his warm breath on my skin and I wanted to scream. I stood up just as the omnibus went over a rut in the street and I lurched forward. James caught my arm and pulled me down into the seat.

'Please stay, Kitty, I've missed you very much.'

I felt the skin on my back crawl beneath the stiff material of my dress as he patted my hand and continued. 'I fear after our last . . . meeting you may have been left with quite the wrong impression of me. I treated you unfairly and I wish to make amends.'

I noticed that he slurred his words as he spoke.

'Very soon after that night, I began to regret the fact that I might not see you again. Truly. Woody and Edward have heard me speak of you so often they think me a love-struck fool. That's why at the club this morning Woody showed me this . . .' James tapped the page on my knees with a gloved hand. His fingers stroked the picture of the plump chick with huge frightened eyes and rose-bud lips caught in a pretty O of terror. The girl on the page looked like a victim. Not a survivor. Not like me.

'I don't mind telling you that the thought of you in danger was intolerable. Woody encouraged me to renew our acquaintance – said this was the perfect time to express my concern. He's a good fellow, eh?'

I didn't answer and I didn't move. I just kept staring at the road ahead as James carried on. The smell of brandy rolled off him into the cold air.

'I didn't think you'd want to talk to me, but Woody, now, he pointed out that a girl like you would be glad to see me again. I hope he might be right? It seems foolish for friends to lose touch.'

James's hand burrowed under the newspaper and he began to stroke my knee. His voice ran on, smooth as watered silk. 'So I came to The Gaudy today to find you. The article here is most specific that your act will continue at that venue. I waited outside like last time and saw you cross the street. When you mounted this omnibus, I decided it was the perfect opportunity for me to apologise and to make amends. What do you say?'

I turned to look at him now. He'd been drinking – a lot. His handsome face was flushed and his copper hair was awry beneath his tall hat. He stared at me and smiled; he reminded me of a lady's lap dog yearning for a tit-bit.

In the sharp light of day, James Verdin looked very young.

Of an instant my head was clear. I pushed his hand out from under the paper and shifted so that we weren't touching.

'What do you say?' he repeated.

I stared up at him and then spoke clearly and distinctly: '*Magna cadunt, inflata crepant, tumefacta premuntur*.'

He looked bemused so I said it again. He shook his head. 'You have me. Is this a game, some private language you theatre people use, perhaps? You do say the most peculiar things. When I told the boys about you that night – I trust you'll forgive my indiscretion, but I had no idea what a very powerful effect you might exert over me – they agreed that it is extraordinary for a girl like you to have such a very vivid imagination. You quite captured their attention. Now, Kitty, I would like us to begin again.'

I shivered, only it wasn't the cold. James grinned. 'Perhaps a sip of this might help?'

He reached into his coat and took out a new flask, finer than the last.

I shook my head. 'No – I don't think so. Not again.'

'Don't worry, this is good brandy, not that medicinal concoction.'

He unscrewed the stopper and took a sip. 'Now, there's a fine fellow too. Do you remember I told you my uncle approves of Edward? He has managed to persuade Uncle Richard that I should receive an allowance while I learn how to run his business affairs. Good Doctor Edward suggested that the only way to . . . interest me was to pay me. And the old boy actually listened – he has been much more amenable recently; I'd even call him generous.'

James took another long pull on the flask.

'My uncle took me to dine at his own club, you know? A stuffy place, full of dust and desiccated corpses. He knew all about my visits to the halls and about you, Kitty – I suppose Eddie let something slip there. They chatter like a couple of old women sometimes.'

James grinned and waved the flask. 'Uncle Richard made me promise not to "lose myself in sin".' He said those last words in a slow, heavy voice that was, I guessed, an imitation of the old man. 'He said I had to renounce all vice before I saw a penny and, of course, I agreed to his terms.'

James wiped his lips and snorted with contempt. 'So I am to be in trade.'

His eyes narrowed. 'But I will use my time and my uncle's money on better things. Art, that is my passion – my vocation.'

He turned to stare at me and this time I didn't flinch or look away.

'You are a sweet creature.' He smiled, but his googling eyes suggested he was finding it hard to focus on my face. I realised then that he had been drinking to get up the courage to speak to me.

The bus lurched and I jolted forward. James put his arm around me.

'Woody says it's easy to set a woman up with a residence. He has experience of these things. Now I am assured of the funds I could do that for you, Kitty. I could find you rooms in a better part of town and visit you there as often as I liked. I could bring you flowers more beautiful than the ones I sent to the theatre and I could sketch you or paint you – then all the world would recognise my talent.'

'Like that drawing?' I asked, looking straight into his eyes. There wasn't a flicker of recognition.

I put it more direct. 'Are you saying you'd like to draw me again? The sketch you sent to the theatre was very fine.'

He shook his head. 'There you go again, riddles. I've never drawn you, Kitty, but I will. When you are my . . . companion you will be my muse, I will draw you every day. Perhaps I could take you to Paris?'

I recalled Fitzy saying much the same thing as James shuffled even closer on the slatted seat and tucked the flask into his coat. 'You have no idea how exciting it is to be near you again.'

I shook him off and stood up. 'And you have no idea at all, do you?'

He stared up at me and his mouth opened and closed. 'But surely you cannot refuse – a girl like you? I am offering you my . . . protection.'

He spoke too loudly because of the drink and a couple of men behind us laughed.

They were an audience and I played to them. I pulled myself up straight, pushed past him and half turned to the passengers on the top deck as I delivered my next line, gripping the front rail with my left hand to steady myself.

'Protection – is that what you call it? *A girl like me* would call it setting her up as your whore. Good day to you, Mr Verdin.'

There was a roar of laughter now and one of the men called out, 'You tell him, girl! Verdin, is it? Vermin more like.'

I made my way to the wooden steps at the back of the deck. A man yelled at me to be more careful when the bus jerked about and I knocked his bowler askew, but I carried on and didn't look back.

At least there was one thing I was certain of now. James had sent me them flowers at The Gaudy, but that picture came from someone else. He was a pink-cheeked fool and the very worst kind of skirt-sniffing toff, but James Verdin wasn't a murderer.

Chapter Twenty-four

'I want to see Sam Collins. Now. Tell him Miss Kitty Peck is waiting.'

The print boy gawped. If he was expecting The Limehouse Linnet to look like the fat little bantam on page three no wonder he didn't know her stood on the other side of his counter in the reduced flesh. He mumbled something about appointments and opened a marbled diary on the desk top. 'There's nothing here, Mrs, er, Miss Peck, is it? Mr Peters hasn't made an entry for you. Not for this afternoon least-ways. Mr Collins is a very busy man. Perhaps you could come back tomorrow?'

I was about to be say something sharp when the door to the street jangled open behind me.

'It's clouding up out there, Ben, so much for better wea-ther. It might even snow again.'

I whirled about to see Sam standing there, rubbing his hands together. 'Miss Peck! You got my message?' He must have seen something spark up in my eyes, because he hurried on. 'Of course you have. A little artistic licence here and there, but otherwise most satisfactory, I hope you'll agree. The block boys in the basement did a lovely job filling out my sketch. Very quick workers they are. And I'm sure it's not done trade any harm, eh?' He flicked his brown fringe aside and winked.

I frowned. 'We'll see tonight, I expect. You certainly know how to pad out a story, Mr Collins, just like you've padded out that girl in the picture.'

'As I said, Miss Peck, artistic licence. Keeps everyone happy.'

I cocked my head to one side. I'd begun to wonder about Sam Collins too, as it happens. How had *The London Pictorial* managed to get the story about my accident into print so fast?

'You were quick off the mark, weren't you?'

He grinned. 'Contacts, Miss Peck, contacts. I like to think I've got your neck of the woods well covered. I have my sources, you know.' He tapped the side of his nose. 'Some of them in the most surprising places. That's what I wanted to talk to you about.'

He loosened his muffler and began to fumble with the buttons on his overcoat. They were all done up in the wrong places making him look like a badly wrapped package. It struck me that if Sam Collins was a murderer he'd need to employ someone with a lot more in the way of physical dexterity to carry his knife bags for him. It took him a long time to get out of that coat and when he threw the muffler at a hook on the wall he missed twice before managing to get it to stay. When he finally succeeded he turned back to me and smiled. 'Please come upstairs to my office. A bargain is a bargain and I owe you, Kitty.'

*

Sam's small office was untidier than the last time, with teeter-

238

ing piles of books and newspapers covering every surface and most of the floorboards. He practically had to burrow under his desk to find his own chair.

'Do sit, please – there's another chair beneath that pile. If you could just pass those papers to me, thank you, there it is. Sorry, I can't offer you tea today. Peters has the most terrible influenza.' He drummed the table and flicked his fringe before adding, 'But perhaps that's for the best, eh? He does make a disgusting pot.'

I smiled at him, despite that picture in the paper. Sam gabbled like a costermonger's boy with a crate full of cabbages to shift, but I liked him the better for it. I don't think he ever managed to think through a fully formed thought before blurting it out and beginning on the next one. His mind was as cluttered as his office, but in both cases I suspected he knew where everything was.

'Mr Fratelli not with you today?' There – he remembered Lucca's name, for a start.

That drawing of Joey unfurled itself in my mind. I shook my head. 'He . . . he couldn't come. But as soon as I got your message after the run-through I took an omnibus west. You say you've got information – about the picture?'

He rustled through some papers on the desk. 'Not exactly. Now where is . . . ah, here.'

He produced a small black book from the midst of the pile and flicked through thumb-stained pages covered with his fat looping scrawl.

'Not about the picture, but about the gallery. Look there.'

He handed me the notebook. It was a list of names.

Sir Anthony Woolley, Geoffrey Manners, Viscount John

Monclear, General Alexander Preston . . . I followed the names down the page with my finger until I got to one I knew – Sir Richard Verdin.

Something fluttered in my belly, something like a crow.

'What is this, Sam? Who are they?'

'They are the trustees of The Artisans Gallery. All decisions taken about the gallery's activities – whether financial or artistic – are taken by that group of men . . . until quite recently, that is.'

I heard the note of excitement in his voice and looked up. Sam was staring intently at me. He twitched, flicked his fringe aside and reached across the desk. 'May I?'

He began to read through the names. 'Sir Anthony Woolley – bed-ridden, crippled by a fall from his horse last summer. Geoffrey Manners – wife's gone off with some minor European princeling and he's followed her. They say he's in Bavaria. Viscount Monclear – he's eighty-seven, never leaves his estate in Scotland. General Preston – went to India last May and not back yet.'

Sam continued down the list for another three or four names explaining why they were unlikely or unable to play a part in the direction of the gallery.

When he got to Sir Richard Verdin he stopped and tapped the page in the notebook.

'Now, here's the interesting one. My source tells me that for the last six months, Sir Richard Verdin has made every decision about The Artisans Gallery and what goes on show there.'

'And that includes *The Cinnabar Girls*?' I asked.

Sam nodded. 'And that's not all. Apparently Sir Richard

was able to make certain stipulations regarding the present-ation of that painting. Done late one night, it was. No one from the gallery was allowed to be present when it was de-livered and hung. He had his own team working on it.'

I could feel blotches of colour spreading up from my neck into my cheeks. I loosened the shawl around my shoulders. The room was suddenly stifling.

'How did you find this out, Sam?'

'As I said, Kitty – sources. It pays to have friends across the city.' He grinned, leaned back in his chair and a pile of papers toppled over behind him. He shot a rueful glance at the mess and continued, as if he'd been prompted to tell the truth.

'Actually, to be frank, this was quite easy in the end. One of Peters's cousins is married to a warder at The Artisans Gallery so I simply took the old chap out, stood him a pint or two and got him to talk very freely. But it is interesting, isn't it?'

It was more than that.

I thought about that meeting with James earlier today. I was certain after talking to him that he wasn't the one be-hind all this, but now I began to see a pattern. Wooden jigsaw pieces bumping around in my head were slotting into place.

'What else have you found, Sam? Anything more about Sir Richard?' I was careful to keep my face a blank as I spoke.

'Only this,' he flicked the notebook again. 'It's really very odd. Until three years ago Sir Richard Verdin showed no in-terest whatsoever in the arts. He is a businessman, you know, very successful, quite ruthless apparently.'

He carried on leafing through the pages. 'Go on,' I said. 'What happened three years ago?'

'He approached the gallery and bought himself a seat on the board with a very significant sum of money. He's interested in new artists, it seems, the younger the better. Likes to interview them personally and nurture their careers. A couple of them are quite the thing at the moment – Robert Rollaston, Clifford Weir, know them?'

I shook my head as Sam continued. 'Can't say their work appeals to me – naked shepherd boys with pan pipes and herds of goats tramping over hillsides – but in certain quarters, I understand works by the Pastoral Brotherhood are very sought after.'

'So you're saying that *The Cinnabar Girls* is by one of his young artists. Do you know who?'

Sam stopped fiddling with the notebook and turned down the corner of a page to mark it. He flung the closed book into the pile of papers on his desk.

'Of course not. I would have run the story by now – after consulting you, Kitty, naturally.' He leaned forward, cupped his chin in his palm and brought his ink-stained fingers to his lips.

'You still haven't told me why you're so interested. You and Mr Fratelli . . .'

Under that fringe his brown eyes were keen with interest. He looked like a terrier on the scent of a sewer rat.

I stared at the only patch of wood visible on the desk top. 'We told you before, we're interested in art, that's all. You might think people from the halls don't have a thought in their heads except drinking and gambling and worse, but it's not true. Lucca . . . Mr Fratelli – he's from Naples originally and very passionate about art. We talk about the Renaissance

– does that surprise you? Leonardo, Michelangelo, Raphael – Lucca, he calls them The Trinity. And he's a painter himself – a good one. When all London was talking about that picture, don't you think it was natural that we would want to find out more?'

I was amazed to hear those names dropping so easy from my lips, but I went too fast and I didn't look at Sam as I spoke. So much for Kitty Peck the great performer – even I could hear the lie.

The office was silent for a moment. 'You intrigue me, Kitty. You really are a most interesting young woman . . .'

I looked up hopefully as Sam finished off, '. . . but I am not an idiot.'

'I don't know what you mean!' I could feel my cheeks burn.

'Oh come on now. At least credit me with a little sense. Tell me the truth – why is it so important for you to know?'

I bit my lip. 'I can't tell you, not now anyway. When this is all over perhaps I'll have a story for you, but I can't risk . . .'

'Risk what?' Sam's eyes narrowed. 'And what do you mean by "when this is all over"?'

The question hung in the air. I regretted saying that.

'Please, Kitty, perhaps I can help you?'

I stood up, flustered. 'I've got to go, there's a show at eight. Thank you for the information about the painting and Sir Richard.'

Sam didn't move. He just watched as I straightened my skirt and pinned my shawl. He looked like he was going over a bit of difficult mental arithmetic. I made my way over to the door.

'Wait, Kitty!'

I paused with my hand on the doorknob.

'There's something else that might interest you. Sir Richard Verdin has a warehouse at Limehouse Basin.' I turned to look at him.

Sam picked up the notebook again and opened it at the marked page. 'I thought that might interest you. It's in Skinners Yard – 3 to 10, Limehouse Basin. According to the register it's been leased to him for the last thirty or so years by an L. Rosen. Verdin imports fur or used to. Any use?'

His clever eyes scanned my face. I nodded and opened the door. As I stepped out onto the dingy, narrow landing I heard his voice behind me.

'I'm expecting another exclusive from you, Kitty, remember that. You owe me now. That's how it works.'

*

The cold hit me immediately when I stepped out into the alley. Turning right, I walked quickly past the dingy window of the Holborn offices of *The London Pictorial*, where a copy of the most recent edition was spread open at page three.

If I could find a street bus heading east I'd take it. I'd even pay the extra to sit inside. It wasn't just the cold that made me quicken my step and pull my shawl up over my head. The air had a metallic tang to it – smoke and soot that filled your nose and scratched at the back of your throat. A mist was licking at the cobbles and coiling round the railings of the grander houses lined up round Lincoln's Inn Fields. The sky above looked like a bowl of porridge. It would be dark soon.

My heels tapped as I swung into Carey Street.

Now I was in a warren of little passages that cut through to Fleet Street. I reckoned it would be easy to pick up an omnibus going my way there, or maybe just a bit further along on Ludgate Hill.

I'd been to this part of town once before – it seemed a long time ago now – with Joey. He was making a delivery to a house of legals off the west side of the Fields. I'd asked him about all the papers tied up with black ribbon, a couple with seals as big as a dinner plate hanging off them. At the time he said he was doing a favour for a friend. I knew who that 'friend' was now – he'd been working for her.

It was closer to the river down here and in places the mist was stirring itself into a fog. I'd step into a patch and come out again a few yards later. It wouldn't be long before all the street fugged up so you couldn't see no more than a couple of foot ahead of you.

That seemed appropriate.

First James, now Sir Richard. Sam had given me more help than he knew, but how did it all come together?

Apart from Lucca, Fitzy and Lady Ginger herself, no one knew I'd made a connection between *The Cinnabar Girls* and the girls going missing from the halls.

But that's not true, is it, Kitty? I heard the sharp voice in my head. You told James Verdin that night, didn't you? He gave you the lixir and you gave him a fantastical story about dancing girls and paintings and murder. And afterwards he told his friends. Oh they all had a good old laugh at the drunken chorus girl and her vivid imagination . . . only someone who heard that story didn't really find it so amusing.

I thought back to what James said about his uncle when we were on the street bus.

He has been much more amenable recently; I'd even call him generous.

No wonder there. It seemed to me that James and his uncle had been on 'better terms' since Sir Richard had received some useful information.

I ran through what James said about his uncle again – *He knew all about my visits to the halls and about you, Kitty – I suppose Eddie let something slip there. They chatter like a couple of old women sometimes.*

Edward Chaston had let 'something slip' all right, but he had no idea what it really meant to Sir Richard Verdin.

Now the old bugger was about to grease his own nephew as a trap to catch me. I wondered just how long I would have lasted as James Verdin's private fancy before another accident happened to me. It was all fitting into place now. I had something 'more' to take to Lady Ginger at last.

A couple of legals stepped out of a side passage and into the alleyway. Their black gowns swirled into the mist around their ankles as they walked ahead of me. I'd like to see Sir Richard Verdin in the dock, I thought. What would his fine friends think of him if they knew?

But what exactly *did* I know? As I walked my mind was flicking through faces, voices, words and pictures like it was the pages of Sam Collins's notebook.

The legals stopped at a tall narrow building. One of them rapped on the door and they turned to watch me pass by while they waited for someone to open it.

The alley was deserted now, the air ahead so thick with fog

that I could just make out the sickly halo of light around a lamp up ahead. I misjudged my footing and slipped on some uneven cobbles, ripping my stocking on the jagged stones. I cursed, and rubbed at the torn cotton. Another shilling gone west, I thought.

I straightened up and pushed my hands under the folds of my shawl to keep them warm. I wondered what time it was. No later than six, I thought, but already dark. I needed to shift to get back to The Gaudy. I took another step forward and stopped again, dead still. The hairs on the back of my neck bristled.

Now I heard it properly – the sound of footsteps behind me. Footsteps that stopped and started up again just at the same moment I did.

Chapter Twenty-five

'Philomel.'

The name slithered off the walls around me. I turned, but there was no one there, no one I could see.

The fog was moving, forming itself into shapes and shadows as it drifted over the cobbles. One moment it was almost transparent and I could see through it to the glistening stones, next thing it rolled itself into a mass that seemed to block off the end of the alley like a dirty grey wall.

'Who's there?' My own voice echoed off the stones. It sounded thin and small.

No one answered. The fog billowed and faded around the gas lamp. Now I could see the sharp black outlines of the buildings marking the far end of the alley. Just there I knew it broadened out into a road that led down into Fleet Street. There were bound to be people about, it wasn't late.

I balled my fists and started to walk, straining to hear footsteps behind.

Nothing.

I quickened my step and then I broke into a run, my boots drumming on the cobbles. At the corner I caught the wall and swung right. I could hear other voices now and singing too. Ahead of me there was a patch of brightness in the fog and as I ran towards it, the patch assembled itself into a tavern – warm and golden with safety.

I thought about dodging inside, but I didn't have to. The door swung open and three men stepped out into the road. I paused for a moment and watched them. They were laughing – a trio of clerks who'd stopped off for a pint or two before making their way back to their lodgings. One of them unhitched his breeches and pissed up against the wall.

I flattened myself against some railings as his friends waited.

'You filling up a tin bath there, Charlie? I thought you'd never stop. Away with you now.'

Which way would they go? I crossed my numb fingers.

They turned left. If I tucked in close behind I could follow them down towards Fleet Street.

I pulled my shawl forward to cover half my face and walked quickly to catch them.

I could hear myself breathe – ragged shallow gulps of rancid air that didn't fill my lungs.

Not far now. I'd take the omnibus going east and I'd be at the theatre within the hour.

Only it wasn't so simple.

Fleet Street was unnaturally quiet, apart from private carriages and the occasional hack rolling past. If any street buses were out in this, they weren't going my way.

But I was glad to make out some other people here, as well as my clerks. Grey shapes flitted through the fog – men and women with their heads down and their coats pulled up tight. Home was the only thought in their heads and I couldn't say as I blamed them.

The street-level windows in most of the buildings, apart from the taverns, were dark blanks and even those above –

as far as I could make out – were shuttered up or curtained tight. It was the kind of evening when London gives up on itself, shuts the doors, lights the lamps and closes its eyes. Nanny Peck would have lit the fire on a night like this and made me and Joey sit cross-legged on her old knotted rag rug while she told stories of spirits and banshees.

I shivered. The clammy air was creeping into the folds of my dress and my shawl was beaded with droplets of silver.

I was grateful that the three gents from the tavern turned east and I made sure they were never more than ten foot ahead of me. At first they talked loudly, but as they tramped along they fell silent, stuffed their hands in their pockets and hunched their shoulders.

All the while I listened out for the sound of steps behind me or the rattle and hollow clop of a street bus. I didn't hear neither. If I'd had money for a hack I would have tried to flag one down, like Lucca that time.

After a few minutes, two of the gents peeled off and headed north. I quickened up so that I could keep the last of them in my sight. We were at Ludgate Hill now, according to the addresses on the fancy shop fronts. There were other stragglers out on the street here too, not many, mind – but enough to make me feel a bit easier. As far as I could tell no one was following. I began to wonder if I'd imagined the sound of the footsteps and the voice in the alley.

The last of the gents turned right down a narrow street into the maze of buildings alongside the river. I thought about following him, but it wouldn't get me back to Limehouse, would it?

I was going to be badly late now and Fitzy would be

waiting. If a street bus didn't come past soon, I'd be dipping into Mrs C's paint box tomorrow to cover the bruises.

Then again, maybe The Gaudy wasn't the first place I should be making for anyway. If I went straight to Lady Ginger's Palace and told her about Sir Richard Verdin and that painting, perhaps that was enough? Surely she could deal with it on from there with her lascar boys and her Chinamen? They could get the truth out of a man, I was sure.

I thought of Frances and Sukie with their shorn, bloodied heads and terrified eyes. That was The Lady's mercy.

'Kitty Peck.'

My name came as a whisper from somewhere very close. At the same moment I felt something brush against my arm. I screamed and pulled away, running blind into the road and into the bank of rolling fog. I couldn't see more than a yard ahead, but I knew I had to keep going. I ran fast and straight into nothing and now I could hear someone following.

First there were cobbles beneath my feet, then flagstones greasy with fog-lick.

I tripped over a broad stone step and fell forward, throwing out my hands to protect my head and face. My palms slapped down onto other blackened steps rising above me. I gathered my skirt and hurried upwards – five, six, eight steps – until I reached the soot-crusted base of a huge column.

I was standing at the top of the steps to St Paul's.

Over to the right there was a glow in the fog – a half-open door. I ran across and stepped through into the soft light. I stood for a moment breathing hard and trying to work out where to go when I heard steps on the stones outside.

I darted forward and ran past more columns and gated

side chapels where marble tombs and great white statues flickered in candlelight. There were sputtering gas lamps here too, but most of them, if they were working, were turned low.

I slipped behind a column and looked back at the door – a black shadow fell across the threshold.

I could feel my heart bumping about under my ribs like a marble in a bagatelle. The vast cathedral appeared to be deserted. I stepped back and winced as the sound of my heels echoed on the marble floor. I knelt to untie the laces, took off my boots and padded softly across the stones to a large memorial – a military man, I supposed, from the over-buttoned uniform and the lions at his feet. I squeezed behind the plinth, crouched low and kept watch on the side aisle through the gap between his stone boots.

After a few moments I heard footsteps; someone was walking slowly towards me. I peered through the boots. A shadow moved across the floor. About thirty foot away I could see the bottom of a gentleman's coat and his dark shiny shoes. Then I saw the end of his cane as he probed the space behind a statue.

I couldn't stay here, he was too near.

I knotted my boots together by the laces and draped them over my shoulders. I slipped out from behind the military type and crawled softly on all fours to the edge of the central aisle. When I was sure he hadn't heard me I stood up and dodged behind another wide pale column.

St Paul's was as silent and dead as all the hook-nosed, stone-faced generals standing about the place. It didn't matter how brave or grand you were in life, I thought, the end was much the same for us all.

A long way ahead somewhere in the forest of pillars a tiny light seemed to be moving about.

A clergy, perhaps, or a watchman?

Careful, deliberate steps sounded over to my right, steps that came closer and closer before moving on past me and further into the dark heart of the cathedral under the dome.

Every nerve and muscle in my body pulled as tight as the strings on Old Peter's fiddle as I leaned out a little way. The man had his back to me now and was walking away between a row of wooden chairs and more statues. Every so often he bent to check that I wasn't hiding in the gaps between the high-backed seats and he used the cane to test the spaces. Even in the gloom, his white gloves seemed to glow.

I watched him for a minute. He was well dressed and broad shouldered. I couldn't see his hair because his collar was turned up and he was wearing a tall hat. I looked back towards the door. I could give him the slip if I managed to get out into the street again.

But then I thought, why not turn the tables, girl? If I could only see his face, just the once, I'd know for sure who he was.

The man with the cane was walking up a central aisle, but there was another to his right and one to his left. If I took the right-hand side and crept up behind him, I'd get a good clear view.

I stepped out from behind the pillar and slipped from shadow to shadow following the man until I was almost level with him.

I could smell his fine cologne – a lot of it, like he'd taken a bleedin' bath in the stuff, but there was something else too, something bitter, sharp and just as strong. The sort of smell you'd want to mask. A familiar smell too, but I couldn't place it.

He was less than ten foot away now. Just a few more steps, Kitty.

The clatter of my boots on the stone made me yelp aloud. One of the knots I'd tied had come loose.

I spun about and pelted towards the door, but I could hear him coming after me, his shiny shoes hammering on the marble. I dodged to the left – there was a small door open in the wall. I stepped inside and shut the door quietly behind me, but at almost the same moment I realised how stupid I'd been. Now I was trapped and I'd done it myself.

Perhaps there was something here I could use as a weapon, an old candlestick or a bit of statue? I whirled around. A single gaslight fluttering against the stone wall showed a narrow flight of stairs twisting up into darkness.

There was nowhere else to go. I put my hand to the wall and began to climb.

After making several turns I heard the door below me open; the sound echoed in the stairwell. I began to run.

Three twists later and the stairs ended abruptly on a landing where an open door led off to the right into a dimly lit passage. I raced through the door and along the passage, which broadened out into a wide set of curving steps. Below, the steps coiled into darkness; above, there was a faint light. I didn't have time to think it through properly – I went where I could see where I was going, winding upwards around and around until my head was swimming. There was no single point to concentrate on here, just endless rising steps.

And then nothing – so much nothing.

I'd come out onto a wide balcony that ran around the inside of the dome. On one side the stone wall curved high above me, on the other a metal rail separated me from the yawning empty space that dropped to the floor of the cathedral yards and yards below. I couldn't see it, but I could sense the vastness of it.

A gaslight flickered over the door, splashing a little yellow pool over the wall and the rail; the rest of the space was black.

There was a noise from the stairwell. I caught up my skirt and ran out of the light keeping one hand on the rail to guide me round the balcony. I ran until I was opposite the door, barely able to make out its shape across the void.

I stopped, gripped the rail with both hands and stared across. There was a shadow in the light now; a huge shape flickered briefly up the curve of the dome and then disappeared. I heard a door shut and the sound of something like a key turning in a lock.

I took a handful of my shawl and brought it up to my mouth. If I started to cry the sound would bring him straight to me.

I backed away from the rail and flattened my hands against the cool solid wall at my back. Which way would he come?

'I have you now.'

The words seem to whisper from the stone itself. I sprang forward and whirled about trying to make sense of the noise and the dark, but there was no one there.

Then I heard laughter from the far side of the dome.

A man's voice, oddly distorted as if to disguise its true sound, rang out across the space.

'You have discovered one of the marvels of London,

Philomel, the whispering gallery beneath the dome of St Paul's. But you will never be able to tell anyone about it. There is a beautiful irony, is there not, in the fact that the daring Limehouse Linnet will dash her brains out on the cold stone floor of Wren's masterpiece?'

Bells began to toll. The great black space filled with a tumbling shower of iron and then a single bell counted out the hour. Seven o'clock.

When the last note sounded, it quivered in the air for a long time before the echo faded. Then I heard the cane scraping across the stones. Where was the sound coming from – left or right?

I couldn't tell. I twisted the ends of my shawl in my hands. I couldn't afford to make a mistake. If I ran the wrong way now I'd likely run straight into him.

I took a soft step to the balcony and looked over the rail – there was a light moving across the floor a long way below – someone carrying a lamp or a candle. Perhaps if I called out?

I took a breath and was about to shout down, but then I stopped myself. The sound of my voice would bring the man in the shadows straight to me and by the time anyone made it up the winding stairs, I'd be spread out on the marble down below as lifeless as one of them statues.

I twisted the shawl again. The thick plaid had belonged to Nanny Peck. It was good strong stuff, not frayed or torn after all these years. I gripped it tight, thinking of her.

I could still hear the scraping.

Strong stuff.

That was it. I didn't mind the height, did I? I proved that night after night, right enough. If I could knot the shawl into a loop and tie it to the rail I could hang there, just under the balcony while he passed by. He'd do a full circuit of the dome without finding me. And it would give me time to think.

I unfurled the shawl and tested it. It was long enough to make a swing, but was it strong enough to take my weight?

I was going to find out one way or another. I looped it round the bottom of the rail and tied the best knot I knew – one taught me by one of the old ship ropemakers who was a regular at The Lamb. Quickly I pushed the material out through the metal rails so that it was hanging down over the edge. Taking in a lungful of air, I climbed over.

I tried not to think of the deep pool of nothing at my back as I clung to the outside of the balcony and crouched low. I don't know why, but just then one of Lucca's stories came into my head – Michelangelo and a chapel in Rome.

Old Mickey – he'd painted the whole ceiling for one of them papals lying on his back a hundred foot up with just a bit of rackety old wooden platform between him and kingdom come. And when I say painted, I don't mean a lick of whitewash. Lucca had shown me pictures in one of his books. Bible scenes, they was – God making the world, Noah and the flood, Adam and Eve leaving the Garden of Eden with an angel hovering overhead pointing out the way.

That was the picture that came to me now. Adam, cast out of Paradise, naked and beautiful, just like Joey in that drawing in Lucca's attic.

Not now. I couldn't think of that now.

I shook my head to clear away the images and felt for the loop in the shawl with my right foot. Carefully I pushed through, sliding down to allow the material to take in my leg and thigh. I tightened my grip on the rails as I shifted to tuck my left foot through the loop and then, gradually, I leaned back and allowed the shawl to take my weight. It felt more like a sling than a swing.

Holding tight to the bottom of the rails with my left hand, I reached out to test the knot for one last time with the tips of my fingers. It was tight as Fitzy's trousers.

I breathed out slowly, cleared my mind, released my grip and slid down into the sling seat.

It held.

Tell truth, it was easier than being up there in my cage at the halls. If I didn't think about the yards and yards yawning open between my nancy and the slabs of marble down below, I was actually comfortable – as comfortable as any girl who found herself in such a position might be, you might say.

Silent as a moth, I swung there, listening.

Slow footsteps sounded above to the left and the cane scratched across stone. He was going clockwise – now I had him. Once he'd passed by and gone on a way, I'd climb back up over the rail, take the other direction and make for the door.

I tightened my grip. What if that sound earlier meant he'd locked it?

Footsteps sounded directly above.

A moment later the rails just overhead were thrown into sharp silhouette by a sudden light. I closed my eyes and began a silent prayer as a voice came from just above.

'Excuse me, sir, the cathedral is closed. Didn't you hear the bell? All visitors should have been out half an hour ago now. Mr Austin! I've found a straggler.'

I heard more sounds and laboured breathing as if someone

large was clattering down some steps just above and to the left. Another voice echoed across the space. 'Good thing you came across him before he went up to the Stone Gallery or, God forbid, to the Golden Gallery up top. I've just come down from there – it's all clear for the night. You done, Mr Thomas?'

'All clear, except for this gent. Now sir, it's a very good thing you didn't go any higher without our knowing. If you'd been locked outside up there you'd have had a most uncomfortable evening of it. This way, please . . .'

There was a muttered reply that rose to a sharp rebuke. I caught the last words, '. . . think you'll find I have every right to be here.'

The second man spoke again. 'I'm sorry, sir, but I think *you'll find* I have every right to be back at home with a nice plate of muffins on my lap. Last entry is five-thirty of a weekday evening and we like to clear everyone out an hour later, except for special services. That's why we lower the lights and close every door except . . .'

The warden broke off for a moment before continuing. 'Ah that's it, isn't it? Old Barker's left the side door at the front open again. We must have a word about that with one of the vergers – he's becoming very lax. That how you came in, is it, sir? I'm sorry, but after six that's for exits only. Now, we'll be going out that way too. I hear it's a filthy night out there. Follow me.'

I twisted in my sling and watched the wardens' lamps as they bobbed around the balcony. Three huge shadows flickered up the curved walls as they escorted the man with the cane back to the door. I heard the sound of rattling and bumping as one of the wardens tried the door.

A voice came again. 'Funniest thing – where is it now?'

The words bounced off the walls. Then: 'Why thank you, sir. Can't think what it was doing down there, must have jiggled out, I suppose? Down we go then, after you. Watch your step there.'

I heard the door open and the fading sound of footsteps on the stairs. Then I was alone in the dark.

Chapter Twenty-six

The windows were barred and shuttered. I stood in the narrow cut and looked up at the flat front of the blackened building with its bent railings and cracked stone steps. If you didn't know better you'd never guess Lady Ginger lived in a palace.

I wasn't sure what time it was now, very late I guessed, but I needed to see her and tell her about Sir Richard and his painter boys. It was enough to exchange for Joey, wasn't it?

Bring me more. That was what she said – and that's exactly what I was doing. *She* could deal with it now.

There was no one else in the dingy passage off Salmon Lane and I can't say I was surprised. Her reputation was enough to patrol these streets – and anyway, only a bedlam would come to Lady Ginger's Palace without an invitation.

I couldn't see a sliver of light from the windows on any floor. I took another step back and peered up to the top where I knew her receiving room was. She was probably there now with her lascars and that bleedin' parrot. I pictured her curled up on a pile of cushions, eyes closed, sucking on her pipe – tendrils of thick sweet smoke weaving up into the air. I wondered if she could tell the difference between her opium dreams and the real world. And even if she could, would it matter?

My feet were raw. I could feel sharp cobbles through the

strips of material I'd ripped from my underskirt and bound over my stockings.

There hadn't been a chance to find my boots.

I'd waited there, dangling under the great black dome of St Paul's until I was sure I was safe and then I'd hauled myself up over the edge of the balcony and untied my shawl.

I bent forward, and my hair brushed the stones as I planted my hands on my thighs and breathed deep. My knees began to twitch and the bones in my legs felt as if all the marrow had been sucked clean out of them. If I allowed myself to dwell on what I'd just done, I thought I might just faint away right there up on the balcony.

I straightened up.

The single lamp was still alight over the open door on the far side, but the wide, spiralling stone stairs beyond were in darkness. I bundled up my shawl and darted round the balcony.

I listened for a moment, but I couldn't hear a sound from the stairwell. I stepped through the door and felt my way down using the wall as a guide.

After an age in the dark I crept out into the vast empty cathedral. At the sound of footsteps I shrank behind a column and watched as a small man with a lamp, one of the wardens I'd heard earlier I presumed, made a final circuit. He was humming a tune, but it didn't sound very reverent. In fact, I knew it from the halls – something about a fella and his girl having a picnic, only when the chorus got to a bit about the unpacking of the fancies, it wasn't just bread and cheese that got laid out on the grass.

I slipped out and followed him as quiet as I could, making sure he didn't catch sight of me. He made his way back to the side door where I'd first come in and disappeared behind a wooden screen. He sneezed twice and I heard the sound of rattling keys.

This was my chance. My stockinged feet didn't make a sound as I flew down the side aisle. The door stood slightly ajar and I slipped through the gap, racing down the steps into the swirling fog. Dodging left I found myself among the tumbledown stones and crumbling table tombs of St Paul's churchyard.

That was when I remembered my boots.

I'd walked most of the way back east and it was hard going. It began to rain as I reached more familiar streets, but at least it thinned the fog to a mist before it washed it away completely.

In Spitalfields by the brewery I took a seat up top with a carter lad. As the big wagon rumbled past he'd shouted out some clever words, but when I looked up at him he must have felt guilty because he asked where I was going and budged up.

The big horses flicked their tails and twitched their ears as the carter boy talked about his employer and some funny business with the wages. When he asked about me and I told him about the halls he asked if his sister could get a start there.

'Pretty she is, neat figure, voice like an angel. What d'ya fink?'

I thought it was the very last place I'd want a little sister of mine to work, but I said I'd keep an ear out.

'You know who I'd like to see?' he said, pulling hard on the reins as the horses spooked at a hack racing out from a side street.

I shook my head.

'That Limehouse Linnet. Kitty Peck, ain't it? They say she's got all London at her feet these days – that she can do just what she wants.'

'Is that what they say?'

He nodded.

I stared ahead. 'She's a very lucky girl then, isn't she?'

The carter boy took me as far as Shadwell and dropped me off just past another St Paul's – the old seaman's church this time. He was collecting a load from the New Basin and couldn't take me no further.

Now, this was a poor place, even compared to St Anne's. The grimy hovels around St Paul's in the east had a reputation for offering entertainment to sailors, if you get my meaning, and I didn't want to linger there for fear of being mistaken for a brass. I tucked my hair under my shawl and kept my head down.

There was no point in going to The Gaudy now, it would be closed for the night and Fitzy would be breaking the china and chewing the cushions in his office. But who knew what hours Lady Ginger kept?

I wondered if she even slept in a bed.

It was past one when I climbed up the steps and reached for the big metal ring in the centre of one of the double doors. I knocked twice and waited for a minute before knocking again four, five, six times. The hollow sound bounced off the damp brick walls around me.

I went back down to the street and stared up at the building. On the top floor there was a momentary glint of yellow in one of the windows as if someone had loosened a shutter or shifted a curtain.

'I see you, Lady Ginger.' I took another step back. 'I know you're in there. It's me, Kitty'.

My voice rang out clearly in the darkness. I was surprised at its strength and the challenge in it.

'I've brought you more, just like you said.'

When no one came I raced up the steps, took hold of the ring and hammered it down again and again with my right hand, all the while thumping on the cracked paint with my left and shouting up.

'Do you hear me, Lady? I've brought you more. I've got a name.' The longer I pounded on the door, the more frantic I became. I didn't care now. 'Where's my brother? Where's Joey? You promised me, Lady Ginger. You owe me!'

I must have beaten on those doors a hundred times before I faltered, crumbling into a little heap at the top of the steps. My voice had dwindled to a cracked whisper of defeat.

I started to cry then, not great noisy sobs, but silent tears that trickled down my face and rolled off my chin into the folds of my shawl. I tried to wipe them away with the backs of my hands but they kept on coming.

I couldn't feel a thing – not the tiredness, not the cold, not my blistered feet and nothing inside neither. It was like I'd been wrung out and cast aside like a rag poppet dropped by a child.

I wrapped my hands around my knees and rocked backwards and forwards on the step. I kept repeating Joey's name again and again. Why had he done this to me?

The doors clicked open and swung silently inwards.

I looked up. One of The Lady's Chinamen stood in the candlelit hallway. He had a scar running down his face from the upper lid of his right eye to the corner of his mouth. It gave off the impression he was smiling, but when he turned to look down at me the left side of his face was blank. Something sweet and musty rolled out into the air.

He reached into the folds of his gown.

Remembering that performance with Sukie and Frances, I stood up sharp and dodged to the bottom of the steps and out onto the cobbles. If he had a blade tucked away I was out of reach now.

But he stayed exactly where he was. I watched as he pulled something from the sleeve – a roll of paper. He raised his arm and offered the paper to me. His black eyes glinted as he stared.

When I didn't move he shuffled out onto the top step and stooped to place the paper on the stone, then he straightened up, bowed his head once, turned and went back inside, closing the doors softly behind him.

I raced up the steps and grabbed the paper. It was too dark to see anything here so I crunched it up in my hand and ran up to Salmon Lane, where there were a couple of lamps.

My hands were shaking as I unfurled it. The page was as empty as the Chinaman's face except for one thing. Right in the middle, written in red and enclosed in a circle, was the number four.

I knew what it meant immediately. Lady Ginger was a subtle bitch – I had to give her that.

The number of death – that's what she called it, wasn't it?

And it was the number of days I had left until my own brother died.

Chapter Twenty-seven

Lucca's face was creased and heavy with sleep. He blinked and rubbed his hand over the scars on the right side of his face.

'Fannella! Thank God, I thought . . .' He shook his head as if to clear away the last remnants of a dream and stared at me. 'Fitzpatrick is as mad as a rabid dog. Where have you been?' He was sharp now.

'You going to let me in or are you going to leave me freezing me out here like a bleedin' slab of hokey-pokey?' Those bold words echoed in the alleyway, but my voice was tight and oddly pitched as if it was going to slide up into something close to a scream.

He frowned, opened the door wider and placed a finger to his lips as he ushered me inside. 'People are asleep. It's late or haven't you noticed?'

Tell truth, I hadn't. After receiving Lady Ginger's message the only thing I wanted to do was find Lucca and talk to him and I hadn't given a thought to the time.

When I'd got to his lodgings everything was dark, so I'd thrown handfuls of pebbles up to his window in the eaves.

I wasn't entirely sure he'd be there or what I was going to say to him if he was, but when he poked his head out I was so glad to see him.

Lucca led the way up to his room, pushed open the door and stood aside to let me go in ahead of him. I sank down on the bed; of an instant there was nothing left in me. I was a candle burned down to the last feeble, guttering spark.

It was dark and cold. Lucca crossed over to the little fireplace and struck a Lucifer to light a stub of grey wax in the single brass stick on the mantle. Then he crouched down, crumpled up some papers and pushed them into the gaps between the scanty nuggets in the hearth. He lit the paper ends from the candle stub and neither of us spoke as the damp coals spat and then, reluctantly, began to glow. Within a couple of minutes a small fire was crackling. He leaned back, folded his arms and watched the flames.

'So, where have you been, Fannella?'

I slipped off the bed to kneel next to him and reached out towards the hearth, but it didn't make much difference, I was numb to the core. My hands were shaking – I noticed that, but it was like I was watching some other girl, not me.

Lucca saw it too. He took my hands between his like we was praying together and rubbed them. I shifted to get closer to the fire and the ragged, muddy hem of my skirt lifted over my feet.

'Jesus! What have you done to yourself?' Lucca dropped my hands, leapt up and fetched a jug and basin from the corner. 'Where are your boots?' Gently he unwrapped the shreds of torn, dirty fabric from my feet and I winced as the material pulled at the crusted blood.

He swore under his breath as he dabbed at the scabbed and grimy skin. The water must have been ice-cold, but I couldn't feel it. I watched as he dipped a scrap of stained linen into the bowl and the water clouded red obscuring the dainty flowers painted on the china.

He looked up and pushed a curl back from my face. 'You have been crying.' It wasn't a question. 'When will you learn that you are not immortal, Fannella?'

I tried to smile. 'I think I learned that tonight.'

I wondered how much to tell him. He unpeeled another strip of material from my right foot and I yelped.

'I'm sorry, but it will be painful. The heat – it makes the feeling come back.'

I bit my lip and nodded. 'It's all right, go ahead – and thank you.'

He dipped the rag back into the bowl and smoothed it over my toes, speaking softly as he worked.

'When you didn't come to the theatre this evening. I didn't know what to do or who to ask. I was worried that you . . . you had been taken like the others.' His dark curls fell forward as he bent to dab at my heel where a blister the size of a penny was raw and bleeding. I couldn't speak for a moment as a stab of pain made me clench my jaw.

'Lucca, I . . . I've been to see Sam Collins again. He sent a message to The Gaudy saying he wanted to see me. I came to find you after the rehearsal but . . .'

(The thought of that drawing of Joey insinuated itself into a corner of my mind. I knew I could trust Lucca with my life, but there was a distance between us now – a secret. I realised with a sudden shock of recognition that Lucca didn't trust *me*.)

'. . . But you weren't there, so I went to Sam's office on my own. I took an omnibus. I thought I'd be back in time for to-night—' I gasped as Lucca ripped another strip from the sole of my foot.

269

He looked up and frowned. 'You took a foolish risk. After the cage . . .' He sighed and tapped his head. 'You are clever, *si*, but sometimes you are like a little child. You act when you should think. You jump before you see. Tell me, how could you be sure that Sam Collins was telling the truth?'

He was right, of course, but I hadn't been of a mind to examine the situation too closely, had I? When I'd gone to find Lucca after the rehearsal I'd found that picture instead. There were questions I needed to ask about that, but whether I *wanted* the answers, now, that was a very different matter. Fact is I wanted to get away from that drawing. That's why I went to Sam Collins on my own, but I wasn't going to tell Lucca that.

I shifted on the rug. 'He asked about you, he even remembered your name. He's a sharp one right enough, but he's not dangerous – at least not in the way you think. I reckon he'd sell his mother for a good story, but he wouldn't kill her for it. He kept his promise too. He passed on some information about the gallery and about that picture. I . . . I think I know who's behind all this now.'

The firelight glowed on the smooth left side of Lucca's face. I couldn't read his expression. 'You need fresh linens on these. I've got an old shirt we can use. You can tell me everything while I finish cleaning you up and make some fresh bandages. I mean *everything*, Kitty.

*

It was the name 'Verdin' that did it. Most particularly the name 'Sir Richard Verdin'.

Lucca had gone quiet when I told him about James and the bus, but as soon as I got to that bit about the gallery and the trustees it was as if someone had chucked a bucket of water on the fire.

I shivered and took up an iron to poke the coals. Little flames were still dancing around in the grate, but the room suddenly felt chill as a butcher's locker.

I set down the iron. 'Sam says Sir Richard's interested in young artists, the younger the better. Apparently he takes a very personal interest—' I broke off as Lucca stood up abrupt and swore in Italian. I didn't understand what he said, but as the curses spat from his lips the meaning was clear.

I sat there in silence watching. Lucca had gone to the far side of the room. Now he stood with his back to me, his forehead resting on the wall and one hand clenched above his head. I could see all the muscles in his arm strung tight. He'd balled his fist up like he wanted to punch a hole in that thin old board right out through to the stairwell beyond.

I stood up and limped over. My feet were stinging like hell now.

'Lucca?' I stroked his back, feeling the tightness of his shoulders beneath the thin material of his shirt. He was like something coiled up and ready to strike. I reached up to his face.

'Don't!'

He stepped away and turned to stare at me. His eye glinted in the shadow.

'Look at me.' He pushed back his hair on the right so that I could see the melted skin that pulled his once-handsome features into a mockery of a face. Deliberately he moved into the firelight and held back his hair so that nothing covered his scars. It was as if everything had slipped to the wrong place. The front of his burned scalp on the right side was patched with tufts of hair, his eye and the side of his nose were fused into a fleshy lump, raised strips of livid red and unnaturally pale skin stretched down his cheek and onto his neck. His ear was a gnarled stub of gristle. I'd never seen him so clearly before. I felt like an intruder.

Lucca's mouth twisted into a smile.

'Verdin did this to me. Look closely, Fannella. This is his artistry.'

'James?' I wasn't thinking clearly.

Lucca snorted and shook his head. 'Collins is right that the great Sir Richard Verdin is interested in young artists. I was one of them, but it's not their painting skills he values. It is something else altogether. He is a connoisseur of the flesh – do you understand what I am saying?'

Another bit of that old wooden jigsaw bumped into place.

I nodded slowly. 'You mean he . . . he used you, like a girl? You were a shilling boy?'

'He paid me more than that, Fannella.'

Lucca sank to the ragged little rug in front of the fire. 'And then he took everything I had.' He stared into the flames and didn't look at me as he spoke.

'I was young, poor and easily flattered. We all were. Giacomo and I had come here to make a new life. In our village we were . . . discovered and it was not good. Our families – they tried to part us, but we were in love. We couldn't live apart. So we went to Napoli, worked hard and then we booked a passage on a ship as soon as we had saved enough money. We hoped that here in London where no one knew us life could be different.'

Lucca paused. 'He was beautiful, Fannella – like an angel.'

I went to sit next to him in front of the hearth and I took his hand in mine. We sat there in silence for a moment looking into the fire. Nanny Peck used to read the flames to me and Joey when we was small. Right then I discovered I could read quite a lot there myself.

I squeezed his hand. 'Giacomo – he's the boy in your pictures in the room over the workshop?'

Lucca nodded.

'What happened to him?'

He didn't answer at first and I didn't want to push it, but then he took a deep breath. 'A short time after we came to London I was . . . introduced to Sir Richard and his circle of artists. At first it was easy. I was one of several boys who posed as models for his protégés. One day, while I waited for my turn, he saw me sketching. He admired my work and he invited me to draw for him. Imagine, Kitty, the great Sir Richard Verdin interested in a boy like me. He said I was talented, a true artist. He said I could be part of his special school.'

He laughed bitterly.

'There were several of us in Sir Richard's "school" – others like me, boys without a past . . . or a future. He invited us to his house, gave us money and made us pose naked for him. He liked to watch as we drew or painted . . . or touched each other.'

He paused and gripped my hand tightly. 'I burned those pictures. I could not keep them afterwards.'

I didn't say a word. If he wanted to tell me more he would.

A coal sputtered in the hearth and a tiny cinder spat out onto the back of Lucca's hand. He didn't seem to notice as he continued. 'Giacomo had found work in a theatre – he was a musician.'

I noted the fact that Lucca said 'was'.

'But he wanted to know how I managed to earn so much more in a single evening than he could in a week. At first I couldn't tell him – I was ashamed. But Giacomo became jealous – he accused me of finding a new lover. The only way I could convince him it wasn't true was to introduce him to the school.'

His voice dwindled to a whisper. 'That was how I killed him.' The room seemed to shrink around us, every peeling, damp-stained wall leaning inwards to listen.

'That can't be true, Lucca.' I turned to look at him direct, but he was knotted up, his hair falling forward. 'You would never kill anyone. I know that.'

I couldn't see his expression as he answered. 'Do you? Then you are deceived. I would gladly kill Sir Richard Verdin and every member of his sick, degenerate family.'

The thought of James in my bed and of him trying to buy me as his whore on the top deck of that omnibus came to me. It struck me then that the only thing dividing the poor from the rich was the fact that a wealthy man could buy himself a nice clean conscience – along with every dirty secret his appetites ran to.

'Lucca, tell me, what really happened to Giacomo?'

He turned to look at me then and his eye glittered with tears. 'You remember I told you once that I liked champagne?'

I nodded and his lips curved up to the left into a sort of smile. 'So did Giacomo. When I introduced him to Sir Richard he acquired a taste for it. And Verdin acquired a taste for him. He became the favoured one.

'For weeks he was Sir Richard's constant companion. It went beyond the school. Verdin bought him fine clothes, paraded him at restaurants, galleries, theatres, the opera. Giacomo was like a pet, a lap dog, a performing monkey, but he could not see it. Quite the opposite, in fact, he adored the life. If people of Verdin's class knew what was happening they closed their eyes and shut their mouths. Silence, like people, is easily purchased.'

He took up the poker and thrust it viciously into the coals. Yellow flames licked the back of the hearth as he continued. 'At first Giacomo told me it was a game. He said he was doing it for us, but he was lying. I knew that he was becoming . . . *infettato* – infected by something. It was like a sickness in him, a greed. We were still together, yes, but day by day the space between us grew wider and deeper. When he looked at me sometimes I could see that he despised me. Can you imagine how that felt, Fannella?

'Then something changed. Verdin took a new companion – someone very different. It drove Giacomo mad with envy. He'd grown used to that life, you see, and it was unbearable to be replaced and locked outside.'

Lucca began to pick at the flaking skin around his fingernails, pulling the flesh so tight he drew little droplets of blood. 'It was like a madness. Verdin had changed Giacomo so much I did not know him any more. I only discovered the truth about that terrible night afterwards, when we escaped.'

He brought his finger to his mouth and sucked at the blood. 'You should never play dice with the Devil, for he will always win.' The thought of Lady Ginger rattling that little green box in her clawed-up fist came into my mind as Lucca spoke.

'I found out later that Giacomo tried to blackmail Verdin. He threatened to reveal everything about the school and about his . . . tastes unless he took him back or paid him a great deal of money.'

He rested his forehead in his hands. I could see his shoulders heaving. 'I have been the cause of so much evil. But I didn't know, I swear to God, I didn't know.'

I put my hand lightly to his arm. 'Go on, Lucca, tell me, please. I won't judge. I'd never do that. Tell me everything.'

He nodded, cleared his throat and took a deep inward breath. 'Verdin invited, no, that's the wrong word, he *commanded* us to attend a . . . celebration. He said we would be paid handsomely. I was surprised. I thought he had forgotten me, but Giacomo was delighted. He took such care preparing himself for the evening like the little whore he was. He told me that our fortunes were about to change, but even then I did not think he really meant that for both of us.

'It was to be a great secret, we were told – a surprise. A carriage was sent to collect us and we were taken to a mansion outside London. The house was set at the end of a long drive and surrounded by trees. It was high summer and the light was just fading from the sky when we arrived. Even now I can remember the scent of *gelsomino* . . . jasmine climbing over the porch. For a moment I was reminded of home.'

Lucca paused and followed the pattern woven into the rug with his finger.

'The house was derelict, but it was still beautiful. The entrance hall had been dressed with vines and candles. The air was thick with musk and we could hear music and laughter. Giacomo was joyful. He thought it was his chance to begin his old life again.

'At the foot of the stairs a young man wearing a carnival mask offered us glasses filled with . . . I don't know what it was. Not champagne, that's for sure. Then we were ordered to remove our clothes and to join the gathering above. You must understand – this was how it always was at Verdin's townhouse and we were used to the rules. It was . . . *Dio mi perdoni*, exciting.'

Lucca broke off and wrung his hands together. 'You said you would not judge me, Fannella. But I am not so sure when you have heard me to the end.'

I reached out to stroke his scarred right cheek and then, gently, I turned his face towards me. 'Go on. I made a promise. Finish your story.'

'The drink – there was something in it, some drug. By the time we reached the room the sounds, the scents and the colours were so intense, almost unbearable, but wonderful too. As we swayed through the doors, it was like entering a magic kingdom, like a scene from ancient Rome. There were cushions and rugs laid out across the floor, a feast set out along a trestle table against a row of windows, and there were bodies moving everywhere. But as I looked, Fannella, I realised, even through the hazy madness that shattered my mind into a thousand brilliant, glittering pieces, that the only people there were the young men and boys from the special school.

'Verdin was there too – watching from a tall chair raised up on a dais. In the red light of the setting sun that came from the window behind him he glowed like the Devil in the old wall painting at the church in my village. He always liked to view us, but I felt then that something was wrong. This wasn't like one of the evenings at his townhouse. This was something different – the room was charged with something wild.

'Giacomo ran forward. I tried to stop him. I caught his hand, but he shook me off laughing as he darted through the bodies towards the dais. Verdin was standing now and he was smiling. While everyone else in the room was intoxicated with lust he was cold and apart. I looked away for a moment as someone whispered my name, a soft hand caressed me and I nearly fell to my knees to become a part of the ecstasy, but I knew, Fannella, I knew then it was a trap. My head was swimming as I tried to see where Giacomo had gone.

'Instead I saw Verdin and in his hand there was a lighted taper. I watched as he stepped slowly down from the dais and deliberately set light to a pile of cushions. No one seemed to notice as the fabric quickly became a golden pyre and then the fire began to spread across the rugs and up the hangings. Thick smoke began to fill the room, a tapestry caught alight and peeled from the wall folding itself over the back of a boy not older than fourteen.

'I couldn't think and I couldn't see, my mind was a carnival. Part of me wanted to laugh and run into the flames and part of me wanted to scream aloud to warn everyone to get out. I tried to find Giacomo, but the room was full of smoke and fire. I staggered back to the doors, but they were closed – locked or barred from the outside. I was choking now as the smoke filled my lungs.

'I crouched low, cupping my hands over my nose and mouth. I could hear screaming and I could smell the terrible sweetness of burning flesh. A hand fastened round my wrist and I was dragged into the smoke. I tried to resist, but the grip was strong. We dodged through the flames until we ducked into the space beneath the table. A choked voice told me to keep my head low and take shallow breaths. Then I felt the grip tighten round my wrist again as the table toppled forward and we scrambled up to a window sill. I heard the sound of splintering wood and breaking glass and I cried out as a ball of fire seared across my head and shoulder. Then I screamed even louder as I was pushed through the jagged panes, falling twenty, perhaps thirty feet to the grass below. A moment later there was a great thud next to me as someone else jumped from above.'

Lucca fell silent and started to pull again at the ragged skin around his thumb.

I tried to take in everything he had just told me. I tried to imagine how he'd lived with himself, with all that festering, pointless guilt eating away at his fish-on-Friday soul. I might not have been the most worldly of creatures, but I knew that when it came to a choice between filling your belly or starving in the gutter there weren't many of us who wouldn't sell our body for bread.

I didn't give a monkey's toss about what he'd done with Verdin and the other boys – after all, there were plenty of types like Lucca in the halls – and the better theatres too – and no one minded much, except the rozzers. And even they turned a blind eye when it suited them.

But all the same, I was angry with him.

Why hadn't he told me any of this before? Didn't he trust me? I thought I'd made it plain I trusted him to the boundaries of Paradise and beyond. Of occasion the thought of me and him being a pair had crossed my mind – and sometimes I got the impression he might have thought that too. He'd certainly let the other lads at the halls think that way – and Peggy too.

I dug my nails into my palms. This wasn't the time to start a fight. And sitting next to Lucca now I found I didn't have the stomach for it. He didn't look at me, just kept picking his fingers and twisting his hands over and over.

I watched him for a moment. It wasn't true what I'd just thought, was it? Lucca had never led me to think we was anything more than good friends and people at the halls had come to their own conclusions. Lucca hadn't said a thing. I'd even shared a bed with him for Christ's sake, and he hadn't made a move.

It came to me then that, sometimes, I wasn't as smart as I thought I was. If anything, Lucca had always been more like a brother to me and that's how I loved him.

The fire was burning low. I glanced over at the little window above his bed and saw that the sky was deep violet shot with streaks of pink and gold. It would be light soon.

Out of the corner of my eye I caught a sudden movement near Lucca's rumpled bed as a mouse darted for cover across the boards, disappearing into a hole no bigger than a ha'penny in the wainscot. Let it be, I thought, we were all of us scrabbling around in a filthy world to stay alive. Lucca had nothing to be ashamed of.

His head hung low and his dark curls had tumbled forward but I could see the curve of his lips and his fine straight nose. No wonder Verdin took him up. He'd been beautiful too once. Like Giacomo.

I took a deep breath. 'Look,' I began, 'this wasn't your fault, none of it was. If anyone was to blame it's Giacomo.'

Something Lucca said earlier repeated itself in my mind: *I only discovered the truth about that night afterwards when we escaped.*

I straightened my back. 'So what happened to him, this Giacomo, then, when you two got out?'

Lucca stopped picking his nails. He was completely still for a moment and then he turned to stare at me. He blinked twice and a shadow seemed to pass across the good side of his face.

He reached for my hand.

'It wasn't Giacomo who saved me that night, Fannella. It was Joey.'

Chapter Twenty-eight

There were rooms in my mind I was careful to keep closed. Looking back, I can see that Ma and me weren't too different there, but in the end she closed so many doors in her head she couldn't find her way out again.

After Ma had gone I'd trained myself not to open the doors that led to memories. It was better that way. In fact, I'd found it was better to keep a lot of things locked away – fear, for example.

When I was up there in that cage I made sure that even the smallest doubt about what I was doing was folded small into such a distant corner of my head that I didn't even know it was there.

There was The Lady too, and this business with the missing girls. I'd dealt with that by watching it from the outside – keeping it away from me like it was all happening to another Kitty Peck.

The girl who worked in the halls, sang in the galleries as she slopped out the vomit and gave the old backchat to Fitzpatrick was hard as an oyster's shell and every year since Joey left her she'd grown a new protective layer. Everything that happened to her was like a barnacle growing on her shell, adding another stony rivet to her armour.

But inside, that girl was soft as an oyster too, and now something was tearing her apart.

'Fannella . . .'

Lucca reached out towards me.

'Don't you dare!' I pushed him away and wiped my cheeks roughly with the heel of my hands. Then I leaned forward and slapped the good side of his face. He didn't move or say a word, so I hit him again on the other side, so hard this time that his head jerked and his hair fell forward to cover his face.

Still he just sat there – and he let me hit him over and over until I crumpled sobbing into his lap. Outside, the shift bell at the docks began to clang.

Lucca stroked my hair.

'I am sorry, Fannella. I should have told you long ago.' His voice was almost a whisper. 'There is so much I should have said.'

'You've known all the time, Lucca, haven't you? You've known he was alive.'

'*Si.*' I barely caught the word.

'I don't understand, why didn't you tell me? You were there with me that day when they came to the theatre and told me about the accident. You knew then it was a lie and yet you let me think he was dead. How could you do that to me?'

Lucca was silent, but I could hear his heart beating fast in his chest. I twisted my head to look up at him and asked again. 'How could you do that to me when you knew he was all I had?'

He swallowed. 'Joey asked me not to. He was my friend. He saved my life.'

'Friend – or more? I have to know.' My voice was sharp.

Lucca shook his head. 'Friend. But he was part of the school. He was . . . one of us.'

That drawing came into my head again. My clever, handsome brother – I hadn't known him at all, had I? All this time I'd been blind to something right in front of my eyes. 'Degenerate' – that's what Fitzpatrick had said about Joey. Now I knew why, and The Lady too, she'd called him a murderer. I sat up.

'What happened next – after you both jumped?'

Lucca sighed. 'I'm not sure what happened immediately after the fire. I was taken to a house in London and Joey cared for me. I was badly burned. This . . .', he gestured to his face, '. . . is what happened just before your brother pushed me through the window. My hair was burned into my skin. He told a doctor that it was an accident with an oil lamp. I was dead to the world for days and there was fever too. I nearly died. Sometimes I wish I had.'

He put his hand to his face and followed the lumps of flesh from his eye to his nose and lips. 'It took months for the wounds to heal and the flesh to grow back. I am a ruin now. It is my punishment.'

I squeezed his hand. 'It wasn't you who lit the fire, was it? And as for punishment, as far as I can tell someone was looking out for you that night. That's when you came to us at The Gaudy, wasn't it? When you was healed up again?'

Lucca nodded. 'Joey – he found me a place. He did it for you, Fannella, because he knew he was going away. He asked me to look after you.'

I stared up at him. 'Going where? If he knew he was going away why didn't he take me with him?'

Lucca was careful not to look at me. 'Many of the boys who died in the fire were the property of the Barons. There are houses across London where gentlemen seek singular entertainment. And those houses are valuable. It was in everyone's interest to keep the events of that night secret, but all the same the Barons wanted a name. Someone let it be known that Joey had started that fire. Your brother's life was in danger. He had to disappear and he asked The Lady to help him.'

I dropped Lucca's hand and pulled my hair back from my face, knotting it at the nape of my neck. A dull throb was beginning at my temples. 'But why would she do that? Why would he ask *her*?'

Lucca shrugged. 'Because, as you know, he was already in her pay. The Barons always look after their own. It's possible The Lady used him as a pawn in some game we couldn't even begin to guess at. All I know is that he made a bargain with her and I promised that when he went away I would take his place and care for you. I owed him my life. It was a debt, and I have been happy to pay it, Fannella, because you became my friend . . . No, that's not right – you became my sister.'

I tried to smile, but the dull pain in my head was growing sharper. There was something else here too, something that Lucca wasn't telling me.

Another wooden piece slotted into place, but I had to hear it.

'Who was it that fingered Joey for the fire, Lucca?'

He pulled at a stray loop of wool in the rug. When he answered his voice was flat. 'You remember I told you that Verdin exchanged Giacomo for a new lover?'

My heart felt like a stone. I nodded.

'It was Joey. He could pass, you see, in society and that made Verdin feel safe.'

The pain was spearing through my left eye now and up into my forehead.

'But you and that Giacomo – with your accents you two could pass for rich folk anywhere in the right clothes. You speak lovely. None of us could tell if you were a lord or a pauper, Lucca.'

Now, Joey was a good actor, I thought to myself, and he could pick up any lingo quicker than a tooler could pick a pocket, but he'd give himself away somehow.

'You'd never take my brother for a real toff, Lucca.'

The room was suddenly so silent that if that mouse in the wall had taken a breath, I'd've heard it.

'But you might take him for a girl – for a woman? And Sir Richard did – often. Your brother was beautiful and the two of them fooled society. For Joey it was a game, for Verdin I think it was more. He paid well and bought him clothes even finer than the ones he gave to Giacomo. In some twisted way Verdin loved your brother. He trusted him enough to tell him about Giacomo's attempt to blackmail him and then he told him about his own plans to wipe every dangerous trace of the special school from the face of the earth so that he could never be blackmailed again.

'He wanted to begin a new life – a public life – with your brother, but he could not allow anyone who knew the truth to live. That's why Joey was there that evening. He wanted to stop it – to save us all. Apart from Joey, I was the only one who lived. I don't think Verdin realised that.'

Lucca stood up and went over to the window. The morning sun showed up the red shades in his dark hair. When he continued, he kept his back to me.

'Joey knew of his guilt and what's more he despised him. Verdin had to make sure he would never betray him, Kitty. What better way to kill your brother than to turn every Baron in London against him?'

I remembered that night again when I woke up and Joey was sitting on the floor by the door crying as he watched me in the dark.

The last little bits of jigsaw bumped into place and the picture they formed was ugly. I don't mean I thought of Joey or Lucca as ugly – they could never be that to me. No, the thought of Sir Richard Verdin running his flint-grey eyes over the bodies of boys who were little more than children and then murdering them to keep his public face as clean as his private soul was filthy made me want to tear him to pieces with my bare hands until all that was left of him was his shrivelled black heart.

I went over to the window and stood next to Lucca. 'Why didn't you tell me any of this earlier?'

'I couldn't. I promised Joey that I would keep his secret. He made me swear an oath . . . he didn't want you to despise him.'

He looked at me now. 'And he did it to keep you safe too. I didn't even know he had a sister until he brought me here to Paradise.'

'Do you know where he is?'

Lucca shook his head. 'The Lady dealt with him. She spirited him away.'

'Just like the girls from the halls?' I laughed bitterly. 'Before I came to you I went to see her last night with *more*, just like she wanted, but it still wasn't enough. I'm going to have to go and fetch them back. I reckon that's the only thing that will satisfy her.'

He was quiet for a moment and his eye glinted in the dawn light. 'Fetch them back from where? You know where they are, don't you?'

The sun was showing clear in the narrow gap between the houses at the end of the street. You could see a glimmering stripe of the river from here and it seemed to shine with that mysterious silver-gilt light the unknown artist used in the sky above *The Cinnabar Girls*.

Only I was certain who he was now. *Infettato* – that was the word Lucca had used about Giacomo, wasn't it? It had a lovely sound in his language, but then he'd explained what he meant by it – infection. This was a sick business all right.

Chapter Twenty-nine

'So, what would you need if you were painting something like *The Cinnabar Girls*? I'm talking practical, Lucca, so don't think about inspiration and passion. What's the first thing that comes to mind?'

I pulled up the breeches and buttoned the fly. Lucca knelt to tuck the flailing ends into the work boots. They were small for a man, but I still had to wear three pairs of woollens to make them a snug fit. Beneath the wool my tattered feet were bound in clean rags.

He looked up. 'Space – lots of it.'

I nodded. 'But what kind of space? If you was working in secret it would have to be where no one would think of looking for you. Somewhere you could move things in and out without anyone thinking anything of it. Somewhere people come and go and don't ask too many questions. Now do you see?'

Lucca stopped pushing the ends of the rough material into the boots and sat back.

'The warehouse – the one Verdin has taken a lease on?'

I nodded again and reached across him to take a brown jacket from the bed, pushing my arms into its over-long sleeves.

'Tell me again about that paint.'

He frowned as he stood to turn up the collar of the jacket to make it cover the bottom half of my face.

'But you already know this. Sicilian Gold was thought to be a fable. There were descriptions of paintings where it was supposed to have been used, but as none of them survived, there was no way to know what it really was, or how it looked.'

He pinched the jacket's shoulders and folded them towards my neck. 'You are thinner than he was. If we wrap a scarf around you too, just here, it will be better.'

I felt a cold breath on the back of my neck. Lucca was dressing me in a dead man's clothes for the second time, but now I knew exactly whose boots I was stepping into. I pushed the thought of Giacomo away like he might bring bad luck. We were going to need all the help we could get tonight and a notion like that was a jinx.

'You mean no way to know how it looked until now. That painting at The Artisans – you're sure that's Sicilian Gold?'

He took a step back to look at me. 'I am certain. The way it shines, the deep quality like a pool or a mirror. The way it seems . . . unnatural, strange. This is what was written of it.'

He paused and then he reached forward to touch my arm. 'I thought it was the only clue we had to help us find the girls, Kitty. That's why I went back to the gallery to see the painting again. I wanted to help you, but I couldn't tell you everything – not then anyway. Do you understand?'

I nodded, thinking of all the secret lives and hidden worlds that had been playing out around me. It wasn't the time to open that door.

I pushed my hair up and knotted it tight behind. I was

going to hide it away beneath the cloth cap lying on the bed. My mind was ticking over like a gentleman's fob.

'That book you stole, Lucca, how did it go? Wait – you don't need to find it. I have it ... "*When Corretti died in 1534, the secret of Sicilian Gold expired with him. Although many have tried to recreate this remarkable, some said 'magical' pigment, all have failed. The only certainty that remains is that the process was riven with danger and involved substances of the most toxic nature. Corretti himself was just twenty-four at his death.*" That's right, isn't it?'

Lucca raised an eyebrow. 'I think that is exactly right. You have a gift – did you know?'

I reached over him for the cap. 'I've got a memory, if that's what you mean. Ma did too. She could read a page in a storybook just the once and then say it all back to us without looking and without changing a word. Joey could do it too.'

I dipped my head so that Lucca couldn't see my face. I pulled the cap down tight, pushing the knot of hair under the rim at the back. Just saying his name twisted a knife. I locked up another room in my mind.

'Listen again: "*The only certainty that remains is that the process was riven with danger and involved substances of the most toxic nature.*" What do you make of that?'

He went to the door to take a coat down from the hook on the back. He shook it and a cloud of dust and dried-out moth wings went up into the air. 'It is as I told you, this artist he must be a magician.'

'No! That's not what you said, is it?' My voice was sharp, but I wanted him to understand why I was so certain. 'You said he was an "*alchimista*" – an alchemist, a chemist. To make up that paint you'd need to know a lot about mixing up poisons and the like, wouldn't you?'

Lucca nodded. '*Si* – all paint is toxic to a degree, but Sicilian Gold was said to be deadly – you remember I told you Corretti's works were feared because they seemed to bring misfortune?'

'Exactly!' I spoke in a rush now. 'But there was nothing supernatural about that, was there? His works brought misfortune, all right, but that's because they were poisonous. Just breathing in the smell of them over enough time was probably enough to kill a person. And what would it do to a mind on the way? Just think, Lucca. Remember the gallery and the way it felt in there? If you were using that stuff, touching it and taking it into your lungs day after day, how would you be?'

'*Mio Dio!*' Lucca flung the coat onto the bed. 'You would go mad . . .?'

I nodded. 'And how would you get access to them poisons in the first place? Have you still got the drawings of me?'

'The ones sent to the theatre? Yes, I have them here. I . . . I took them with me.'

I knew he'd kept them. Something told me that even though Lucca was revolted by the man who drew those pictures, he was fascinated by him too. I wouldn't go as far as to say he admired him, but there was something there that drew him like a magnet. It was professional appreciation, I suppose.

'Can you find them for me? I need to show you something.'

Lucca knelt to pull a sheaf of papers from under the bed. The two drawings of me were on the top. He handed them over and I knelt down in Giacomo's breeches and flattened the papers out on the floor.

I poked a stray ringlet up under the cap and looked from one drawing to the other. I knew I was right.

'When I was practising again after the cage slipped, Lucca, something about these drawings kept going through my mind. Look at them carefully – what do you see?'

He crouched next to me and pulled the sketch of my head and shoulders towards him.

'You are right, they are both by the same hand, that's certain, but . . .' He paused and brought the side of his thumb to his lips.

'But something's changed from one to the other. I'm right, aren't I?'

Lucca nodded and reached over to smooth the second sheet, the drawing of me in the cage. His finger caught on a tear where the pen had slashed through the page in the word 'songbird'. The gash in the paper pulled wider.

'Thing is, when I was up there practising, something Madame Celeste told me about performing kept going through my mind. "No jerking about and no hard angles – they'll give you away, expose you for what you really are."'

Lucca looked up. His face was blank as I continued. 'Don't you see? The first drawing – it's all fine and delicate. It's a pretty thing.' I sat back uncomfortable at what I was going to say next. 'Lucca, I think the man who drew this . . . well, he admired me. You might even say he was quite taken with me. And there's the name too, Philomel – the nightingale – the bird who can't sing. I reckon he didn't much like my dirty song, but he liked me. He's made me look like a lady here – all quiet and demure. Untouched.'

Lucca looked at the paper and bit his thumb.

'But when he drew *this* picture . . .' I pushed the drawing of me in the cage towards him. 'He was angry. Look at the lines – see the way his pen rips through the paper? It's all hard, jagged angles. The first picture – it's like he was . . . caressing me, it's all delicate lines and little inky kisses. But in this one . . .'

'He wants to hurt you?'

I nodded. 'Or kill me. So what changed?'

Lucca nodded slowly. 'When he drew this . . .', he tapped the torn paper, '. . . he knew about you and James. You were tainted.'

'Not just that. He knew about James all right – but he also knew about me and *The Cinnabar Girls*. He knew I was on to him. When he drew this and left it for me he hated me, and he was frightened of me too. That's why he's tried to kill me – twice.'

'Twice?' Lucca's head shot up.

I didn't have time to explain. 'Look at the window. It's getting dark – we have to get going.'

I took the drawing from his hand and began to fold it again. I didn't want to see that girl in the cage or those spite-filled lines a moment longer than I had to. As I turned the sheet in on itself I noticed a faint stain running along the bottom edge – too regular and neat to be an ink splash or a thumb mark.

I held the paper up and looked closely. Then I took it to the window and flattened it against the glass. It was a watermark running through the grain of the paper. A lion's head and the name of a company: *Leo Rosen Imports*.

I was right.

*

There was a nice irony to the fact that my brother and me both took to the attire of the opposite sex so easily. 'Degenerate' – that's what Fitzy said it was, but I liked to see it as 'flexible'.

It was certainly useful. I remembered Lucca's advice from the last time I went about dressed as a boy and I was careful to walk broad and heavy.

This time it was easier. The clothes Lucca had chosen for me were the gear of a working lad, not a gent. There weren't so many buttons to fiddle with and under my coat there was a loose shirt open at the neck.

He had arranged a scarf around my shoulders and it hung down at the front of the coat, disguising my shape. Giacomo's old clothes were loose on me and that helped to keep my secret too.

We stepped out of his lodging and onto the cobbles. I could hear the river slapping against the stone steps at the end of the passage. The tide was in and the water was high tonight. Arching my neck, I took a deep breath to clear my head.

'Remember to keep your head down.' Lucca nudged me as a big man came towards us.

He wore the close black cap of a stevedore and his boot

steps echoed from the sooty walls. The last shift had ended a couple of hours back.

'If anyone recognises you on the streets word'll get back to Fitzpatrick and he'll send a party out to look for you.'

I pushed my chin into the folds of the scarf. If Fitzy went to The Lady and told her that I'd hadn't turned up at The Gaudy, what would she do? I thought about the note her Chinaman had left on the step of The Palace. Surely she knew then that I hadn't been up in that cage – and she'd given me time. Or was it a warning?

The number of death.

Lucca's low voice came again. 'You've already missed a night.'

I shook my head. I wasn't going to think about that, couldn't allow myself to.

'After tonight that won't make no odds. If I'm right, Fitzy can squeeze himself into my stockings and sequins and go hang himself up that cage every night from now on. I'm not going back to the halls. Once I've got Joey and we've . . .'

I stopped. I was going to say 'found them girls'. Tell truth, I wasn't sure what we might find at Sir Richard Verdin's warehouse. I only knew we had to go there.

After Lucca told me everything about Joey, Giacomo and Sir Richard Verdin it was like seeing a map of the Empire laid out in front of me for the first time and being able to give a name to nearly every little patch of pink, no matter how far away or how small and inconsequential it might be. I doubt that Queen Victoria herself could've made a better job of it.

But there were still a couple of places that troubled me.

Bodies – that was the word that kept coming at me now. If he'd killed the Cinnabar Girls, where were their bodies? God knows that grey old river can keep a secret, but there were six of them in that painting. You'd think at least one of them would have turned up by now, bobbing around in the scum like that cellarman from The Carnival?

And then there were the others – little Maggie, Polly Durkin and Peggy – a lot of women there to keep hidden away.

(It was important that I didn't allow myself to think they might be dead, 'specially not Peggy.)

We'd sat tight in Lucca's room all morning and all afternoon.

The paint, the lixir, The Artisans Gallery, Verdin, the warehouse, the pictures – I talked myself hoarse setting it out for him and then going through it again and again to be certain I hadn't left a loose end trailing that could pull it all apart.

I had the right man, didn't I? It couldn't be anyone else. The question was *why*? I circled that point until my head felt like a bucket of eels.

Eventually I slept for a short time when the afternoon sun slanted across the bed and brought some warmth into the attic.

When I woke Lucca was laying out clothing for me – plain, homespun pieces that belonged, I guessed, to Giacomo before he became tainted by Verdin.

'It's time, Fannella.'

*

We walked fast. Out on the river huge ships were riding four deep in shadow. I could hear the creaking of rope and smacking of canvas as wind caught at the rigging and rattled through the forest of masts. Waves slapped at the piers and sucked at the lowest stones of the slime-covered steps that led from a network of crooked alleyways down to the water. If you met a man coming up from the river at one of these black mouths of a night-time you didn't ask what he was doing or where he'd been.

We dodged into a side court and I lowered my head as a party of sailors lurched into view. Even in the gloom their white-blonde hair gleamed bright as the moon, marking them out as arrivals from the North as surely as the angular sound of their ragged drinking song.

Lucca pulled me close as they passed and we melted into a gap between the buildings. We both knew that when sailors have money in their pockets, drink in their bellies and the liberty of the shore, a sort of madness comes upon them.

This part of London was a labyrinth, but there was safety in the winding passages and shoulder-wide cuts, if you knew them by heart. I pushed the jacket collar higher and stepped back into the alley. Of a sudden one of Ma's stories came to me. Something about a monster hiding at the centre of a maze. I shivered.

The shipmen were gone now but these streets, the gateway to London, were never quiet. Wagons rumbled through arch-ways, chandlers stayed open for the tide, and gin shops of the lowest type – where punters stood upright to swill their guts through with Christ knows what – didn't take much notice of the hour. Tonight it seemed that every third doorway was the trade pitch of a bobtail. One of them pulled at my sleeve.

'It's a brisk night. Five ships in today. You gents up for a quick one?'

I pulled away and sank my chin deeper into the coarse fabric of Giacomo's jacket. Lucca quickened his step.

She called after us. 'I'll do you both for a penny.'

We walked on in silence trying not to draw attention to ourselves. The oversized boots rubbed my skin through the layers of wool. The blisters on my feet were opening again. The night was thick with the scent of trade. Every step brought a sharp new tang – coffee, spice, rum, sweat, tar, tobacco, stale wine and the meaty, fatty smell of wool – if you could bottle the air of the docks you could carry the world in your pocket. Old labourers boasted you could blindfold a regular, set him down on any corner and he could tell you exactly where he was from a single lungful.

I took in a deep breath now. Coal and smoke. We were getting close. I could hear machinery whirring too.

Limehouse Basin never rested – smaller boats were still built here, coal barges queued in the cuts night and day and the engine that drove all the lifting gear wheezed and bellowed round the clock. I could feel it now, throbbing like a great beating heart through the soles of my feet on the cobbles.

'There is just one thing that worries me.' Lucca's hushed voice made the air steam around him as we walked.

'Just the one?' I tried to make light of it.

He sighed. 'When we get there. If you are right about this. What are we going to do?'

I didn't answer. Lucca had me there. I wasn't sure of that myself. I just trusted my instinct that I'd know.

There weren't many lamps down by the basin entrance where narrow buildings huddled close together. With their black arched windows and load doors gaping high above the street they looked like old women keening at a graveside.

Platforms jutted out over the passage almost touching across the gap in some parts. During the day they blocked out the light, but tonight they gave the darkness substance – like you could hold out your hand and feel it slipping through your fingers.

I reached out to the right, rested my hand on the bricks and stepped forward, letting the wall guide me. 'This way, Lucca, keep close.'

'Do you know which side?'

'No, but once we get out into the open we'll be able to read the numbers.'

The passage broadened out at the end and we found ourselves on the south side of the basin. The smooth black water at its centre reflected the viaduct that cut above the northern edge.

Over to the left there were lights and people moving about. Heavy lifting gear clanked and groaned as men scurried like ants over mounds of coal. Rows of open barges lining the edge of the basin were filled with more glittering black piles of the stuff.

We shrank back against the walls, careful not to be seen. I looked up. Flaking paint letters over a loading door above told me that the premises of *The Samuel Carter Coal Company* occupied numbers 34 to 36. Just to the right the Jeffries family (father and son, according to their sign) were at number 33.

'This way.' I pointed right and we began to edge our way around the basin. A train screeched across the viaduct, filling the air with steam, as we reached the double wooden doors of Warehouse 21.

'Run, Lucca!' We took advantage of the smoky cover and the noise and pelted round the stone wharfside. I looked up again.

'Number 2 – we've gone too far.'

Lucca peered up, uncertain. 'But the next one back is 11, Kitty.'

'That can't be right.'

The warehouse to my left, a squat sturdy affair, was definitely number 2 – *Millett & Co.* – but, as Lucca said, the next warehouse along to the right was a tall building clearly marked as number 11 – *Francis, Kenyon & Beedy*.

'Sam said Verdin had a lease on a warehouse at Skinners Yard, 3 to 10, Limehouse Basin. In that case, where is it?'

I scanned the flat brick fronts of the buildings. One thing was clear – this section was older and not as well used as the southern edge.

I took a step back so that the water was just behind me and counted the warehouses again from the end – one, two, eleven, twelve . . .

That was when I noticed it. Attached to a wall about ten foot away to the left there was a wide enamelled sign all rusted over with trailing weeds poking through it. I couldn't read the words from here, but I could see the arrow running along the bottom.

I motioned for Lucca to follow me.

I pulled away the weeds and rubbed at the layer of green

slime that covered the metal. The sign creaked and dipped sharply to the left as a rusted bolt worked its way out of the wall and rattled down onto the stones. It didn't matter, no one could hear us over here – not with the sound of all that machinery hammering away – and I very much doubted they could see us in this shadowy corner.

I pushed the sign straight as Lucca rubbed with an old bit of cloth revealing three words. *Leo Rosen Imports*. There was a picture of a lion's head too – just the same as on that watermark.

'That's it, Lucca! This is the one we want. Sam said Verdin leased it from someone called Rosen. So where is it?'

Lucca squinted doubtfully in the direction the arrow once pointed.

'It must be down there.' He nodded to a crack between the first two of the warehouses.

I stared at the black slit between the walls. It didn't look like a passageway to me, more like a place where a man caught short would take a piss.

'I'll go first, Fannella. Stay just behind me.'

Lucca stepped into the gap and I followed. The air was rank and at the fifth step I felt something soft underfoot. Giacomo's boot sank into something that made a wet sucking noise when I pulled free. I gagged and brought my hand to cover my nose and mouth as the stench of decay rolled up.

'It was a dead rat – a big one. I did that too.' Lucca's low voice came from just ahead. There was a sudden yellow flare as he struck a single Lucifer. He held it up and stared back at me, the scarred side of his face hidden in shadow. He turned and carried on, holding the match high. We were in

302

a passageway about a foot and a half wide. Sheer black walls reared up on either side.

The Lucifer fizzled and died.

'Don't look down.' Lucca's voice was steady and reassuring. 'There are all manner of things at our feet here. Come. It doesn't go on much further. There's a sort of corner here and beyond that I can see – well, not light exactly, but the dark seems to be thinner.'

We came out into a little courtyard of buildings that mostly looked like shrunken versions of the warehouses round the basin. Overhead, the moon – half of it – came out from behind a rag of cloud and I could see quite plain. There were buildings lined up on either side of the yard and a single taller building at the far end. There was a stone well in the middle of the cobbles with a broken wooden cover balanced over the opening.

These buildings were older than the ones around the basin and they were derelict. The ripe smell of damp, rotting wood, mould and dead vermin filled the space. Most of the doors hung open on rusted hinges and broken glass from the lower windows crusted the stones. It glittered in the moonlight. A couple of the loading platforms high above were missing most of their boards, and several of the wide double doors, where once, a long time ago I reckoned, goods had been hauled up from the yard and taken into store, had been crudely barred over with slats of wood.

I doubted anyone had done business at Skinners Yard for a long time, not even a working girl looking for a quiet corner to trade her glove.

Only the tall, narrow building at the end seemed to be

complete. I noted the ropes and pulleys dangling from the solid platform four levels up and the fact that the ground floor windows were still glazed.

There was a long sign painted direct on the bricks running down the whole left side of the warehouse too. The writing was slanted and in the old-fashioned style. In places it had worn away, but not so as you couldn't read it: *Leo Rosen Imports. Fancy Goods and Oriental Silks. Est. 1834.*

For a moment I froze. My hair prickled beneath Giacomo's old cloth cap, something cold slithered down my spine and I had to force myself to breathe. It wasn't the smell in that closed-up space that choked me. No, it was the thought that I'd found them at last.

We'd found them. If they were anywhere in London, the Cinnabar Girls – Peggy, Maggie, Alice and the others – were here. I could feel it.

Chapter Thirty

'Have you gone mad?'

Lucca hissed at me as we crouched behind the well. I was taking Giacomo's boots off.

'No, and you'd better do this too if you're coming in there with me. The sound of these boots could wake the dead.' I thought of Peggy and I bit my tongue.

For some reason we were both whispering, even though the only signs of life in that God-forsaken yard were the rats turning over the bloated bodies of long-dead pigeons in the corners. It must have been the thickness of the walls around us, but you couldn't hear the machinery out on the basin here.

I winced as I pulled off the left boot. Blood from my blisters was already beginning to seep through the wool, all three layers of it.

'But there is glass everywhere – and worse.' Lucca swore under his breath, yet he bent forward to remove his own boots.

'How are we going to get in, Fannella?'

I pointed at the rope pulley hanging from the loading platform high on the wall.

'Up there and in through that opening on the right side – second floor. Easy.'

'Easy for you, maybe, but you forget I have not had the benefit of Madame Celeste's training.'

Lucca's face was hidden by his hair as he untied his left boot.

'And I cannot climb a rope.'

'You won't have to. I'll get in and make my way down to let you in. There must be a door down here out to the yard.' I scanned the building uncertainly. The only opening onto the courtyard side of the building appeared to be the doors of the loading platform high above us.

Then I saw a way. 'Look! Over there to the left, just by that spar of wood leaning against the wall. There's a row of wooden shutters half set into the stones leading to the vaults under the warehouse. If I can get in up there I'll make my way down to that level and let you in. You can slide through.'

The half-circular openings along the base of the wall looked like a row of eyes staring at us.

Lucca bit the side of his thumb. 'What are you expecting to find in there?'

Bring me more. Lady Ginger's voice came sharp into my head. But the old bitch hadn't even opened her door to me when I came to her with *more*.

I looked up at the building behind us. If he really was using it as his 'studio', Christ knows what we'd find. It would be *more* all right, but would it be enough?

I clenched my fists. 'I don't know exactly, Lucca, and that's the honest truth. Evidence, I suppose – maybe something more . . .'

I felt my guts coil into a knot as The Lady's own word sprang from my lips. Admit it to yourself, girl, I thought.

306

You're expecting to find Peggy's body in there, her and them others too.

I busied myself with the other boot, not wanting Lucca to see my guilty face.

'We should just go to the police and end this now. Let them find . . .' Lucca paused, obviously thinking the same as me and not wanting to share it.

I stared at him. 'And what about Joey? I can't bring the rozzers down on Paradise or Lady Ginger, can I? This has gone too far for that. And Verdin would only buy them off, like he's bought everyone he's ever come into contact with. Think about Giacomo, Lucca. Do it for him. You still love him, don't you?'

Lucca took a deep breath and felt into the folds of his coat. 'I brought this. Take it with you.'

I looked at the little ivory-handled gun in his hand with horror.

'No!'

I didn't want to think where he'd got something like that, but the thought came to me that I knew exactly who he might want to use it on. Like I always said, Lucca kept more secrets than one of his Roman father 'fessors. I was beginning to suspect I only knew the half of them.

'I'm not taking that. You keep it.'

He tried to press it into my hands, but I held them behind my back. 'No. It's not for me.' I'm not sure why, but I was definite on that. I didn't even want to touch it.

'Then take these, at least.' He handed me the box of Lucifers. 'It will be dark in there. You'll need them.' I nodded and stuffed the little box into the pocket of the jacket.

'I'm going up there now,' I whispered, pointing at the rope dangling in front of the painted sign. 'Wait for me over there. I'll try to get that half-shutter open and then we'll go through the building together.'

*

Getting inside was easy.

The ropes hanging down from the platform were new and strong. Now I was close to, I realised Rosen's warehouse wasn't the forgotten shell it presented to a casual view. The gear connecting the ropes was well oiled – which is why I didn't make a racket as I climbed – and some of the platform boards overhead had been replaced.

When I got to the opening I'd pointed out to Lucca I shifted my weight and swung forward catching the brick sill with my foot.

The gap was tall and thin and not glazed over and when I managed to pull myself inside I realised why. It led direct to a wooden staircase. The opening was the only source of light and air.

A warehouse owner wouldn't spend a penny to keep his workers warm, but he'd like them to breathe, 'specially given the fumes coming off some of them goods.

Joey had taken me with him to a skin house once when they were unloading a cargo of hide. I'll never forget the stench of it, worse than a sewer it was. All around us were bins full of horn sorted for shape. Some of them were black and twisted, others were creamy white – ivory, I guessed. The sour smell coming off the horn bins was worse than the hide.

It got into your nose and worked its way down into your throat so that everything you put in your mouth for hours afterwards tasted of death.

I felt into the pocket for the box of Lucifers and struck one against the wall.

The wooden stairs were broad and strong. Like the ropes and pulleys outside they were good, none broken or missing as far as I could tell.

The match sputtered and died. I shook the box in my pocket – plenty there. I was about to strike another when I noticed that I could make out the outlines of the steps below. The opening allowed a gash of faint grey moonlight to fall across the twisting stairwell.

I stood there for a moment allowing my eyes to grow accustomed and then I began to go down, keeping one hand on the wall to guide me. At every ninth step the stairs turned and led to another level below.

It got colder as I went down. After three or four turns the air changed. The tarry wood and sawdust smell of the stairs faded and now there was a metallic, bitter scent in the air.

It was pitch black. The moonlight couldn't reach this level so I struck up another of Lucca's matches and held it high. I was in the store vaults beneath the warehouse.

The floor beneath my feet was stone and just ahead of me a row of great brick arches leaned into the shadows. I counted three of them, but I knew that old storage cellars like these often followed a different plan to the buildings above them. Some of the vaults under the docks stretched for miles. People said there were passages too where it was easy to move your gear out from under the eye of the Customs men.

The match burned down to my fingers and I dropped it. By my reckoning, the row of half-moon windows where Lucca would be waiting outside should be just behind me to the right. I felt my way back to the steps and struck up another match. There was nothing – just a blank wall of greasy brick. I must have gone down too far. The match fizzled out in my fingers.

I sat on the lowest step, dipped into the pocket again and fumbled with the box, but just as I was about to strike I realised that there was another light down there with me.

I stood up and took a step forward; perhaps it was a trick of the mind or an optical illusion like one of Swami Jonah's magic tricks?

The light disappeared, but then it came again when I moved a couple of steps back to the right. There *was* a faint light far across the cellar – when I moved, the curved stone pillars blocked it from view.

I dodged behind a span of arches and carefully followed their line across the cellar, slipping from one black space to another until the light was clear ahead. It came from a partly open door – a great wide metal thing covered with studs and straps. It put me in mind of the box in the wall in Fitzy's office where he stashes the takings of an evening.

The sour smell was stronger here and there was something else: the air was thick with a sickly sweetness. It wasn't the fragrance of flowers, nor even like Lady Ginger's opium smoke; it was a harsh, unnatural scent and I'd known it before – that night in St Paul's.

I froze. Was he down here now?

I dodged under an arch and flattened myself against the

ice-cold bricks. You should go back now, girl, I told myself, you can't do this alone. You need Lucca . . . and his gun.

I took a deep breath but that stink coiled into my lungs and made me want to gag. I heard a scrabbling sound at my feet and looked down to see a rat staring up at me. The sheeny black creature blinked, snuffled at my foot and skittered away across the stones when I kicked out. It watched me warily for a moment, then it pressed its body close to the wall and slunk to the open door. I watched in disgust as its thick, grey, hairless tail slipped around the metal and disappeared.

'Oh Jesus! Another one. Get it away from me, please.'

I heard a muffled scraping as if something was dragged across the floor.

'No! Please!'

'It's no good, I can't move, Peggy. Keep still and it might . . .'

There was a sharp scream.

Without thinking, I ran forward and pushed the door further open to reveal a long, narrow chamber with a barrel ceiling and another studded, barred door at the far end. The walls were plastered and whitewashed over. An oil lamp placed on the stones about halfway down cast a flickering circle of light across the three kneeling women whose hands were tied above their heads and roped to great metal hoops in the walls. Their bodices gaped open and their skirts were soiled and ripped. Even in the gloom I could see the scratches and bruises on their skin.

But they were alive – all of them.

I stepped into the circle of light. The women moaned and shrank back against the walls, lowering their heads.

'Please, not now. Not again.' The cracked voice came from a woman behind me.

I turned and found myself looking down at Peggy. Her lovely thick hair was matted into a filthy knot and there were long scratches down her arms. The cord at her wrists had cut into her flesh and the wounds were crusted and weeping.

'Peggy!' I fell to my knees and gently lifted her head.

Her eyes were sunk so deep into their sockets that they were almost closed over and her bottom lip was split and swollen.

She didn't look at me, but she whispered the words, 'Don't. Please, sir.'

'Oh Peggy.' My eyes filled with tears. 'I'm not him.'

I ripped Giacomo's hat off and pulled my hair free. 'Look. You *know* me – I'm Kitty.'

Peggy slowly raised her eyes to mine. At first she didn't seem able to focus. Her blank eyes rolled across my face as if trying to find something there she recognised.

After a moment, she whispered, 'Kitty? Is that really you? Oh thank God. Thank God.'

*

The ropes binding the women at their wrists were tied so firmly that I had to burn them with Lucca's matches to make them break. When I'd finished on Polly Durkin she slumped onto the stone floor and kept repeating the name of her boy, Michael, over and over.

'It's all right, Polly.' I crouched next to her and stroked her hair, knowing full well that it was not all right in this stinking pit. 'You'll see him again, soon. I promise. But we have to get you out of here first. All of us, we've got to go.'

I'd never seen the other girl before. I reckoned she was about the same age as me, maybe a year or so younger. She was a redhead with that fine chalk-white skin that bruises like a peach. She wasn't as badly hurt as the other two – so far as I could tell. There was a welt on her shoulder and blood at her wrists where the rope bit too deep, but he'd left her face alone.

The veins in the skinny arms stretched above her head showed blue as I burned the rope.

She winced when the flame licked too close.

'What's your name?' I tried to distract her.

'Anna. Anna March.' She flinched as I struck a new Lucifer. I knew that name – Tally March was a comic singer at The Carnival.

'You Tally's girl?'

She nodded and tears came into her eyes.

'How long have you been here, Anna?'

'I . . . I'm not sure. Not long . . . not as long as the others.' She looked across at Peggy and I saw a tremor go through her.

'There's no daylight, see. Just the lamp and he lets that go out sometimes, so we're left in the dark.'

'When was he last here?'

Anna shook her head. 'I don't know. When he comes to take one of us he gives us all something to drink and then it's like everything in your head goes wrong. He could have been here a day ago or . . .'

The rope burned through and Anna fell forward. Like the

others she cried aloud as she moved her arms again and the blood came rushing back, but she was more alert.

'Anna, listen. I need you to help me. We have to get out of here before he comes back, but Peggy's in a bad way and Pol's not much better.'

Anna rose stiffly to her feet. She pulled the ripped material of her dress together at the neck, folded her arms around her and rubbed her aching muscles.

'You're Kitty Peck, aren't you? Mum says you're a wonder. The bravest thing she's seen.'

'Most foolish, more like. Do you think you can let Pol lean on you?'

Anna nodded.

'Peggy.' I ran over to where she sat against the wall and gripped her hand. 'We're getting out. You've got to try to stand. Can you do that?'

Peggy pushed herself up from the stones, held my arm and hauled herself up. I felt her grip tighten and I knew she was in agony. I reached down for the oil lamp.

'Anna, can you take Pol now?' The pale girl slipped down beside Polly Durkin and whispered. Polly nodded and staggered to her feet. Anna put her arm around her shoulders and looked across at me. 'Where are we going?'

*

The lamp made things easier.

Me and Peggy went first and Anna and Polly stuck close behind. It was slow going, but as we went back across the cellar Peggy became more herself with every step. I imagined she'd given up hope in that prison and now every yard away from it put a little piece of her spirit back.

The stairs were the hardest bit. Polly's leg was bad and climbing the wooden steps made her cry out loud.

We got Peggy up first and then me and Anna went back.

As we supported Polly up the two flights, one of us on either side of her, I hoped to God that Lucca was still waiting.

I was right about the half-moon windows. At the top of the next flight of steps the lamp showed a row of them set into the wall at head height. They were shuttered from the inside but not glazed. If you removed the lock bar you could open them out to the yard.

I placed the lamp on the boards and looked around. We'd need to stand on something to get out that way. Against the wall there was a bench and an old crate. The faded letters *OSEN4* on the side suggested that a long time ago the crate had been packed with Rosen's goods.

I pushed it over to the first half-moon window, clambered on top and freed the lock bar, pushing the shutters outward.

'Lucca.' I called his name softly and then again when there was no answer.

'Lucca, you there?'

Nothing. I leaned forward and scanned the yard. 'Lucca!' This time there was a movement in a corner but it was only a mangy old cat poking around for rats. I looked down at the women standing around the crate.

'He came with you then?' Peggy tried to smile despite her broken lip.

I nodded. 'He was supposed to be waiting here for me.' I looked out into the shadowy yard again. It was deserted.

I couldn't worry about that now.

'Polly – you first. Me and Anna can help you through.'

I hauled Polly onto the crate and together we pushed her up and out through the window onto the stones.

'You next, Anna. I can push you through and then you can help pull Peggy out into the yard after that if I support her from below.'

Anna nodded and pulled herself up. I pushed her from below as she struggled to clear the last inches.

'Just you and me now, Peg.' I tried to smile at her.

Peggy shook her head. I couldn't see her face properly in the shadow as she spoke. 'The others, Kitty. They're still there. Alice, Martha, Jenny, Maggie – all of them. They're in the other room.'

At first I didn't understand what she was saying. 'They're all alive – the Cinnabar Girls?'

Peggy didn't answer. She had no idea about that picture.

I started again. 'All them girls who went missing from Paradise – you're saying they're still here?'

She nodded and looked back down the stairs. 'Maggie – she was here when he brought me. Only fourteen. Like Alice.'

The thought of that faded scrap of a thing came to me then. I remembered the last time I saw her trying to dodge round the tables in The Gaudy while I watched her from the cage.

'And she's still in that room – the one beyond the place I found you?'

Peggy nodded.

'I'm going back.'

'No!' Peggy gripped my hand. 'You can't, Kitty. It won't make no difference, not now.'

I wasn't listening properly as I shook her off. I'd failed Alice, but if I could still save Maggie . . .

All that time I'd been up in that cage lapping up attention like a kitten in a whorehouse and imagining myself to be a proper little victim when Maggie and all the others had been here.

I owed little Alice Caxton that at the very least.

'Listen, Peggy.' I pulled her up onto the crate and turned her face towards me. 'I know you're in a bad way, but when you are out in that yard you're going to run. I want you to run through the gap in the wall opposite and out onto the basin – all three of you. Run without stopping. Go to The Gaudy, find your Dan and get him to take you to The Lady. Tell her everything you know about this place, every single thing you can remember happening to you here.'

Peggy shrank back. 'Not Lady Ginger. I couldn't go there.'

I took both her hands in mine.

'You can, Peggy, and you must. I won't be far behind. And this is important: you must tell her that I've got *more*, just like she wanted.'

Chapter Thirty-one

The long stone room where I'd found Peggy and the others reeked of piss and worse. I hadn't taken it all in before, but I shuddered now when I went back and saw the way they'd been kept. You wouldn't treat an animal like that.

I raised the oil lamp so it threw more light around the walls. There were marks on the plaster where Peggy, Anna and Polly had been bound to the rings above their heads and there were other stains – dirty ghosts of women who'd been there before them.

The door at the far end of the room was metal like the door behind me. It was barred across by a single band held in place by brackets on either side. I went towards it and set the lamp on the stones. I tightened my fists. Did I really want to see this? I thought about Maggie again. I had to know.

I reached for the bar. My fingers tingled, I could feel my hair crackle and my ears rang. Lady Ginger's dice tumbled into my mind, the little red squares rolling over and over – every side of them showing the number of death.

Warehouse number 4, Skinners Yard.

'My congratulations, Miss Peck, on yet another brilliant performance.'

Edward Chaston's voice was soft and pleasant.

I didn't turn as the sound of his footsteps came closer.

'Allow me to help you with that.'

I felt his grip on my shoulder.

Reaching across with his other hand, he lifted the metal bar and propped it against the wall. His cufflinks glinted in the light as he pushed the door and it swung inward, a cold wave of decay and that peculiar, sweet-metallic scent came rushing from the black hole beyond.

Now I knew what it was. When we laid out Nanny Peck before sending her 'home' to Ireland to be buried in her village, I'd complained to Joey and Ma that the funeries had painted her face wrong and doused her with a lousy cologne. Joey told me what it was and why they'd used it.

Embalming fluid– that's what Edward Chaston smelt of.

'Do you want to see them?'

I could feel his breath on the back of my neck but still I didn't turn to look at him. Every muscle in my body felt as if it was aflame. The room shrank around me as I tried to concentrate.

Draw it all in, girl, feed on it and make it work for you. The Fear is your greatest ally, Kitty, if only you knew it. I'd never needed Madame Celeste and her 'state of perfection' more keenly.

'Then again, perhaps not?'

He was all reason and smooth politeness, his voice comforting as a fox fur trim as he continued. 'Some of my earlier pieces are now quite disappointing, to be frank. They present a sorry sight. But I am in the process of perfecting my art.'

He reached around me, caught at a leather loop set into the metal and pulled the door shut again. It closed with a heavy sigh that whispered off the stones.

'As I am sure you already know, clever little Miss Peck,

this used to be my father's fur store. The cool, even temperatures here are ideal. To preserve animal hide you need a cold, dry place and this is most certainly that. My intention was to keep them all here – my school of silent models – and then to arrange them in a variety of compositions. I apologise for the scent, but it is most necessary. I have tried a number of fixatives. I found cavity solution to be very successful, but, of course, the fumes tend to attach . . .'

He paused for a moment. 'Do you know, Miss Peck, it is extraordinary but the younger the body the faster the rate of decay.'

Alice and Maggie. Christ! What had this madman done to them?

'Well, no matter. It has been an interesting experiment – we learn through our mistakes, don't we? For my latest work live models have proved more . . . malleable. Look at me, Kitty, when I speak to you. It is most impolite to ignore a gentleman.'

He whirled me about. Edward Chaston's clear blue eyes glittered in the lamplight.

I'd thought he had a kind face, the face of someone with a ready laugh and an easy nature. When I'd first known it was him that was the one thing that kept coming back at me to make me doubt. Sir Richard Verdin – now, he had the face for a murderer – but Edward Chaston, he looked like a scrub-cheeked choirboy all grown up.

I stared direct at him. In the lamplight the crinkled skin around his eyes was pitted and heavily lined. Deep grooves ran from the side of his nose to his mouth. When he smiled at me now he looked like one of them half-size marionettes from Signor Malinetti's act. They were supposed to be a comic turn, but, tell truth, I always found their slack mouths and button-black eyes most unsettling. I didn't like to come across them hanging up on their own out back when I was clearing up of an evening.

'A pity.' Chaston sighed and brushed a ringlet away from my face. 'And so beautiful too, until you speak . . . or sing. I hoped you might be different, Kitty, but you are just like the other filthy bitches from the halls. James tested that for me. You lost me a guinea, did you hear?'

His fingers followed the line of my cheek and caressed my neck. I shuddered, but I didn't take my eyes from his and I couldn't stop my tongue.

'And I thought you just said you was a gentleman, Mr Chaston.'

He grinned, showing a neat row of little teeth that struck me as too dainty for a man. 'Doctor Chaston, please, or soon to be anyway. I have many interests, Miss Peck – many talents. I am more gifted in every way imaginable than that idiot James.' His voice suddenly became hard. 'But you liked him, didn't you?'

I didn't answer as Edward's clammy hand crept into the neck of Giacomo's shirt. 'Still, I suppose I must be grateful that you threw yourself at him. The drug I supplied loosened your tongue as well as your morals, did it not? James's account of your . . . congress was most enlightening, in so many ways.'

He brought his hand up again and tipped back my chin. I flinched, but it wasn't his touch. Not only that, leastways. It was the sight of his hand – all flaked and scaled over. The big gold ring on his smallest finger was loose and moved as he stroked my cheek.

I saw Lucca's book again, the words clear in my head like the page was open in front of me. *The only certainty that remains is that the process was riven with danger and involved substances of the most toxic nature. Corretti himself was just twenty-four at his death. Fellow artist Brancazzo wrote that his body had grown old before its time.*

Just like Edward's.

His blue eyes narrowed and the dry skin puckered around them. There was no humour there now.

'Just when I was on the brink of my greatest artistic triumph I will have to start over again. You set my birds free, Kitty. I cannot forgive that.'

'Forgive, *Doctor* Chaston?' I heard myself laugh. 'That's a fine word coming from you, isn't it? There was I thinking a doctor saved lives. Call yourself a man of many talents, do you? Well, let me tell you what I call you – a murderer.'

He slapped my face and I felt the ring cut into my cheek. I didn't budge – I didn't want to give him the satisfaction of seeing my fear. Instead I spat up at his face, catching him on the chin. Then the words came tumbling. I couldn't stop them and now I didn't care.

'And your picture, *The Cinnabar Girls*, do you want to know what I really thought of that? I'm going to tell you anyway. I thought it was a pile of horse shit – an evil, stinking smear of rot and misery. All them fine gentlemen at The Artisans – they weren't looking at the "*ambition*", they were buying flesh like a punter pawing at a backstreet doll. Only they cleaned it up for themselves and called it artistic appreciation to make it nice, make it legal. But that's what you people do, isn't it? You buy your morals by the yard. Well, don't fool yourself on that score. Meat – that's all they came for and that's all they saw – not what you'd really done. You think you're so clever with your chemicals and your fucking Sicilian Gold, but what does it all amount to? Nothing. And I'll tell you why, shall I? A real artist needs to create, not destroy. A real artist deals in life, not death. A true artist has a heart – has a *soul*. But you're barren. There is nothing living inside you but hate.'

When I stopped he didn't move and he didn't say a word, he just stared at me. Then he wiped the spittle from his chin and looked down at his glistening palm where the bubbled flecks of saliva caught the lamplight. He balled his fist up tight and began to laugh.

'Bravo, Miss Peck – a passionate recitation. What a fiery actress you would have made. I think tragedy would have been your forte. And I must thank you for your artistic . . . insight. The thought that a girl like you would be familiar with the work of Corretti. I confess I am astounded.'

Chaston clapped slowly like punters do in the halls when they're tired of an act.

'But how would you know about Sicilian Gold?' He cocked his head to one side. 'Ah, I have it – your friend. The one with the ruined face. Mr Fratelli. The art-lover.' The last two words were mocking.

He lunged forward and grabbed my arm. I tried to pull away but he was surprisingly strong, forcing me back against the wall next to the door. He moved his hands to my throat and tightened his grip so that I couldn't breathe. I kicked out but he held his body rigid against mine, flattening me to the wall.

'I don't know how you found me here, little Philomel, but I do know that it will be the place where you sing your last song.'

Reaching into his coat he produced a syringe and jabbed it quickly and viciously through the coarse material of Giacomo's jacket into my shoulder. I yelped at the sudden pain.

Chaston stepped back. 'Don't fight it, Kitty. It will only hurt more.' I tried to scream but the room was already fading around me. As I sank down the wall, his voice seemed to come from the end of a tunnel. 'I didn't use enough to kill you here. That will come later.'

*

When I moved it was as if my head was full of fireworks. Great blooms of pain exploded behind my eyes and shot my vision with coloured sparks that distorted and fractured the room.

I was laying on my side on a pile of rags. My hands were tied behind me. The air smelt like the workshop at The Gaudy. It was thick with sawdust, paint and turps, and I would almost have found it a comfort if it hadn't been all mingled up with that other stronger scent, the one that meant bodies and decay.

Gradually my sight began to clear. I was in another part of the warehouse now. From the tall, double-shuttered opening over to my right and the network of beams overhead I guessed I was on the top floor where the loading platform overhung the yard below.

There were oil lamps and candles placed on work benches

by the wall and on the floor. In the centre of the room, propped against two thick wooden pillars, there was a huge rectangle half shrouded with grey cloth.

Edward Chaston's new work was half the size of *The Cinnabar Girls*, but if the broad strip of sickly, transparent gold clearly visible along the entire length of the lower edge was anything to go by, he'd perfected his mastery of Sicilian Gold.

The paint reflected the gleam of the candles on the floor and seemed to shiver with an unnatural light of its own. As I looked, there seemed to be movement in the pigment as if there was something coiling in its depths. I wanted to keep looking at that strip of gold until I was lost in the paint. I'd been wrong earlier; Edward Chaston had created something after all – but the fact that it was almost alive was repulsive.

The boards behind me creaked.

'Awake so quickly? Good. I wasn't sure how long that would last. When it is administered directly the dosage can be difficult to calculate. It is all a question of scale. I am grateful that you are lighter than most of your friends.'

Chaston crouched down next to me. He took a handful of my hair and yanked my head back. 'The dark one? Peggy, was that her name? She was a dead weight. I made a mistake early on in making her one of the central figures. I began to dread the days when I needed her up here. But the red girl was promising.' He pulled my hair up tight and I cried out. 'I had plans for her, but you ruined that.'

He stood abruptly and rubbed his hands together. He'd taken off his coat and rolled back his shirt sleeves. The skin of his arms was raw and crackled over and he scratched at crusted patches of scales at his wrists and elbows. 'We don't have much time. I should begin.'

He walked over to a bench, took up a sheaf of papers and leafed through them, frowning occasionally, tossing some to the floor and carefully placing others back on the pile.

'Tell me, Kitty, how familiar are you with the work of Corretti?'

Even if I'd wanted to I couldn't answer him. My tongue felt like a lead weight in my mouth. Chaston continued brightly as if he was explaining an effective cough remedy to a mother whose baby had a bout of the croup. 'Little is known of him as a man and as none of his paintings survive it is difficult to judge his work. But his contemporaries spoke of him with awe. They feared him and they feared his genius. They thought his Sicilian Gold was the work of a devil. It was lost until I found a way to create it again – and it is beautiful.'

He glanced at the shrouded canvas and smiled.

'Corretti's greatest work was said to be *Persephone in the Fields*. I have chosen to paint a companion piece as an act of homage. *The Rites of Eleusis* is a bolder, more direct work than *The Cinnabar Girls*, as you will see.'

He held two sheets of paper in front of him and looked from one to the other, holding his head on one side and squinting. The lines around his eyes folded into deep channels.

'In myth Persephone was the daughter of Demeter, goddess of the earth. When Persephone was compelled to spend part of each year in the world of the dead as the bride of Hades, her mother's grief was so terrible that the earth mourned with her. When Persephone rose from the underworld again, the sun returned and crops grew once more. In ancient times, the Eleusinian Mysteries were performed each year to ensure the return of Persephone. They were rites of birth, death and sacrifice.'

He dropped another one of the papers to the boards and looked from the remaining sheet in his hands to me.

'This figure, the supplicant, for you, I think. I'll work straight onto the canvas tonight. They'll have to be careful when they move it, the paint will be fresh.' He frowned and looked around. 'My father will arrange for everything to be cleared as he has arranged for so much else. Power is a wonderful thing, Kitty.'

My father will arrange. It was the second time he'd referred to his father, but hadn't James said Edward's parents were dead?

Chaston smiled coldly. 'Did you imagine that stupid little Jamie might be a rich man one day, Kitty? Is that why you wanted him?'

He set the paper down on the bench and walked back towards me. 'My guardian, Sir Richard Verdin, has been like a father to me and in return I am his dutiful son. I keep his secrets and he keeps mine. Together we are formidable. He realised many years ago what James is. The allowance will enable James to ruin himself, to show himself for what he really is – my father has given him a rope by which to hang himself.'

Chaston crouched in front of me. 'I am the Verdin heir, Kitty, and I will inherit so much.'

They say that madness is carried in the blood, don't they? That it can be handed down from one generation to another in the way of freckled cheeks, curled hair, crooked teeth or an over-large nose. Edward Chaston taught me an important thing that day, and I often like to think of it now. It's not blood that counts, it's nurture. When you raise a child, you shape it like a bit of clay on a potter's wheel. Every touch of your fingers, every ridge, every groove, every print becomes a part of the finished piece.

Sir Richard Verdin had moulded a child in his own image – whatever that boy saw as he grew to manhood in that bastard's house, it warped him, twisted him out of human shape and made him wrong. It made him the monster standing in front of me now.

Chaston glanced at the canvas and then back at me. 'My father is an art-lover too, did you know that?' He began to laugh quietly as if at some private joke.

'He is a true connoisseur, although it must be said our tastes . . . differ. Nevertheless, he has taught me much; he has taught me to appreciate the delicate balance between pleasure and pain and he has taught me that the only thing that truly matters is the moment. There is no heaven or hell, Kitty – no Hades.' He looked over at the painting again. 'There is only appetite.'

He knelt and began to rub something against the side of his boot. I could hear the scrape of metal against the leather as he continued.

'To live without conscience is a liberation. Whether in the public domain or in private, it frees you from the petty morality of the masses. It is the precise quality of omission you need to run a business empire – as, one day, I will. My father taught me this lesson well and now he encourages me to develop my own enthusiasms, to seek my own liberation.'

He stood, took a step towards me and grinned, showing those dainty white teeth again. The room swam, but now I could see he was fingering the stubby blade of a knife.

'Stand up.'

I didn't move.

'I said stand.' Chaston took a knot of my hair again and pulled. The room billowed as I struggled to rise. I managed to kneel but the drug he'd punched into my shoulder had weakened me. There was no fight left now, just a flickering hope that whatever he might be about to do to me, it would be over quickly.

'Prepare yourself, Miss Peck—'

An odd hollow bumping sound came from somewhere behind him and to the left. Chaston paused as a large glass jar rolled from the shadows beyond the painting. It was unstoppered and as it circled slowly over the boards it left a trail of glistening gold. It came to a halt against the lower edge of the picture and more liquid pumped out, pooling around it.

Chaston dropped me and ran to the bottle. He set it upright and tried to scoop the spilled liquid up in his hands, forcing it back into the neck. He gasped as he did so, as if it burned his skin. He knelt in front of the painting, scrabbling in the liquid, and his hands were coated in gold to the wrist.

The air was filled with bitter fumes. My eyes began to water and I started to cough. There was a huge crash and the sound of splintering glass as another bottle crashed onto the boards in front of the painting.

Chaston looked up in confusion and then at the broken bottle that had missed his head by inches. A great slick pool of glistening gilt spread around him now like the cloak of a pantomime prince.

And then the fire began.

It happened so fast. The edge caught first – a blue flame danced at the fringe of the golden pool, fizzing and gathering strength as it sucked greedily at the liquid. The flames grew taller, wavering gracefully and shooting off extraordinary colours as they spread swiftly across the surface of the spilled paint. Chaston just knelt there in the centre of the glinting mess. He stared dumbly at the flickering circle of fire around him trying to understand what was happening.

Even when the flames skipped up into his hands like a ball of light he didn't move, he just looked down at the brilliant, beautiful fire that ate his skin through to the bone in a matter of seconds. It was only then that he began to scream.

'Fannella!'

Lucca was at my side cutting the ropes that bound my wrists. 'Try not to breathe it deep into your lungs. It is poison.'

I felt something tingle through my veins bringing strength and sense back to every part of my body. It was hope.

'There!'

Lucca pulled me to my feet. The room was filling with smoke now. He covered his nose and mouth.

'Quickly. This way. We'll have to use the ropes outside.'

'But you can't climb.' I began to choke as smoke filled my throat.

'I'll have to. It must be easier going down.'

He pulled me over to the double doors that led out onto the loading platform at the top of the warehouse. He lifted the bolt and rattled one of the doors back, pushing me out onto the wooden boards high above Skinners Yard.

Behind us the room took in a shuddering gulp of air. I could feel it rushing through us as the fire began to feed. Lucca pushed me forward and I caught at one of the ropes dangling from the pulley overhead. I wrapped my legs around it and swung free.

There was a splintering noise from the room. I hung there just off the edge of the platform mesmerised as Edward Chaston's last painting was consumed in flames. The wide canvas pulsed from side to side with an eerie green light and then, quite delicately, it began to peel away from the burning frame, gracefully folding itself down upon his glowing, jerking form.

'Go, Fannella!'

I tore my eyes away and began to climb down, feeling the rope pull tight above me as Lucca caught at it too.

As I climbed down I could hear howling. Chaston's agony ripped into the night air around me. The sound was animal, not human.

Then there was a single gunshot and the screaming stopped.

Chapter Thirty-two

We stood by the well in Skinners Yard. Looking back, it's the colours I remember most – green, flecked with sudden spurts of dazzling orange and gold going off like rockets on Guy Fawkes. It was something to do with that paint I supposed, all them medical fluids that Chaston used to make his Sicilian Gold.

The yard began to fill with smoke and even though it made my eyes smart and forced its way deep into my throat, I was rooted to the stones. I couldn't drag my eyes from the roof timbers of the old warehouse as they burned against the pale dawn sky. Lucca gathered up our boots, grabbed my hand and dragged me into the alleyway. When we got out to the basin we gulped the clean air.

'How did you get in – how did you find me?' My words came in ragged gasps.

'I heard your voice – and the others too.'

Lucca coughed and wiped his mouth. 'The well – the sounds seemed to echo from the stone. I looked over the edge and saw iron rungs set into the side so I decided to go down a little way. But it's not a well, Kitty, it's a sort of chimney with passages leading off towards all the warehouses in the yard. Once I was inside I could hear you speak quite clearly so I knew which opening to take. And then I heard him.

'The passage opened out into the vaults under Rosen's

warehouse. I think there must have been a fire pit there once. I hid in the shadows and watched as he carried you upstairs and I followed. He was too busy making preparations to notice me as I slipped behind the canvas and it was easy to hide there in the shadow while I thought about what to do.'

I was quiet for a moment.

'And you shot him?'

Lucca stared at the black water of Limehouse Basin. 'I did not mean to. At the end it was an act of mercy, even if he was, truly, a Verdin.'

I didn't say anything, but I knew he was telling the truth. I don't think I'll ever forget the sound Edward Chaston made as the paint and the flames consumed him.

'Fire!'

The shout of warning brought us up sharp. We heard more calls and whistles too as others took up the alarm and then the sound of heavy work boots thundering on stone as men ran towards the flames. We ran too – in the opposite direction, skirting round the basin and shrinking into the shadows to hide from the men rushing towards the blaze.

As we crouched behind some wooden stairs beside one of the warehouse buildings, I gripped Lucca's arm.

'I have to go to The Palace. I have to tell The Lady it's over. I've done what she wanted.'

Somewhere behind us there was a huge explosion as the brilliant burning carcass of Rosen's warehouse collapsed upon its secrets.

Lucca nodded, took my hand and together we fled.

*

The sky was light overhead as I hammered on the double doors, calling her name. Lucca tried to stop me, but I kept on battering until my knuckles were raw.

'Give me my brother!' I shouted that too, over and over, but my voice was hoarse and cracked from the smoke. Soon I was just mouthing the words.

I felt Lucca's arm about my shoulders. He pulled me round to face him. 'You must stop this, Fannella. It's obvious she will not let you in.'

'Why not?' I could feel my eyes burning now, but it wasn't the fire. 'I've done everything she wanted.'

There was a clicking noise behind me as the doors to The Palace opened at last.

But it wasn't Lady Ginger who looked out at us. She'd sent down another one of her old Chinamen and there were a couple of dark-skinned barrel-chested lascars with him this time.

The Chinaman shuffled forward, hawked some black stuff onto the steps and bowed, first to me and then to Lucca.

'Lady knows all and is grateful.'

That's all he said – his peculiar voice was thin and high. He reached into his sleeve just like the last time and knelt to place a square of paper on the step. As he did so I noticed that he never took his hooded black eyes off me. He straightened up, bowed once again, turned his back on us and began to shuffle inside.

'Grateful! Is that all the old bitch has to say? Well, I've got plenty to say to her.' Lucca caught my sleeve and tried to pull me back, but I darted up the steps and tried to push my way past the Chinaman and into the hall.

'Joey. I'm here!' I kept calling out his name as if he was a prisoner in there. I kicked and struggled as the silent lascars closed ranks and blocked the way. From a great distance I heard myself scream and spit and swear at them like an alley cat, as – gently but firmly – they forced me back out and onto the step.

The door closed in my face and I crumpled to the stones. A ringing noise began to fill my head. The sound pulsed and clanged so loudly that I crouched low and covered my ears to block out the pain of it. Then everything went black.

*

When I woke I was in Lucca's bed.

Sunlight streamed across the shabby blankets and just above me a fat bluebottle buzzed against the glass of the little window, battering the same pane again and again until it dropped, exhausted, onto the pillow. I brushed it away and sat up. The sudden movement made me cry out and fall back again; my head felt as if it was split in two. Lucca was hunched at the other end of the bed, watching. His arms were wrapped around his knees and his narrow shoulders were level with his ears. He'd pulled his hair back from his face and caught it up at the neck like one of the old-time sailors round the docks. He reminded me of an owl.

'H . . . how long have I been asleep?'

It was difficult to speak. My mouth was dry and my throat burned.

'Six hours. And that's not enough. You need to rest.'

I struggled to get out of the bed, pushing at the tangle

of blankets. 'No. I have to see her. I have to tell her it's over before it's too late – Joey . . .'

'You don't have to do anything, Fannella.'

Lucca handed me a square of paper. I opened it out and tried to make sense of the black curling lines. My head swam as the writing gradually came together in my eyes. Lady Ginger's elegant hand looped across the page.

Miss Peck

It has come to my attention this evening that you have concluded your part of our recent business agreement. I write to relinquish you from your bonds and to assure you that you will receive full recompense as previously agreed.

Joseph Peck is safe and, if it is still your wish, you will be reunited. Do not come to me. I will send word when the time is right.

Your contract to perform at my theatres is now rescinded. Mr Patrick Fitzpatrick will be informed of this in due course.

There was an unreadable flourish at the end of these lines – her signature I supposed – and then a postscript.

It may be of interest for you to note that your colleagues Miss Margaret Worrow, Miss Polly Durkin, Miss Anna March and Mr Daniel Tewson have also been fully remunerated for their part in this matter. Like you, they will never speak of it again.

*

'You cannot go alone, Fannella.'

Lucca twisted his hat around again and picked at the frayed band.

'I have to. That's what the message said. And I don't want you following me this time.' I stared out across the flat, stone-grey water. It's a funny thing – the Thames is never the same twice, not quite. Sometimes it's crumpled and green, sometimes heavy mud-brown waves wallop and suck at the stones, sometimes it's yellow, bound at the edges with a froth of dirty cream lace and sometimes, not often mind, it's silver-blue and shot through with ripples of light.

I watched as the wooden lid of an old packing crate from the docks floated past the base of the steps. There were some odd, foreign letters stamped diagonal across it in red and next to them a picture of a dog's head, or perhaps it was meant to be a fox or a wolf.

The lid got caught up in a little eddy of weed and sticks. It twisted round and round in the same spot for a minute or so and then it bobbed free, twirling gracefully away into the smooth silent water. I found myself wondering where it had been and where it was going. That old crate lid had probably seen more of the world than me, I thought. But that was going to change. Once I had Joey back, we were leaving. All three of us were getting out of Paradise – and I didn't much care where we went next.

I squeezed Lucca's hand.

'I'll be all right. After all, I did everything she wanted, didn't I? *"You will receive full recompense"*, that's what Lady Ginger said. Do you think that means she'll bring Joey with her today now she's called for me?'

Lucca frowned and picked at the hat band again. 'Who can tell? For three days you've heard nothing and now, this morning, a summons – to that place? At least let me come part of the way – please.'

I shook my head. Tell truth, I wanted to do this alone. Why would The Lady demand to meet me there if she wasn't bringing my brother? It was probably some twisted joke, I thought, another one of her bleedin' mind traps – reuniting the Peck family of puppets with a final twitch of the strings. I knew her ways now and I wasn't frightened no more. All the same, if she really was giving Joey back I wanted him for my-self. Just me and him, even for the shortest time, like the old days.

I pushed up closer to Lucca and leaned forward so that I could see his face properly through all that hair.

'Look. You saved me once already, Lucca Fratelli, and don't think I'm not grateful that you came after me in that warehouse and . . .' I broke off. I didn't want to think about that night, let alone speak of it.

'Thing is – it's over. I've got to do this on my own. He's my brother. Do you understand?'

'But The Lady . . .' Lucca rolled the brim of his hat over his knees.

'The Lady is playing a game, putting on a show, that's all. You know what she's like.'

Lucca sighed and shifted on the step. 'As you wish, Fannella.' He smiled ruefully. 'At least she has already granted you one thing. Fitzpatrick has been complaining that the takings are down.'

*

I'd never been to Ma's grave before. Not since the day we buried her. It was cold then and it was cold now.

I remember the frost covering the mound of earth about to be shovelled back over her coffin after we left. There weren't many of us there that day. Me, Joey, a couple of Joey's friends and a legal all got up in shiny black with a tall hat bound with a crêpe band. The trailing ends of the band fluttered about behind his head as he stood there grim-faced and silent.

Joey said afterwards that the legal put him in mind of a beetle. Neither of us knew who he was and we didn't much care. Tell truth, I suspected he was at the wrong funeral but I couldn't talk to him. I couldn't talk to anyone that day.

By the time the vicar had said his piece and Joey had rattled a handful of earth down onto Ma's box, the man had gone. I reckoned he realised his mistake and felt embarrassed.

That drab winter day was five years ago.

A keen wind whipped down the avenue of cypress trees now as I made my way to her plot. The bell in the little chapel of rest at the entrance had gone off just after I came through the gates. Three strikes. I was early. The Lady wasn't due until the quarter.

For some reason I'd dressed myself up. Not in one of them bright, blousy outfits I'd bought with Lady Ginger's purse, but something plain and decent. Dark blue with a high neck, buttons and good gloves. My hair was tied back and away from my face and I was wearing a hat with black feathers at the side and a scrap of net across my eyes. I had Nanny Peck's shawl pinned around my shoulders too. That seemed the right thing to do.

I counted the avenues until I came to the right one – number 50, west side. Ma's grave was over to the left somewhere ahead. I remembered the hatchet-faced angel with wrestler's wings who stood as a perpetual body guard to some poor soul whose family had more money than taste.

We couldn't afford a stone for Ma. But I remembered at the service there was a wooden cross with her name on a tin plate stuck into the earth mound at a jaunty angle. I thought they'd use it as a marker after we'd gone and I looked for it now.

I didn't feel sentimental about the spot. As far as I was concerned she wasn't there. Anyone who's been at the deathbed of someone they love will tell you the same. One minute there's a person with you, next minute they're gone. It's like a candle flame going out and the sudden absence is shocking. But there's an odd sort of comfort in that because you know they must have gone somewhere else.

I don't claim to be a divinity but one thing I do know is that Ma, the best of her, went off somewhere that night and she wasn't here with me now in the cemetery.

I stepped off the gravel path and walked along the tree-lined row beyond the winged prize-fighter. It was one of these, I was certain.

Henry Trott had a nice big stone with a carving of a flaming urn set into the top. It came back to me now. Ma's grave was three plots further along. I paused, confused. They all had stones here – fine ones at that. Not a single grave in this row had a simple wooden cross.

I stepped forward to check. After Henry Trott came Martin Benyon, brewer, then Hannah Dyson, beloved wife and mother, then Mary Clifford – a pillar the size of a man, but not much more there than her name and a couple of dates – and then a tall grey triangular block set on a plinth. Simple it was, but elegant, the corners carved sharp and clean. Must have cost someone a year's wage, but they'd set it up in the wrong place. This was Ma's grave. I was sure of it.

There was some lettering on the base hidden by greenery. I knelt down and pushed the leaves and grass aside.

Elizabeth? Ma's name had been Eliza. I tugged at the weeds growing up round the base of the stone and a clump came away from the ground, roots and all.

ELIZABETH REDMAYNE

1836–1875

BELOVED DAUGHTER AND MOTHER

SHE TOOK LITTLE BUT WAS OWED MUCH

Redmayne? I straightened up and stared at the stone. It was good work, quality marble, beautifully cut letters filled in gold. The dates were right too, but the name was all wrong. If this was a mistake it was an expensive one. I clenched my fist over the weeds, furious that some family had taken Ma's grave and planted a stone to a stranger on top of it.

I heard a crunching noise as someone came towards me down the gravel pathway. The noise grew louder, heavier. It was more than one person, perhaps two or three. *Joey?*

My heart pounded under the starched blue bodice as I flung down the weeds and darted back to the cypress avenue.

Four Chinamen set down Lady Ginger's chair.

It was that same black one I'd seen before, carved with dragons. Their hooked talons gripped at the feet and at the ends of the arms. The men carried the chair on long poles set through metal hoops at the sides.

Lady Ginger sat there like a queen. For a moment she was still, then she nodded, raised her hand and the Chinamen bowed and moved off silently, melting into the garden of stones.

Today her grey hair was coiled in a plait on the top of her head and I could see the strands of pure white winding through it. She was dressed in heavy black lace sewn over with tiny glittering beads of jet so that she seemed to shimmer in the pale winter light. Like before, her face was painted white, although her cheeks were daubed with bright, unnatural spots of crimson.

Ma had an old doll – a wooden one with real human hair and glass eyes – that put me in mind of Lady Ginger now. That doll still gave me nightmares.

She watched me for a moment and then she moistened those cracked black lips that looked like something sewn onto her face.

'Good afternoon, Kitty Peck. I trust you are well?'

That light girlish voice, so sweet yet so sour.

I nodded curtly. I could feel my palms sweating in my gloves.

'Come closer.'

I walked slowly to the chair and stood just in front of her. She stared up at me. Her eyes flickered across my face like they were reading the lines in a book.

'As I remarked once before, you are so very alike – you and your pretty brother, Joseph.' Her eyes half closed. 'But he was weak, Kitty. And you are strong.'

'*Was?*' I couldn't stop myself. 'You promised me, Lady, you told me he was alive. "*Full recompense*" – that's what you said.'

She began to laugh, but it became a cough that wracked her tiny body and made her lean forward. I could see her skinny shoulder blades all knotted up beneath the lace.

When she straightened up she took a square of cotton from her sleeve and dabbed it at her mouth. There was a black stain on the material as she folded it away.

'Forgive me. It was a figure of speech. You brother is still very much alive. But I am afraid he is not here with me today.'

I knelt down in front of her, gripping the arms of the chair. One of the Chinamen appeared just to the right but The Lady flicked a hand and he shuffled back into the shadows.

'Where is he? You owe me, Lady. The things I did – they was for Joey, nothing else.'

She was silent for a moment and then she smiled.

'Do you really mean that? Look into your heart, can you honestly tell me that you did not revel in your fame? I watched you, girl. You were the perfect choice. It has been most diverting.'

She reached into her sleeve and pulled out a thin black roll.

'I knew a girl very like you once. You will light this. Here.'

She handed me a small silver box full of matches. My hands shook as I lit her opium stick. It was smaller than her usual pipe, but I'd seen enough men in the backstreets dragging on a tarry stub to know what it was.

Lady Ginger inhaled deeply and the tip of the black stick glowed. A trail of sweet smoke coiled around us. I saw a tremor go through the old woman's frail body and her eyes rolled back in her head, then, of a sudden, they snapped open again.

'I will return your brother to you . . . in due course. But whether you will accept him, now, that is another matter.' She grinned, showing her black gums. 'You will find him much altered.'

I thought of that finger and felt the bile rising. The cemetery seemed to spin around us. What else had the old bitch done to him?

'If you want your brother you will come to The Palace tomorrow at noon. Not a moment before. You may bring the Fratelli boy with you, it will be useful.' She paused and held her head to one side, like a crow sizing up a morsel of carrion. 'There – you see, I know all about you, Kitty *Peck*.'

She made my last name sound like something you'd want to spit out of your mouth.

I stood and took a step back. The wind gusted through the cypress trees and a little storm of dust and gravel blew around my feet lifting the edge of my skirts and billowing them out around me. I didn't know what to think any more. Was she lying again, playing a game?

I curled my fingers tight around her silver strike box. 'Why are we here, Lady? Why couldn't you just bring Joey here with you today and let us be? What have we ever done to you?'

She brought the stick to her lips again and sucked greedily. Then she threw it down onto the gravel beside her chair.

'Pain comes in many ways. I find that the opium helps. You will do well to remember that. Now, you will help me, please. I cannot walk without assistance.'

She raised herself from the chair and I saw her mouth twist with pain as she forced herself to her feet. She shook a little as she gripped the left arm of the chair and reached out towards me. I took her gloved hand and felt the lumpy knots of rings and bones through the leather.

'Walk with me to your mother's grave.'

She leaned heavily on me as we went the little way back to Ma's grave. I realised then how frail she was. The great Lady Ginger was fragile as a baby bird fallen from the nest.

'It's here. I know it is.' I pointed at the stone. 'But it's all wrong, someone's made a mistake. She was Eliza, not Elizabeth – and her name was Peck. We didn't put that thing there.'

She was silent for a moment. 'No, you did not. I did. When she was born I gave her my own name, because, at the time, it was all I had left.'

Lady Ginger looked at me and her eyes glittered. I couldn't tell if she was on the edge of tears or if it was malice there.

'Elizabeth Redmayne was my daughter.'

I handed the paper to Lucca without a word and watched his face as he read to the bottom, and then read it again. I stood and went over by the window where something standing on the floor and covered in a slump of dusty velvet propped open the shutter. I passed Lady Ginger's dice box from hand to hand. The shagreen case was rough to the touch and I could hear the dice rattling inside.

I looked out across the jumbled roofs and smoking chimneypots of Paradise. It was a fine day.

When we'd got to The Palace the doors were wide open. Two of The Lady's Chinamen stood waiting in the hall at the base of the broad oak stairs. One of them took his right hand out of the opposite sleeve and pointed to the floors above; the yellowed nail on his first finger was long and curled.

As we passed, he bowed. They both did.

I felt Lucca's hand tighten on my arm as we made our way up. On every landing corridors lined with china pots and oriental rugs stretched away into the depths. Every time we halted, uncertain where to go, another of The Lady's men stepped out of the shadows, bowed and pointed the way upwards.

At the top of the stairs the doors to The Lady's receiving room stood open.

Lucca caught my hand. 'What if this is another trap, Fannella? We have walked into it.'

I shook my head. 'It's too late for that now.'

I pulled him forward across the threshold and into the room.

346

In daylight The Lady's chamber was a dreary, musty place. The ceiling and walls were stained, cobwebs hung in garlands in the corners as if no one had ever noticed them to clear them away and the air was heavy with the sickly smell of her. Only she wasn't there.

The room was empty apart from a square of red cloth set out in the middle of the bare boards. There were three things on the cloth arranged in a triangle.

I went forward and knelt down. My fingers tingled as I reached for the small, gilt-edged card nearest to me. It was an address: *17 rue des Carmélites, Paris*. I turned it over.

Two words in Lady Ginger's looped hand scrawled across the back.

Full recompense

I flipped it back and stared at the address again. I felt for Joey's Christopher and his ring in the neck of my dress as Lucca crouched next to me.

'The letter is for you, I think, Fannella?'

I looked down at the name written neatly in the centre of the folded paper on the cloth – *Katharine Redmayne*. Was that really who I was?

Elizabeth Redmayne was my daughter.

God forgive me, but when Lady Ginger said that in the cemetery, I began to laugh. There was a furious wildness in the sound that I could barely control and I brought my hands to my mouth to stop it and to stop myself from lashing out at her chalk-white face.

All the while she had just stared at me, her doll-black eyes dead and unblinking.

After a moment she raised her hand and one of her China-men appeared from nowhere. She reached for his arm and turned her glittering back on me as he guided her to the chair.

I called out to her then. Now it was my turn to demand *more* – just as she'd done, but she never looked back, not once – and she didn't speak another word to me.

Katharine Redmayne – if I touched the letter would that make it true?

Lucca decided. He leaned across the square of red silk, took up the letter and handed it to me. For a moment I stared at the name and then I ripped it open.

February 14th 1880

I have tested you, Katharine Redmayne, and found you worthy, better than your brother, whom I return to you in full recompense.

I knew a girl like you once who came to London with nothing more than a child in her belly, a purse full of coins and a loyal servant called Bridie Peck. That girl built an empire for herself where all worlds meet. She gave up her own daughter, but she became a mother to many.

When she is gone her family will still need a careful parent to guide them. For a long time I thought Joseph would be the one, but I was wrong. Your brother has a weakness that can be exploited and a Baron must be strong.

You are strong, Katharine.

When you leave this room today you will find my solicitor, Marcus Telferman, waiting for you in the entrance hall. I believe you met him once before at the burial of my daughter, your mother. Telferman knows my wishes and will be ready to act for you should you decide to accept my terms. The documents of transfer must be signed within the day or this offer will be rescinded.

The choice is yours, Katharine. You can walk from this room today and live a small, narrow life or you can build your own empire. Perhaps a better one. You have proved yourself capable in more ways than you know.

Before you decide, think carefully on this: men like Sir Richard Verdin are not unreachable.

You have only to give the word and your will shall be done. I believe Mr Fratelli will have an interest in this matter.

Her signature wound across the bottom of the page, underlined twice. Like before there was a postscript.

The dice and the other are yours, no matter your decision today.

Lucca looked up from the letter. The good side of his face was lit from the window.

'What will you do, Fannella?'

I turned Joey's Christopher and his ring between my fingers and looked at the dingy room around me. The stains up the far wall where Lady Ginger had leaned into her nest of silken cushions and smoked her opium pipe was a dirty ghost of the past.

The whole place needed a good clear-out and a lick of paint.

'I'll deal with it,' I said, turning to push the shutter back further to let more light into the room. There was a scratching noise at my feet and the sound of something rasping on metal. The noises came from beneath the mound of velvet that was propping open the shutter. I pulled the fabric free and found myself staring into the glinting black eyes of Lady Ginger's parrot. The bird fluffed out its tatty grey wings and held its head to one side.

'*Pretty girl, pretty girl, pretty girl, pretty girl, pretty . . .*'

Epilogue

The London Pictorial News: February 28th 1880

DEATH OF PROMINENT PHILANTHROPIST

London mourns the loss of one of its most distinguished and generous benefactors.

Sir Richard Verdin's interest in the work of young artists and his energetic nurture of emerging talent will be a supreme loss to the artistic firmament. This correspondent understands that Sir Richard's body was discovered by a manservant at his London home, late on Friday last. A single gunshot wound to the head will have killed him instantly.

Sir Richard's death is presumed accidental. Servants have confirmed that the gun found at the scene belonged to the prominent businessman and philanthropist. Initial investigations suggest he sustained the fatal wound while cleaning the piece.

In a cruel twist of fortune it has recently come to light that Sir Richard Verdin's ward and godson, Edward Chaston, soon to be admitted to the Royal College of Surgeons, also died in an horrific accident not two weeks ago. Interested parties have confirmed that Sir Richard was left 'devastated' by this loss, describing Edward Chaston as 'the son he never had'.

Dr Chaston, for let us award him that title in death if not in life, can be revealed, for the first time by this newspaper, as the reclusive artist whose extraordinary work, *The Cinnabar Girls*, has set London aflame.

It is with regret that your correspondent notes that *The Cinnabar Girls* is, apparently, destined to be the last and only work from the hand of the 'unknown genius'.

ACKNOWLEDGEMENTS

Writing *Kitty Peck and the Music Hall Murders* has been an adventure and I'd like to thank everyone who has helped me on the way.

First, the team at Faber and Faber, whose enthusiasm, optimism and wise counsel has been invaluable – Hannah, Katherine, Becky, John . . . and everyone at Bloomsbury House.

Also, massive thanks to *Stylist* Magazine for setting Kitty free, to Tamsin and Sarah for their forensic attention to detail, and to Eugenie for her excitement and encouragement.

Finally, I must mention my family, friends and work colleagues, whose unflagging support, interest and amazement kept me going through a long dark winter at the keyboard.